SARATOGA.

A Story of 1787.

NEW YORK:
W. P. FETRIDGE & CO., PUBLISHERS,
FRANKLIN SQUARE.
BOSTON:
WILLIAMS & CO., 100 WASHINGTON ST.
1856.

STEREOTYPED BY
THOMAS B. SMITH,
82 & 84 Beekman Street.

PRINTED BY
GROSSMAN AND WILLETT,
82 & 84 Beekman St.

PREFACE.

THE general characteristics of American life and manners at the period immediately succeeding the Revolution, have been often and well portrayed. But every section of the country then presented special local peculiarities, arising in part from the various races of the settlers, partly from the different relations in which they stood to the Aborigines, and partly from the character of the country itself. These local peculiarities afford an inexhaustible field for the historian and novelist.

It has been the aim of the author of the following pages to present a picture of a particular time and place. Most of the incidents narrated have been handed down by tradition as veritable facts; and the principal personages introduced are drawn from actual prototypes. And even in those parts which are more purely imaginary, it is believed that no historical probability has been violated. For all artistic purposes, whatever might be true is true; and this book is presented to the public as a faithful, though of course an incomplete, picture of Saratoga in 1787.

CONTENTS.

CHAPTER VIII.

CHAPTER IX.

CHAPTER X.

CHAPTER XI.

CHAPTER XII.

CHAPTER XIII.

CHAPTER XIV.

CHAPTER XV.

CHAPTER XVI.

CHAPTER XVII.

CHAPTER XVIII.

CHAPTER XIX.

CHAPTER XX.

CHAPTER XXI.

CHAPTER XXII.

CHAPTER XXIII.

CHAPTER XXIV.

CHAPTER XXV.

CHAPTER XXVI.

CHAPTER XXVII.

CHAPTER XXVIII.

CHAPTER XXIX.

CHAPTER XXX.

CHAPTER XXXI.

CHAPTER XXXII.

CHAPTER XXXIII.

CHAPTER XXXIV.

SARATOGA.

CHAPTER I.

A MEETING IN THE FOREST.

One summer morning in the year 1787, a party of four persons were traversing the forest, near the spot where now stands the gay watering-place of Saratoga. Two of the party were young women, mounted on horseback. Their attendants, who were on foot, consisted of a white man and an Indian, or rather half-breed.

"How soon do you think we shall come to the rock, James?" said the taller of the two horsewomen; "it seems to me that we have been riding long enough to be there by this time."

"No, no, Miss Marion, not quite;" replied the man who was addressed; "no doubt it may seem a long way to you, who are not used to it; but, Lord bless you! I know every foot of this here ground, as well as you know the road to church. We are now full a mile to the southward of the spring yet. We need n't hurry, for the colonel won't be able to jine us till arter we've been there some time."

"Are you sure," said the fair interlocutor, "that we

are in the right way? For, to me, one of these paths looks just like another."

"Sure, Miss Marion!" was the reply, "why Indian Joe here, could find his way blindfold, I'll be sworn. Besides, you can see the light in the east shinin' through the tops of them hemlocks, so you may be sartąin we're not turned round, and that our heads are still looking towards Skeenesborough."

"What blindfold mean, you say?" asked the person designated as Indian Joe, who now joined in the conversation.

"The Lord love us, miss!" replied the other man; "you see the ignorance of them savages. Why, Joe, where was you edicated? Blindfold means walking with somethin' tied over your eyes, all jest as if 't was pitch dark now—"

His further explanatory remarks, on that head, were cut short by a slight exclamation from the second young lady. Her horse was standing still, while she was pointing with her riding-whip at some object by the side of their path. Her eyes seemed to be riveted upon this, whatever it was, as if by a kind of fascination, while her cheek was slightly blanched with the fright which it caused. Within a few feet of her, in fact, was a fallen tree, now old and decayed; but which in its descent had broken off a yard or so above the ground, so that, as it lay, the top of the trunk was nearly as high as a man's head.

"What is the matter, Lucile? what is it?" exclaimed her companion, observing her alarm, and approaching her in anxiety. Lucile made no reply, but continued pointing at the object which fixed her attention, apparently unable to do more.

"What's got into the gal?" said the man who had been addressed as James: "don't be skeered, Miss Valcour; sit still, and I'll see what it is in a jiffy."

But, in the mean time, the Indian, whom nobody, just then, noticed, had taken a short turn toward the head of the prostrate tree, and with silent but rapid steps, was now seen approaching the group, walking along the elevated trunk. When within a yard or so, he paused, making a quick motion of his hand toward Lucile, as if to beckon her away. But she either did not understand the sign, or was unable to obey it. She did not stir. "Have a care, all on ye!" said James; "have a care, for it may be a painter or some tarnal thing of that kind. You jest move off, miss, while Joe and I takes charge of the creetur. What is it, Joe? Let's know at once."

But Joe seemed too much occupied to heed what his companion said; for, casting a few hasty glances around him as he stood balancing himself on the timber, and apparently not discovering what he sought, he slowly removed his rifle from the hollow of his left arm, where it lay, and keeping his gaze fixed on some object hitherto undiscoverable to all but him and Lucile, he steadily pointed it a little downward and fired. There was a scrambling among the bushes, a loud, ferocious snarl was heard, and then the sound of rapidly retreating footsteps. The Indian, as soon as he fired, had bounded backward on the log where he stood, loosing his hold on his gun, which was caught by the bushes and held fast.

"That's what I call Indian shootin'," growled James: "if he'd been behind a stump or a log, now, he might have done it. Faugh! Catamount! you'll never wear that wolf's tail in your belt. It 's as good as ten dollars gone."

"What is it you say about a wolf, James?" asked the first speaker; "surely you do not mean to say that Lucile has been so near one as that?"

"Don't I, miss? Ask the Indian, then, if you don't believe me. But I ought to know the critters by this time. Joe, how on arth could you miss him? I thought you'd white natur enough in you for such a job as that."

"Too much talk!" said the savage, with some ill-humor; "you big brag: why no see dat?" he added, pointing to a large limb, which had intervened between him and the animal, and which was marked with the charge which had been fired at the wolf.

"That's true, for once," said James; "this time I admit there's some excuse for you, specially as I see the leaves below are covered with the varmint's blood."

"James, I think you are too rough with Joe," said the fair speaker again; "he seems to have saved Lucile's life, and—"

"Lucile's life!" exclaimed the man: "No, no, my young lady! Who ever heard of a wolf attacking folks in broad day-light? 'Taint their way. Take my word for it, the gentleman was as glad to get off, as you to see him go. 'Taint in the natur of them critturs to set on human bein's, onless when they come in droves like, and find a man alone. I'll be bound this one was as frightened as Miss Walcour herself."

"Ah! Lucile," said her companion, "how frightened you must have been! How did you come to see it? I'm sure if I had been in your place I should have fainted away!"

"No," said Lucile, who had now recovered from her fright, and whose spirits revived with her release from danger, "I do not think you would have fainted away; but you would have run away, as I should have done if I had thought of it. But I never saw such a horrid thing before, and it is no wonder I was startled."

"Do you know, Lucile," said the other, "that you will be quite a heroine after this? But James, I thought that fellow said there were no wild animals in this region?"

"Lord! miss," replied the man, "do you call a wolf a wild animal? why he's as harmless as a woodchuck, compared with some that used to be in these woods. Hows'ever, the crittur's bein' here shows we must be pretty well on our journey; for it 's seldom they ventur' far from the rocks and hills in daylight, and this chap must have been caught out late a gallivantin'. What do you say, Catamount? Arn't we pretty near the Rock Spring by this time?"

The Indian to whom this question was addressed, was, at the moment occupied in disengaging his gun from its entanglement, and in examining whether it had sustained any injury. After some delay, he replied without deigning to turn his face toward his questioner:

"What I tink, you say? Indian no *tink;* he *do.*"

"Yes, I know," said the man, "but you need n't be huffy about what I said about your shootin'. I mean, don't this wolf bein' here show we must be near the eend of our journey?"

"You know how shoot," replied the savage, "why you no see path clear, eh? Why you no see sky out dere? Big tree dere, what you call rock, too, plenty."

"The redskin seems to think, miss, that the mountain

is clus by," said the white man, turning to the young ladies under his charge. "I used to be this away often enough, and knew every deer track then. Them ledges he speaks on, are nigh hand to the Rock Spring, and the hill country beyond used to be full of varmint. But I'm a little onsartain now, for I don't think I've been here since Colonel Mooer's division camped up in Palmertown a mile or so above these springs, soon arter the battle of Sarotogue."

"Well, well!" said the young lady, "I understand all that, but when once you begin to talk, there is no stopping you. If Joe, now, had a little of your tongue, and you a little of his thought, it would be a great deal better for both of you."

"Thought, miss?" said the man, "why thought in a savage would give him the stomach-ache. He ain't used to it."

"That may be," said she, interrupting him; "but I have known your talk to give others the head-ache. But, Lucile, what makes you so silent? Has the sight of the wolf tied your tongue, or locked up all your smiles?"

"No, Marion," was the reply, "but you know, one is naturally a little stupid after a fright; I was only trying to be thankful that the danger was not very great, after all. I was wondering also, why the dog, who went ahead of us did not give us some notice of the presence of this creature."

"I can tell," said the man, still pushing himself into the conversation.

"You can tell," said Lucile, turning to him; "well, what is it then?"

"Why, you see. miss, the dog is city bred, that's all;

he may be a very good dog for smelling out a thief who gets into your hall; but as for the wild varmint, I ventur to say that he never so much as put eyes on one yet."

"Well, James," said she, "let that be as it may, he's a good dog in his way. But what can be the matter with him now? I'm sure it is his bark I hear out there ahead."

"I think," said Marion, "we must be coming to some house, or clearing as they call it; for there seems to be an opening among the trees a little further on. James, what is it we are coming to, there where you see the woods lighting up, and where you hear the dog bark?"

"I kind o' think," said the man, "that we must be coming to some bit of low ground. There can't be no clearing hereabouts, and I remember a little swamp a quarter of a mile or so this side of the Rock Spring."

All now moved forward. At a little distance they found the path more plainly defined, and freer from obstruction. It came out upon the south-western edge of a small piece of marshy ground, covered with a thick growth of alder and tamarack. The upland about it was dry and sandy, and along its margin ran a footpath, into which our party passed from that which led away to the south. They followed the path along the western side of the swale which by a slight descent conducted them down to a small rivulet that emptied into it.

At the point where they struck the low ground, they had found the dog whose bark had attracted their attention. With nose to the ground, he was making courses up and down along the trodden track, giving a yelp now and then, as if he was on the scent of some object, the character of which he could not well make out. However, he uneasily followed the travelers down to the little brook, where the tired horses had been watered. A few rods beyond this, where the ground again gradually ascended, was a fine clump of magnificent beeches, beneath which the ground was free from brush, and was covered with a rich green sod. The beautiful situation, and the vicinity of the running stream, made this a desirable halting-place. By this time the sun had so far risen as to shine full upon the spot. The sky was clear, and the morning was delightful.

"What can be the matter with Prince, Marion?" said Lucile; "he stopped at the creek and keeps running up and down the path whining and barking. I have a great mind to follow him and see where he will go."

On this same morning Arthur Walcott was in the forest alone. He had been there through the night. His couch and his covering had been of hemlock boughs. He is standing among the high trees on the eastern side of the little swamp. The light of the morning sun comes down warmly through the open branches. He is gazing upon, and enjoying the scene. Youth and health are always fond of things pleasant—of physical comforts and animal delights. He basks in the warm, perfumed air, and the cheerful sunlight, just as a horse, a snake, or a vegetable might do. And yet, in character, he is far above the ordinary grade of even the human animal. The reader will find out in what respect, as we go on.

He is of medium height, perhaps a little more, and is both lightly and strongly made. His shoulders are broad and his limbs tapering. His forehead is high and wide; his eye, large, well-opened, and gray, easily dilating, brilliant and steady. (We describe him almost zoologically.) We must add a little more, however. His complexion is brown by exposure; and his hands and feet, though the first are well tanned and the last are encased in tough woodsman's boots, are small and delicately made, and would not seem to belong to a laboring man, or one whose occupation was either humble or menial.

His countenance is composed and quiet, though its whole expression indicates uncommon resolution and firmness of purpose. It is thoughtful, and even, to some extent, dignified. His dress is composed mainly of coarse, strong, gray, woolen cloth, such as was then the usual product of the domestic loom.

At the moment when our attention is called to him, he was carelessly surveying the scene around him. On all sides but one it was a pine forest. The trees, for the most part, were large and tall, and had but little underbrush between them; but, although for this reason, the view between their trunks was tolerably clear, yet it was not of any great extent, on account of their thickness and proximity to each other. To the west the ground fell away, and sunk for a space, into the little marsh of which we have spoken.

After trying what further views he might obtain from the tops of hillocks, and of fallen trees, and finding that he gained little or nothing thereby, our forester, in order to gain a more distinct notion of his whereabouts, determined to climb up among the branches of some of the taller trees standing near at hand. Being light of foot, and strong of arm, the task was an easy one. So depositing his gun, his pouch, and his forest tackle upon the ground, he swung himself readily into one of the neighboring saplings; and after a few moments, might have been seen near the top of a tall, yellow pine, perched upon a limb, like a look-out upon the mast-head of a ship at sea. The view before and around him was, in fact, like a wide sea of forest green. To the north and the south it lay level and uniform. To the west and north-west, at the distance of a few miles, it was bounded by a low range of wooded hills; while eastward it stretched away for many a league, growing hazy in the distance, until it was terminated by a long chain of misty mountains, that lifted their blue and billowy tops against the silver brightness of the morning sky.

The sun shone cheerfully, though with slanting rays, over all the wide expanse; but it touched no visible house-tops, sunk down into no rude clearings, and brightened up no fields of waving grain; for that whole region was a wilderness. The chirp of the squirrel, or the twitter of the wild birds, could be heard among the leaves; but no other sounds broke the stillness. On one side, and in one particular alone, was there any evidence of the vicinity of human beings. At a considerable distance to the southward was to be seen a thin column of smoke, winding lazily up into the air above the trees.

Unexpressive and indefinite as the view may seem to the reader, it appeared to satisfy the young man who was gazing upon it; for after a few hasty glances, he descended from his perch to the ground.

Here, as the day was now beginning to advance, he proceeded to set about such preparations for a morning's meal as his situation admitted of. The means to that end, it must be confessed, appeared meager enough; but, nevertheless, he seemed in no wise embarrassed by the circumstance. Upon a limb hard by, were suspended the remains of a saddle of venison; from which, with a sheath-knife, he soon cut a few slices; and, after striking a fire among the dry leaves by aid of his gun flint, he was soon enabled to effect a hasty broil, using such expedients as are familiar to hunters in like situations.

While partaking of this primitively prepared meal, his attention became, from time to time attracted by slight sounds that faintly struck upon his ear. They seemed to come from the direction of a foot path, which wound around the eastern and southerly side of the alder swamp; and he was led to the conjecture that some one might be advancing along it. As every meeting amid those solitudes, was one of interest, he kept from time to time glancing in the direction in which any new-comer would be likely to appear. Very soon afterward his watchfulness was rewarded, and there emerged into view, the tall, gray form of a hound, that, with nose to the earth, came speeding along the path, directly toward where the young man sat.

The latter immediately sprang to his feet, and seized his gun, exclaiming to himself as he did so:

"As I live, that must be Mr. Valcour's dog! Prince! Here! Don't you know me, old fellow? Aha! I thought so!"

The animal, with many signs of friendly recognition, at once ran to the young man, and leaped and fawned around him in great glee.

"Keep down, you outrageous dog!" said the latter, "be quiet, sir! But what the deuce has brought you off here alone? Where's your master, Prince? What! down there is he? coming this way, I suppose."

The brute appeared to have some idea of the purport of the question thus addressed to him; for, skipping away in the direction indicated, he turned, and looking back, uttered a sort of half bark, as much as to say "Come on."

"No, no, my fine fellow," said the young man, "not till I have finished my breakfast, at all events."

At this moment, however, the sounds of a horse's footsteps, coming at a gallop, began to be heard; and soon after, and before the person of the rider could be seen, a clear and pleasant female voice, called out through the trees:

"Prince! why, Prince, you truant, where have you gone? Prince! There's a good dog! come back here at once!"

But Prince was indifferent to the call, or at least deferred answering it for the present; for stepping aside from the path, he seated himself upon his haunches, and with his red tongue lolling from his jaws, awaited with composure the course of events.

Meanwhile, the young man hastily arose again, for the voice of the new comer admonished him that she was to be received with more ceremony than her four-footed courier had been.

When the horsewoman emerged into view, she caused him to start with surprise, for the apparition which she presented, was not one often seen in the wilderness. Aside from the superior quality of her dress, and the delicacy and beauty of her form, her cheeks were now flushed with exercise, and her eyes shone with excitement. The meeting to both was unexpected, and the embarrassment was consequently mutual. The young lady was the first to recover from it, and feeling the absurdity of a prolonged silence under such circumstances, she said, as she reined in her horse,

"I beg your pardon, sir, for so suddenly intruding upon you; but my dog, that I see sitting there, and with whom you seem to be acquainted, ran off from me, and I was merely following him for a little way up this pleasant path."

"Were any apologies necessary," said Walcott in reply, "they should come from me, who should have been astir like you, instead of idling over a hunter's meal. You are as free of the forest as others. But I thought I was far enough from places where young ladies rode out alone."

"Oh, as for that," said she, "I am not alone, by any means; the dog there, for instance—"

"It is the sight of that very dog," he replied, "which excites my curiosity; for, as you surmise, he is an old acquaintance, and I thought I knew every body that knew him. So, when he came up, I expected to see him followed by—"

"By some more agreeable person, I dare say," she said, laughing as she interrupted him; but added, after a slight pause, during which she sat patting the neck of her horse, while now and then she stole a glance at her new acquaintance,

"So, you can form no idea who I am?"

"You will pardon me," he answered, "if I confess myself at fault on that head; but—may I take the liberty of tightening the girths of your saddle? For I perceive them to be loosened, and I fear if you should ride back with the same mad-cap speed as that with which you came, that some accident might happen."

Here he made a movement toward the side of the horse, which, from the suddenness of his approach, shied. As the young man had feared, the loosened girths proved dangerous, for the saddle turned and the rider was thrown off. The other, however, was too close and too quick to permit any serious consequences; for while with his left hand he caught the bridle-rein and so stopped the horse, with the right he caught the young lady round the waist, and lifted her gently to the ground; all had been the work of but a moment. Her color went and came with the suddenness of the danger, and the immediate relief. She found at the moment, no words to express either fear, censure, gratitude, or pleasure.

"No injury is done, I hope?" said the young man as he gazed anxiously in her face; "I was to blame for the way I approached you."

"You have, I must say," she answered, now beginning to laugh a little at her situation, "an expeditious way of dismounting your opponents. But be assured, I am not at all incommoded, and must thank you for your timely aid. If the accident had not occurred here, it would somewhere else, where I might not have found assistance."

"You are very good to say so," he replied; "but I can hardly forgive my own awkwardness; but let me now repair the mischief."

Saying this he speedily readjusted the saddle, and rendered it secure against the recurrence of a similar mishap. He then gave to the fair rider his assistance in remounting, noticing as he did so, her small buskined foot, and the agile spring with which she regained her place. He almost wished to himself that she might then and there, fall off again; it was so pleasant to catch her in his arms, and so delightful to help her to remount.

"This seems destined for a day of adventures with me," she said, "for this is my second one since daylight."

"What was the first?" he asked quickly.

"Nothing but a great fright, after all," she replied, "a thing not worth telling of now; but I fear some one may be expecting me down yonder, and so I must hasten my departure. I think, sir," she added, looking archly in his face, "I think I have the advantage of you—for I imagine that I know who you are, while you seem not to recognize me. I have the better memory, or the warmer heart! Good morning to you!"

"Stay one moment!" he said, as she started; "can I not know to whom I have been so pleasantly introduced; at least so much?"

"Not now," she added laughing, as she rode away; "our camp is not far off."

So saying, she galloped rapidly away, and soon disappeared around the turning of the path. The young man gazed after her as long as she was visible, and almost sighed as the little plume in her riding-hat at last became undistinguishable among the leaves of the forest. He found, on turning round, a little to his surprise, that the dog had not followed his mistress, but sat as coolly as if in his right place, or as if, by instinct, he had divined that the young man would soon have occasion to travel the same road as himself. The remains of the morning's meal were soon disposed of, the larger portion being given to the dog, who, without scruple took upon himself the character of a guest. The young man then gathered up his few accouterments, and prepared to follow his late visitor.

"It must be little Lucile," he said to himself musingly, as he went along: "she knows me, and goes accompanied by old Valcour's grayhound. That explains it all. But what a charming girl she has grown! I suppose Marion, and the rest of them are with her. Heighho! how beautiful she looked on that Canadian pony! I wonder what other adventure she met with. But I shall soon know all about it."

After threading his way for some distance along the path, and following it around to the opposite side of the valley, he suddenly came upon the party to which the young lady was attached.

Before proceeding further, it is proper that we should give the reader some fuller explanations of the characters and circumstances of the various personages already spoken of.

Lucile Valcour, the younger of the girls, was the only daughter of a French Canadian refugee, who, during the war of the American Revolution, had espoused the cause of the colonists; and had, in consequence, during the continuance of the struggle, been compelled to abandon the provinces north of the St. Lawrence, and to take up his abode within the limits of the United States. This he had been enabled to accomplish without material pecuniary loss, as most of his property was of a personal and movable character; and, for the little that had been confiscated, he was afterward liberally rewarded by grants of land from the State of New York.

He was now somewhat advanced in life, living in retirement and affluence at a country seat near the city of New York, and not far from the Huguenot village or settlement of New Rochelle—a place recommended to his favor by its name, and by the example of his compatriots, who, exiled for a different cause, had formerly established themselves there.

At the period when our story opens, it was already

customary for gentlemen and men of leisure, during the summer months, to bring their families from the towns and the sea-board into the interior; and the mineral springs of Ballston, having already attracted attention, had thus early made that neighborhood one of considerable resort.

Thither had Jules Valcour and his daughter repaired.

Among those by whom they had been accompanied were Colonel Henry Belden and his daughter Marion, with whom the reader is partially acquainted. This gentleman had served, with some credit, in the American army during the war. He was now living in comfortable circumstances in one of the southern counties of the State; and was an old friend and neighbor (as neighbors then went) of Mr. Valcour.

In respect to the two men who accompanied the riding party, on the present occasion, the one was a thin slightly made man, with a bronzed and hardy countenance, and a wiry, athletic frame. He was partially dressed in the livery of a groom, for such things had not then gone out of fashion. The other, though to appearance an Indian, was in reality a half-breed. His white blood, however, did not show itself so much in his appearance as in some of his habits. He was a large, powerful man, with thick stolid features, and small, fiery black eyes. His garb was chiefly that of the white people, with whom, when occasion offered, he liked to associate. He was armed with a long rifle, and a hunting-knife stuck in his belt. The groom was also provided with a pair of horseman's pistols.

In respect to our young woodsman, Arthur Walcott, we have also a few more words to say. He was of a good New York family, the only son of a widowed mother, and a distant relative of the Beldens. His father, who had been a physician of some distinction, and who was particularly noted for his treatment of the insane and persons of diseased minds, had been dead many years; and the young man had been brought up with a good education, but with much indulgence, and with but few restraints upon his inclinations. Natural good sense had, however, in part, remedied the evil caused by early license.

When quite young, suitableness of age, of social position, and supposed compatability of temper, had suggested to his mother, and to the father of Miss Belden, the propriety of a marriage between them. Hence they had been taught to regard themselves as affianced. Beyond this, they gave but little thought to the matter. This relation, instead of kindling any positive attachment between them, seemed, on the contrary, to have lulled their passions, and to have superinduced in their conduct, in spite of a real and mutual esteem, a certain indifference of bearing.

Marion, in temperament, was gentle; quiet and lady-like in manner; with no lack of sensibility, but with much reserve and self-possession. She was tall, well-formed, with light complexion, brown eyes, delicate features. She might easily have excited the admiration of any young man of taste and appreciation.

Her present companion, young Lucile Valcour, was younger, less tall, and more sprightly than herself. Her temperament was warmer and more mercurial; her features less regular, but more mobile and expressive. Her eyes and hair were dark, and her complexion less clear; though her lips and her cheeks possessed a warmer and richer tint.

She knew of Marion's engagement to young Walcott;

though of the latter she knew but little else. She imagined, however, that he must be something of a hero, and handsome of course. That he and Marion were ardent lovers she did not doubt. She had not seen the young man for some years—not, in fact, since she was quite a girl; and she had almost forgotten him, while he had wholly forgotten her. When she met him in the forest she had merely guessed at his identity; and, as we have seen, he had arrived at her own by the same process.

So much by way of introducing some of the persons with whom the reader is to become acquainted in the course of the story, the thread of which we now resume.

When young Walcott approached the group beneath the beech-trees, Miss Belden called out to him, saying:

"Why, Arthur, who would have expected to meet you here? I thought you had gone up to the lakes fishing. You are a gallant man indeed! Lucile says she found you eating your breakfast out there in the woods alone. Why could n't you either invite us to join you, or go up to the cabin and take it with us, like a Christian?"

"Pooh! Marion," said he, as he sauntered in among them, "how was I to know you were here? And as for the hut, I take it that I know how to broil a venison steak as well as Sandy Brigham, or any of his men. But, I say, where the deuce are you all traveling to, in this Amazon-like manner?"

"We did not come quite as badly attended as you think," replied Marion; "for we left my father only a little way back."

"Well that's fortunate, as far as it goes," he answered; "but I have special reasons for wishing that even he would not stray off amid these wilds quite so much. Where did he stop?"

"Only a mile or so from here," answered Marion; "he took a path to the right, to examine some bottom land, as he called it; and he promised to meet us here by this time. So we came on with James and the guide."

"Well," said the young man; "I hope he understands the paths well enough to find his way here; for these woods are not, at this time, quite so safe as they might be."

"Why," said Marion, quickly; "what is there to harm him?"

"Many things," said he; "even your wandering friend on the pony there, came nigh meeting with an adventure just now."

"Oh! I forgot," exclaimed Marion. "Lucile, this is Mr. Arthur Walcott, of whom you have heard me speak."

"He ought to know me without any introduction," said Lucile, poutingly. "But these men are so indifferent! I knew him at once, I am sure; but he only stared at me, without manifesting any interest, instead of speaking to me familiarly at once, as he should have done to my father's daughter."

"But, pray, how was I to know your father's daughter?" asked Walcott.

"How did you know his dog?" retorted she. "Am I of less consequence than Prince?"

"Ah! but you know," he said, "that Prince did not hesitate to acknowledge his acquaintance without pretending mystery."

In this manner the young people, for a few moments,

conversed together, sometimes seriously and sometimes jokingly; but their conversation was at length interrupted suddenly, and in a manner a little remarkable.

The hound, which had been for a few seconds uneasily snuffing the air, all at once began to yelp, and then broke forth into full cry. Taking a few turns around the party, with his nose to the ground, he then set off at full speed, through the open woods.

The Indian, who was only known by the English name of Joe, immediately started to his feet, and, without a moment's hesitation, ran rapidly away, following the course taken by the dog, which was in a south-westerly direction.

"This is 'tarnal strange," now exclaimed M'Carty, the little groom, as he ventured to intrude into the conversation; "I never knowed Indian Joe to be riled up so sudden before. And that oneasy dog seems to have got the hydrophoby all at once. Here, Mr. Walcott, if you' ll look arter the young women, I'll try and see what's the matter."

But it was already too late, for young Walcott had disappeared, leaving the two girls in no small alarm, at the turn affairs had taken; but without any definite idea of what the cause of the sudden tumult or the danger might be.

"Well, to be sure," said M'Carty, grumbling; "when a feller's young, he's more fit for runnin'; but I rayther think I understand matters here in the woods better than any on 'em. Hows'ever, let 'em have their own way and I'll just wait and see the end on 't."

"Do you think any thing could have happened to my father, James?" asked Miss Belden, with much anxiety.

"There's no tellin', miss," replied M'Carty. "Them houn's is odd critters, and I never hear 'em cry out that way without feelin' sort of onsartain. And Joe, too, is a parfect bear-ometer, as they says at sea; and can tell when any wild critter's about by the feel of the air; and especially bears, as the name shows. Now miss—"

"But," said Marion, interrupting the loquacious attendant, "if any thing has happened, had we not better ride that way?"

"Not a bit on it, Miss Marion," replied the other, "that 'ud only be tanglin' things up worse. Keep in the traces, says I, and then they'll know where to find us."

"But what *can* it be?" persisted the alarmed girl. "There can be no danger from Indians, and I hope there are no wild animals about?"

"As I said, Miss Marion, there's no tellin'," replied M'Carty, "but—whew! there goes that yelpin' hound again! Can't nobody take these hosses? But no! I'd better look arter his gals. That 'ud be the Colonel's orders, I know."

CHAPTER II.

CRAZY JAKE.

To explain what was the real cause of the little commotion we have noted, it will be necessary for us to refer to some events which had preceded the time at which our story opened.

Colonel Belden, with his daughter and her friend, accompanied by the groom and the guide, had early that morning set out from their quarters at Ballston, on an excursion through the woods. Their purpose was to visit the "Rock Spring" at Saratoga, which had already become known, and was an object of much curiosity. It was situated some seven or eight miles distant in a northeasterly direction. As the day was likely to be extremely warm, they had taken this early start, in order to arrive at their place of destination before the full heat of noontide could be felt. Their route thither lay through a heavy pine forest, which was traversed by numerous paths, worn by the feet of animals, or those of the Indians, in their different migrations and hunting excursions over the country.

For a part of the way, the path lay along the western bank of the stream now known as the Kayaderosseras Creek. When they had accomplished about half of their journey, they reached a point where the track which they were to follow, diverged to the northward, and left the stream some distance on the right. The Colonel, who affected an agricultural taste, here left the others to pursue the regular path, while he went to examine the "bottom lands" along the creek. He accordingly rode down some distance in the required direction, and after having accomplished his object, he again leisurely resumed his journey, but by a route somewhat to the eastward of that taken by the young people, supposing that he could arrive at the place of rendezvous, at the worst, within half an hour after them.

When, however, in following down the course of the stream, he came to a point where it diverged considerably to the east; and where, in order to pursue the right course, it was necessary for him to leave it, he sought out some path by which he could mount the high bank, which there bordered the valley. He soon found a narrow, rough, dry water-course, by which he hoped to ascend the sharp acclivity; and into this he immediately turned his horse.

The hour was still early. The air was fresh with night dews, and the copse was still dim with lingering shadows. Daylight was broad upon the hills, but crept more slowly down through the bushy slopes of the rocks, and the tangled brakes of the valleys.

The Colonel, without much difficulty for an old gentleman, as he indeed was, rode up the steep and stony way; but when he had nearly reached the top, at a point where the path was unusually narrow and rough, there suddenly stood before him an apparition which might well have caused a younger and stronger man to pause in alarm. It was that of a man of large size, clad in the skins of wild animals. His hair was long and tangled, and his beard unshaven. His head was bare, and his feet were rudely swathed in moccasins of untanned hides. In person he was squalid beyond description; and although he was apparently a white man, yet so weather-beaten and sunburnt was his face, and so disfigured and distorted by brutal habits, and unbridled passions, that one might almost fancy that he was some upright beast of prey.

He maintained his ground square in the pathway; eyeing with a fierce and mocking smile, the appalled traveler whom he had thus suddenly confronted. It must be confessed that the latter had sufficient cause for terror. Although a man of nerve, and tried courage, he was not a little alarmed at his present position. Rumors had indistinctly reached his ears, of a crazy man, who, for some years, had infested these woods; and had, on several occasions, been found to be extremely ferocious and violent. These rumors, however, had been so vague that Colonel Belden had been inclined to consider the whole story as fabulous. Now, however, there was before him a living and startling proof of their truth.

The horse, also, upon which he rode, seemed quite as uneasy as himself. At the first appearance of the wild man, he had snorted and plunged with violence, but after a short struggle with his rider, he stood trembling, as if in some sort familiarized with the danger, or fascinated by it. The gorge where he stood, was too narrow and steep to permit of turning around; and the thicket was on all sides close and apparently impenetrable. The place was a natural ambush.

At last, to put a bold face upon the matter, Colonel Belden accosted the stranger, saying:

"Well, my friend, how do you do this morning? My horse was a little frightened at your sudden appearance."

"Fine morning," said the lunatic, his face suddenly flushing, and becoming covered with a hearty look of welcome and good-will; "fine morning, sir, he! he! I say, come in to breakfast!" With that he stepped back a few paces, and opening the bushes on one side, disclosed a passage into the adjoining thicket, on the top of the acclivity.

Colonel Belden moved forward, scarcely knowing what course to pursue, or how to get rid of his dangerous companion.

"Ha! ha!" shouted the latter, as he led the way onward, making the woods resound with his loud, sonorous laughter. "You 're not too late for breakfast arter all, I say! Put on the kettle there! ha! ha! ho! ho!"

At every utterance of his stentorian voice, the horse would start and tremble, as if aware of the dangerous presence of that most fearful thing—a wandering human intellect.

The strange man now led the way forward over the level ground, shouting with wild merriment, and leaping, as he went. His appearance indicated him to be a man of immense strength, though his head was already prematurely bald. His face generally wore a smiling or a mocking look, but was subject to great and unexpected changes of expression.

"Did you ever see the Doctor?" said he, suddenly

turning to Colonel Belden, as they went along. "Now, do you know the Doctor has got a notion that he is a stronger man than I am. Ha! ha! ho! ho! But let me once catch him out here in the woods alone, as I do you"—(here he paused, and his countenance changed from its ruddy color and smiling expression to the whiteness of death, and an appalling scowl of mortal hatred)—"and by the God that sits in the sky," he continued, stretching his bare arm high above him; "I'd tear him to pieces like a bundle of leaves! But, I say" (here his face again resumed its old expression and color), let's hurry in to breakfast! ha! ha! ho! ho!"

They had now reached a small open space, on one side of which the lunatic had erected a kind of hut, of bark and boughs.

"How do you like my house?" said he, turning to his unwilling guest; "some think it's too clus in here; and some," he continued, turning to the south side and parting the bushes; "some don't like the prospect from this window! Ha! ha! ho! ho!"

By opening the bushes, he disclosed that on this side was a deep gulf or precipice, extending sheer down into the valley of the creek. This was deep enough and precipitous enough to render a plunge or fall from its brink inevitably fatal.

"That's my cellar," he added, "where I keep my fresh game. I'll soon give you a chance to try it, so dismount and join me in a glass of tea first, ha! ha! ho! ho!"

Colonel Belden now found himself compelled to dismount, for the strange being, who had seized the horse by the bridle, was at each moment becoming more wild and ungovernable. The horse was then turned loose in the woods, and was driven from the spot by sticks and stones hurled after him. Meanwhile the lunatic kept leaping and laughing through the open space, and making the woods ring again with his shouts.

The old man was wholly unarmed; and even if it had been otherwise, he might, perhaps, have hesitated about making use of deadly weapons, except in the last extremity. At the same time he could not but entertain serious misgivings as to the issue of his present dilemma. His thoughts also painfully dwelt upon the alarm and distress into which his daughter would be thrown by his prolonged and unaccountable absence.

The place where all this occurred was a little less than two miles from the spot where Marion and her companion had halted. The air was, at the time, still; not a breath of wind stirred the trees; and not a sound disturbed the forest where they were. The harsh, dissonant shouts of the wild man, rendered faint by the distance, had reached the acute ears of the hound, and of the Indian; while they had made no impression upon the less trained senses of the others. Arthur Walcott heard nothing; but readily divining that something unusual must have attracted the attention of the dog, and aroused the sluggish apathy of the savage, he had followed their footsteps closely, to meet, with them, whatever danger might exist.

After going for some distance in a direct line, he began, at length, to hear the cries and shouts which had startled the Indian. Then, for the first time, a faint glimmering of the true character of the danger began to dawn upon him. This only increased his anxiety; and it was now, almost with the fierce agility of a panther, that he sprang forward. In appearance, even, he became greatly changed. His eyes dilated and assumed a steady look of menace. His lips were compressed, and the veins in his forehead swollen and knotted, like whip-cord. His movement, which before was laborious, now became light and easy; and he even gained upon the Indian.

At last the dog suddenly stopped upon the verge of a thicket, and sitting down began, continuously, to raise his long, mournful, howl. The savage, immediately afterward, dashed through the brake beyond him; and then was heard the loud cry of the lunatic again; which Walcott was in doubt whether to attribute to the arrival of the Indian, or to the execution of some plan of mischief previously prepared.

It was one of the peculiarities of the lunatic that he was generally silent except when he met with some human being, or was meditating some violence. This Walcott well knew; and from Colonel Belden's long absence, he apprehended that some danger from that quarter might threaten him. The shouts of the maniac were now loud and obstreperous, and as Walcott approached he could distinguish the following:

"Try it again, old bald pate! ha! ha! Try it again! next time you may reach it! Oh! how jolly! Reach higher, I say! But ho! ho! who's this? Take that, for coming without an invitation! There 's hell behind you, yellow dog! Ha! ha! Try it again, old white-top! Ho! ho!"

His raving and merriment appeared to have reached a climax, he fairly screamed with delight; and the savage came bursting back from the thicket, with every mark of mortal terror in his looks and actions.

Walcott now dashed forward, and pushing aside the bushes, he saw Colonel Belden, bound to a tree, in a curious and alarming way. The sapling, when in its natural position, inclined far over the brink of the precipice; but the lunatic had contrived to bend it back, so that, while holding it, he tied the body of the poor old man to it with a stout thong. In his muscular grasp, his victim was like a child; and the feeble resistance he met with, hardly impeded his operations. When the lashing was securely accomplished, the tree was released from his hold, when it immediately began to assume its natural position, over the rock. The struggle was now between the elastic force of the young sapling, and the failing and nearly exhausted strength of the old man. As soon as this should fail, he would be dragged by the recoil entirely over the precipice, where the suspension would cause a lingering and most painful death; or where the breaking of the cords which held him, would precipitate him upon the rocks and broken stones far below.

It was just about the time when the waning energies of the victim had become almost exhausted, that young Walcott arrived upon the scene. The Indian had previously made his appearance, but one thrust of the lunatic had hurled him back as if he had been a child; and, cowed by what appeared to him supernatural strength, he had then turned and fled.

With Walcott, however, it was different. After emerging upon the open space, he walked stealthily but rapidly up to where the wild man stood, and laid his hand firmly upon his shoulder. The latter turned fiercely about, as if to grapple with this new intruder; but meeting with the fixed, unflinching glare of his eye, he suddenly changed his manner; and with unaccountable marks of submission and fear, he exclaimed:

"The old Doctor, by the Lord!"

Young Walcott, turning him about, and pointing away, said—

"I told you not to come here again! Do you understand me now? Go!"

The madman was ruled as by magnetic power. When released from the hold of the other, he slunk away, cowed and silent—and after getting a few rods distant, fled at the top of his speed, and soon disappeared in the distance.

The savage having seen through the bushes what had taken place, now made his appearance again; and gave an emphatic evidence of his astonishment by the characteristic exclamation of "ugh!" Walcott, in his eyes, was a mighty "medicine man."

By this time the attention of both had become necessary to rescue the old man from his perilous position; for his strength had at last utterly failed; and after endeavoring in vain to clutch some bushes to stay or retard his descent, he was swung, with a heavy lurch, far over the brink of the rock; and was now suspended from the branches of the swinging tree. Here his situation was dangerous in the extreme, for besides the circumstance that life could not long be sustained in such a position, it was found that the cord by which he hung was composed of thongs of bark rudely twisted together; and that at every oscillation of the tree, they continued slowly to unwind. It was obvious that as soon as they should become sufficiently untwisted, to bring the weight more unevenly upon them, the separate strands would break one after another, and the weight which they held would drop. He could not be reached from the top of the rock. There was nothing which could be thrown to him, by which he could be hauled up. The least additional strain upon the bark rope, it was feared, might cause it to snap at once. Time was precious, and it seemed that nothing but instant, and almost miraculous action, could be effectual.

The course now pursued met the emergency. Walcott did what, at first sight, appeared to be most calculated to hasten the catastrophe. He sprang into the young sapling itself, and climbing out upon it, caused it gradually to sink down beneath his additional weight. By this means the old man was lowered some distance down the chasm. The young man finding, however, that his own weight was insufficient, called to the Indian, who had been looking on, with curious attention, and who, now that he comprehended the object of the proceeding, sprang lightly into the branches of the tree. This, under the new load, slowly bent over like an enormous withe, till the old gentleman, more dead than alive, was lowered to a table or shelf of the rock, near the bottom of the gorge; while Walcott, swinging himself downward after him, soon released him from his bonds, and the tree was then allowed to resume its old position. In all this manœuver, there was little or no danger, except to the person to be relieved. The sapling would bend, but ten times the weight put upon it, would not have broken it.

As soon as they were all safely landed below, Colonel Belden, in the reaction which followed his severe struggles, and in the sense of a sudden relief from a great danger, fainted away. He was in that state carried to the top of the bank, where the two men busied themselves in effecting his restoration. Shortly after he had been brought to his senses, and as soon as he was sufficiently recruited to walk, they all started, at a slow pace, for the spot where his daughter and her companions had appointed to meet him. The horse which he had ridden had fled, and it was deemed useless, at that time, to look for him in those uncertain wilds.

"Arthur, my dear boy," said the old man as they slowly and painfully pursued their journey; "nature has intended you for a soldier. I noticed, even in the extremity of the peril, the coolness and promptitude with which all your measures were taken. But how, in the name of all that is curious, have you acquired such control over that crazy man? That puzzles me more than all. And, by the way, who, and what is he? I had often heard vague reports of such a person, but never, until to-day, have I believed them. Do you know any thing about him, Joe? You live in these parts, I believe, and must have met him often before."

"Indian know him," replied Joe, "been here five, six, tree year. He kill bear, kill white man, kill Indian, kill all. He de debbill! He big medicine man! no good, see him; no good fight him. He de dibbell! ugh!"

"There 's a satisfactory answer, any way; eh, Arthur? Well, Joe, I suppose he must pass for the devil in your opinion. But, Arthur, my lad, it seems to me that your influence was a little singular. I should like to know how you acquired it; and, above all things, it strikes me that this poor fellow should be properly cared for, and put under such restraint as will prevent him from doing further mischief to himself or others."

"Why, sir," replied the young man, "it would be a long story. I am afraid to give you a full account of him. As yet, so far as I know, he has not done any great harm, though they tell strange stories about him. I believe he was known to my father; and he seems, in some way, to confound me with him: for, when I spoke to him to-day, he called me 'the old Doctor.' It is, no doubt, owing to this delusion that I was able to control him. In fact, this is not the first time I have met him. I believe he would be a little dangerous with most men. I should much dislike to have him meet with any persons who should be weak enough to manifest any fear of him. And it seems that even your coolness, Colonel, was no protection against him. But, good heaven! what is that I hear? There is his shout again! He must certainly have met some one else! Can it be?—It must be Marion or one of the party!"

Saying this, he sprang hastily forward, and, without making further explanations, disappeared through the trees.

CHAPTER III.

THE ABDUCTION.

It will be borne in mind that when our attention was last withdrawn from the party of the young girls, they were still under the "beech-trees" with their horses, and the groom, M'Carty. Naturally, all felt much alarm at the sudden departure of Walcott and the Indian; and their anxiety was intense, to ascertain the cause of the disturbance, and what connection, if any, Colonel Belden might have with it. For some time they continued to hear the yelp of the hound, as he receded further and further away; but, at length, all sounds died out in the distance, and the poor girls were left alone to painful conjecture. As, however, silence prevailed for a long time, they began, gradually, to resume a little courage; and, at last, they so far forgot the causes of their anxiety, as to observe with more curious attention, the character of the spot in which they were. They also had the curiosity to look for some of those new and celebrated springs with which the neighborhood was said to abound, and which they had, in part, ventured so far to visit.

One of these they found by following the deer path into the edge of the marsh. The fountain itself was plainly indicated by the redness of the earth which surrounded it, caused by the deposition of the copious solution of iron, with which it is charged. But the water, which rose up and burst forth, like a boiling Geyser, was bright and sparkling, and as clear as crystal. It gushed up in great abundance, and flowed off in a steady and copious stream. The fixed air broke in continued bubbles from its surface, as from a glass of sparkling wine. It is now known as Columbian Spring.

For some time they amused themselves about this spring, drinking of its water, and wondering at its liveliness and exuberance. At length, however, the three—for the groom had fastened the horses, and gone with them to the fountain—returned along the rude pathway. When they came forth from the thicket of alder bushes, they were surprised not to find the horses which they had left tied to the trees. Every thing around them was still, and nothing gave a clew to the mystery. The groom was the first to observe the fact. He immediately endeavored, by means of the tracks, to find out in what direction they had gone. He soon ascertained that the course taken was backward, and around the circular beaten path. The animals must have been untied, for no remnants of broken bridle reins were left behind. They seemed, also, after a short distance, to have gone away at a rapid pace. He followed the tracks till he came to a place where the ground was much trodden by them; and as footprints led thence in all directions, it was impossible to divine what way further they had really gone. Selecting those footmarks which appeared the most distinct, and which went off through the underwood, quite away from any regular course, he followed them for ten or fifteen rods. When in a part of the woods more close and impenetrable than usual, he suddenly felt himself seized from behind, and thrown, with violence, to the ground. In a twinkling he found himself pinioned and helpless.

"Ha! ha! ho! ho!" shouted a stentorian voice beside him. "So, my little lamb, I've got you again, have I? This time I'll give you a tether you won't get rid of so easy."

"Well," said the undaunted M'Carty, "for a cussed hoss thief, I must say you've done it pretty considerable well. But, I say, you're a pretty lookin' object, hain't you? But what in darnation is the creatur about now?"

This question was elicited by the unusual proceedings of the maniac, who had caught hold of a young tree close at hand and pulled it over, till, as he sat on it, the top lay on the ground. When he had got it in this position, he proceeded to make arrangements for fastening his new prisoner to it. By this time, however, M'Carty had begun to comprehend something of the nature of the contrivance; but, as his hands were securely tied, he was not in a situation to render any very effectual resistance. Watching his opportunity, notwithstanding, as he was pulled to the tree, still lying upon his back, he succeeded in giving his captor a violent thrust with his feet, which sent him to some distance; and the bent sapling sprang back to its upright position. M'Carty, meanwhile, got upon his feet, and started off in hope to make good his escape by running. In this, however, he found himself egregiously mistaken; for he had scarcely made a dozen steps, before he was recaptured and flung again to the ground, with as much facility as if he had been the merest child.

"And so, my little pet," exclaimed his tormentor, "you

thought to get away did you? Would n't it be nice though? ha! ha! But I'll give you a beautiful swing this time, eh? so that even the Doctor can't get you loose."

Saying this, he lifted M'Carty in his arms and carried him back; and after tying him to a tree, he again proceeded with his plan, which seemed to be a favorite with him. This time, M'Carty could not defeat the operation, and he soon found himself securely lashed to the elastic sapling; and having a strong suspicion that though the weight of the lunatic had bent it down, his own would not suffice to keep it there. Such, in a few moments, proved to be the fact. For, no sooner was the sapling loosened from the hold of the lunatic, than it swung the little groom up into the air, like a scarecrow on a pole. As, however, he was tied by the waist, he did not, immediately, experience any special inconvenience. To be sure, he felt absurd and helpless enough, thus dangling about among the bushes; and he also entertained some apprehensions as to how long his remaining in that "bad eminence" might continue; or rather, how long he might be able to endure it. His position, however, seemed to afford his captor infinite amusement. He laughed, shouted, and screamed in the most frantic manner, and even fairly rolled upon the ground, in the excess of his enjoyment. The woods again resounded with his unearthly glee.

Meanwhile the two helpless girls, who were now left entirely alone near the Spring, were in a condition little to be envied. Of the meaning of those strange, wild shouts they were utterly ignorant. There was something in the sounds too unnatural to encourage them to approach them. But the agony of suspense at last overcoming all the other feelings, Lucile proposed to go and ascertain, if possible, what had happened. After much debate, this course was consented to. She, accordingly, stepped lightly and cautiously forward toward the spot whence the noise proceeded. She had gone but a short distance, however, before those formidable sounds had altogether ceased, and the woods had become hushed and silent. Still, though with trembling footsteps, she pursued her course; but paused in uncertainty at the place where the horse-tracks led away in different directions. The sudden silence oppressed her with the sense of some new danger. The stillness was as mysterious as the preceding noise had been, and seemed much more to be feared. While she was in this state of uncertainty and apprehension, her attention was attracted by a slight rustling among the leaves close at hand, and looking that way more steadily, she discovered a pair of large, fierce, wild eyes, gazing upon her through the foliage. Her first thought was that they belonged to some wild animal; but gradually the outlines of a human countenance became faintly recognizable through the leaves. The character of the expression, however, was not at all calculated to reassure her. In the look of madness there is always something more painful and startling than in the gaze of the wildest and most untameable beast of prey.

Lucile, without knowing whom or what she was to encounter, felt herself, nevertheless, mysteriously influenced by the singular stare, of which she found herself the object. To a certain extent she was paralyzed. She was not of a timid nature; but at that moment she experienced the fascinating power of a real, or supposed, great peril. She was unable to withdraw her look or to move her limbs. She would have cried out, as much for aid for herself, as in warning to her friend, but her tongue was stricken as with palsy, and she was incapable of uttering a sound.

The spell at length was broken. Slowly parting the bushes, the maniac came forth and stood confronting her, wild, hideous, and mocking. He gazed upon her with mingled curiosity, admiration, and menace. The object now presented to his sight was, it would appear, new to him; but, at the same time, his manner was that of one who had unexpectedly fallen upon a prize, which he did not indeed quite understand, but which he had no idea of relinquishing.

Poor Lucile! If alarmed before she knew the danger, how much was her apprehension increased, now that it stood before her. The madman certainly presented no pleasant object of contemplation, though his conduct was so far unusual that he indulged in none of his sardonic laughter, and uttered no wild shouts. All his merriment had passed away. Solemnity sat upon his rude features. Even an apparent effort to recover some lost train of ideas was perceptible on his countenance. Perhaps the beautiful object before him vainly and ineffectually touched some chord in his ruined memory; recalling dimly and, perhaps, unconsciously, not the images, but the emotions, of other days. What may have been the struggle to connect that which he saw with what he had seen before; or how the sweet look of woman may have had reference to the tenderness of a mother's early caresses, can not now be told. Alas! for the poor wandering lunatic! no mother's heart would ever again beat—no mother's eye ever again light up with affection and pride. On earth no consoling voice was destined to soothe his passions or alleviate his sorrows; or sympathize with him in his struggles and his joys. The lamp of intellect had gone out forever, and he was left in the darkness of solitude and abandonment.

Whatever may have been the connection of his present conduct with the dim and confused recollections of his past life, there he stood, still silent and gazing at the frail and beautiful being who trembled before him. Can it be believed? From his dark and solemn eyes, so saddened by unaccountable sympathies, roll forth tears, that still hang upon their motionless lashes! But no! a deep gulf separates him from all the tender, treasured memories of the past, and he may never, on earth, re-cross it!

Not long, however, did this unwonted mood continue. The charm was soon broken; for the tramp of hasty steps, and the cry of a running hound, not far away, caused him to start. The old expression of mingled fatuity, malice, and cunning came back. In an instant, and before she was aware of his intent, he caught the young girl in his arms, and darted away with her through the forest. One scream of terror was all she could utter, before, in the extremity of her apprehensions, nature came to her relief; and she fainted, and, for a long time, knew no more.

When Walcott had, as we have related, left Colonel Belden and Indian Joe, on their way to the place of rendezvous originally agreed upon, he hastened on before them at the top of his speed. The others followed him as fast as they could. The dog alone kept pace with him. On arriving at the "beech-trees" he found Miss Belden there alone, and almost wild with apprehension. A few words reassured her as to the fate of her father. Of what had occurred near her, she knew little or nothing, except that Lucile had departed and had not returned. The untying of the horses, the search and absence of M'Carty, and the absence of Lucile were the facts. How far the maniac might have been concerned in those events, was left to conjecture. But Walcott knew his almost diabolical ubiquity, and his activity in evil; and had no difficulty in attributing to him, most, if not all, of those untoward occurrences. That it was he who had let loose the horses, he had no doubt. What had become of M'Carty, and what had befallen Miss Valcour, were very different questions. But it was no time for idle conjecture. If any thing serious had actually occurred, he knew himself to be the one most likely to remedy it. So, without loss of time, he made his way in the direction in which the missing groom and his young mistress had disappeared.

We have, thus far, neglected to state, that the name by which the lunatic was then generally known, was "Crazy Jacob," or "Wild Jake;" and we take this occasion to adopt it, for the sake of greater brevity and clearness in our narration.

That he had encountered either Lucile or M'Carty, Walcott felt very confident, from the outcries which he had heard. Further than this he was, for the present, unable to conjecture. When he reached the spot where the others had paused he was, like them, at a loss how to proceed. While hesitating there he was joined by Indian Joe. Colonel Belden, faint and exhausted as he was, had met and remained with his daughter. Though the young man and the guide were both, for a moment, at fault, the hound kept moving rapidly about in a circle; till suddenly pausing, and looking upward, he set up a furious barking at some object overhead.

Turning his eyes in the same direction, Walcott saw the body of M'Carty suspended from a small tree, motionless and apparently lifeless. To cut him down and relieve him from his precarious position was, for the two active men, but the work of a moment. The body was laid upon the grass; and while Walcott felt for some lingering sign of life, he directed the Indian to go for water. In the course of a few minutes, M'Carty slowly and painfully opened his eyes; but it was fully a quarter of an hour before he was able to speak. It seems that in his struggle in the tree, the thong around his body had gradually tightened, till his breathing had become extremely difficult; and he had, at last, been rendered speechless, though still retaining his hearing and his eye-sight. From this cause he had been unable to give any sign of his whereabouts; but most of what had occurred between Jacob and Lucile he had witnessed.

During the delay which was necessary for his full restoration to speech, and that which was further caused by his recital, it may well be imagined that young Walcott was impatient enough. The fate of the young girl, in whom he already felt a lively interest, was still wrapped in uncertainty. She had disappeared, leaving no present trace behind.

"Then you have no idea," said Walcott, after a diligent cross-examination of M'Carty; "you have no idea what direction he took with her after he started?"

"None more than I telled ye," replied the other; "I was n't myself in no condition to be particular sharp about the young woman. But, so near as I could judge, the varmint made off toward the lake; and I 'm afeard it 'ill be hard tracking him through the fly."

"It's difficult to say what course he will take," said Walcott, thoughtfully; "he often changes his mind; and sometimes is quite as apt to be found in a position directly opposite to that for which he starts, as anywhere else. But did he show any signs of violence with her, Jim?"

"None, that I see, on t' other hand, he seemed quite dumbfounded when he first laid eyes on her. I did n't hear any more of his 'tarnal yellin', which, I suppose, he means for a laugh; but whether I grew deaf, or he grew dumb, I can't say. All I know is that he kept his eyes on her, and carried her away as softly as a kitten. Away he went over that hummock yonder, and clus by the yaller pine, like a two-legged moose. Cuss me, if I think he's human. What do you think on't, Joe?"

Thus addressed, the Indian, laconically replied:

"He debbill."

"Well, you may n't be far off the trail there any how," said Jim; "but what I want is to meet him agin, when he can't get behind me to take an onfair advantage."

During this colloquy, Walcott had remained silent and musing. He now interrupted the speakers, saying:

"It won't do to leave her in his power a minute longer than we can help. He may at any moment kill her in one of his caprices. He might even take it into his head to tie her up, as he did you, M'Carty. But, I suppose you are too much frightened to go near him again?"

"Not, if I know my own mind, Mr. Arthur. Do you think you 're the only man that ain't afeard of nothing? I'm ready to start this minute. Joe there, may stay behind with the colonel and his da'ter. You jest lead off, and we 'll see if the varmint trees me agin like a cussed raccoon."

Arthur Walcott was, in one sense, rash. In imminent danger, he acted promptly; but even in the most pressing circumstances, he did not act unadvisedly. Whatever precipitancy might appear in his conduct, now existed in fact. Upon occasions, where instant action was indispensable, his power of mind, and rapidity of combination, were equal to the emergency; and his plans were only developed by their simultaneous execution. But when it was not necessary to act on the instant; when the case admitted of reflection, or required delay, he was not one to omit an opportunity of coming to a correct conclusion. In the present case, therefore, before adopting any plan, he took time for reflection; since pursuit made in the wrong direction would be worse than useless; and from some experience of the habits of Jacob, he had arrived at the conclusion that it was not always safe to trust to probabilities or appearances.

CHAPTER IV.

THE SPRINGS IN 1787.

In those days, as we have already said, Saratoga was almost a wilderness. It is true that about a quarter of a mile from where Colonel Belden and his party were now assembled, there was a small clearing and a rude hut, the work and the property of Indian Joe, the guide. The latter, notwithstanding his thorough aboriginal habits, had white blood flowing in his veins; and this might explain his partiality for something like a garden and a fixed abode. The rude shelter which his cabin might, in the present case have afforded, was uncalled for, as Walcott knew they were not far from more convenient accommodations, and had made up his mind to take the old colonel and his daughter thither. Since the first adventure of the morning, he had virtually assumed the direction of all their movements. He was unwilling to expose them for a second time to the hazard of meeting with the maniac; and he could not very well leave them unsheltered even for the coming night. It would also probably be useless to attempt tracking the fugitive during the darkness. He therefore determined to place the old man and Marion in safety for the present, and to commence the search as soon after as practicable.

During the fatigues and excitements of the recent events, the day had insensibly worn away, and was now fast verging toward nightfall. It was therefore prudent to take immediate steps to procure some proper place of shelter.

Having succeeded in recovering the horses, which had not strayed very far, the whole group began slowly to move northward along the western side of the valley, following the woodland path so often mentioned. To the left, the ground was rough and rocky, and rose with a gradual ascent. It was everywhere covered with large, old trees, the views between which were not interrupted by any underwood. To the right, as they went along, still lay the narrow swale or marsh.

After proceeding for a quarter of an hour or more, they began to perceive signs of the vicinity of some sort of habitations. The distant barking of dogs was heard. Presently they could occasionally see an Indian boy gazing at them, with his great round eyes, from behind some distant tree. He betrayed thus early the instincts and habits of his race. He was not noisy and prattling like the child of the white man; but taciturn, shy, and watchful. The everlasting bow and arrow seemed inseparable from him. Its practice was the education of all. The forest was their only university; and the young savages grew up to take their degrees, not on scrolls of parchment, but in deer's hide and bear-skin.

Presently the travelers came to a more open place; and here was seen, at a short distance ahead, a small clearing, and a large log-house. Further on, and up the slope to the left, were some twenty or thirty wigwams. It was, in fact, a sort of Indian town which they approached.

Here were visible all the various and picturesque objects which characterize such scenes. The men were grouped together in lazy clusters, either dozing upon the ground, or sitting in sluggish silence, leading just the life of unoccupied animals. The women were busied with the various labors of their position, making or staining baskets, cooking their rude meals, hanging out strips of meat to dry, or working upon gayly-fringed moccasins.

It was not, however, toward the cluster of wigwams that our party continued its way. The log-house, which stood in the clearing, and on the verge of the valley, seemed to be their point of destination.

On coming nearer, it was found to be a huge four-sided edifice, constructed of round logs, rendered impenetrable to the weather by wedging and plastering. Its roof was composed of long poles covered with strips of bark, and its chimney of rough stone, laid up in mortar. At one side, and a little away from it, was a large shed of hemlock bushes and poles, which answered the purpose of a stable. Here the horses of the new comers were, shortly afterward, bestowed with such care for their comfort, as circumstances admitted. At the door of the cabin itself, the guests were met with a sort of reception which did not partake, either of the obsequiousness of the modern publican, or the churlish ungraciousness of a man receiving unwelcome company. In those days, it was the custom to receive and entertain freely all who required shelter; and the act was neither a condescension or an homage. Their arrival, therefore, excited no remark. No extraordinary movements were perceptible in consequence of it. In the mean time, night had begun to set in as they approached.

By the side of the entrance, on a log which answered the purpose of a bench, sat a man in his shirt-sleeves, quietly smoking a pipe. He gave directions to a negro about the horses, and rose up as the old man and his daughter came to the door.

"Them cattle, I take it," he said, "ain't had no great matter of traveling to-day, eh! squire?"

"None to speak of," replied Colonel Belden, "but we ourselves feel a little fatigued, and would be much obliged to you for such accommodations as you can give us."

Upon hearing the sound of the other's voice, the man suddenly pulled his pipe from his mouth, and after looking at the colonel steadily for some time, took off his cap respectfully, saying:

"Your sarvent, captain; I did n't at first know you; these still times so alter a man. What can I do for you?"

"Eh, what?" exclaimed the old colonel, looking sharply at his interlocutor, in his turn; "whom have we here? Upon my word, I think it's Brigham? Why my old friend, how do you do?"

"Who would have thought of meeting you here? Marion, this is one of my old soldiers of '77. I am indebted to him for many an important service. But, Brigham, you don't mean to say that you've turned landlord again?"

"Yes, but I do tho', captain; a man must turn his hand to any thing, when the campaign is over, you know."

"Why, I should have thought, Brigham, that services like yours would have put you in a position to live at your ease. What I did was no great matter, you know; and yet they have given me a colonel's commission for it."

"And how much pay does that bring you now?" quietly asked Brigham.

"As for that," replied the colonel, "why no great matter—nothing at all, in fact; but then the honor, you know."

"Yes, I know," said the other, "but in the way of getting a living, I don't see that your services have been any better paid for than mine. Hows'ever such is the fortune of war, captain, or rather colonel, since they have made you one, which I'm glad to hear. But I never counted my little enterprises as any great thing. I would do the same over again just for the fun of the thing. You know I was always fond of running a little risk."

While this dialogue was going on, the rest of the party had dismounted, and passed into the rude hostelry. The building was divided into two compartments, nearly equal in size. The first, or ante-room, like the other, occupied the whole width of the house. Beyond it, was the inner apartment or with drawing-room, which, as it appeared, was set apart as the place in which any female guests who might be present, were to be accommodated. In the outer room, the meals were not only taken, but cooked; and when the tables were cleared, the apartment was turned into a bed-room. The simple habits, and the narrow circumstances of the occupants, rendered this arrangement convenient and proper. Whatever could serve as a shelter from the rain, was then deemed a fit place for eating and sleeping.

The men, as a matter of course, paused in the outer room, and began to make themselves at home. Coats and hats were doffed and hung on huge hooks or spikes of iron, driven into the timbers of the building. Suspended over the back of a maple chair, was an iron candlestick, in which was burning a tallow candle, that shed but a faint and flickering light through the apartment.

While M'Carty had been busy providing for the comfort of the quadrupeds, Indian Joe, true to his savage instincts, had quietly declined sharing in the menial services, and walked with the gentlemen, into the house.

Colonel Belden and Walcott speedily informed Brigham of the painful suspense under which they were laboring in regard to the disappearance and fate of Lucile Valcour; and, as they had expected, he immediately took a lively interest in the affair.

"You must know, colonel," he said, "that I always thought crazy Jake would end by doing some great mischief, and I've often tried to secure him, but all to no purpose. Where on arth he has gone to now, there's no tellin'. Hows'ever, if Arthur here (hitching his elbow toward Walcott) will go with me to-morrow morning, I'm agreeable to have one push after the old varmint. But we'll have to make an arly start, as the old chap, to my sartain knowledge, gets up considerable soon himself, and we must nab him afore he smells us over the dew."

"Start as early as you like, my friend," said Walcott, "and I will be ready. In fact I would go now, if it would do any good."

"No, no," said Brigham, "there's no use in being off yet. The moon isn't up till near three in the morning; and as for going off through the woods in the dark, we might as well stay where we are, for Catfoot himself could n't foller game without something in the way of eyesight."

"Well, Brigham, my old friend," replied Colonel

Belden, "manage it your own way. Only I wish you to understand that in this business, I take success particularly to heart; for I would as soon leave my own body lifeless in the woods, as to go back to Jules Valcour without his child."

Soon after, preparations having already been made for that purpose, supper was served up for the guests on a long table of pine, set out in the middle of the room. It is needless to detail the various preliminary operations which met the eye of the travelers, and which forcibly impressed upon them the fact, that they were already a little removed from the comfortable habits of well-organized society. It is enough to know that the preparations were at length achieved.

Grateful to the appetite as may be the dishes which are sometimes spread before the well exercised sportsman, after a hard day's chase; we doubt whether the most exhilarating hunt could give a keener appetite than that which certain of our party brought to the discussion of their evening meal. In true democratic style, all sat at the same board; though, as in all democracies, there was still a distinction. One end of the table, was, even there, looked upon as especially to be honored. There was no daïs, and no canopy, yet good manners and gentle breeding, on the one hand, gave a separate position; and on the other hand, natural respect and deference, accorded a tacit superiority to those whose previous position and habits had qualified them for maintaining such an ascendency.

During the meal, little was said by any of the party. Marion Belden was too much excited, and at the same time, too much exhausted, by recent occurrences, to partake, except in a very slight degree, of the food placed before her. Anxiety also prevailed in the hearts of her father, and of Walcott. The mind of the latter was impatiently busy with thoughts and devices for the morrow. Brigham was moving about the premises, sometimes within, and sometimes without the building; and occupied with the various little cares of his establishment, or the weightier duties of a host.

"Why, here comes little Jim M'Carty as sure as I am alive," said he, as the groom, after having made proper provision for the horses, now entered the apartment to take his place at the table with the others.

"It's me for sartain, Sandy Brigham; and there 's nothing so very wonderful about that, I take it."

"Yes there is, though, Jim," replied Brigham; "for nobody has hearn on ye, since you was carried off by the Winedots (so he pronounced Wyandottes), just arter the war."

"Well, it's true," said M'Carty, seating himself, and commencing his meal without ceremony. "It's true, them varmints did do something like what you say; but I made up my mind not to go with 'em clean to the lines; and so I gin 'em the slip one fine morning near the Sawble (Ausable) Forks."

"But how did it all happin, Jim? I thought you was too sly for any redskin to get hold on. Tell us all about it. You and I used to conceit we understood the cunning ceremony of the critters as well as any body."

Brigham now flung himself down upon a large wooden chest, to hear M'Carty's account of the adventure. As for the others, they were too busy with thoughts of their own to pay much heed to what was said. M'Carty, with many interruptions, caused by the necessary business of eating, then gave something like the following account of his capture and escape.

"Why, you see, the way it happened was jest this. You remember there was parties of them British Injuns hangin' about for a while arter the war was done. How-s'ever, when some months had passed over, without any scalps being lost, the country folks began to think there was no more risk, and to go back to their clearins. I happened, about that time, to be down Fish Creek with some pelts; and General Schuyler wanted me to go out with his gals and some chaps up from Albany, on a visit to Quakers' Springs—them salt licks, you know, 'tother side the lake, near Bemis's. Well, when they started, I was for takin' the gun along, knowin' how things was with the savages better than they did; but they downright laughed me out on't; so between their jokes and the heat of the weather, I left the shootin' iron behind. We followed the old army track through the woods, all on 'em bein' mounted but me. As I knew every foot of the ground, I nat'r'lly led the way. They came on, laughin' and jokin'; and laid out to have a knick-knack, or somethin' of that kind, when they got to the Springs. As we come up within a mile or so of the spot, I begun to notice marks in the path which I did n't at all like the look on'. I know it's hard tellin' a Huron's trail from an Oneida's; but I had had some experience that way, and from what I saw, I begun to wish I had brought the rifle along, in spite of their jokes. Hows'ever, the trail led straight ahead, whoever made it; and I thought it was likely the savages themselves, if so be there was any of 'em about, had n't any notion of our party being near. Acting on this idea, I kept carefully ahead, detarmined to keep a sharp look out. I know'd the gineral would expect me to bring back his gals, safe and sound, or I would never he'r the last on't. So I just cautioned the young folks to make a little less noise, and told 'em what I thought was in the wind. This only made 'em laugh the more; and they rode along, singin' and shoutin' like mad. They war a high set, I tell you. There 'll be a devil's dance soon, and somebody will have to pay the piper; but let 'em laugh as wins, thinks I, and says no more. Well, whether the redskins were too far off, or whether they only played shy, nothin' on 'em did we see while goin'. We got to the spring, and all the things was spread out on the grass; and they begun to eat. Up to this pint the trail had been strong; and there was every sign that a party of Injuns had been about. I judged there might be seven or eight of 'em at least.

"Leaving the young folks to enj'y themselves, I thought I'd jest take a turn in the neighborhood, and see what had become of the Hurons, if Hurons they was. As I went quietly along a path, I caught sight of somethin' brown poppin' behin' a fallin tree to the right; but it did n't get out of sight before I diskivered it to be an Injun head. I never let on, but made as if nothin' had happened, and walked steadily for'd, lookin' carelessly about me. For all that, I took good care to go no further than a rod or so; when, turnin' coolly around, I strolled back. In wheelin' about sudden like, what should I catch a glimpse on, but the leg of another savage around the edge of a small white pine, clus to the track. Thinks I to myself, this is gettin' rather warm; may be the whole gang is skulkin' about within a stone's throw. At that minute, I was somethin' like thirty rods or so, from where the rest on 'em was takin' their refreshment. As good luck would have it, the ground 'twixt was open; so that they were in clear sight; and I calc'lated they would have no trouble in seein' me, on a pinch. I still made as if I saw nothin', but detarmined, as soon as I was a little more clear, to give the alarm, and make a run of it for myself. I was a little nonplushed to find they let me quietly go on; and so begun to suspect some trick. Sure enough, in a moment arter, I sees a tall feller, every minute or so, when he thought I was n't lookin', glidin' from one cover to another, in the direction of the party of young folks. The game was plain enough now. They wanted to catch the whole on us.

"There was n't a second to be lost. If I gave alarm at once, the young folks might have time to mount and get away before the Injuns could come up. But in that case, it was putty clear that I myself would have to be nabbed. But there was no other way; so, jumpin' on a big stone in the middle of the path, I gives a screech loud enough to wake the dead. It turned out jist as I expected. The Injuns at once jumped from their hiding-places, and what between my yell and the sight of the redskins makin' toward them, the young men understood it all in a jiffy. They got on horseback in no time, the Injuns arter them at a keen jump, and thanks to the open army road, they soon left the redskins far enough behind.

"As soon as I saw this, thinks I to myself, this time the gineral can't say but what I did my best. Meanwhile as long as the savages thought there was a chance of catchin' the rest, they did n't seem to mind me; maybe they thought I was sure game enough any how. We differed a little in opinion on that pint. I never yet knew even a Mohawk, who could outrun me in an open woods. So when they begun to turn and make preparations to get me in their clutches, I quietly pulls out my jack-knife, and rips down the legs of my leather breeches to near the bottom, both fore and aft, as a sailor might say; and then, arter a full consideration of my course, I made tracks. This, at once, brought the whole pack of yellow wolves howlin' at my heels. Instead of goin' toward Schuyler's I took the other trail tor'd the narrows, where I calc'lated to dodge the critters by takin' to water. Almost anywhere down the creek, I fancied they could wade, and that I would not stand so good a chance of fallin' in with help. Some Oneidas was ginerally foun' near the outlet, fishin'; and if they saw the tuft of a Huron's scalp, they would n't sleep till it hung at their belt. Besides that, I began to think they would n't fire at me for fear the report might awaken inconvenient 'tention. They was in the midst of an inemy's country.

"As the race was likely to be one of some length, I thought best not to put forth my greatest speed on the start. The savages are famous for their wind, and though I knowed I would leave 'em far behind in a short run, I felt some oneasiness as to the upshot of this long one. Hows'ever, away we went, and I just kept them their distance behind, knowin' that until I should tire out, I could leave 'em at any moment. To my surprise, while I was tryin' exper'ments on their speed, one short feller seemed to keep the same distance whether I went fast or slow. To put him to the proof, I then went at the top of my speed for ten or fifteen minutes; but I found to my sorrow, that he kept as near me as ever. That means somethin', thought I, for if the villin was n't sure of catchin' me somewhere, he would, most likely, have tried to come up with me before.

"In the course of half an hour I came in sight of the Lake, and shaped my course for that part of the outlet, to which I knew the friendly Injuns was in the habit of goin'. For half a mile, before reachin' the water, the ground was low, and covered with thick bushes. Into this thicket I made my way as best I could, trying to shape my course, so as to throw the Injuns out, if possible. I met with no trouble in soon gittin' to the side of the water, and begin to think it was all right, when all along the shore, beneath the bushes, for ten rods or more just in front of where I came out, a long file of Injuns riz up. They had laid hid among the reeds and bushes, and completely barred my way. For some time back, also, without my noticin' it, the short chap behind had been gainin' upon me; so that durin' my confusion at sight of the trouble ahead, he came up, and almost before I had made up my mind what to do, he coolly laid his left hand on my arm, while, in his other hand, he swung a long-handled, bright-edged tomahawk, with which he made circles over my head. I felt queer-like. But in a twinklin' I was surrounded by the others, who seemed astonished as they came up, but said nothin'. By signs, they soon gave me to understan', that the least noise would cost me my scalp. I did n't want to sell it at that price, and so kept still. But, all the while, I could see across the outlet, and not more than five hundred feet from where we stood under the shelter of the alder bushes, several of our own Injuns quietly fishin' on the other shore. The temptation to blow out was strong but as my very winks was noticed, I, of course, did n't dare to think on't.

"Well, the long and short on it was, that they hid in the bushes till dark, when they pulled out some light canoes that lay under the bank, and dropped down the stream; so that by daylight, we was far enough on the road to Canada."

"But, Jim," said Brigham; "did n't the gineral send scouts to see what had become of you?"

"To be sure he did, but as we had taken the route by Skenesborough, and not by Lake George, they found nothin'; and after sarchin' a few days, they finally concluded it was not likely anything more than a lock of my hair was travelin' toward Canada, while the rest of me was takin' a rest in the woods."

"A lock of your hair, sir?" said Colonel Belden, who for some time had been listening; "what do you mean by that?"

To this M'Carty replied by making a significant motion with his table-knife around his own scalp.

"But," interposed Walcott, for the first time joining in the conversation; "were you quite sure that your young ladies and their friends got back to Schuyler's without meeting with any further trouble?"

"Sartainly not," replied M'Carty. "How should I? But arterward I heerd that they was waylaid by another branch of the Huron gang, and that the young fellers had to shoot two or tree on 'em with their pocket-pistols before they got off; but I never heerd the particulars on it."

Here the conversation began to flag, and after a little while dropped. Colonel Belden took that occasion to withdraw. His daughter had done so some time before. The old gentleman, however, before laying down for the night, came back to consult about the proceedings for the morrow, as his anxiety was so great as almost to destroy any disposition to sleep.

"Then you say, Brigham," he remarked, addressing the latter; "that you are willing to join in this search yourself?"

"Sartainly, colonel; that's what we're agreed on; and we must be off, as I said, just as soon as the moonlight will let us. But I've been thinkin' whether we couldn't get some of the Oneidas or Mohawks up in the village to jine us. There's a chap or two there with an uncommon keen scent. Indian Joe is good, but he won't answer in the present case. We want some one with the nose of a hound, and the cunnin' of a fox. I think I'll jist step out and see if Catfoot has got back from his moose-hunt to the north. I won't be gone long. If we get him, the business will be sure."

So saying, Brigham went out of the cabin, on his projected errand; and Walcott, after some urging, induced the colonel to lie down and endeavor to get a little rest.

As good luck would have it, Brigham found the Indian whom he had designated as Catfoot, within his wigwam, to which he had apparently just returned. There was a haunch of venison slung upon a pole in the corner; and some fine moose-steaks were already broiling on the coals of a fire built against a large stone outside.

The chieftain, for such was his rank in the tribe, had a countenance at once impressive and inscrutable. His air was listless, and his whole manner quiet and composed, as he reclined upon a pile of skins within the hut. But, though his face in the rigidity of its muscles, and the smoothness of the skin was like bronze, his quick, bright, uneasy eye, gave to him still the appearance of possessing an active, wide-awake mind; and contradicted the impression made by his motionless body. Brigham walked into the wigwam, which was lighted by a small bunch of pine-knots, and, with the freedom of an old acquaintance, said, as he seated himself:

"Well, Catfoot, I see you've had plently of luck this time. Did you have to go far arter that moose?"

While asking this question, Brigham pulled out a short pipe, filled it with tobacco, lighted, and handed it to his friend; after which he produced and prepared another for himself. The Indian took the pipe quietly, and after a few whiffs, replied:

"'Cross Lake George." Then pointing to the saddle of venison, continued, looking at Brigham. "Take him."

"Thankee, Catfoot, I'll take a slice or so when I go; and in particular, because you and I may want it to-morrow."

Upon hearing this, the eye of the Indian was turned with quick curiosity upon his companion; but he said nothing, and Brigham continued:

"The fact is, Catfoot, them strangers down at my house are old friends, and have got into a scrape about a gal that came along with them from Balltown. Crazy Jake, that you know of, has took her off, and gone down into the mash, or to some other hidin'-place, and they want us to find him and bring the gal back."

"Where you tink him hide?" asked the Indian.

"Why, between you and me," replied Brigham, evasively; "that's been the reason of a good deal of thinking with me. Old Jake is a cunnin' varmint, for all his shakiness about the head; and I've known him afore now to throw sharper eyes than ourn off the trail. He got her this arternoon near the lower clearin', and he started toward the lake. That's all I know, though, of course, I have my notions besides."

"What you call notions, eh?" pursued the Indian, puffing away steadily at his pipe.

"My notions, Catfoot, is my own private thoughts; though not being well worked up yet, they ain't worth mentioning. But, I reckon, you'll have no objections to go with me in sarch of the runaways?"

To this Catfoot replied: "Good; go when you ready."

"So I thought," replied his companion; "so that's settled; but we'll have to be off awhile before daylight."

As Brigham knew his Indian friend was no great hand at upholding his end of a conversation, he soon after took his departure, with the understanding that all were to be at his house, prepared to start, an hour or so before sunrise.

The night was a quiet one. As Brigham walked back, enabled to pick his way by the dull light of the stars, the air was serene and still, except as it was disturbed by the numberless voices of insects, toads, and other like tenants of the woods. Occasionally, also, high overhead, could be heard the cry of the night-hawk, as he pursued his spiral circles in the sky; or the loud, rushing sound of his wings, as, after diving for a fly or a bug, he suddenly arrested his downward career, and resumed his spiral upward course to attain another elevation. Now and then could be heard voices, calling from the neighboring huts; or the low song of the Indian mother, as she hushed her children to sleep beneath the waving and murmuring pines. The sweetness of that simple melody might, perhaps, have arrested the attention of ears more delicate than Brigham possessed; but custom had made him indifferent to such sounds; and a life passed upon a wild, disturbed frontier, had not inclined him to gentle sentiments, or given him a poetical taste.

The valley, before spoken of, on the margin of which the Rock spring was located, stretched its dark belt in front of Brigham, as he returned to his house. At that hour, it was to the eye one dense, impenetrable mass of brake and bush.

Though he had long been accustomed to situations in which great care and constant address were required, yet the morrow's undertaking was one wherein his previous habits and experience could not be of their usual avail. Besides, though he had every confidence in the sagacity and skill of his friend, Catfoot, under ordinary circumstances, he well knew the superstitious awe with which the aborigines regarded those who were afflicted with aberration or imbecility of mind; and he had his doubts as to how the conduct of his associate might, in the present case, be affected by it. A few rods to the southward of where the log-house stood, the western side of the valley was quite abrupt; and in descending into it there, it was necessary to avail one's self of a fallen tree, which had been uprooted on the brink, and had dropped so as to lie inclined down the slope. On both sides of it were broken rocks and thick brambles. This was not, in fact, the ordinary place of descent, which was nearer to the cabin, and was less precipitous and bushy. Brigham, in a kind of brown study, had strolled southward along the high ground, past the fallen tree. As he paused there, in deep thought, his attention became attracted by a low rustling sound, coming up from the valley, as of some one cautiously walking through the tangled brushwood. He listened attentively, though without attaching any importance to the sounds, as they might be caused by any stray Indian wandering by the spring at a late hour. His act was mechanical, and, more than any thing else, the effect of habit. Two or three times, the noise again became audible; and he even thought he could distinguish the shuffling of footsteps on the rocks of the declivity, and the low sound of a solitary voice. The distance, however, was so great as to prevent him from catching the words spoken.

But at length, every thing became silent again; and Brigham, supposing that he heard only the tread and soliloquy of some belated native, thought no more of the circumstance. Soon after, he returned to the cabin, where he found that all, excepting Walcott, had retired for the night. The latter was anxious to know the effect of his host's visit among the Indians, and to conclude the arrangements for an early start in the morning.

A few words sufficed to let him know of Brigham's success in finding and securing the service of Catfoot; and after a brief conversation about their plans, the two men at last laid down, to catch, in their turn, a few hours' sleep before starting.

CHAPTER V.

THE NIGHT-MARCH.

A LITTLE after three o'clock, the next morning, those who were to assist in the intended search after the missing girl, were collected in front of the log-edifice. Brigham, Catfoot, Walcott, M'Carty, and Indian Joe, composed the party.

There was one principal path which led to the outlet of Saratoga Lake, which was then, and is now, commonly known as the "Narrows." The general course of this path was along the edge of the valley we have mentioned; a valley which was traversed by a brook, that ultimately, and after a considerable detour, emptied into the lake. Upon this route, it was deemed important that some one should go, so as to intercept Jacob, in case he should take it into his head to return by it. Accordingly, Brigham himself determined to proceed toward the Narrows, on this line. Meanwhile, it was not impossible, that the lunatic, following the impulse of habit, might have repaired to the spot where Colonel Belden had so narrowly escaped being made his victim.

To meet this contingency, it was decided that M'Carty and Indian Joe should take that direction; but if unsuccessful there, they were to follow down the Kayaderosseras creek to its outlet, and so join the others at the Narrows. To Catfoot was intrusted the task of following up the trail which the fugitive had left; and by signs, inappreciable by any other than an Indian's eye, to trace out the route which he had followed. As, however, success was more probable on this route than on any other, and one man would be inadequate to the capture of Crazy Jacob, in case he should be found, it was determined that Walcott should accompany him.

The path to be followed by Brigham formed an irregular curve with its concavity toward the south; that to be taken by M'Carty and Joe formed a similar curve, with its concavity toward the north; while the path which it was supposed the fugitive had taken ran in a line nearly equidistant between the two. The distance between these three was so small, that there was hardly a point where the loud shout of a man, or the report of a rifle, could not be heard from one party to the other next adjoining it. It was therefore hoped, that in the event of any important discovery, communication might take place between them all.

It will be recollected that the hour of starting was long before daylight. The moon had indeed risen, but its light was feeble and uncertain. Thin vapory clouds were scattered over the sky, sometimes gathering into clusters of a deeper shade; and as the moon sailed behind them, the whole leafy forest below was shrouded in thick darkness—all the more intense from contrast, and all the more palpable from the profound stillness which prevailed.

It seemed, indeed, a hopeless task to make much progress under such circumstances; but it was hoped that by the time they could be fairly engaged, the day would begin to break. As to Brigham, who was to follow the regular path, there was no difficulty; as to M'Carty and Joe, who were to travel over ground familiar to the latter, and to a point which had often been visited, there was also scarcely any embarrassment; but as to Catfoot, it was quite a different affair. He was, indeed, familiar with forest life, and with the particular locality; but it was impossible to divine what track the capricious brain of a lunatic might induce him to follow; and the indices which he might have left behind, would be difficult, if not impossible to find except in broad day-light. It had been determined that Colonel Belden, in spite of his urgent persistence, should remain at the house. The service required young and vigorous limbs; and besides, in case of his absence, his daughter would be left in a lonely cabin, among wild bands of savages, with no protector but a servant. Thus precluded from taking an active part in the operations, the old man had still watched, with interest, the preparations and departure of the others. The path pursued by Brigham, for some distance, was visible from the house; and the colonel could trace his receding form, by the pale light of the moon, until, having reached a spot where the path went down into the valley, it disappeared as suddenly as if dropped over a precipice.

The two other parties had started at the same time. Until they should reach the spot where Lucile had been seized, their paths lay together. They also, for some time were visible from the house, and as their forms became indistinguishable in the distance, or lost in the foliage, Colonel Belden turned away and sighed, as if his hopes were vanishing with them.

While pre-occupied with many unpleasant thoughts, and

engrossed by anxiety as to the result of the efforts about to be made, he heard, or fancied he heard, the sound of distant, but loud and sonorous laughter—a sound so peculiar, that when once heard, it was not likely to be forgotten. In a moment, all his senses were on the alert. Faintly and distantly it seemed to die away and become hushed. Was it fancy? Could his ears be thus deceived? So faint was the sound which had reached them that their evidence was not wholly to be trusted; but he still conceived anxious suspicions that the object of pursuit might not, after all, be far from the starting-point; and the sound of that unearthly laughter seemed like the mocking of an evil spirit, at the futility of human efforts, when directed to thwart its diabolical plans.

Slowly, and with many painful thoughts, therefore, did the old man turn back into the house, and endeavor to seek that rest, which for the earlier part of the night had been denied him.

From the point where Catfoot and Arthur had separated from M'Carty and Joe, they had to travel eastward nearly a mile, over a level and heavily-timbered plain. Of underbrush there was but little. The trees lifted their straight branchless trunks to a great height, their tufted tops spreading in thick canopies overhead, through which occasionally the faint glimmer of a star could be seen. Now and then a low rustling sound, gave token of the passage of the light breeze of a summer night. The cadence of the wind among waving pine-branches, is the most solemn, religious, and cloistral of all the voices of the great woods. It seems like the sigh of hopeless prayer; like the dying away of distant anthems; like the almost inaudible rush of spiritual wings. In the dead hour of midnight, and especially, in the long silent watches which precede the dawn, are these effects most appreciable.

It must not be supposed that the heart of the Indian scout was alive to such emotions of solemnity; or that his mind could trace in any thing he heard or saw, remote spiritual analogies. Sensibility was nearly exhausted in gratitude for a favor, and in vengeance for an injury. But it was far otherwise with his companion; who felt, as he followed silently on, that the shadowy arches through which they swiftly wended their way, had all the grandeur of an ecclesiastical fane. He imagined himself moving through the vast aisles of some Gothic cathedral; and, with a deeper sense of reality, he felt that the wilderness, in its wide desolation and utter solitude, was, withal, a solemn temple of worship.

The two men kept close to each other. This, even in the comparatively level space through which, at first, they had to pass, was no easy thing. In the shadows of the thick tree-tops, the darkness was intense; and it was more by the faint sound of his footsteps than by the aid of the eye that Walcott was able to follow his companion. Occasionally, too, he was liable to be misled, as some startled denizen of the woods crossed the path; and it required all his attention and skill to distinguish the muffled tread of his leader from the many noises of the forest. To provide against the accident of separation in the darkness, a signal had been agreed upon between them. It was to be an imitation of the cry of an owl; and more than once was Walcott recalled to the true course by that preconcerted sign.

While proceeding in this manner, at a place more than usually obscure and obstructed by bushes, Walcott became confused and distracted by sounds of footsteps leading, at once, in several directions. After a little hesitation he determined to follow those which he imagined to be most in the line of his course. As he followed on, the sounds receded, and he was thus confirmed in the idea of being on the right track. He was, therefore, considerably annoyed when, after having gone some distance in that direction, he suddenly heard the signal from a point entirely different, and apparently at a considerable distance. He immediately changed his course, and made the best of his way toward the spot from which, at short intervals, the cry of the owl continued to be heard. As he went in this new course, the footsteps which he had prieviously followed, seemed, on the contrary, to be following him. At the same time, they made so little noise, and appeared to drop so softly on the leaves, that he could not tell whether they belonged to a man or to an animal. He supposed, however, that if an animal it would be nothing more than some raccoon, or other small quadruped following him from curiosity. It gave him, therefore, no concern, and but little thought.

Although by this time the moon was up, and shed bright pencils of light, here and there, through the openings of the tree-tops, he had not yet been able to see objects around him with any distinctness. After a walk of some ten minutes, he reached the spot whence the supposed signal proceeded; but, to his surprise, found no person there. This was singular, and by no means agreeable. Having stood, for a moment, in a state of perplexity, listening to the mysterious tread of whatever was following him, he suddenly felt his arm touched; and the guide, in a whisper, enjoined silence, while, with a tight grasp, he drew him rapidly forward.

Walcott, in much surprise, permitted himself to be thus hurried along, and began to think that the Indian had made some discovery important for their enterprise. Their present course was toward a small opening in the forest, where the bright moonlight formed a strong contrast with the thick gloom of the surrounding woods. The footsteps behind, continued to follow as they went. No other sounds were heard. Apparently, they remained at about the same distance; and, though their progress was now more rapid, it seemed to make no difference in the facility with which the proximity was maintained.

They soon reached the open ground; which might, perhaps, comprise about two acres. Without halting, the Indian led the way directly across it. On the margin of the clearing, the pursuing footsteps ceased. Hitherto not a word of explanation had passed between the two men; though Walcott observed that his companion was a little disturbed. As soon as they reached the center of the clearing the Indian paused; and as Walcott was about to ask the meaning of it all, he laid his hand upon his arm, saying:

"Listen!"

At that moment, there arose a wild inhuman scream, which not only startled the two men, but which appeared to awaken the whole forest for miles around. Hundreds of animals, seemed suddenly to be astir. The outcry was like nothing which Walcott had ever before heard. To his untrained ears it was neither that of a human being, or of any known animal. Sometimes it would begin in a low wailing cry, then gradually swell, till it rose into an appalling volume of unearthly noises, to which no name could be given or simile applied. At the same time it had something in it, so startling as to disturb the steadiest nerves; and seemed to come from a creature of great power and ferocity. Walcott did not ask the Indian what it was: but to his inquiring look, the other replied, simply by pronouncing the word

"Painter."

The whole mystery was at once explained. Walcott had never before met with the creature known as the American Panther; and had but an imperfect idea of one. The recollection that he had been tracked for a long distance through the woods by the terrible creature, which must often have been near enough to spring upon him, was unpleasant enough, even though the principal danger was now past. He felt a sense of faintness like that which one experiences after having narrowly escaped falling from a precipice. Had he, while near the animal, paused for any considerable space; or had he, on the contrary endeavored to run, or do any violent act, he would probably at once have been attacked by the animal. But as he had continued in a quiet walk until joined by the guide, and as the two had then moved steadily, though rapidly away; it is probable, that the animal like all of the feline species, had hesitated in his purpose, watching an opportunity for a surprise, or a sudden assault.

The Wild Cat or Catamount, as in common parlance, it is sometimes called, still continued its outcry on the edge of the woods, walking round and round the clearing as if searching for a means to get at its prey without crossing the open space. It may well be imagined that the two men, did not dare to stir from their position. In the open ground, and in the full moonlight, where they stood, there was little or no danger of an attack.

They therefore determined to stay where they were until the dawn, which was now just breaking in the east. With daylight, the animal would doubtless slink away, and leave them free to proceed. It was during the interval, in which they were thus waiting for morning, that they had an opportunity of observing the sly and cat-like habits of their dangerous neighbor. Now, that she had no longer a chance of falling upon them unawares, she stole around their place of refuge, as a domestic cat would creep around a cage in which two mice had been insnared, but were still beyond her reach. Ever and anon, as she paused, she sent forth into the night, her wailing shriek; which at different times resembled the cry of a child, the lament of a woman, and the howl of a wolf. After each of these outbreaks, there would be entire silence for some minutes; and when it was again heard, it would be from a different direction. Each projecting clump of bushes and each shadowy point, was apparently tried by it, to ascertain whether under its cover, it might not crawl within leaping distance of its victims. Once even, an approach was made so closely, that its two eyes shone like fire, full upon them.

Walcott prided himself upon being a good shot, and at that time he drew his rifle to his shoulder, with the half formed purpose of firing; but his more prudent and experienced companion, prevented him. Unless the shot should take instant and fatal effect, it would surely cause the death of one or both of them. Besides the object of their expedition would then be unaccomplished; and it was too important to be forgotten, even at that hour.

Thus were they compelled, impatiently, to watch their enemy, and to wait for morning.

Slowly the gray light continued to creep up the eastern sky—all the more slowly to them because of their impatience. It was long before the black woods even changed to a dusky brown. Gradually did the nameless and countless noises of wild animals which had been stirred up by the appeal of the panther, die away; and give place to the tamer, but more welcome, echoes of morning. The sky was luminous long before the tree-tops became traceable; and when, at last, the light slowly descended, clump after clump of trees, and bushes, came out dimly from the darkness; till, in gray obscurity, the whole vast fretted vault of the wilderness became traversable to the human eye.

CHAPTER VI.

THE TRAIL.

WITH the darkness, the panther disappeared; but so silent and stealthy was its departure, that the direction taken could not be ascertained.

The path which had been followed by our two adventurers, hardly deserved the name. No eye but that of an Indian could have discovered its outlines by day, and no foot but his could have followed it by night. But Catfoot had never once lost the path. Its course lay nearly east and west; and if continued in a direct line, must have terminated in the vicinity of the lake outlet. This outlet, or "narrows," so often spoken of, was that part of the lake in which it suddenly contracts and pours its heavy volume of water through a deep, narrow channel.

As soon as it was sufficiently light, Catfoot set about the task of finding the trail of the fugitives. Hitherto, he had only pursued a general course on which they had started, and which, it was likely, would have been followed. The present task was no light one. To an ordinary eye, the woods presented only a trackless blank. Whatever faint indications of passage were left, could only be observed by eyes familiar with every feature of the wilderness.

From the point where they then stood, Walcott and the scout went in opposite directions, at right angles with the main path. It was thought that in this way, one or the other of them would be likely to fall upon some trace of the fugitives. This was the more important proceeding, and the more likely to succeed, because, at a short distance eastward, beyond the open ground, where they had been compelled to take refuge from the panther, the level plain, over which they had been passing, suddenly sunk down by a considerable declivity, and the ground became low and marshy. Beyond this point the woods became tangled and bushy, and the ground rough, and interrupted by sluggish streams and muddy water-pools. It was thought probable that somewhere along the brink of this morass, or "fly," as Brigham had termed it, some trace of Jacob might be found; if, indeed, he had gone, as was supposed, to the narrows. It was agreed that as soon as either of them should light upon any thing important, he should announce the fact to the other, by a howl, in imitation of that of a wolf. By adopting this precaution, there would be less danger of their search being discovered. Walcott took a southerly direction, and examined every inch of the ground along the brink of the hill for some distance without success; and he had just began to think of retracing his steps, when he heard a sound like the low, distant howl of a wolf. Having, for a moment, forgotten that this was the concerted signal, and his ears being familiarized with the sound, he did not, at once, comprehend its meaning: nor did its import occur to him, until after it had been twice repeated. He then retraced his steps as rapidly as possible, to the spot where he and his companion had separated, and there paused, awaiting some further signal by which to be guided. This was not long in coming. The same cry which had already been twice heard, could now be distinguished, much louder than before. As it came from the direction which the Indian had taken, Walcott hastened forward toward it, without hesitation. As he went on, it was from time to time repeated. At length, after having gone thirty or forty rods, it was no longer heard; and he paused in some uncertainty; as by this time he supposed himself to be near the place, whence the sounds had proceeded.

While looking about him for some sign or token of his mysterious companion, he heard a dull sound upon the earth behind him; and on turning around, saw the Indian quietly standing there. It was as if he had risen from the earth, or descended from the sky, so sudden and unaccountable was his appearance. He well deserved the name which he bore; for in the present instance, probably for the sake of effect, and to impress the "pale face" with a high opinion of his stealthy activity, he had swung himself upward into the branches of a tree, from which, to the surprise of Walcott, he had so made his silent descent.

"Why, Catfoot," exclaimed Arther; "where the devil did you come from?"

The Indian smiled, and pointed to the branch overhead. He then proceeded, with much apparent satisfaction at his late theatrical performance to call his comrade's attention to some marks upon the earth, which had given occasion for his signal. This was more to the purpose. The ground where they stood, was sandy and soft. Close along the edge of the slope which led down to the low ground, the Indian now pointed out, what Walcott would, at first sight, have taken for the track of a bear, but that the strides were too long for that usually sluggish animal. Evidently, the impression was made by some heavy creature, for it was deep and well defined. It was traceable only for a very short distance, and that where the ground was more than commonly bare and free from leaves and broken twigs. The Indian led Walcott along the whole extent of the visible appearance of the tracks, pointing out each impression, and often disclosing one where his companion would have seen nothing. During all this while he continued silent.

"Well," said Walcott, with some feeling of irritation, when they got through, "I see nothing in all this. Some heavy animal has passed this way without doubt; but I don't see how the sight of his footsteps can do us any good."

"What you think him?" said Catfoot, seating himself coolly upon a fallen tree, and looking his associate full in the face.

"What do I think him?" answered Walcott, impatiently; "why some bear, to be sure; or perhaps that infernal wild-cat; or perhaps a moose. But whatever it was, it is hardly worth our while to bother our heads over it. We have something more important to think of. I wish to heaven, Brigham or M'Carty would give some signs of themselves."

"Bear, moose, wilcat, all got four leg," coolly replied the pertinacious Catfoot.

"Well, what of that?" said Walcott.

"No make two step like man; make tree, four," continued the Indian.

"Why, what the devil, then, do you suppose, did make these confounded tracks?" asked Walcott, testily.

"Jake," replied the other.

"You don't mean to say these are a man's footmarks,

stretching five feet apart, and looking more like the marks of a falling stone than any thing else, do you?"

"No; him Jake's," said the other persistently.

"But whatever made these, must have been as heavy as an ox," still urged Walcott.

"Wild Jake, I say, carry load; run like moose," said Catfoot, with emphasis.

It was, after all, quite possible that the crazy man, with the burden which he bore, might have caused the trail. Walcott also, by this time, recollected that Jacob had worn large, shapeless moccasins, such as might not very clearly leave behind the impression of a human foot.

For the rest, the Indian was quite positive, and evidently had come to a conclusive opinion upon the point. Walcott recollected that, in the interpretation of any of the signs of the woods, Catfoot was not one likely to be mistaken. He therefore at length, yielded a slow and reluctant credence to the theory so sententiously propounded to him in the matter.

"But, Catfoot," he said, after some pause, "I do not see how this is to benefit us; for the marks stop the other side of this fresh ground; and there we will be left as much in doubt as before. It seems to me that he would not keep this course long, if he meant to go to the lake. Perhaps we had better push straight across the swamp, as we have now daylight before us."

The Indian shook his head, saying:

"No find him that way; better keep trail."

"But how are we to do that?" asked the other. "Time presses; and we must do something. If this is really Jacob's trail, he must have carried her, as you say, while he passed this spot; and that shows that he had not yet killed her."

Catfoot now rose; and going to the place where the footmarks seemed to disappear, turned to his companion, and motioned him to follow. Hereupon, he again moved forward; but now with greater apparent confidence and rapidity; for a while, following the edge of the swamp, after which he turned gradually to the northwest, curving more and more, till at length, the course lay almost directly back toward the springs.

Walcott, during all this while, did not in the least understand by what impalpable signs, or savage instincts his companion felt himself guided; but for the time he had nothing better to do than to follow. From the other two searching parties no signal had as yet been heard. In Brigham great confidence was to be placed; and as he would undoubtedly visit the narrows, it was still hoped that before night he would be able to report what was discoverable in that quarter. In M'Carty and Joe, not so much faith could be put. The former, though shrewd enough upon occasions, was too careless and rattle-brained; and the latter labored under a superstitious awe of the madman. Their search, however, would have the effect of determining a question of fact; and if Jacob should have visited the place which they were directed to examine, they would probably be able to give some notion of his present whereabouts, or of the disposition which he had made of his captive. It was quite certain that if they had encountered any thing of importance, they would, ere now, have been heard from.

Without doubt, therefore, not only they, but Brigham also, had already gone forward to the lake; and one, or all, were confidently expected to make themselves visible during the day.

These reflections occurred to Walcott, as he and Catfoot continued their pursuit. After a considerable period, the latter began to move slowly, and to pick his way with more care. At times, he even appeared to be at fault. It was, at the same time, some satisfaction to Walcott, at long intervals, to discover in some piece of soft or sandy ground, the same rude impressions which had first attracted their attention. It showed, at least, that their course was not at random, and directed merely by caprice. It also increased his confidence in the skill of his associate.

When at length, therefore, he found the latter becoming baffled and uncertain, he felt all the more annoyed and disappointed; for it was certain that if the Indian's sagacity should fail him, there was no other immediate thing to rely on.

A broken stick, an upturned leaf, a bush slightly put aside, or a cobweb torn asunder, to the keen eyes which there observed them, were like monuments, plain as guide-boards and mile-stones: but when they became faint and only discoverable at long intervals, and after close search, the result became again involved in doubt.

The ground had now become more open; and the few traces which they met were quite as much calculated to confuse as to enlighten them.

After passing over a small interval of dry plain which was destitute of trees, and bore only a few stunted shrubs, they came to the brink of another valley through which flowed a small stream. As they stood there they could hear its low ripple deep down among the somber bushes, mingling with the hum of insects and the twittering of birds among the sunny branches.

Walcott knew it to be the same creek along the other side of which Brigham must have passed the night before; and by following up which, they would come out at the place from which they started.

Here they confidently expected to find some evidence that Jacob had descended into the valley, and turned to the right, so as to follow the run of the rivulet, toward the Lake.

In this expectation they were a little disappointed; for the trail, though they now came upon it again, and found it more marked and decided than before, led in no one direction, but pointed forth in all. The earth was much trampled; and Walcott had the unspeakable satisfaction of finding, in several places, a small imprint, apparently that of a female foot. Here was almost a certain proof that their efforts had not been in vain. Here Jacob must have paused, and let down his burden. The spot was, doubtless, a point of departure; and, in every view, worthy of close observation.

But the slight consolation afforded by this discovery, was soon destined to be forgotten in anxiety, when they found that precisely there, all further trace of those they sought seemed to be entirely lost. The trail in one place descended to the creek, and was traceable across it; but it was also found, radiating forth on the plain above in several different directions, on each of which it finally disappeared.

The savage began to manifest signs of surprise. His eyes became like those of a lynx—quick, uneasy, rolling. Not a scratch in the sand, not a blade of grass from which the dew had been brushed, not a leaf whose down had been rubbed; seemed to escape his scrutiny. But after much fruitless search, and much delay, they were still compelled to pause and consider what was next to be done. It was idle to wander on at random, when every step they made might take them further from their object.

Both were silent; and the Indian even laid himself down upon the ground, as if in the intense labor of reflection. For some time he was entirely quiet, so much so that Walcott bent over him to see whether he was asleep; but found his small, black eyes still wide open, and as restless and fiery as ever. They alone wore a look of thoughtfulness; for his countenance was as still and expressionless as wax.

"I see no other way for it," said Walcott, at last, "but to follow up our first plan, and go down the stream. It seems to me more likely that he went to the narrows than anywhere else. He would not go back to the springs; and, at the north, he has no hiding-places that I ever heard of. What do you say, Catfoot, shall we try it?"

The other slowly rose from the ground, saying:

"Try him? Yes. Ugh! no find him, though; must be debbil; no leave trail."

With this determination they descended into the valley of the stream, and pursued the route toward the Lake.

CHAPTER VII.

THE FLIGHT.

We must now return to poor Lucile Valcour, who has been left, all this while, at the mercy of a being more to be feared than a beast of prey.

When she was first seized by Jacob, nature had come to her relief and deprived her of consciousness. For some moments after she became restored to the use of her senses, she was too much startled to be fully conscious of her situation, or to reflect upon the imminent peril to which she was exposed. She felt herself in the power of one who seemed to possess more than human strength and agility. He dashed through the woods with the speed of a deer, bearing her as easily as an ordinary man would bear a child.

In the confusion and alarm of the moment, Lucile could not tell in what direction they were going; and even when she sufficiently recovered herself to look about, owing to the rapidity of the flight, and the thickness of the trees, she found it impossible to form any thing like a reasonable conjecture upon the point. Though apprehensive of some act of violence, the intrepid girl, when she found herself beyond the immediate reach of relief, refrained from screams and outcries; but turned her mind resolutely to contemplate her actual situation, and, if possible, to devise some means of averting its dangers. After the few struggles, which she had impulsively made in the beginning, she concluded that entire, apparent passiveness, at least for the present, was her best policy. She spoke to her captor firmly, but entreatingly, in a voice so gentle and touching, that the rudest heart should have been moved by it. But he heard or heeded nothing, as he crashed through the brush, and swept like a phantom past the dark and somber trees.

When, at length, his speed was somewhat slackened, and when she renewed her entreaties to be released, or to be taken back to her friends, he only answered by his wild laugh, though its extreme loudness was now suppressed; and, in other ways, he gave indications of that cunning, so often manifested by madmen. As will have been conjectured, he pursued the route which was afterward so successfully followed by Walcott and his guide. When he arrived at the place near the creek, where the skill of the Indian was baffled, and the patience of his comrade so severely tried, he released the trembling girl from his arms, and allowed her to walk.

"So, so, my pretty puss; you and I have given them all the slip," he exclaimed; "we've beat 'em all to Gretna Green! Ho! ho! The old Doctor will have to be sharp to find me this time."

"But you don't mean to take me away any further now, do you?" Lucile ventured to ask.

"No further? Ha! ha! ha! Why what should we go further for? Ain't we here already? My poor little pussy! you have got a nice pretty face" (and he patted her under the chin, with his huge, long-nailed black fingers), "but a little soft" (touching her on the forehead), "just a little flighty, you know, here, eh? Bless me, what a pity!" he continued as if speaking to himself. "I must take care that she does no mischief. They say crazy women are sometimes the devil. So, for all she looks so innocent and tender-like, I'll just keep an eye on her. Poor thing! poor thing!"

Lucile was not ignorant of the fact, that it is a common delusion for the insane to imagine others around them to be out of their wits. This reflection, while the idea was grotesque enough, was still fraught with consolation, for it was not likely that any violence would be offered to her, so long as she was supposed to be such a natural object of compassion. With such armor has beneficent wisdom shielded those from whom the mind, their ordinary protector, has been withdrawn.

Whatever might be the issue, Lucile immediately determined to assume, or at least not to contradict, the character, which the delusion of her captor had assigned her.

"I am hungry," said she, following up her thought; "can you take me to some place where food can be obtained?"

"Poor thing! poor thing!" was all the reply which Jacob, for the moment, vouchsafed to make.

"How far is it," she said, "to my father's house? Please tell me, brother."

"Ho! ho!" he now noisily laughed, in reply; "the poor little puss is already thinking of her father's house. We ran away to get married out here in Gretna Green, and she begins already to talk of her father's house! ha! ha!"

"But, you know," she continued, trembling at the turn

he was giving to affairs; "you know that you are my brother, and we can not get married."

"Ha! ha!" he replied: "she is so flighty she thinks I am her brother. But no matter! I'll take her to my mad-house and cure her. Then we'll be married. But it's a pity she's wild, and has no one to care for her; so, I must sacrifice my own feelings, for her sake. There now! little pussy! come along, and we'll have it seen to right away."

The poor girl was greatly alarmed, and had gained no reassurance by what had been said. She followed him slowly. Her limbs trembled as she walked; her cheek was pale; and her eyes half blinded by tears. She was in the power of a madman; and nothing but the utmost prudence and circumspection could avert the danger which at every moment threatened her. What if the marriage should be insisted on? How could she evade it? And what ceremonies might he imagine to be necessary or suitable for the occasion?

In the mean while he led the way down an easy, sandy slope, upon which grew a large pine-tree—large enough to have stood there for centuries. It had reared itself for nearly a hundred feet into the air, without a branch, and apparently, without a knot. But, either from its enormous weight, or from the washing away of the earth from its roots, it had lost its perpendicular position; and now leaned far over down the hill. Its vast bulk, hanging thus in mid air, was like a natural tower of Pisa; and gave to one standing under it, a constant uneasy apprehension lest its supports might give way, and the enormous shaft itself, topple over, and fall with a crash to the ground. Around its base, protected by the shadows of thick bushes, had been arranged poles and strips of bark, so as to form a rude kind of hut, which was something more than the bare shelter of open branches and rustling leaves. The leaning tree formed nearly one side of the conically shaped cabin; and although its base was at the outer margin of the creek valley, its shaft swept slopingly upward, by the peak or apex. To this rude abode, or rather, place of concealment, was Lucile led by her captor.

To divert his thoughts, if possible, from the channel in which they had, for some time, appeared to be flowing, she still continued to complain of hunger; hoping thus, to set him to the task of providing food—a task, which, in their situation, she thought, could not fail to keep him for some time occupied. In this design, she was, to a certain extent, successful.

As soon as she had entered the cabin, and sat down to gather her thoughts into order, as well as to recover her exhausted strength, he departed from the hut, often cautiously looking back, and re-ascended the bank down which they had come. In doing this, however, he practiced a precautionary maneuver, of which she was at the time ignorant, and which, had she known of it, might have rendered her still more unhappy, as it showed the cunning and determination to retain her, of the creature who had, so suddenly, become the controller of her movements, and, perhaps, the arbiter of her fate.

Instead of walking up the acclivity, in the ordinary way, he walked backward, carefully placing his feet in the tracks which he had made in descending. He was familiar, it seems, with the Indian method of pursuit by trailing; and, with a foresight almost diabolical, had anticipated that he would be followed, not only with the energy and force of white men, but with the sagacity and experience of the aborigines.

At the spot where they had halted, it was his design, that his pursuers, whoever they might be, and whenever they might come, should be thrown out, and utterly baffled. As soon as he reached the level ground at the top of the ascent, he moved boldly off into the woods, leaving a plain trail—at least plain to the eye of an Indian. After he had continued on thus, for thirty or forty rods, he returned upon his footsteps, in the same manner, as he had ascended from the cabin; that is to say, by walking backward. This operation he went through several times, on each occasion taking a different direction.

When all these various maneuvers had been accomplished, the next task was, to depart from the vicinity in such a manner as to leave no clue to his course.

The place of concealment in which he had left his captive, was so cunningly devised, and so carefully hidden, that it was quite unobservable from any position which his pursuers were likely to take; and all his approaches to it, he had scrupulously rendered indistinguishable.

It was his present purpose to proceed alone. During his absence, which he intended to be a brief one, he had no apprehensions of the escape of his prisoner. In fact, he hardly looked upon her in the light of a prisoner. The notion which seemed paramount in his mind, was, that they were two lovers who had run away to be married. Besides, she was now surrounded by a wilderness, which was to the inexperienced eye utterly trackless, and beset with difficulties which rendered traveling, in any given direction, almost impossible to a novice.

These considerations were not, properly speaking, distinctly palpable to the mind of the lunatic; if it may be said that the unregulated chaos of sensations and fancies which he experienced belonged to such a thing as mind. He appeared rather to be guided by the instinctive impulses which move animals, and often seem to inspire them with what looks like superhuman cunning.

It will be recollected that, at a short distance from the old pine-tree, at whose base the cabin stood, was a small stream, flowing, in its general course, toward the lake. Jacob, while making his false trails, had also bent his steps to this creek. He even went beyond it, and again retraced his way. The stream was ten or twelve feet in width, and was generally fringed with a thick border of willows. Its bottom was hard, and was of a stiff clay, except where, now and then, it was paved with a deposit of white pebbles. The water was only about six inches in depth; and when Jacob, on his return, reached nearly the center of it, he made a powerful spring sidewise, and alighted some distance down the stream. He then carefully walked away in the water, avoiding places where his weight might make some marked impression upon the bottom.

Poor Lucile had, meanwhile, remained almost in a state of stupefaction, arising from terror and exhaustion. Night was now coming slowly on. Its approach is always heralded among the shadowy recesses of the forest, long before it becomes apparent in the open plains, and on the hill tops. Utterly helpless, as she was, she reclined upon a pile of boughs and rough old deer skins, which formed a rude couch. Her despondency, for the moment, was such as to disincline her to any further exertion. The drowsy silence around her, save as it was disturbed by the low ripple of the neighboring brook, combined with the fatigue, and with the shades of early evening, to lull her into an uneasy half slumber, like that produced by narcotics in a person suffering great agony. Her intense feeling of the peril of her situation, grew gradually fainter and fainter, and finally, passed away from her consciousness, somewhat as the surrounding landscape became shrouded, first in shadows, and then in darkness.

And as this outward night, which now began to vail the world, was not all mystery and silence, but was lighted by innumerable stars, and was disturbed by the hum of insects, the whir of reptiles, and the distant howl of awaking beasts of prey; so the mind of Lucile was not wrapped in dreamless slumber; but visions shone out like stars through the mist; and her repose was agitated by confused and multitudinous thoughts of pain and danger. Hers was the sleep of fever. Her body alone rested; and even that not fully. The confusion in its citadel, the brain, communicated itself to her whole system, and shook her limbs with convulsive starts. Her lips moved, with the struggles of memory, and with the efforts of her senses to resume their offices.

How long she lay in this state, she did not know. Every thing around had become shrouded in utter darkness. Her breathing was just audible within the hut. Outside of it, from different directions, could be heard the howl of the wolf—the almost universal denizen of the primitive American forests. Nearer at hand, a nice ear might, perhaps, have heard the low sound of stealthy footsteps, pacing slowly and cautiously about the cabin. Occasionally there was a pause, and then the walk would be resumed. But of all this, the sleeping occupant of that rude abode was happily unconscious.

At length the bearskin which hung across the entrance was thrust aside; and a pair of keen, black eyes, dilated, and blazing with eager curiosity, shone through the opening. Presently a shadowy form crept through. Then there was a pause and silence. Again the form was in motion; and, after some slight rustling, interrupted by periods of listening, a light was struck, and the huge ogre-like form and fierce countenance of Crazy Jacob became faintly discernible in the dull glimmer. Still, the tired girl slept on, unconscious of any change about her.

No sooner was the light obtained than Jacob turned it so that its beams fell upon the face of the sleeper, which he, for a moment, contemplated with a look of mingled admiration, ferocity, and pity. In a few seconds, however, the torch was extinguished, and all was again left in darkness.

The madman then crept quietly up to where she lay, and took her gently up in his arms and bore her, still unconscious, from the cabin. But, as the chill night air fell upon her cheek, she woke with a start and with a slight scream.

"Ha! ha!" laughed the maniac, as he heard her voice, and felt her feeble struggling; "the poor little kitten is afraid to travel in the dark."

The sound of his voice at once recalled her to a full consciousness of her situation.

"You are going to take me back to my friends, now, are you not, good Jacob?" she ventured to suggest.

"To your friends, little puss?" he replied; "why, no,

you silly thing; you don't know what's good for you. I have a house fit for a princess, and I'm going to take you there. Ho! ho! What gay times there will be at our marriage, to be sure! Nobody is to be seen there; but there are voices there which always answer; and when one laughs, they are such jolly company! Voices all around, coming from everywhere; and such good creatures that you never hear 'em unless you say something yourself, or show yourself inclined for a bit of fun. Ain't it a jolly place?"

"But you do not mean to take a poor girl like me there without seeing her father, and asking his consent?"

"Flighty again, by jingo!" said he. "Consent? Why, didn't you run off with me without leave or licence, you silly little puss?"

During this short dialogue he had set her down, and was busied in so arranging the bushes in front of the hut, as to conceal it as much as might be, from observation. She perceived that he was doing something near her, and partly divined what it was; but could see little or nothing.

To him, darkness and daylight seemed as one. He did not talk much to himself, as maniacs are apt to do; and save now and then giving vent to his hoarse and dissonant, but slightly suppressed laughter, he worked away in silence.

The position of the hut itself was admirable for the purpose of concealment. By a slight arrangement of the bushes it could be made entirely to elude the notice of any ordinary observer. The only difficulty was in so arranging the trail as to induce any who might be in search, to pass by it. For this purpose, he was careful to make distinct footsteps leading past it, and toward the brook. The number of indications pointing that way, only rendered the confusion greater; but while the trace was plain, it would be rapidly followed up; and the pursuer would only think of pausing where, like a hound, he began to lose the scent.

All these dispositions were soon made; and again he took the helpless and trembling girl into his arms, to bear her away. She found it vain to resist, and more vain to entreat. Her earnest beseeching, and irrepressible sobs, were only met by wild laughter, or wilder answers to her questions. Whither he was now going to take her, she could, of course form no conception; but her startled imagination pictured to her beating heart unspeakable horrors. Danger is always more formidable when we are called upon to face it from out of slumber. So it was now with her. When she was first seized, the terribleness of her position was not so strongly depicted to her fancy. Now she felt faint with fear, and, at length, permitted herself to be borne along in speechless apprehension. Their course was, at first, to the creek. Once in the water, however, instead of following the current, he faced it, and went in the opposite direction.

The horrors of that night-passage—her fatigue and faintness—the thick darkness which reigned around, the howl of pursuing wolves, which, like sharks in the wake of an ill-fated wreck, hung upon their traces, were too much for the nerves of the frail and delicately nurtured girl. She soon became unconscious in the arms of the maniac, and for many succeeding hours knew no more.

CHAPTER VIII.

SARATOGA LAKE.

It was past midday when Walcott and his Indian companion reached some high ground overlooking the lake. It was the spot which had been agreed on, as the place of rendezvous. They found no signs of the presence of their associates, and every thing around was quiet and still. They stood upon a slight knoll, free from trees, which commanded a fine view of the beautiful sheet of water. At this time, it was not, as it is now, surrounded by a cultivated country, with fields, farm-houses, and orchards to humanize the view. A thick wilderness of green trees hemmed it on all sides, and the glassy water looked like a vast mirror set in a frame of emerald. A summer sun was pouring its fervid effulgence over all the landscape; which, as a wilderness, was no less pleasing than it is now. The bold promontory of Snake Hill, alone, lifted its dark mass in the distance, to give any thing like an air of ruggedness to the otherwise gentle picture.

Many years have since passed away. The ancient race which formerly peopled these regions, has disappeared. The land is occupied by men, not only of another generation, but of another blood, and complexion—a nation, powerful, industrious, intelligent. Revolutions have taken place in governments, and political institutions have been overthrown; but the vast and noble physical features of the land which has witnessed these mutations, have remained the same. Times may, as the proverb says, change, and men change with them, but the lakes still reflect the headlands; the rivers still flow, and the mountains still stand, almost unchanged, since the dawn of the creation.

"I wonder," said Walcott, "what has become of Brigham; he ought to be somewhere about, and should have been here since daylight."

"Him there," said the other quietly, pointing down the slope before them, to a thick clump of sycamores.

"Where?" asked Walcott, as he looked at the place indicated, but failed to discover any indications of his friends. "I can see nothing, I am sure. Besides, it is time for the others to be here. What can keep them all loitering in this way?"

"All there," replied the Indian, again glancing his eye at the spot.

To remove all doubt, however, they now walked down to the cluster of trees; and, sure enough, found them there, and all fast asleep. The ashes of an extinct fire was near them, and the remnants of a breakfast of fish were still visible. As Walcott and the guide came up within a few yards of the sleepers, they were accosted by the voice of Brigham, who said, springing to his feet:

"Hooray! Catfoot, my old boy, where have you been all this while? We had made up our minds to leave at noon, in case you did n't come, and so detarmined to lie down and take a little nap, till the time was up."

The Indian made no reply, but sat down by the remnants of the fish, and commenced to break his fast, as a thing of the first importance.

"What are you in such a hurry there, for?" exclaimed Brigham, at this procceding; "are you so near starved that you can't wait for something more to be cooked? I thought you 'd more control over your appetite, Catfoot."

"No time to cook him," was the other's brief reply.

"Why not? But there's no use tryin' to get an explanation from an Indian. Can you," he said, turning to Walcott, "tell what he means by being in such a tarnal hurry all at once? If you 've seen any thing, you 've done better than I, for I'm blowed if I 've hit upon the ghost of a discovery all night—not so much as a giggle from that laughin' hyener, crazy Jake. Them fellers there," pointing to M'Carty and Indian Joe, who were by this time awake, and had risen up, "ain't any wiser than two blind cubs afore nine days is out, eh, Joe?"

Joe vouchsafed no reply; and Walcott proceeded to explain, in detail, the result of their night's adventure, and their morning's search. Brigham listened, with deep attention, to the recital, and, when it was ended, he asked:

"Did ye happen to notice there was a big pine-tree near where the trail led down to the kil?"

"Yes," said Walcott, "I noticed that particularly, because it leaned over so far that it seemed every moment about to fall."

"There's a kind of hut there," replied Brigham; "and if I'd 'a had any notion the trail led thereabouts, I should n't have passed without a visit. It lies at the foot of the tree, and you would n't notice it unless told on't beforehand. I've a consate that Jake is or was somewhere about there. Catfoot's right; there's no time for cookin'."

"But," said Walcott, "we followed the tracks this way, down the creek, afterward. He could n't very well have stopped there long, without leaving some mark, which Catfoot would have noticed."

"How was it, old boy?" said Brigham to the latter, "had n't you eyes enough to see the hut?"

"Hut empty," said the other, in reply. "Medicine man been there—gone."

"But about the trail," continued Brigham, "how did you happen to lose it, when once you found it in the kil again?"

"He de debbill, don't I say?" replied the Indian, testily; "he leave one, tree, six, four trail. Gone anywhere."

Having said this, Catfoot, who had now finished his meal, or, rather, finished the fish, rose up, tightened his belt, and seemed prepared for a new start.

Walcott, in the mean time, hastily partook of some smoked venison which, through the prudent foresight of Brigham, had been brought along. Though feeling but little appetite, he still thought it best to avail himself of the present occasion, to make provision against such fatigues and fasts as the expedition might yet call upon him to undergo.

No sooner had he finished, than Catfoot, who was evidently waiting for nothing else, having put himself in complete marching trim, took the lead, and beckoned the others to follow.

"Something is in the wind," said Brigham to Walcott, as they also were preparing to start; "I never knowed him to act so prompt-like unless he had some good idea at the bottom. All we've now got to do is to foller the best way we can. Come, Mac, you and Joe must stir yourselves to keep up, for I can see in his look that we're to have a hard pull."

What project was really on foot, Walcott could not divine; and the Indian's natural taciturnity and reserve, when questioned, rendered it difficult for him to ascertain. He had, however, already sufficient experience of the skill of the Indian to give him great confidence in the propriety of any course which he might judge it expedient to pursue; and so, without comment or inquiry, the preparations for the departure of all were hastily completed. These, in fact, were very trifling. A belt tightened, the cold food gathered into a package, the sheath-knife secured, the rifle dropped into the hollow of the arm, and all were ready.

Away, then, went Catfoot, no longer with slow tread, and searching eye; but with the confident air, and long, loping trot of the American savage, when upon an assured trail. The pace was not only rapid but constant —such a pace as, during a day's journey, would sometimes accomplish more than the gallop of a horse.

The course, for a short distance, lay due westward. Passing over a few light hills of sand, they came upon the high shore of a dark, deep pond of water about half a mile in width. Here they diverged to the right, keeping upon the brow of the bank. Sheer down through the trees could they see the glassy water which all around the border of the little lake was overhung and shaded by thick trees. In the center it was as smooth and unruffled as if no living thing occupied its depths. It was a gloomy place at that time; and such as we have described it, it will be found at the present day. Through this sluggish pool, one of the creeks we have noticed, flows, in its passage to the Lake.

Traveling in those days was a very different thing from what it is now, even without the aid of steam. A journey of four or five miles, in a thick forest, through swamps, down slopes, covered with brambles, over fallen logs, and across deep and muddy streams, was not the labor of half an hour. Ten miles of such traveling often occupied a long summer day. It will not, therefore, be surprising that several hours elapsed before the five men had come near to the place where the trail of Jacob had eluded the keen eye of Catfoot. Though their course was still direct, they now moved more slowly. In some places the stream up which they traced their way, had become choked by brush and fallen trees, and expanded into small natural basins or ponds. As they were passing by one of these, M'Carty inquired:

"What sort of fish do you catch in these 'ere ponds, Sandy?"

"Why, nothing in particular," replied Brigham. "Bull-heads, I believe, and like enough, a sucker now and then; but why do you ask?"

"Because I see somebody has been down here fishing lately."

"Somebody been here fishing?" exclaimed Brigham, coming to a full halt. "Halloo! there, you Catfoot! wait a minute! Where have they been fishing, Mac? Let 's see how you come to know?"

Thus appealed to, M'Carty led the way back for a rod or so, and pointed out something that had escaped even the sharp eyes of the Indians. This was the mark of a fish-pole, set in the bank. By the time they had begun to gather round it, Catfoot also joined them, and instantly began to scrutinize the adjacent ground, in order to get some further clew to the character of the fisherman. In a short time, they heard from him, the Indian expression of surprise, uttered with peculiar emphasis.

"Ugh!" said he, as he pointed to some marks upon a bit of sand hard by. Brigham and Walcott immediately joined him in the examination; but neither could make any thing out of it. Walcott, indeed, thought it bore some resemblance to the footprints which he and Catfoot had followed in the morning; and upon turning a look of inquiry to the latter, he received an affirmative nod.

All now set themselves to see what more could be made out of the discovery. The single indication found, was not sufficiently defined to prove any thing. It was, therefore, all-important to obtain something more, by way of verification. The impression formed might have been old, though it did not appear to be so. But in the case of a character like Crazy Jacob, any sign was worth attention.

For a few minutes, the men spread in different directions, so that every inch of ground might be carefully examined. Presently, Indian Joe, as if tired of the search, sat down upon the limb of a fallen tree, and lazily watched the disappointed looks of the others, as, one by one, they began to show evidence of failure.

"What are you sitting there for, you lazy varmint?" exclaimed Brigham, indignantly, as with much annoyance at his own want of success, he observed the cold indifference of the other.

"No good look," said Joe, in reply.

This question and answer having attracted the attention of Catfoot, he walked up to Joe, scanning his face, as if he was reading it; then, laying his hand upon his shoulder, while he looked him full in the eye, he asked:

"Where?"

Joe rose up, and pointed below the branch on which he sat. There, in fact, was discernible a pole and line with the necessary appliances for fishing, of the rudest and most primitive character. They were at once seized upon. On inspection, it was obvious that they had but recently been used. The marks of the earth upon the pole were still fresh. It was then carried to the hole in the border of the pond, and found to fit it exactly. If then it had in reality belonged to Jacob, as the footprint in the sand would seem to indicate, he must still be within a short distance. How had he left the spot? That was the question. He could not have flown into the air; and on earth, almost every thing leaves a trace discoverable to the practiced eye. No such trace, however, had yet been seen, though already Catfoot had discovered in the bed of the stream above the pond, footmarks which led down to it. They corresponded with those previously seen. All proved that Jacob had come thither, and to that extent were important; but they did not show how he had departed. That question still remained unsolved.

A sudden thought occurred to Walcott. Taking a small stick, he carefully measured the length and width of the impression they had first discovered in the sand, and afterward those which were formed in the bed of the stream. They differed materially both in length and breadth. He also, in this way, ascertained that no two of them corresponded.

"Brigham," said he, "what do you think of the notion of a man walking backward? It has occurred to me as just possible in this case. The tracks here all differ in size; and it may be that this has been caused by an endeavor to step twice in the same place."

"A good idea, by Jove!" exclaimed Brigham: "Catfoot!" he continued, calling to the latter, "come this way a minute."

As soon as the other came up, Brigham, in order to convey his meaning more readily, walked forward a short distance on a strip of soft ground, and then went back, step by step, treading in his tracks.

The eyes of the savage immediately lighted up with intelligence, and he placed himself to re-examine the traces in the creek. After looking hastily at a few of them, he rose up, saying:

"Good—now we go."

Again the whole troop resumed their course, now quite confident that Jacob could be nowhere below them; and full of hope that, with the last clew which they had obtained, they would soon be enabled to find him. From time to time, as they hastened on, did they observe the old trail, in or near the stream. Wherever the ground on the shore was dry and hard enough to leave no trail, it was supposed, that the water had been left. In fact, as a proof of the probability of this theory, in one place, they found the mark of a footstep upon a broad flat stone, as if some one had trod upon it, after coming out of water. All this evidence was confirmatory. The last fact was something more than that; and was regarded as proof positive, for the track pointed up the stream.

The place where Walcott and the guide had at first followed the trail to the brook, was soon reached. Near at hand, stood the large leaning pine-tree. To Walcott and M'Carty, the discovery of the embowered hut at its base, was matter of much surprise; but the Indians took it quite coolly. One, certainly, and probably both, knew of it before. In fact, Catfoot had, as he had already intimated, examined it in his former visit; but he had not seen fit to communicate the fact to his companion. It was now eagerly revisited by all; but as neither of those they were in search of, was expected to be there, no disappointment was felt, at the place being found tenantless and deserted. Catfoot, in a short time had again examined the different trails which led from the spot, and found the same evidence of a return upon them, which had been observed in the brook. Indeed as he now held a clew to this proceeding, the fact was quite obvious. All the courses on the plain above, were therefore, speedily given over; and the men betook themselves again to the water. They now turned their attention to the examination of the upward course of the brook. For nearly twenty rods they proceeded without discovering any thing. At last, as a reward of their persevering search, the trail again became visible; and this time, leading plainly in the direction they were then pursuing.

The footprints, wherever they could be seen, differed from those they had been following all the morning, in now being of a uniform size. Clearly then, in this case, whoever had passed up before them, had not returned; at all events, by the same path.

By this time, the sun was approaching the western horizon. If any thing satisfactory was to be accomplished before it reached that goal, no time was to be lost. After nightfall, the pursuit could not be continued. Walcott already entertained the keenest apprehensions, as to the consequences of delay. It is true, that the missing girl was a stranger to him, except so far as a previous knowledge of her family, and the casual encounter on the morning of the previous day, may be said, in some sort, to have made them acquainted. Still he thought to himself, that any person of proper feelings would do, and ought to do all in his power to rescue one so young and interesting from the dangerous companionship into which she had been forced, or the frightful fate, which might at any moment befall her, in consequence of it. All this might be true—doubtless was so; and yet among those now engaged in the same pursuit, and exerting themselves so energetically on her behalf, any disinterested person might have observed widely different degrees of interest in the result.

The Indians had embarked in the undertaking, partly upon Brigham's persuasion, and partly from their natural love of difficult and adventurous enterprises, in which their prowess and peculiar skill might be called into play. Brigham was chiefly interested on account of old Colonel Belden. Why M'Carty was there, has already been shown.

Walcott thought to himself that his own conduct was quite natural; and so, in fact, it was. At the same time the recollection of the bright eyes, which, at his first interview with her, had shone upon him; of the gentle smile which had greeted him, and of the lithe, pliant, but graceful and harmonious form, which the Canadian pony had borne away, contributed not a little to warm his enthusiasm. More than once he found himself dwelling upon these things, and he permitted his fancy to depict her now in attitudes of distress and supplication; and the touching intonation of her voice, already vibrated, so to speak, over the very chords of his heart. In fact, her beauty, and real or imaginary perfections, formed, at the time, the material of his pleasantest thoughts; while the fright and suffering, which in all probability she now underwent, and the imminent peril which hung over her, formed a stimulus to exertion, which drove all ideas of hesitation from his mind, and all fatigue from his limbs.

It was remarkable, and so it appeared to all, that Jacob should have pursued a course which must very soon have brought him to, or near the Rock Spring. It was not imagined that he would thus voluntarily seek the vicinity of the friends of his prisoner; and the pursuers, now, at every moment, anticipated that the trail would lead away in some other direction. Such, however, was not the case. It continued to point directly on. Soon, in fact, the smoke of Brigham's log hut, began to be visible, above the trees; and the distant bark of dogs, at intervals disturbed the stillness of the evening air.

Lower and lower, sunk the descending sun, and as the space between it and the western horizon grew less, the anxiety of those who felt a personal interest in the recovery of the abducted girl, grew more and more intense. More than twenty-four hours had already elapsed since her disappearance; and the moods of insanity during this long interval might have devised a thousand reasons for her destruction.

The condition of Colonel Belden and his daughter, in the mean time, had been one of anxiety and apprehension, which grew deeper, as time wore away, and brought no information, and no grounds for hope.

The sun was near setting as those who had been engaged in the search came again in sight of their point of departure. All this round appeared to have been run to no purpose. They might not now be nearer their object than when they started. But yet they brought back with them a trace or clew, slight enough to be sure, but one which they hoped to follow up to some issue.

The course pursued by Jacob did not ascend the side of the valley or swale, so as to go near the cabin; but continued on the line of the stream, till it led fully past it. Here the party halted. They had already, for some time, been seen and recognized from the house; and the old man was well-nigh giving way to despair when he saw them thus returning without his protegée, and, as he imagined, without the design or the inclination, to continue the pursuit further. But he was no less astonished than they had been, when he found that it was the trail itself, which had brought them thus strangely back to their starting-point.

CHAPTER IX.

FOUND, BUT NOT CAUGHT.

"WELL, colonel," said Brigham, after a long discussion, "I suppose you may be right that the gal is made way with; and in particular, as we hain't lately seen no signs on her. But whether that's so or not, I'm determined, for one, to get at the bottom of the matter, and to cage this wild varmint, if we do no more. He ain't fit to be loose. And so, whether any body else keeps on or not, I mean to follow up the chase."

"Why," exclaimed Walcott, "you don't for a moment suppose that any of us mean to abandon the poor girl, do you?"

"As for that, every man must make up his own mind. I've my own notions as to whether we shall find her alive if at all; and most likely so has most on us. Maybe she will turn up, and maybe not. Not seeing any tracks of her lately, I confess, is rather a bad sign."

"That proves nothing," said Walcott, "she has not walked; she could not, of course, keep up with Jacob in traveling through the woods, and he is strong enough to carry her anywhere; and that too, at a pace that you or I could hardly equal. Besides we have not seen any sign or evidence of violence anywhere; and a murder leaves upon the earth, marks deeper and plainer than footsteps in the sand. I'll not give over the search, while I've a foot left to travel on—so there's two of us."

"Catfoot," said Brigham, "what do you say? You are worth all on us, at a pinch; and, old fellow, if you'll just stand by us now, for old acquaintance' sake, why, you know, I'll make it up to you some other time."

"Good," replied the Indian. "Catfoot no want sleep like squaw—always hunt with his brother."

"I knowed you'd do it. You're clear grit; and I'd do as much for you," answered Brigham, his face flushing with pleasure: "So now we are coming on, and if Joe and Jim here will join us, we'll be all right."

"In course, we're ready, if you are, Sandy," replied M'Carty; "and so you'd better see what can be done afore dark."

Upon this the pursuit was again resumed. The trail was traceable for a short distance, when it entirely disappeared. At the suggestion of Catfoot the party now separated; and M'Carty, Joe, and Brigham, each going off different ways, took up positions that, in some sort, enabled them to surround the spot where the trace was lost. This was done in consequence of the information which Colonel Belden had communicated in regard to the strange noise and laughter which he had heard near there, during the preceding night.

At this point the whole of the valley of the creek was occupied by a dense thicket of alder, with here and there clusters of wild scrubby tamaracks; and it was not unreasonably supposed that Jacob's actual place of concealment might be here, or near at hand.

While this movement was taking place, and while Walcott was busily scanning the brake, Catfoot had held himself apart, and was considering the ground, which being on the west side open and free from trees and brush, extended from the brook to the margin of the valley. This open ground was about six rods in width, and about a hundred yards long. Its inclination was very slight, and it might almost have been called a level. Along the creek was a fringe of willows, through which the water could be seen sparkling by day, and from which its low ripple could be heard by night. In the midst of this natural court, thus walled and hedged in by a steep bank on the one side and by a stream and close copse on the other, stood, what in those days was an object of almost superstitious wonder, and what, in our time, is still one of scientific curiosity.

A few paces from the bottom of the ledge was a large rock, in shape much like a common hay-rick, but only about four feet in height, by, perhaps, five in diameter. Down through its apex was a round hole about six inches across, through which came welling forth a column of limpid and sparkling water, that poured in all directions over the lips of this natural well, and kept the sides of the rock laved with its ceaseless flow. At times the stream came up in beats or pulsations, so as to seem not unlike blood flowing from an opened artery. All around it the ground was much trodden by the feet of wild animals, who were, apparently, in the habit of coming there to drink, just as domestic cattle will gather round a pump and trough.

A little to the northward of this, at the time of which we speak, was the white canvas of an old military tent, which was then unoccupied, but which gave token of recent habitation.

This was none other than the marquée which General Philip Schuyler had caused to be pitched upon that spot, for the accommodation of himself and his family, when he chose to visit this celebrated spring. Such a visit he had made only a day or so before the events of our story; and from the fact that the tent had been left standing, it was supposed that he or some of his friends might be seen there again within a short time.

As the sun sank behind a heavy bank of clouds in the west, its last rays illuminated the tall ridge pole and the white canvas-top of the tent, while they shone full upon the high green pines which shot their tall shafts into the air on the opposite side of the swale. In the interval lay the alder marsh, now dull and shadowy, but alive with the hoarse croak of frogs, and the wild and peculiar whir of countless camelion toads. The approach of evening, or of a summer storm never fails to call forth these lugubrious sounds.

Quietly but keenly did the eye of the Indian peruse, in the open ground, each visible object and mark; for, to him, they seemed as significant and full of meaning as to a scholar are the printed words upon the page of a book. He was absorbed in deep reverie. Unlike the others, he paid but little attention to the alder thicket. For some reasons of his own he appeared either to doubt its being the place of the lunatic's retreat, or to have sufficient confidence in the dispositions already made, to prevent his escape from it in case he should be there. After some moments of consideration he slowly passed over the little slope to the base of the ledge, where the ground was more or less covered with broken stones and rotten sticks. Here his attention became again fixed; but after a short pause he began, like a hound recovering the scent, to move slowly along in a southerly direction, keeping his eyes riveted upon the ground. Having gone in this manner for five or six rods, he was compelled again to pause; for the real or imaginary trace which he had just followed, again became invisible. But this hesitation was only transient, for the lost thread was soon recovered, and now so plainly and unmistakably as to bring him to a full stop, and to cause him to utter an exclamation of surprise. He even, by a cry or whoop, gave notice to the others that he had come upon something unusual. They soon gathered upon the spot; and he pointed out to them where a man had trodden upon a bit of yielding sod, just above where they stood. It was plainly Jacob's footstep. Its size and shape were sufficient proofs of the fact; and they had now studied it enough to be quite confident. It led still up the bank which, at this place, was not very precipitous, and along which lay the decaying trunk of a large tree, which years before had fallen slopingly down the declivity.

Catfoot and Walcott instantly and eagerly followed up the trace, but could not find it beyond the prostrate tree. They carefully examined the trunk itself, to ascertain whether or not he had scrambled along upon it, and reached the level ground above, in that way. No evidence of such a proceeding, however, could they detect, after the closest scrutiny.

They, therefore, turned back to make a re-examination. The old log, at the point where they first approached it, was, in consequence of the peculiar way in which it had fallen, and of a concavity in the ground, nearly as high as a man's breast; and beneath it, was a sort of lattice-work of bushes, so thick as to be impenetrable to the eye. Catfoot, kneeling down, put these aside, and peered through. In this attitude, he remained for some seconds. Then, to the amazement of Walcott, he seemed suddenly to be seized with a strange tremor, and to be laboring under some violent agitation. His eyes became fixed, dilated, and glaring; and his whole countenance for a single moment, gave token either of great pain or great fear. These signs of emotion, in one of his race and temperament, were all the more remarkable. Walcott, therefore, to clear up the matter, thrust his companion aside; and looking through the bushes himself, saw there perched like an ill-omened bird, in a hollow of the rock, the fantastic figure of Jacob himself. In the deep shadow where he sat, his form and proportions looked gigantic; and his great wild eyes, sparkling with excitement, as he watched his pursuers, wore an expression of malice, mockery, and menace. No wonder the courage of the Indian had failed him. The apparition appeared to his excited fancy superhuman, and appealed to those sentiments out of which alone all his fears arose. The danger also was not unreal; for Jacob was within striking distance, and was crouched like a tiger, preparing for a spring, or like a coiled rattlesnake just drawing back in order to make the dart of its fangs more fatal.

The moment, however, that his eye met that of Walcott, his whole attitude changed; and uttering a loud cry, he flung himself backward in the darkness, and disappeared. It was done so suddenly that he seemed to have sank in the earth. For an instant, but for an instant only, did Walcott pause; then, tearing aside the brush, and springing under, he succeeded in rolling the old tree from its position. Beyond it was then disclosed the narrow entrance of a cavern.

During this time, Walcott had been closely followed and actively assisted by his companion, who, when the first trammels of his superstitious fears gave way, had recovered his self-possession as if by a rebound.

The remainder of the party were now called, and soon gathered upon the spot.

"We've got him at last, I think, Brigham," said Walcott, as the others came up.

"I heard his yell from t'other side of the mash," replied Brigham; "but where on earth is he?"

"Not on earth at all," answered the young man; "for unless he is a wizard, he disappeared down that dark hole there."

Brigham then approached the opening, and with a long stick, sought to sound its depths.

"It's big enough for sartain," he said, after having vainly sought to find its bottom.

"He's as bad as a four-footed varmint," said M'Carty, "to crawl into such a burrow; he can't be much better than a woodchuck, though he's got the cunnin' of a fox; and I dare say he'll die game. We'll have to get our shootin' irons ready in this case."

"What do you mean by shooting irons, M'Carty?" asked Walcott; "we are not about to shoot him as if he was a beast, notwithstanding your comparisons."

"Well now, that's odd, any how," answered M'Carty; "I should say, for one, that a critter as made away with a young woman, where nobody could find her; and like enough has eaten her half up by this time, could n't be no better than a cannibal, which I take to be next thing to an animal. And I dare say Sandy there is of my notion."

"Pooh! M'Carty," answered Walcott; "let us hope that the poor girl is still safe and unharmed somewhere; and at all event, whether Jacob is a cannibal or not, we must use no fire-arms, nor commit any unnecessary act of cruelty. Taken he certainly shall be, and well secured. But for the present, we must think more of his prisoner than of him. Has any body here any notion of the extent of this hole?"

"Why, as for that," replied Brigham, shifting his quid of tobacco from one cheek to the other; "I've heern tell of something about this cave afore, but never made no account on't. In fact, I did n't know where the mouth was, and did n't believe in it. Hows'ever, if all the rest they tell about it, be true, the place is sartainly big enough, and not onpleasant neither, when once you get in there. Great rooms filled with crystils and dimings, and sich like; and, may be, gold, for all I know. All this, I take to be nonsense; but what we know for sartain is, that here's a real hole, with the man we're in search of, inside of it. But still I consate we sha'n't find the young woman alive, and should n't be surprised to find Mac's notion half true."

"From all this, it would seem that the place is extensive enough to hide Jacob, unless he is carefully sought with torches," answered Walcott. "It is lucky we got here before dark; for once inside the cavern, night is as good as day; and so, we shall lose no time. Where can we procure lights?"

"Plenty of pitch pine up at the house," replied Brigham; "M'Carty, do you and Joe go up and bring down a lot of it. But I'm thinking, Mr. Arthur, we had all on us better take a bite of something to eat before venturin' further. I feel a mighty cravin' myself."

"Well," said Walcott, "perhaps you are right. We have now got all sure, and as a few minutes can probably make go great difference, do you all go up and get something to sustain your strength. I feel no need of it myself, and but little appetite."

"That won't do, Mr. Arthur," said Brigham; "either you go up, or we all stay. M'Carty here can watch in the mean time; and, especially, as we sha' n't want him or Joe, any more to-night, in all likelihood, as three on us will be enough to go into the cave."

This arrangement was, accordingly, concluded upon. M'Carty and Indian Joe, for the present, remained where they were, to prevent an escape; while the others went to Brigham's cabin, to procure food, and the necessary lights.

By this time, darkness had begun to spread over the landscape. The woods had become shadowy, and the pathways dim. The pursuers had not been in the slightest degree, too eager; nor had they arrived at the mouth of the cavern one moment too soon. In a very short time later, the trail which led to it, could not have been traced; and in that event, the evening of the second day would have left them in as much doubt and uncertainty, as that of the day before.

Anxious were the faces which met them at the door of the house. The colonel and his daughter were eager to know the meaning and results of the noises they had heard, and the movements they had witnessed. A few words sufficed to apprise them of all. Still the great problem remained unsolved. The fate of Lucile, and not the pursuit and capture of Jacob, was uppermost in their thoughts, and weighed upon their hearts. They entertained none but the gloomiest anticipations.

The old gentleman thoughtfully and sadly paced the floor of the apartment; while Marion, after many fruitless endeavors to glean some materials for hope out of the events of the day, could not repress a few tears, born of fear and anxiety.

During this while, all the others, save Walcott, had been busy in satisfying an appetite whetted to a keen edge by eight or nine hours of continued exertion in the woods. The young man, as he had said, really felt but little inclination for food; and he was only persuaded to partake of a morsel, just as they were about to start. Meanwhile, he had remained silent and thoughtful. To Marion, he proffered none of those sympathetic attentions which, considering their relations to each other, might under present circumstances have been looked for. Their want, however, was neither felt or observed by her. Each was pre-occupied by special subjects of anxiety, and gave no heed to the conduct of the other.

Meanwhile, Brigham had gathered together, and prepared, the material which would be needed in their contemplated subterranean search. When every thing was ready (and all had passed with rapidity) the three men left the cabin to repair to the mouth of the cave in order to relieve their temporary sentinels, and to commence their operations. They were provided with bundles of pine roots, and knots, for torches, with cords and ropes; and, notwithstanding what Walcott had said, with firearms, to be used in a case of emergency.

Soon after starting, they heard from the valley below, and in the direction in which they were going, a violent stamping of feet, a sort of scuffling sound as of men struggling together, and then a half suppressed cry for help. They immediately hurried forward, but had taken only a few steps, before meeting Indian Joe, who came up to them so panic-stricken, that he was at first unable to explain what had happened. He, however, immediately turned about, and beckoned them to follow him. Down the bank, they all accordingly rushed. When they arrived near the opening of the cavern, they saw a dark object rising from the ground, which on examination, proved to be the form of M'Carty.

To explain what had occurred, we are compelled to recur to the time when the others had gone up to the house.

When M'Carty and his companion had found themselves alone, they sat down quietly on the tree, which had been rolled from the mouth of the hole; and prepared to spend their time as agreeably as possible, in conversation and in smoking.

"Well," said Jim, "whatever becomes of the gal, we've got the old one fast, for a while, any way. But, Joe! I say, do you know where this hole leads to?"

Joe raised his arm, and pointed away in a westerly direction, saying:

"Mile off."

"Come, old boy, that's a whopper to tell to a man like me," replied M'Carty; "I rather reckon it's some fox-hole, dug, perhaps, in the days of Noah, when foxes, by all accounts, was bigger than they are now."

"Fox nebber make dis hole," said Joe, by way of rejoinder.

"And why not?" asked the other. "Do you suppose the varmints of the Bible could n't do more than the puny critters of our days? It 's a most onchristian notion of yourn, Joe, if you think so; and you ought to have a regular missionary to larn you better."

"Fox nebber dig trough big stone," was the pertinacious reply of the Indian.

"And how far into the arth," said M'Carty, "do you mean to say the cussed tunnel goes to? You talk about its going through big stun as if you'd been inside, and knowed all about it."

"Bin in—bin trough," answered Joe.

"Through to what?" asked M'Carty.

"To t'other hole—mile off," was the answer.

"All gammon, my old chap," said the other; "that 'ud be a pretty story to tell. A hole under ground a mile long, and comin' out, goodness knows where in the woods! Don't try it again, I tell you. I should rather say that old Jake just crep in here for a short hide; and like enough he and the old fox is havin' a row to see who's boss."

"Tell you, no fox," said Joe. "Big hole—take in wigwam—high as tree, and full of glass."

"Joe," said M'Carty; "you're in liquor. Tell us where you got it, for I'm rather dry myself."

"No whisky, tell you! where you s'pose get him?" testily answered the Indian, now getting excited at the bare idea that such a luxury should be supposed to have been near him. "Dis captain nebber hab whisky—he good hunt, but big fool."

"There you're right, old feller," answered M'Carty, "whatever you may say about the woodchuck hole here; to my notion it's not sensible to be out in the woods without something to drink; and if I had my way, I'd always carry whisky; and if I could n't get that, then I'd have brandy; or, as the Canucks calls it, 'Oh Davy.'" (*Eau de vie.*)

"Oh Davy better than whisky," said Joe, now entering into the spirit of the discussion.

"That's your ignorance, and Indian larnin'," answered M'Carty. "Why, you ought to know that 'Oh Davy' is nothin' but French whisky arter all; and a man can't fairly get drunk on it without an intarpreter."

"Wish had him, though," said Joe, "try him hard."

"Why, old boy," said Jim, "you talk nothin' but sense ever since you left off gabblin' about this mouse-trap of a hole. Wish you had him, do you? Well, there's two on us in the same way; though, as I was sayin', whisky is better and more natural unless, perhaps, when a man's a foreigner. But, heigho! there's no use talkin' about such things, when we can't get 'em. So we'd better speak agin about your whopper of a story about the toad-hole there."

"Better look and see toad no jump," said Joe, feeling a little spiteful at his companion's incredulity.

"How, jump?" asked M'Carty. "But, now that I think of it, old Jake must have got the better of the fox and scared him out, to judge by the scratchin' we hear inside."

"Look sharp—told you so before," still said the Indian.

"Why, Joe," said the other, "to my thinkin' the old

chap would n't like a tussle with me the second time, and in particular when you 're by to lend a hand at a pinch. So never fear. He took an onfair advantage on me before; but let him try it again."

At that moment the speech of M'Carty was interrupted by the sight of a dark object which suddenly issued from the cave, and striking against the burly figure of Indian Joe, sent it rolling down the hill like a sack of sand. M'Carty was not lacking either in activity or courage. He instantly sprang at the form which caused the mischief; and, at once found himself grappling with his old enemy, the lunatic. He practiced upon him all his tricks of wrestling, and put forth his utmost strength; but every thing was unavailing. In a twinkling he felt himself borne down the bank, and flung with violence upon the ground below. It was at this moment that he had uttered a half-suppressed cry.

When he recovered from the shock and rose up, he found that his opponent had disappeared; and that torches were approaching from the house.

CHAPTER X.

THE CAVERN.

"WHAT on 'arth can be the matter with M'Carty?" exclaimed Brigham, coming up. "Why are you rolling there, like a fly-bitten horse? Could n't you get exercise enough in eighteen hours' run? But, I say, this looks queer. I'm blessed if I don't think they 've let the critter out of the hole!"

Meanwhile, the new-comers gathered around their crest-fallen comrade, who, with looks half foolish and half sulky, was still unwilling to confess that he had been, for a second time, foiled and worsted.

"How did it all happen?" asked Walcott, perceiving that Brigham's conjecture was not unlikely to be true: "I thought you was too old a soldier to be caught napping at your post."

"There's no soldiering, and no napping in the case," answered M'Carty: "Joe, there, can tell you that he pitched him down the hill like an empty barrel. Tit for tat, thought I, and so, I pitched into him. But what's the use trying falls with the devil? Before I could get one good grip, he was off, like a great black hawk; and there's the whole on't."

"But he didn't by any chance, carry off the girl with him again, did he?" asked Walcott.

"How was it, Joe? for I'm blessed if I got sight of anything," said M'Carty.

"No got squaw this time," said Joe.

"Well, that's satisfactory, any how," broke in Brigham; "we'll now have a clear field to go into this dog hole of a den of his; though I'm still thinkin' it ain't of much use."

Preparations were now accordingly made to engage in that enterprise. The pursuit and capture of the lunatic, not being of such immediate importance, was deferred to another time.

Long before this, it had become completely dark. The tall trees and thick bushes, around the spot where the party stood, were lighted up by the red glare of the torches which they bore. The rough rocks and equally rough faces of the men, were also, now and then, illuminated by them. The scene might perhaps have been called picturesque. In the distant woods could be heard as usual, the howl of the wolf, the low hooting of the owl, and the far off wail of the catamount. Near at hand, all the thicket and marshes were alive with other wild sounds, not so loud, but equally harsh and discordant. In the midst of the ceaseless din, which rolled upon the ear like uninterrupted platoon firing in a great battle, could occasionally be distinguished a loud, but retreating shout of laughter, which there was no difficulty in attributing to the escaped maniac. It seemed more inhuman and fearful than any other of the sounds which disturbed the night.

But these things were scarcely heeded by those whose operations we are endeavoring to trace. With the exception of Walcott, none there present had, for such scenes, the least appreciative taste. And even upon him, there was made at the time but a slight impression—an impression then immediately forgotten, but long afterward recalled in full force, and remembered in all its details.

The three men now crawled into the cavern; for M'Carty and Indian Joe, not being needed there, were left behind, and had it in charge simply to watch the entrance so as to prevent Jacob from going in again. The others groped their way onward without any apprehension, as they had left Jacob, the only formidable obstacle, behind them. The opening at first descended at an angle of about forty-five degrees for nearly ten feet, at the bottom of which, as at the bottom of a pipe-bowl, they found a narrow passage leading thence horizontally—a passage but little more than wide enough to permit one person to proceed at a time. This narrow drift or funnel, of a variable size, continued for about a rod; and during their slow passage through it all bore their torches with difficulty ahead. It was plain that had Jacob remained in possession of this subterranean stronghold, their further progress could have been rendered impossible, as each would have been entirely at his mercy at this spot, and might have been brained as he crept along. As it was, however, they got forward without any serious impediment. The rock below was worn smooth apparently by use; and overhead, as the smoke of their torches curled up among the dripping crevices, they found indications that their present way must have been opened by some vast convulsion of nature, as each side in projection and indentation corresponded with the other as if once torn apart; while between them now hung glittering masses of white felspar and transparent crystal. At the termination of the tubular passage, the ceiling abruptly rose up to seven or eight feet in height. Here they were enabled to elevate their lights above their heads, so as at once to look before and around them. The passage also grew rapidly wider, until it attained nearly, though not uniformly, the breadth of an ordinary room. The surrounding rock, save in the sparry interstice above mentioned, had been hitherto dark, and was almost everywhere dripping with water, but as they proceeded, the character of it began to change. The walls and the roof became comparatively dry. Occasionally, also, new fissures or breaks were visible, which were filled with the white or yellowish spar. The sparkle of quartz here and there sent back to the eye a white reflection from the torches. These doubtless were the diamonds of public rumor alluded to by Brigham.

The human voice, in the close arches where they now moved, when raised but a little above its ordinary key, sounded loud and stunning. When they stood still, even the ticking of a watch could be heard. They were getting far beyond the reach of all the noises which disturbed the upper world.

The further they proceeded, the more were they astonished at the extent and magnificence of the grotto. Brilliant stalactites began to glitter around them. They seemed to be moving through the gallery of an illuminated palace, where utter and almost magical silence reigned.

They carefully scrutinized every nook and shady crevice as they passed, lest, in some of them, might be found a side opening leading away to other chambers, where the object of their search might be concealed. None such, however, as yet, appeared. It was an encouragement to them to know that their chances of success were so much the better, as the cavern, to all seeming, consisted of but one grand passage. There was no labyrinth of apartments to be traversed, in which a solitary wanderer might be lost; and amid whose mazes, the anxious searchers might prosecute their examinations in vain.

Meanwhile, the path they traveled was not an easy one. The floor was encumbered with loose rocky fragments, with numberless stalagmitic cones, and with rough outcropping ridges of golden-hued mica slate. Nor was it otherwise level, but ascended and descended; and although its general direction was westerly, it still wound onward in an irregular zig-zag; so that there was scarcely a single point where the view could have reached to any great distance, even had their lights been powerful enough to penetrate the dark arches which yawned before and behind them.

As they moved slowly through those subterranean abodes, with the red smoking torches which they bore, and the various characteristics and contrasts which they exhibited in dress and in manner, they would have formed a fine subject for an artist's pencil.

In front was Walcott, youthful, athletic and compact in figure; with the ruddy light illuminating his glossy hair, and his clear complexion; while his thoughtful brow and anxious eye betrayed the absorbing interest which he took in the enterprise. Next came Brigham, large, swarthy, rude, intelligent, cunning; his eye blazing with passion, and his countenance sobered by experience; powerful, resolute and adroit. After him could be seen the Apollo-like form, the stoic face, the flashing eye, and graceful, composed movement of the Indian. From the sparry roof and the glistening sides, from the encumbered floor and the sable vaults, arose the bright lights and deep shadows of the picture—evoked by the red blazes of the torches, like contending spirits, from out of the surrounding space.

The countenances of all were more or less clothed in wonder. Even Indian stoicism had given way before the dazzling phenomena which thus unexpectedly greeted them in these solitary vaults far under the habitable world.

From the utter silence which they had previously encountered, they were, at last, but only by degrees, awakened to the consciousness that something like the sound of rushing water was gradually, and from the distance, stealing upon their senses. More clear and more musical did the liquid melody become, as they proceeded onward. With their senses absorbed by these sounds of enchantment, they sometimes forgot the object for which they had ventured thither; but they still mechanically moved on.

At length they came to a place where the echoes of the rushing water, like the swell and cadence of an Æolian harp, filled the whole air. Immediately in front, they beheld a narrow stream, clear as glass, but running like a torrent. From its surface arose a thousand sparkling bubbles, so that it looked like a rivulet of effervescent wine. It issued from the right, or northerly side of the cavern, out of dull porous rocks, painted over with a red deposit of iron oxyd. On the other side it poured, with a loud brawl, into a close, full-throated funnel. They heard the sound thereof, but could not tell whence it came, or whither it went. They tasted of the water, and found it of a pungent, saline flavor, but quite palatable and exhilarating. To judge from this, the stream might well be imagined to be one of the full-charged subterranean arteries, out of which issued the numberless veins that bore, through uprising strata and sinuous crevices in the rocks, the various waters of the mineral springs, which burst out so abundantly upon the surface of the earth above.

After a slight pause they crossed the stream, which was not very deep or broad. Beyond it, the cavern grew wider; and, with the smoky lights which they carried, they could hardly perceive the extent of it through the gloom. Before venturing further on their course, they carefully passed along each of the sides, to ascertain the possible existence of any openings. In this the sharp eyes of the Indian were found to be of great avail. On one side he detected a small low orifice, of a size sufficient to admit the entrance of a man's body. It had escaped the notice of the others. On closer examination it was found to be of a considerable length, and was suspected to lead to some other compartment of the grotto. It lay close by the mineral brook, and in a position not to be easily seen.

After a little hesitation, Walcott crept into the opening, and passed out of sight; the others immediately followed, and soon found themselves in a small vaulted chamber, possessing no other outlet than that by which they had entered. It was brilliant with crystals. On the sides, the ceiling, and the floor, were huge, pointed, translucent masses of sparkling quartz. As the flaring light of the torches spread around the little apartment, and was reflected back from a thousand points, the eye became painfully dazzled by the luster; and the three adventurers paused as if they had unwittingly burst in upon one of nature's secret treasures. What added singularly to the air of enchantment which the place wore, was the sound of the rivulet, which penetrated thither through concealed fissures in the rocks, and, varying with the ever-changing flow of the water, came to the ear in soft, melodious, ringing murmurs. With little aid of fancy, it might have been taken for the tones of a musical instrument, softened by distance, and rising or falling upon the variable winds.

CHAPTER XI.

LUCILE.

When we left our poor Lucile, she was borne quite unconscious, in the arms of Jacob, from the bough-hut in the direction of the Rock Spring. Her fatigue and anxiety had been more than nature could endure. How long she lay in this merciful trance, she never could tell; but when her senses began slowly to return to her, she could hardly believe that the objects she saw around were real. It must be that she looked upon the pictures of a dream, or that her mind was wandering—so wonderful was every object which met her eye. She saw herself in what appeared to be a vast chamber or vault, around which shone myriads of sparkling objects, of every conceivable color and brilliance. The light by which they were beheld, came from a large fire of sticks, built in the center of the room against a cluster of stones. A tall flame rose from it toward the roof, where it sent a thick canopy of smoke, which, after creeping slowly along the arches, seemed to escape through unseen crevices; for the quantity of it, in the apartment, was in no wise increased, even after the lapse of a considerable time. Under her was a pile of skins, thick enough to form a soft and comfortable bed; and, no doubt, it had contributed not a little to prolong her sleep.

Before endeavoring to scan the marvelous objects which everywhere met her eye, or to unravel the mystery which surrounded her, she tried to compose her startled thoughts, and by recollecting where she was last, to follow up, if possible, the thread of events which had led her hither. For a long time she was quite unsuccessful; the vail which shut out the past, seemed too thick and impenetrable. But at length, it lifted slowly like a rising mist; and faintly, and one by one, did the painful incidents of the last few days, take their proper place in her memory. But still there was a point where they ceased to be distinguishable; and the picture which she had thus been able to retrace, faded away in those last miserable moments of consciousness, when the lunatic had carried her, in the darkness, away from the lonely hut of boughs. What had since happened? and where could she be now? Upon her person were the same clothes she had worn on the morning of the ill-starred excursion; and she could not therefore doubt but that the adventure, by some inscrutable means, had brought her where she was.

To her wondering eyes, the place, though so wild and solitary, was still mysterious and magical. It would seem that she had in reality been transferred to a fairy palace. Around her, were none of the appliances of civilized life —none of those devices and productions which the human race is constantly, and from generation to generation, accumulating in its abodes, and scattering over the world.

Of all that she saw, the fire alone, and what lay on and around it, gave token of the presence of man. In the midst of the space it blazed and crackled away in sullen industry; while before it on rude spits were to be seen three or four small objects which, on a closer inspection, proved to be fishes thus exposed to a primitive broil. It was so far consoling, as it showed that she was not beyond the reach of human attention, and was still an object of care. But when she looked around upon the magnificent solitude of the vast apartment, and sought to divine by what means she had been translated to it, the mystery became appalling, and a cold awe crept like ice over her heart.

For a long time she listened in silence, hoping, in that way to learn if any other living thing might be near; but no sound disturbed the stillness save the roar of the fire and the crackling of the sticks. Yet, somebody must have been present, and that not long since; for there the fire lay burning, and fresh fish were broiling upon the spits. Who this provider might be she trembled to imagine.

She walked about the apartment and on all sides she met solid, impenetrable rocks. No door—no apparent means of entrance or of egress did she encounter. It seemed like a gorgeous tomb in which she was buried. Or, was it all, rather, the delusion of a disordered brain? and could she suddenly have become as crazy as the lunatic? To assure herself of the contrary she still continued her examination. Each object, she could distinguish, define, and describe. The couch, the fire, the broiling fish, were all considered. Her mind quietly and clearly performed its office, in respect to the things which she saw. She even turned her attention to details as a means of further convincing herself that her thoughts were still healthy and sound. She examined the fish by the fire. One side of them was raw and the other was burned to a crisp for lack of turning. This she saw; she could comprehend and explain it. Thank heaven! reason still held its sway in her mind, and she was not the victim of disordered fancy, but of some unexpected natural misfortune. So far, well; but could it be that the mysterious purveyor had purposely left her to the care of supervising the preparation of the half-broiled meal? There was a grain of hope, or, at least, of consolation in the thought. His presence was more to be feared than solitude and desertion.

It will be borne in mind, that a long time had now elapsed, how long, the poor girl herself had no means of measuring, since she had partaken of any food. It will not, therefore be surprising that, in spite of the perils to which she had been exposed, and in spite of the dubious and agitating circumstances in which she was at present placed, nature gradually asserted her power and proclaimed her wants, and that she felt a strong and growing appetite.

So it was without reluctance that she, for the moment, endeavored to forget her unhappiness in attending to the preparation of the food which she found before her. When would be her next meal? Who would be her provider? Might not the malignant designs or the unthinking caprice of her captor leave her, perhaps, soon, or, perhaps, at some later period without sustenance, a victim of starvation? There was hunger in the very thought; and she began to regard the little that was before her with an eye of longing, and yet with a feeling that, like a poor man's wages, or a miser's wealth, it was to be economized and carefully hoarded. When, therefore, the food was sufficiently cooked she partook of it but sparingly; though either a long fast or an alarmed apprehension as to the source from which her future supplies were to be derived, gave to that little a flavor which no sauces could have imparted, and which only served to whet the appetite it was intended to allay. Thirst, too, with its feverish requisitions, began to be felt. How was it to be slaked? No limpid pool, like the few treasured fishes, seemed ready to invite her attention; and her eager eye in vain surveyed the mysterious rocky walls which shut her in, for some collection of the desired element, or for some trickling drops which might serve to satisfy her thirst. She took up one of the half-burned brands from the fire and commenced a tour of exploration. It was with a feeling of joy and gratitude that she found in a remote corner a thin trickling thread of water, falling in limpid drops over the white rocks of the side, and collecting in a little hollow near the bottom. In this was sufficient to satisfy her thirst, and one source of anxiety was relieved by observing that as fast as the basin was exhausted, the tinkling cascade which fell into it served to renew the supply.

This prime want being for the present, gratified; and, for the future, provided against; she resumed her reconnoissance. Closely and carefully did she peer into every nook and corner; and, with uplifted torch, she sought to penetrate the shadowy recesses of the high roof. But, to her alarmed eye, no sign of outlet or means of access, was anywhere visible; and it was with lowered hopes, and a gathering sense of misery that she continued her round, till the circuit was quite completed. Not the least success had attended the effort. To all appearance, her prison was as much without opening or aperture, as an unbroken nut-shell. She did not, for a moment, doubt the existence of an opening; but the ground of alarm was that it might be so difficult to find, so hard to attain, or so carefully secured, as to prevent her from deriving any benefit from it. In the fullness of her grief, she at last sat down upon the pile of skins which had served her for a couch, and burst into a fit of violent and uncontrollable weeping.

During the occurrences which had taken place, a vast change had been wrought within herself. From being a girl, she felt herself to have become a woman; from being giddy, thoughtless, and dependant upon others, she had become considerate and sober; and had been forced to look into her own mind for resources, and for grounds of hope. In two days a new life had swept over her, leaving, like an angel of wisdom, its manna of experience and its store of strength, behind. So the poor girl felt; and under the influence of the new-born impulses, she desired to act; but the sorrow of the hour lay too heavy at her heart, and she could not restrain a few tears of bitterness, and a few sobs of anguish.

But here, the course of our narrative compels us for the present to leave her, and to turn our attention again to the movements of the other actors in our story.

Jacob, after having made the preparations for an evening meal, which we have noted, had taken a kind of cup made of the hollowed shell of a species of squash, commonly called a gourd, and had made his way back through the cavern to the rivulet of mineral water. Arriving there, some impulse of caution or curiosity induced him to continue on to the mouth of the grotto, for the purpose of seeing what his pursuers might be doing; for, by a sort of instinct, he had long since divined that eager eyes were already upon his footsteps. What occurred when he arrived at the outlet and was about to emerge into the open air, we have before related. The excitement of those few events had driven from his mind all thought of the errand which had called him forth, and of the circumstances which required his return. The helpless prisoner, in her solitude and sorrow, was utterly forgotten. For a long time, neither pity for an innocent sufferer, nor eagerness to repossess a beautiful victim, was felt in his heart; and it was not until, when far off in the woods, he looked back and saw the lights of the moving torches, and the forms of his pursuers about the entrance of the cavern, that an indistinct comprehension came back to his disordered mind of the purpose which they had in view, and of the contemplated mischief which he had left behind him in the grotto.

CHAPTER XII.

JACOB AT HOME.

Walcott and his associates, when last we left them, were still in the crystal chamber, which they had found by the side of the subterranean brook. Full of amazement at the splendor which everywhere met their eyes, they for some time remained, absorbed in new emotions, and in forgetfulness of the pressing errand which had brought them hither. To the young man especially, whose mind was still open to the seductive charms of romance, there was a singular fascination in every thing by which he was surrounded. He was, therefore, the last that turned to leave a place which had taken such strong hold of his fancy. Though full of fairy sounds and latent glories, it was without occupant of any kind; and by any further delay there, the enterprise in which they were embarked could only suffer.

In going out of the chamber the Indian took the lead. When he had crept nearly through the orifice, and was about emerging on the other side, as he held his torch before him, he saw, or fancied that he saw, standing in the open space and within a few feet of him, the fantastic figure and mocking face of Jacob. So deep was his superstitious dread of this creature, and so startled was he by the unexpected apparition, that by an involuntary impulse he hurried back into the closed chamber before the others had started to follow him, exhibiting in his countenance every mark of surprise and fear.

"What the deuce is the matter now?" exclaimed Brigham; "you ain't bit by a rattle-snake, are you?"

"No: seen Jake though," was Catfoot's perturbed reply.

Brigham instantly rushed into the opening, and crawling hastily through into the darkness, leaving the others to follow with the lights, was about rising on the other side, when a large and heavy fragment of rock came crashing against the wall beside him and broke into pieces sending its very splinters into his face. It was lucky that he had left his torch behind!

"Halloo!" he exclaimed, as he scrambled up; "the cave ain't tumbling in, I hope? But it must be the critter Catfoot saw. Sheer off!" he added, in the darkness, "or you'll find it ain't Jim M'Carty you've got hold on this time."

In a moment after a faint light shone through the opening, and Walcott and the Indian hurried out to join their companion. It was then by the aid of the torches that Brigham was enabled to catch sight of the shadowy figure of Jacob, as with the speed of a phantom, it disappeared in the darkness ahead. His loud dissonant laughter also burst like a sudden explosion upon their ears, and in continuous reverberations, rolled through the vast vaults of the cavern for some minutes after he was gone.

There was no time for consideration. The men all rushed on in hot pursuit. This, however, they found to be no easy task; and overtaking the fugitive was a feat not likely to be soon accomplished. Beside the roughness of the way, they were at this point much embarrassed by its width, which exposed them to the risk of leaving some lateral hiding-place unexplored as they passed; and so their whole labor might go for nothing, and their whole scheme miscarry.

"I think," said Brigham, as they hurried along, "that I shall give them lazy villains, Jim and Joe, a piece of my mind, when we go back. It's a pity if they could n't keep this crazy devil from getting in here a second time. I dare say they've got hold of a rum-bottle somewhere, between 'em, and are both sound drunk and snoring before now."

"They are certainly much to blame for letting him in," replied Walcott. "He will embarrass and, perhaps, entirely thwart us here."

Again busied with the labor of the search, each relapsed into silence. They got forward slowly, but without meeting any serious impediment and without catching another sight of the fugitive. At length the cavern became suddenly much narrower and led abruptly up a narrow ascent. On the top of this acclivity it was found that the character of the rock had become greatly changed both in color and in composition. Instead of white and transparent spar and crystal, they found dull coarse masses of marine limestone, and dikes of flinty trap. A breath of air was also felt to be blowing past them, which had a fresh, damp, and earthy odor. As they passed a little further on they saw, in the distance, a faint, dull glimmer of light. On proceeding thither, they found a small hole leading upward. Into this Walcott clambered, and soon emerged into the open air. It was at a small cleared space in the forest, upon which at that moment the light of the moon was falling in full effulgence. In the surrounding woods a ghost-like silence prevailed. The dew, like a misty vail, lay upon the grass and upon the leaves; and all nature seemed too peaceful and too slumberous to have been recently disturbed by the passage or presence of human beings.

The three men now set themselves to examine the outlet of the cavern, in order to see whether it contained any indications that the fugitive had escaped through it. In a few moments they had the satisfaction to find that there were no discoverable footmarks leading outward, except their own; but that, on the contrary, a fresh trail led inward. A part of the mystery was at once cleared up. By this means had the crazy man effected his second entrance, and not by eluding the vigilance, or overcoming the resistance of the two sentinels who had been posted to guard the eastern inlet.

The pursuers must have passed him in the cavern, where, doubtless, he had many hiding-places, and in some of which his hapless prisoner must still be concealed. There was nothing to do but to turn back, and to make a re-examination. Down the vaulted way, accordingly, was their course again bent; but they retraced their steps with no strong hopes of success. That all their movements had been watched, they had no doubt; and considering the facility with which they had been eluded, and the thousand shadowy recesses with which the vast cave abounded, through any of which some secret passage might lead to other compartments, they all felt that the chances were strongly against them.

After descending to the bottom of the slope, and gaining the point where the passage became high and wide, they resumed their scrutiny, and this time with much greater care than before. It was supposed that Jacob had slipped behind them, while they were eager in pursuit. They felt confident that his hiding-place could not be on the other side of the brook, where the gallery was narrow and easily explored. Its greatest breadth was, perhaps, at the very point where they were now prosecuting their search. In consequence of this, they had separated, not only for the purpose of extending the space to be illuminated by their torches, but so that, while one traversed the center, the other two could explore each of the sides. Walcott was a little ahead of the others, and in the center; Brigham was upon the right, and the Indian upon the left. While occupying these relative positions, it was suddenly observed that Catfoot paused, with very much the air of a dog, when first catching the scent of game. He stood perfectly still, while the others approached; and when both came round him, he said, snuffing the air,

"Smoke."

"What?" said Brigham.

"Smoke," was the reply.

"What do you mean by that?" asked Walcott.

"Mean somebody cook, get ready eat," answered Catfoot.

Walcott, hereupon, stepped to where the Indian stood, and after a little attention, did, in fact, perceive the smell which had arrested the attention of the other. The discovery was important. There could be no smoke without a fire, and no fire in that place, without human hands to kindle it. And whose could it be but the lunatic's? The conclusion was almost certain. But where, after all, was the place whence it issued? and by what avenue was it to be reached? Here was a still unsolved, but most important, question.

"Brigham," said Walcott, "just step a little further on, and see if you can discover any smell of smoke there."

Brigham accordingly took up a position in advance as requested; and then, shaking his head with a negative sign, he moved slowly toward his associate, and did not pause until within a rod or so of him, when he replied,

"Here, Mr. Walcott, I consate there's something like smoke. Hold a minute! I'll bet I can tell what the critter is roasting. Venison? No. Brimstone, perhaps? No. 'Taint that kind—too fresh like. By thunder! it 's fish. I'll swear to it. Catfoot, come here, and give us your opinion on't."

The Indian approached, and after a moment's hesitation, quietly replied:

"Pike."

"So it is, old boy," said Brigham, "fresh pike, by all that's natural! It must be the fish he caught in the pond where we found the pole and fixins."

On the left hand side of where they were now standing, the rocks, as they rose up, receded so that, by aid of the ledges, one could, without much difficulty, climb up it, to a point near the ceiling.

"Catfoot," said Walcott; "will you be good enough to examine these rocks along here, while Brigham and I watch?"

The Indian prepared to perform the task. Brigham took up his position further on in the cavern; and Walcott moved back toward the western opening, so as to command the spot, if necessary.

"I say, Mr. Walcott," shouted Brigham from the distance; "shall I shoot the varmint this time, in case he shows fight?"

"Not under any circumstances," was the reply; "our first business is to find the girl, and our next to take him, if we can; and no violence must be used, except in self-defence."

"Oh, very well, then!" said Brigham; "if you don't want him hurt, I'm agreeable."

Meanwhile, according to the young man's request, the Indian was engaged in a close examination of the side of the cavern, where the smell of smoke had first been perceived. On the other side, no trace of it was discoverable. For this reason he did not deem it necessary to give the latter more than a hasty observation. Most of his attention was turned to the former, where he traversed the whole distance between Walcott and Brigham, and was slowly returning, apparently without success, when a small piece of rock not larger than a walnut shell, came rolling lightly down the sloping side. Almost simultaneously, his eye swept the dark space overhead; but instantly after dropped again, while he, with much deliberation, and apparently, with more care than ever, continued his scrutiny, till he came again up to where Walcott was awaiting him. When there, without pausing, and without looking at him, he said in a low voice:

"Jake on big rock, just where you see me stop and look up. Place there to climb."

Having said thus much he slowly crossed to the other side of the cavern, and then went so far back in the direction of Brigham, as to be immediately abreast of the spot he had indicated. There, with his face turned the other way, he appeared to be engaged in examining each nook and suspicious shadow, as he had done in other places. His torch was held high over his head, in such a manner that what light it gave fell directly upon the place where Jacob was supposed to be.

Meanwhile, Walcott had not only observed the start which the Indian had given at the falling of the pebble, but had narrowly watched his movement since; and when the latter took up his final position, he was not slow in divining the purpose for which it was done.

Moving then slowly toward Brigham, with a manner as careless as he could assume, he was soon enabled to satisfy himself that the Indian was correct; for high up on a shelf of the rock near the roof of the cavern, he saw the shadowy figure of the maniac, perched there like an ill-omened owl. He was careful, however, as he approached, not to direct his look full upon the place, or by any other sign or token to indicate that he was at all aware of his presence. But when he found himself at the base of the shelving rock, almost immediately beneath the other, he paused and called upon Brigham to come near. Then, without an instant's delay, he dropped his own torch and sprang boldly up the acclivity, ascending by the aid of a few natural ledges, or stepping-places found on its face.

"Ha! ha! ho! ho!" shouted the wild creature from above, "it's old Arthur, all over! See how he comes! But I'll show him how to go down again, without the help of steps!"

So saying, he planted himself in a position where he could grapple at great advantage with the young man, as soon as he should be within reach.

The latter still went up rapidly and resolutely, but with

no hurry or scrambling. Though the situation was critical and even fraught with the utmost danger, his manner was quiet and his countenance composed, though it wore a look of unusual determination. Below him, his two associates had advanced to a position where the light of their torches now illuminated the place where Jacob stood, throwing his huge, fierce, and fantastic figure, in high relief against the white rocks behind him. He was fearful to look upon, and the two men held their breath with expectation and alarm, as they saw Walcott draw nearer and nearer in his giddy ascent. Whatever power he may have possessed over his adversary seemed to have been lost, for the latter still maintained his ground firmly and even fiercely; and Brigham apprehended nothing less than to see the adventurous young man dashed down the craggy precipice, as soon as he and Jacob should encounter.

When, however, they were within a few feet of each other, Walcott fixed his eye steadily and unwaveringly upon that of the maniac, whose glance, in a little while, began to quail, and finally dropped to the ground.

"Jacob," said the young man, quietly, "you will be good enough to come with me. It is quite necessary. I have been looking for you some time, and so we are well met."

During this address, and even for some seconds before it, the lunatic appeared, in some sort, to be transfixed and subjected to an influence which he could neither resist or shake off.

"Ugh!" exclaimed Catfoot from below, where he was watching these proceedings with astonishment. "Big medicine!"

"I'm blessed, if he ain't done it!" said Brigham. "It's like medicine, as you say, Catfoot. But who'd a thought of such a thing? It must be the very devil is in it."

"Mr. Brigham," exclaimed Walcott, as he came with Jacob down the shelving rock, "allow me to introduce you to my friend here, Jacob Whittaker, a man of eccentric habits, but one who can behave like a gentleman when he tries. You understand me, Mr. Whittaker? And this, sir," said he to the latter, "is also a particular friend of mine, Catfoot of Mohawk. You will treat him with proper respect as a friend of mine, you know."

"Oh! certainly, doctor," said the now submissive Jacob, "any friend of yours will be treated civil enough by me. He's welcome to this castle of mine, which being in a republican country, you know, I have been obliged to have built under ground, as you see."

"By the way, Whittaker," said Walcott, "since we are here in your apartments, suppose you show us your wife and the other members of your family. You know, sir, this is what politeness requires, and I never overlook any breach of that; so lead on."

Upon saying this, he took Jacob's arm, who, half reluctantly, and half foolishly, still yielded to the influence of the other, and led the way, for a few steps, again to the base of the shelving ledge of rocks which they had just descended.

"You see, gentlemen," he said, pausing and half turning round, "I am obliged to take you up a somewhat rude stair-case; but the arrangement was a freak of mine. Is it," he added, stopping and turning to

Walcott; "is it really necessary that the gentlemen be shown up?"

"Absolutely," was the reply.

Hereupon Jacob resumed his progress, and they all clambered up the ledge. The shelf near the top formed a species of platform or landing where they could stand with ease.

In an obscure corner of it lay a large loose rock. To this Jacob at once applied himself with the intent of rolling it aside.

"Why, Whittaker," said Walcott, "for such a fine house as this you ought to have a door-bell to announce your coming."

"You see I have a knocker instead," was the reply, as the huge mass of stone was heaved one side, and struck, as it rolled over, resounding against the rocks. "It's rather loud, to be sure, but I like it myself. Ha! ho!"

"No more of that, if you please," said Walcott, sternly. "We can dispense with that kind of laughter. You forget yourself strangely."

Jacob stood rebuked.

Meanwhile, by the removal of the loose rock, there was disclosed a hole large enough for any one to pass through; and below it a large apartment or chamber, from which rose up a strong light. Through the passage thus made they all went in succession, Jacob leading the way. When within, they found themselves standing on a gallery or shelf not unlike that on the outside. Though high up, it was still some distance from the top of the apartment, and from it by an easy slope and rude projections, a descent could be effected.

CHAPTER XIII.

THE RESCUE.

A few hours before the events with a relation of which the last chapter is closed, the young girl, who had been so suddenly spirited away, and whose disappearance was the cause of so much anxious exertion, was still, with many sighs and half-suppressed sobs, weeping at the hard lot which had befallen her. To her it seemed inconceivable that no effort at her rescue had apparently been made. Her attendant, M'Carty, she knew to be active and faithful, and as such, he had been intrusted by her father with the care of watching over and protecting her. Why, with his zeal, under the guidance and experience of Colonel Belden, had not something been accomplished? Any effort which might have been made, even though unsuccessful, would have been so far fraught with consolation as to show that, in her misfortune, she was not forgotten, or left without sympathy. Many were the painful reflections which passed through her mind, in that hour of depression. All her recollections came up one by one, shaded with melancholy associations; and each with its particular train of unhappiness.

What, she thought, would be the anguish and despair of her bereaved father, so near at hand, and yet without power to relieve her, when he should learn of her disappearance? She knew herself to be his greatest treasure; and she felt herself to be his only stay on earth. Who would dare to disclose to him the most unhappy fate of his beloved daughter? Who would face the grief and despair which would be manifested at the first annunciation of her loss? And when the first burst of passionate sorrow should have passed away, what would be the life—what would be the lot of that poor, companionless old man? Who, for the future, would pay him those little caressing attentions which habitual affection had rendered necessary, and the absence of which must continually revive the bitter recollection of his loss? What hand would assist his feeble footsteps, and soothe his bed of sickness? And what gentle heart, with cheerful encouragement, would lighten his journey, as he traveled down the dreary pathway to the grave?

As the affectionate girl thought of all these things, her anguish was even more on his account than on her own. Hitherto, she had not even dared to fancy what fate she might be called upon to undergo, or how the unhappy drama was to end. From such a contemplation, she instinctively shrank, and turned her thoughts rather, though it was with a new pang, to the friends who might lament her loss, and to the distant home which that loss would render desolate. She imagined to herself that as her father would be returning thither, he would look to the window for her greeting smile, and pause at the door for her welcome kiss, in vain. The empty mansion would echo to lonely footsteps; and the old house-dog even, as he should see his master come back alone, would look curiously and suspiciously upon it; and at nightfall, in the heaviness of his heart, would he lift up through the stillness, his long and mournful bewailment. Sorrowful eyes would gaze into her empty chamber, where the unwound clock would be hushed and motionless; and where, for lack of a fostering hand, the flowers by the window would be faded and dead.

In the apartments of her father, in busy imagination, she already fancied that she could hear his lonely tread all the night through; and even his low moan, as, at intervals, the recollection of his irretrievable sorrow came back to his bursting heart.

And then, too, she felt it to be hard, in the springtime of life, and in the bloom of her hopes, to be buried thus alive in this solitary tomb.

At times, moved to the quick by the many sad thoughts which came so thickly upon her, she would spring from her couch, and like a caged bird, hasten round and round her brilliant, but most inexorable dungeon. Again, without consolation or relief, would she return to her resting-place.

And through all these sorrows, these futile searches for the least hope of escape or relief, would she wonder why the young Walcott, the lover of her friend, who, she thought, was so generous, and who, at their slight interviews, had looked upon herself so kindly—why he had not, in some way, traced her out, or given some tokens of interest in her fate. To him, after all, was it most natural that the others should look for guidance and direction. Colonel Belden was old; and his zeal, rather than his ability, was to be trusted. At the first alarm, when his safety was supposed to be concerned, Walcott had shown himself active and prompt. Why should he not do as much for her? Was it that his zeal for Marion's father was more than his zeal for Marion's friend? It might be; and yet, one so alive to the welfare of others, must surely be mindful of the melancholy fate of a poor helpless girl like herself. She imagined that she had even read thus much in his open, manly features, and in the gentle gaze of his thoughtful eye. Any suspicion against him, must therefore be an injustice. She was doubtless the victim of some remorseless destiny. Premature sorrow was to attend, and, perhaps, premature death, was to close her career, thus bringing to a miserable conclusion all her young hopes, and scattering to the wind her, as yet, incompleted plans. How, indeed, could any one, not gifted with supernatural knowledge, or prophetic vision, be able to discover the place of her concealment and confinement—a place so entirely unknown and inconceivable to herself? And then, again, could the capricious jailor, who had thus mysteriously immured her, be moved by her entreaties, or guided by her suggestions?

No; the first had already failed; and against the second he seemed to be armed with a diabolical cunning. She had more to hope from his absence, than from his mercy or simplicity.

Still, was it not just possible—was it not even probable that such a remarkable place as that in which she found herself, was known to some one who dwelt in the vicinity of it? And if known, was it not also likely that the search for her, would sooner or later be directed thither? Here, indeed, was a ray of hope; faint and far off, like the first glimmer of a light-house at sea; but like a shipwrecked sailor, she hailed the distant harbinger with gladness. In sanguine confidence, she reasoned that even because her disappearance had been remarkable, it was all the more probable that she would be looked for in some remarkable hiding-place.

She had often heard that young Walcott himself was deeply versed in all the mysteries of the forest, and the secret places of concealment which lay buried within its recesses. Who then so likely as he to break the spell of the enchantment, and to force open the stony doors of her dungeon? And, in that connection, did she recollect him as he was, or as her fancy pictured him, on the morning of their interview. She recollected the promise of activity and energy, given forth by his fine form; the manly candor which reposed upon his countenance; and above all, the glad flash of his sympathetic eye, as it shone in genial luster upon her. His generosity would preclude him from overlooking her fate, and his knowledge, forethought, and power, must make his endeavors successful.

With these happier thoughts, was her poor heart, at least, a little quieted; and she again reclined in uneasiness upon the rude couch spread for her reception.

Amid the flickering of the fire through the cavern, and the equally uncertain flickering of her hopes, through the darkened recesses of her own heart, did she at length drop away into busy dreams and uneasy sleep. Then was faintly reproduced and recapitulated, the events of the last few days. She imagined herself again to be riding on horseback through the forest, as on the morning of the actual expedition. She then fancied herself carried swiftly in the darkness, through the bush and copse of the brook, and soon was wandering around her stony cell. Then by a wide sweep of its electric wing, did busy fancy bear her away to the hearth-stone of her father's house. Birds sang amid the flowers by the window, and cheerful voices rang in happy converse around her. But again a mighty change! Invisible arms encircled her, and some inhuman power bears her away screaming for help. It is her persecutor. She knows his wild laughter, as he bounds away, leaping like a gnome through the black arches of the rocky cavern. The mystical music of running waters was also mingled with other fancies.

Anon, she was walking, wearied and nearly fainting, over a hard and stony path, in utter darkness. She was dragged through narrow passages, and lifted down unseen precipices. Then a sudden light shone around her, developing on all sides high, inexplicable, glittering, stony walls. But in the midst, like an angel of darkness, was again shadowed forth by the merciless dream, the terrific form and features of Jabob, the maniac!

Again was she seized with an irrepressible terror, and she imagined herself to be calling for help on Walcott, when lo! before her waking eyes, stood the real image of her dream—the abhorred Jacob! But there too—oh! blessing—stood the Walcott she had invoked! It must no longer be a fancy! It must not be delusion now! Aught but reality would be death or madness. She rose up hastily, brushing her hair from her forehead; there was wildness and hope, terror and gratitude in her eyes, as she fixed them upon her deliverer. To him she rushed, for the evidence of vision was too deceitful and unsatisfactory. She clung fast—in his arms the poor girl sought to shelter herself; lest, like her dream, the precious image of hope, and harbinger of deliverance, should also pass away. Like a child, she even sobbed upon his bosom, and in unsubdueable bursts of gratitude and gladness, sought for his protecting touch, and seemed to petition for his consoling assurances.

The scene was too much for all—too much for Walcott whose younger heart and fresher feelings had left him open to livelier and, perhaps, more endearing emotions; too much even for the rude men by whom he was surrounded, men who made it a point of pride to smother sensibility, and whose outer nature had been case-hardened into stoicism. While Brigham hastily brushed a few rebellious tears from his eyes, the face of the Indian was marked by rigid gravity mingled with respectful sympathy. Over both, nature was asserting her power, though its influence might be brief. But with the younger man of their party it was different. While the outward effect of the scene upon him was no less than it was upon them, its influenee upon his heart was deeper and likely to be more enduring. He felt in his inmost soul the beseechings and sobs which shook the poor girl's frame, and made her tremble as she still hung upon his bosom.

For some time all attention was given to soothe and restore her to confidence. Constant assurances of safety and protection, the gentlest and almost womanly cares, and even caresses were necessary to effect it.

When at length she had become somewhat more calm, and the men had leisure to look around them, to their astonishment Jacob was nowhere to be seen!

Even the vigilance of the omniscient Catfoot had been eluded. The maniac was, indeed, gone, and none knew how or when. At that moment, however, there was little disposition to inquire into the matter, as weightier considerations pressed upon them. Their own position began to grow unpleasant and embarrassing. They might, in that peculiarly-formed cell, all easily be made and held prisoners; and the late fugitive now had it in his power to hold his pursuers fast in the trap into which they had entered. One man at the passage might prevent the egress of a hundred. Their apprehensions on this score were, however, groundless, as soon appeared by Catfoot and Brigham ascending to the opening which they found still uncovered, and outside of which, to prevent future accidents, they now established themselves as sentinels. Although this precaution relieved any immediate cause of uneasiness on account of Jacob, it was necessary, or, at all events, desirable that they should make a speedy exit from the cavern. The poor girl who had been so strangely immured, and so providentially discovered there, though hope now lighted her eye and flushed her cheek, must have suffered too much already from fatigue, exposure, and apprehension; and the damp air and doleful recollections of the grotto were not at all calculated to restore or to benefit her, and their prolonged influence might be seriously injurious.

"Do you feel yourself able to go now, my dear young lady?" said Walcott, after a while.

"Certainly," she eagerly replied; "let us get out of this horrid place at once. If I were dying I would still try to crawl out to see the beautiful world and to breathe the fresh air once again."

As she said this, tears forced themselves into her eyes again, and Walcott could not help thinking her, at that moment, by far the handsomest, or, at all events, the most engaging and lovable girl he had ever met. The trust which she reposed in him he felt to be a most grateful one; and no obstacle seemed too imposing, or danger too imminent to prove the zeal which he cherished on her behalf. To serve her was a happiness, but to have saved her was a blessing. Tenderly, therefore, did he half guide and half carry her up the rude steps of the side which had to answer the purpose of a stairs. Tenderly again did he watch her trembling foot as, awed by the darkness and agitated by the sudden change in her situation, she unskillfully sought her way down the outer rock. At this time, Walcott bore no torch, and he saw, with much concern, that those of his associates were already nearly burned out. He, therefore, determined to take the shorter route to the open air, though it might expose his charge to the chill of the night atmosphere and the further fatigue of a walk through the damp woods. They, therefore, bent their steps toward the western opening. Brigham and the Indian now went on as before, answering the purpose of the link-boys of ancient days.

Lucile, meanwhile, still clung closely to the arm of her deliverer. She felt no embarrassment in the act. She was still very young, and was yet but half relieved from her first great grief. She was walking by the side of her preserver, and already felt a kind of property in him. All barriers of reserve and distance were annihilated. She spoke but little, for she was still too much agitated and too doubtful of the issue—almost too doubtful of the present reality. It might all be a cruel mocking dream!

To the young man who witnessed her emotions, who felt her little hand trembling upon his arm, who overheard her half-suppressed sobs, as they walked slowly along, her gentle clinging and her trustful looks, were fraught with dangerous excitement, and awoke every generous and sympathetic emotion of which his nature was capable.

If it was a dream, as her fears would still cruelly suggest, to him the dream was most delightful. Ah! what joy it was to have saved her from danger! What a rich compensation for the exertion, already shone in the tender light of her loving eye!

But it was not long before those, who had been so long buried in the recesses of a subterranean world, found themselves clambering up the steeps of the outward passage. When they issued from the cavern, their eyes were dazzled by an unexpected luster; and it was some time before they could appreciate that the sun was already high in the heavens, and that an effulgent morning was illuminating the world! No morning ever shone in the Hades they had left behind. There, all was gloom, and "the blackness of darkness forever." The music of its mysterious streams, the brilliancy of its crystal chambers was forgotten. They saw the glorious day, the upper world, the emerald woods; and their anxious hearts panted for nothing more joyous or more beautiful.

CHAPTER XIV.

WHAT FOLLOWED.

By the side of Brigham's log house, that morning, stood M'Carty, holding by the bridle one of the horses on which the excursion party had made their way thither. The sun was already more than an hour high; and the man as he waited, began to manifest some signs of impatience at the delay of others which kept him there. At length, however, Colonel Belden came out of the house bearing a letter in his hand.

"I have written a hasty note to Mr. Valcour," he said; "and I hope, M'Carty, that you will take care that he gets it as speedily as possible. So long as there was a rational chance of recovering his daughter, I wished to spare him the pain of our apprehensions. But I am convinced that any further hesitation would be a mistaken kindness. Break the news to him as gently as you can, and do not allow him to imagine that the case is entirely hopeless, bad as it now looks."

"There's just a chance, as you say, colonel," said M'Carty in reply; "but between you and me, it's mighty queer that Walcott and the rest on 'em ain't back before now. Don't you think I'd better wait till we hear from them, at least?"

"I see no great use in it," answered the other. "I

presume that the reason of their delay is, that their torches have burned out, and that as they have to grope their way back in the darkness, they move but slowly. My great surprise is that a cavern should be found to exist here, of an extent sufficient to cause the consumption of so much time in exploring it. It can hardly be that the lunatic has managed to inveigle three strong and active men. It is very remarkable. Still, all that remains to be done, after you are gone, is simply to make up another party of exploration; and with a more ample supply of lights, ropes and perhaps ladders, to go in after them, and either show them the way, or furnish them the means of getting out. I purpose to be one of the new company myself, to be sure that every thing is done properly."

"If you'd take my advice, colonel," said the man, "you'll do no such thing. A new sarch is well enough, to be sure; but you can do more good where you are than under ground, you may depend on't. By all means, let me stay, and see to this business, and send Joe to Balltown."

At this moment their conversation was interrupted by a noise, coming apparently from the valley below. Turning their eyes in that direction, they saw the individual just spoken of, running up the bank, with might and main, and making directly for where they stood; while, as he came, every now and then, he turned his head, and looked behind him, as if apprehensive that some pursuer might be close upon him.

Hardly a moment had elapsed after his ascending the brow of the hill, before another became visible, whose appearance would seem fully to justify the haste and fear which poor Joe had manifested. It was none other than Jacob himself, who, contrary to his usual habits, did not trumpet forth his presence by his usual burst of laughter. When he came in sight of the other two men, he paused, while an expression of baffled rage came over his features, as though he had been suddenly thwarted in the execution of some fixed purpose. For a moment he glared upon them as if half inclined to attack all three. But apparently convinced that the odds were too great, he abandoned his purpose, and turning about, disappeared behind the crest of the hill.

The whole had occurred so suddenly, and had passed so rapidly, that Colonel Belden and his attendant had not determined upon any course to pursue toward the crazy man before it was too late to do any thing.

Meanwhile, Joe had not paused until he had placed the other two men between himself and the danger. Once there, he awaited with them the upshot of the affair. When Jacob had disappeared, and M'Carty had had time to acquire a faint comprehension of the affair, he turned indignantly to the Indian, saying:

"Why, Joe, you sneaking varmint you, what do you run off that way for? Ain't you got the pluck to stand up for yourself like a man?"

"How you fight medicine man, eh? No remember tumble last night?" said Joe.

"He's no medicine man, as you call him, at all, Joe," answered M'Carty; "he's nothing but a poor crazy devil, and a little pluck would keep him quiet."

"Yes," said Joe, "he de debbil—no keep him still though. He come out hole dis time too. How he get in there, you think, eh?"

"Get in there!" said M'Carty. "Why, did n't you tell me that there's another entrance to the place somewhere in the woods? You see, sir," he continued, turning to Colonel Belden, "Joe here, pretends the cave is as big as all out doors, and has another outlet about a mile to the west. It 's a tough story; but I begin to think there's something in it."

While this short dialogue was going forward, Marion Belden had also issued from the cabin, and joined the group; her attention having been attracted by the slight stir which had been caused by the reappearance of the maniac. Her countenance was pale, and exhibited traces of watching and anxiety.

"Have you heard any thing of Lucile yet?" she asked. "I thought from the noise just now that Arthur must have got back."

"No, my child," answered Colonel Belden. "It was only the wild man, who has made his appearance again; but he seems to be alone. And I am sorry to say that we have had no word of Arthur or his companions, since their departure last evening."

"Ugh! see!" suddenly exclaimed the Indian, interrupting the conversation; while he pointed to the opposite side of the valley, where his trained eye had detected the retreating form of Jacob going up through the bushes, and pausing among the thick shadows of the pines.

It is perhaps needless to say, that the savage, when he had been suddenly startled by the second apparition of the maniac issuing from the cavern, had, in the terror of the moment, forgotten what might have furnished a sufficient explanation of the circumstances, namely, that the place was possessed of two entrances. This, in fact did not occur to him, until it was recalled to his mind by M'Carty. It then served in some measure, to relieve him of his superstitious fears; but as his enemy thus became more human in his eyes, and less an object of awe, he became more an object of hatred and of revenge. Over this the mind of the savage, from that moment, began to brood.

Meanwhile, across the little valley, all could now see the fantastic figure pointed out by Joe, moving stealthily among the open trees like a baffled beast of prey. To get a clearer view of him they moved to the verge of the ledge, and watched him somewhat as spectators in a menagerie gaze through the bars of a cage at some ferocious beast. The object of their scrutiny did not at all belie the simile. He coolly moved about, sometimes at a less, and sometimes at a greater distance, but always with the apparent intent of watching their movements or of waiting for an opportunity to perpetrate some further mischief.

"Had we not better get away from this dreadful neighborhood?" asked Marion, trembling at the sight of Jacob, though he was at a distance; and remembering with a pang, the fate of poor Lucile, who might yet be in the power of the frightful creature.

"No, my child," replied Colonel Belden, "we are entirely secure where we are; and we must let no clew escape us, by which it is possible to find out something of the lost one. But in the mean time, do you go to the house and endeavor to rest yourself, for your eyes are heavy and your cheeks are pale."

So saying, the old gentleman kissed her affectionately on the forehead, and she was about turning away to obey his injunction, when they were startled by the sharp report of a rifle shot, which exploding just beside them, sent its long, crashing echoes to a distance through the forest. On looking around they saw Indian Joe rising from behind a stump, with the piece in his hand; the smoke of the burnt powder slowly rolling away from the spot.

"Ho! ho!" shouted the hoarse voice of Jacob, from the other side of the little valley (for at him the shot had been aimed). "Ho! ho! how nice! Trying to hit the moon in broad day light! Next time, shoot puss for me, for she's gone off with the doctor. Let me catch him though! But ha! I'm off."

Upon saying this he suddenly disappeared in the distance. The cause was soon made manifest.

"I thought," said Walcott, who unexpectedly stood behind Indian Joe, and now laid his hand upon his shoulder, 'I thought I told you not to use fire-arms?"

On hearing the sound of his voice all immediately turned about, and saw the whole searching party standing behind them, as if they had been produced there by magic; but what was more, Lucile was also present. With her eyes full of tears, and her heart full of gratitude, she awaited the eager and affectionate salutations of her friends. Nor were those salutations long in coming; for with a half cry of delight, she was instantly caught in the arms of Marion.

"Lucile! darling Lucile! Are you here at last? Are you really here, safe and unharmed again? You disappeared so strangely, and remained away so long, that we almost ceased to hope. Oh! my darling! I should have died if you had been lost!"

"Oh! Marion," she answered, while she sobbed at the painful recollection; "it was dreadful. It seems yet like a long and frightful dream! I am almost afraid to trust my senses now. And yet," she added as she pressed her friend to her heart, as if to assure herself of the reality of what she felt and saw; "and yet, I must be awake at last! for this must be you, Marion. Oh! heaven be thanked, it can not be a dream! But, Marion, what horrors I have experienced! And if it had not been for Arthur—for Mr. Walcott, I mean—I might still be in that frightful cavern."

Leaving the two girls to communicate to each other their mutual experiences and anxieties, as they made their way to the house, we proceed to call the attention of the reader to other things which were said, and other events which transpired around them.

It being no longer necessary to send off a messenger to Monsieur Valcour, as had been contemplated, the horse which M'Carty had paraded, was now restored by him to the shed which served as a stable. The three men who had just returned with the abducted girl, and who had been so long awake and in active motion, were glad enough to seek a little repose.

Lucile herself, as the excitement by which she had been buoyed up subsided in the sense of safety, soon sought a couch, and fell into a long and deep sleep. Every tired muscle lay in a trance as profound as that which vailed her eyesight, and suspended the worn and weary mechanism of her mind.

As the sun rose higher, the heat grew intense. Colonel Belden had sauntered down to that ever wonderful phenomenon, the Rock Spring. The cool ripple of the neighboring brook, and the gushing sound of the sparkling water that poured up from the stony hydrant, were no less grateful to his ears in the fervid heat of that summer day, than was the mineral water itself to his thirsting palate.

Catfoot had withdrawn to the Indian village hard by; and M'Carty, after some while, might have been seen emerging with many a stretch of his limbs and many a lazy yawn, from some unknown dozing-place among the horses. The drowsy influence of the hour upon him could only produce a few short cat-naps, from which it would seem he was not yet fully relieved. With idle and loitering steps he also bent his way to the spring, where the old colonel, like a sentinel on duty, was pacing to and fro.

CHAPTER XV.

INDIAN JOE.

M'Carty belonged to a class of men whose self-esteem is not lessened by any occupation or relative position in which they may be placed. Without positive impertinence, he felt himself to be every man's equal; and he would have had no more scruple in addressing the highest above himself in station and character, than in accosting a stable boy. A talk was all the same to him, whether with the one or with the other.

"Nice day this, colonel," said he, as he came up; "and one feels it in particular, arter the tarnal tug we've had for a day or so. Have you any notion whether that crazy critter is hanging about us yet anywhere?"

"Indeed," replied Colonel Belden, "it would be difficult to say; but I imagine he can not be far off, especially after what Mr. Walcott has told me of his habitation in the cave."

"By the way," broke in the other; "where's Joe? as he and I are the only ones beside yourself fit to be about, one or other on us ought to be keeping a lookout."

"He has not been seen since Brigham lay down; I suppose, like the rest of you, he felt tired, and has gone somewhere to rest himself."

"Them Injuns, colonel," answered M'Carty, "don't

need no rest between times. I've knowed 'em to be on a run for a week, day and night, and then sleep it all out when the scurry was over. And it's mighty convenient for 'em, I can tell you, seein' the life they lead."

"Why, M'Carty," answered Colonel Belden, "it seems to me that sailors are not the only persons who spin yarns. You tell a tough story now and then yourself: this about the Indians going a week without sleep, for example."

"Not a bit on it, colonel," was the ready answer; "not a bit on it. I've seen things as strange myself; and Sandy Brigham here, if he was awake, could tell some things a great deal more astonishing, which happened to himself. He's been a man of mighty active habits, and has an obsarvin' turn of mind, I can tell you, and you know it too."

"I've known him for a brave, prudent and skillful man all his life; but I have never known him to tell such wonders as you talk of," said Colonel Belden.

"Leaving it to his friends, I reckon," answered M'Carty, "to blow his horn for him—for Sandy Brigham ain't a bit of a brag. But I've often hearn tell of some of his doin's, afore the scrape he got into with Burgoyne; in fact afore the war came into these parts, when the red-skins was decently quiet and civil-like."

"What, for example, did he do so very remarkable?" asked Colonel Belden, by way of encouragement to his companion, who was obviously bent upon a story.

"Well, among other things," said M'Carty, catching at the implied permission, like a fish at a hook—"among other things something like this happened. It seems that afore the war there was two neighbors down in Clifton Park who differed in politics and often had disputes about it. One was for the country, and the other for the king; and after the battle of Bunker's Hill the neighborhood became too hot with the king's friend and he had to make tracks for Canada, leaving his farm and every thing behind him. There he staid for a year or so, hoping for quieter times, but as none came he thought he'd just go back, in a secret way, and look arter his property a little. He was mighty sly about it, as you can guess; and so nobody knowed any thing of his being about till one day in shying across a meadow of his old neighbor, who should he come plump upon but the man himself, who was there mowing. The old grudge between 'em came up worse than ever, and the old quarrel soon grew hot between 'em, till the neighbor, in his fury, was on the pint of hacking off his legs with the scythe. Upon this, the Tory begged for his life, and was let off. He soon sneaked away and went back to Canada again. But he did n't relish the fright he had got; and so he detarmined on revenge.

"With that he gets together a gang of Injun runners and come down to the Mohawk country again. Meantime his old neighbor had crossed the river and was now living on the south side. It so happened that he was the only one who kept a boat along there, and though the stream was not deep it was wide and rapid, and full of sharp eddies and deep holes. When they came to his house, which they did on a dark night, they made a great ado, and got him up out of bed under pretense that they was in pursuit of a damn Tory, as they said, and wanted him to come out and take them across the river in his boat Up he jumps, hearty enough at such a call, and fairly rowed them to the other side without suspecting any thing wrong. But when once over, lo and behold! his old inimy, whose legs he was so near mowing off, makes himself known, and the astonished farmer, all at once, finds himself a prisoner. There was no help for it, away he must go. His scalp hung loose upon his head, with half a dozen tomahawks whizzing about his ears. Away they started for Canada which lay rising of two hundred miles off, straight through the woods.

"But you see the prisoner's wife waited and watched for him till broad day-light. Then she grew oneasy; no boat was in sight, and every thing, fur and near, was hushed and quiet. She grew scared and hurried off to tell the neighbors. They all begun lookin' and sarchin', but not one of 'em could tell what to make of it, and they about give it up. But it happened that Sandy Brigham was down that morning at Schenectady selling some pelts. He heard the news and guessed how it all was; so taking a few Oneidas, friends of his, with him, he made arter the runaways. As soon as he struck the trail, which he had no trouble in doing, he found out pretty near what was the matter. The Injuns knowed a Huron's footmark at once. Brigham had carried along some dried beef for the journey, as they would have no time to hunt, but the Injuns took with them nothing to eat, and they did n't dare to use their guns for fear of letting the Hurons know they was after them. They found the trail pretty fresh nearly all the way. It took nigh on to eight days to perform the journey, and though Sandy had but just enough provision to keep himself alive, the Injuns took nothing unless, maybe, a root or so now and then."

"But," said Colonel Belden, interrupting the narrative which was fast bordering upon the extravagant, "did not Brigham offer them a part of his own fare?"

"Sartain," said M'Carty, "but they would n't let on that they was hungry. They only pulled their belts tighter and pretended that goin' without victuals kept them in better running order, and made their scent keener."

"And did they," asked the colonel, "after so much running and fasting, come up with the fugitives after all?"

"Not exactly," was the answer; "they only caught sight on 'em as they was pulling across the St. Lawrence in a canoe, though they had the satisfaction of sending a few bullets arter them. But it was of no use."

"But what was the termination of it all?" asked Colonel Belden.

"The end on it was, that the man had to stay in Canada till arter the war; and when he got back, his wife thought it was his ghost. And he said that all the way to the St. Lawrence, when they first took him, he was compelled to carry a smoothing iron in each hand, as a kind of punishment."

"I have heard something like the same story before," said Colonel Belden, "but I never heard that the Indians fasted during the journey; and I did not even know that it was Brigham who led the party, though such enterprises were then common to him."

"But, colonel," said M'Carty, with a slight twinkle of the eye, as he shifted a quid of tobacco from one cheek to the other, "the most curious part on't was, that arter the hunt was over, what should the Oneidas do, but shoot a lot of deer, roast 'em whole, and eat for almost twelve hours without stoppin'."

"M'Carty," said the old colonel, laughing, as he

paused in his little walk, "it seems to me that you have made a great mistake in life; you should have been a sailor, or a romance writer."

"I reckon I can navigate the woods as well as any sailor, colonel; and I never yet knowed the clark who could bring down a buck at a hundred yards better than I can. So I'm satisfied as I am."

"No doubt," replied the colonel, "it 's easy enough to see that. But, M'Carty, whatever your friends, the Oneidas, might do, I feel at this time greatly inclined to get something to eat, as it is past noon. And I dare say the rest of our people up at the house would like to do the same."

So saying, he moved away, inviting the other to follow him to the log-cabin. But the latter, after walking a few steps, paused, saying:

"Don't you think, on the whole, colonel, that I'd better stay behind, and keep guard like; for I'm not yet quite easy in my mind about wild Jake. The vicious sarpint may be arter more mischief."

"Do as you like, my friend," said the colonel; "perhaps you are right to keep a good look-out."

M'Carty accordingly staid behind, taking his post a little beyond the Rock Spring, in the direction of the mouth of the cavern.

"The colonel is a nice man," he muttered to himself, as the other disappeared over the brow of the hill, "and I dare say, was a brave officer; but he's no good listener, that's sartin. His faith would n't move mountains by a long shot. I suppose young Walcott, or captain, as folks sometimes call him, as soon as he is rested, and has got a little to eat, will be for hunting up this wild Jake again, to get him caged. I should n't object to having a hand in that job myself; and so, as soon as they've got through dinner, I'll try and get a cold snack, and be ready to jine 'em, in case they want another scurry. Meantime, I'll keep my eye open, and in particular watch that wolf-hole yonder."

After Colonel Belden had departed, M'Carty continued, as he had intended, upon the lookout, sometimes pacing slowly across the open space, and sometimes resting beneath the shadows of the neighboring bushes. Every thing around him remained quiet; and nothing louder than the humming of bees or the ripple of water was heard. There was no sign of the vicinity of Jacob; and although the self-constituted sentinel kept his eyes fastened upon, or wandering over the alder copse, in search of him, he was neither gratified or alarmed by a glimpse of his uncouth figure.

He soon saw Indian Joe emerging from the thicket and bearing in his hand something which at first was undistinguishable, but which, on a nearer view, turned out to be nothing more than a large decayed leaf. He was puzzled to know for what purpose such a trifling object had been picked up and preserved. The Indian bore it carefully in the open palm of his hand, for the leaf seemed to be of the last autumn's shedding, and was so tattered and dry that it threatened to be blown off with every puff of wind, or to fall to pieces upon the slightest agitation. Without uttering a word he brought it forward and held it up before the eyes of his wondering companion, who saw nothing in its shape or character to justify so much care and attention. It was in no respect different from any other old leaf, unless, perhaps, that its ashy-brown hue had been in several places dyed to a sort of rusty purple.

"What tomfoolery is this you are at now?" asked M'Carty at length, with a little impatience.

"Don't see him?" answered Joe, interrogatively.

"Don't see what, you copper-head?" asked the now irritated M'Carty.

"Look again," said the Indian.

Hereupon M'Carty renewed his examination but could make no more out of it than he did before.

"You no see nothing dis time?" asked Joe again.

"What the devil should I see but an old rotten oak leaf which you have picked up for some Indian witchcraft or confounded humbug!" answered the other.

All this Joe took quite coolly; while sitting quietly down on a stump, he continued:

"White men big brag, but big fool!"

"Come, come, you varmint," answered M'Carty, "none of your colored talk to-day, but if you've got any thing to say, why out with it at once, and don't be sitting there like a goose upon an egg ready to be hatched."

"Well, den," answered the unmoved Joe, "look on him agin."

"Oh blazes! go to the devil with your old leaf," replied the other, impatiently.

"Him stain red in the middle—you no see dat?" continued Joe.

"Well, what if I do?" answered M'Carty. "What does that mean?"

"Him blood, dat's all," replied Joe.

"Blood!" exclaimed the other, "and pray whose blood is it; and how do you know it, eh?"

"Big Jake—medicine man—debbill, what you call him?" answered Joe.

"But what makes you think it is his blood?" asked M'Carty.

"Find him over dere," said Joe, pointing across the valley; "hit him wid gun, you know."

"Eh? what?" asked his companion. "And so you suppose you hit the critter, do you?"

"Yes, know him," answered Joe; "see blood drop, drop on ground, on leaf, on bush."

"By George, Joe," said M'Carty, "if you're right that shot of yourn was n't thrown away, arter all. It may help to catch the critter."

At this moment the two men saw Walcott approaching from the direction of the house. It would seem that he had already obtained sufficient rest and refreshment for the time being. When he came up he was made acquainted with the new incident of which the Indian had produced the evidence. But the young man, instead of manifesting the satisfaction which the others expected, and which M'Carty had not only felt but plainly expressed, showed some degree of displeasure. The veins in his forehead swelled, his eye lowered, and his voice fell to a note of sternness as he said:

"This, you see, is the consequence of disobeying me. You have wounded the poor creature with as little thought as if he were a brute. You have come near committing a cowardly murder! Hereafter, sir, I shall not ask for your help, and the sooner you get away to your cabin the better."

Joe understood but imperfectly what was said; but still he comprehended that he was, in a manner, dismissed, his acts disavowed, and his future aid repudiated. Neither the rebuke or the manner in which it was administered, was agreeable to him. His Indian blood received a spark which might soon kindle it to a blaze. The feeling which was aroused within him was not one of gratitude, or remorse, or humiliation, or shame. He was no whipped spaniel ready to lick the hand that struck him, or to fawn upon the master who drove him from his presence. His form became more erect, and though his look was sullen and fierce, his manner was cool and a little truculent.

"No tink Joe good friend, eh?" said he, turning round to Walcott before going away.

"You are not a safe friend; and, at all events, you are not fit to engage with me in the search I am about to make after this poor creature you have just shot," answered Walcott.

"No good to look for young squaw, eh?" asked the Indian.

"Why, yes, Joe," said the young man, slightly blushing; "I must say you behaved like a man there, and I would gladly reward you for it; but you should not have fired upon a man who does not know what he is about. It is worse than a common murder! But we won't say any thing more about that now. Here is something to buy you some powder and tobacco; and I hope you will make good use of the first."

Saying this, Walcott approached the savage to offer him some money, by way of acknowledgment for his services.

"No want him," was the surly reply of the Indian.

Without waiting for any further parley, Joe slung his gun over his arm, and slowly walked away. After proceeding a few rods he again turned, and, with his voice a little raised, he asked, as he touched the barrel of the weapon with his right hand:

"Ain't you 'fraid, captain? Ain't you 'fraid Injun shoot, eh? Take care! Joe no friend: he be worse, may be."

"No, you infernal sneak," exclaimed Walcott, now irritated in his turn at the threat which had been used; "you had better look to yourself, and mind that you don't come in my way again, or it will be the worse for you."

The Indian, upon this, again wheeled about; and, resuming his walk, in a short time disappeared in the forest.

"Captain," said M'Carty, "don't you think you was a little too hard on poor Joe? If you had spoke to Catfoot that way, you'd have had a bullet through your head afore now, like enough."

"I would not have spoken in that way to Catfoot, because he never would have given occasion for it," was Walcott's answer; "but this fellow, after all I had said, must needs go and shoot at the poor devil, when there was no earthly reason for it. Besides, I half think he's a coward, and would do us no good."

"I don't know that," said M'Carty, "it's redskin natur to shoot at whats'ever they 're in chase of; and I did n't quite like Joe's look when he left. Besides, he's a half-breed, and so much the worse on that account. If I was you, I'd sort of be on my guard agin him."

"Why Jim, you have turned adviser, have you?" said Walcott. "But I imagine I can take care of myself, especially here in the woods. I have had experience enough, I am sure."

CHAPTER XVI.

THE STORM.

THE day had, by this time, considerably worn away. Noon was long since past; and, though the sun was getting near the tops of the high trees in the west, its rays continued to beat upon the earth with unabated fervor, while the heat was as great as at high noontide. The whole forest—and when we speak of that, we speak of all the visible landscape where our scene lies—was hushed and motionless. No wind could be felt to fan the cheek; and not so much as a leaf, or the long tender swinging limbs of the weeping willow, stirred, to announce its passage. Yet the sensations of the beholder were not those of repose. In the western sky, below the points where the fiery disc of the sun seemed burning its way to the horizon, was a long, dark, ponderous bank of cloud, which was slowly rising higher as if to meet the descending sun, and threatened soon to hide that burning luminary in its dusky folds.

Walcott saw and noted these indications of the coming storm, as he was returning toward the cabin; and he felt most grateful in the thought that Lucile had already been restored to shelter and to friends.

A summer tempest, in these latitudes, always has in it something beautiful, even when most violent and imposing. Its distant approach inspires the observer with emotions of awe; and the solemn mutterings of its thunder puts to silence all the minor noises, and hushes to rest all the smaller passions of the world. It comes over the tops of the distant hills in majestic progression, like the regulated march of an embattled host; it moves through the leafy arches of the wilderness, whispering to the leaves, groaning with the trees, and swooping with the wind, like myriads of innumerable spirits let loose, in madness and riot, upon the earth.

When Walcott reached the cabin, he found all there astir. The electric, forerunning influence of the wide storm had already touched their eyelids, as with a wand, and sent the enlivening, wakening blood in full pulses through their veins. Far away from them yet, was the power which had thus chased slumber from their limbs; for still all nature seemed hushed; and on the tall green pine-tops to the eastward, the sunlight fell, in soft golden fullness. To the eye in that direction, it was yet the mild, the beautiful, the glowing summer afternoon; but to the heart, and to the nerves, those telegraphic wires of the human frame, there was wildness in the air, and loudness, and motion, and violence, close at hand. Unconsciously the eye looked forth to discover something new, something startling, and shone the brigher, both from the excitement which caused the act, and from the expectation which accompanied it.

So, as Walcott came up to the door, was he met by a pair of glittering, grateful eyes, which sparkled upon him with still another luster than that so mysteriously imparted to them by the approaching commotion in the elements. An internal agitation gave a new glow to their electrical light. And so he felt it to be, though the knowledge took no form in his thoughts, and suggested no phrases to his tongue.

And to whom did those bright eyes belong? Their proprietor stood here almost tremulous with pleasure—with grateful pleasure, for such she took it to be. Was it Marion Belden! Marion was looking forth at a window with her father's arm in hers. Her manner was serene, her voice even; and though her eye was also bright, it was not with any peculiar luster; her cheek was not flushed; she made no eager step of gladness and pride to the door, as her affianced lover came in. And yet, gratified she certainly was, but with a degree of emotion which a sister might have felt. How different a picture did her face present from that of the little eager, proud, and trembling girl who met the young man at the door, and who, like one who had a species of right in him, a sort of franchise in his heart, still unconsciously barred his passage.

"Here you are all safe and happy, and wide awake at last," said Walcott, after a pause. "And you, too, Marion, have got your eyes open about the time when birds think of shutting theirs."

"No doubt you have had your sleep too, if it comes to that," said Marion.

"I suppose," continued Walcott, "I ought to ask how you all do, after the late events, but my eyes have already answered that question. You all look as bright and wide-awake as if it was morning, and you had just been sounded to breakfast by a gong."

"Listen!" exclaimed Lucile; and as she paused, with

her finger lifted up as if to enforce silence, the deep rumble of the distant thunder began to be heard.

"Is that," she said, "the gong you spoke of?"

"It is certainly loud enough to have answered as a summons to a repast of the ancient gods; but it is also heavy enough to suggest less pleasant ideas, such as the deep note of midnight fire-bells, or the distant boom of breakers upon a rocky shore, during a storm at sea."

"Why, Arthur," said Marion, "what has made you so romantic all at once? According to Lucile's story, she did not find you writing poetry the other morning when we first came upon you here, though the spot, she says, was a lovely one."

"The scenery was fine, certainly," said Walcott; "but though I had not my eye 'in a fine frenzy rolling,' I might have been thinking poetically enough for all that. Venison and verses go well together, when the first is cold and the last warm. But touching the thunder, which we are just beginning to hear, it, somehow or other, always impresses me with feelings which are not quite apprehensive, but which are serious and solemn. It represses all levity in me as effectually as the deep bass of a church organ during service."

By this time, shadows began to creep over the landscape, as the rays of the sun were cut off by the clouds, and its round red disc began to dip into the dark line of the uprising bank of vapor.

The few domestic animals about the cabin now began to seek shelter and to prepare for rest, as if the night had already set in. The creak of the cricket and the whir of the tree-toad, filled the air with their uncouth but not unmusical sounds.

The inmates of the cabin now came forth to enjoy the coolness, which, from the withdrawal of the sun and the approach of the rain, began to pervade the atmosphere. It was worth while also to observe the slowly lifting clouds, and the swelling storm, that, like a mighty raven had already spread its vast sable wings to the north and south, and threatened soon to overshadow half the visible world. Above the white line of its top, where the heaving vapor looked like huge fleeces of snowy wool, the sky was intensely blue, and the tempest seemed to be rocking and rolling up into it, just as a dark-hulled ship is launched upon the crystal surface of a still sea.

In front of the cabin, then, all save Walcott, sat absorbed in the interest of the scene. He, with equal appreciation, but with fewer words, now stood, and now slowly walked to and fro, with his looks sometimes turned to the sky, and sometimes toward the group of friends close at hand. In each direction his eye found objects of admiration; and to the one his imagination, and to the other his heart, acknowledged an impulsive inclination. Both heaven and earth, at that moment, were full of attraction for him. The mystery of this impulse and attraction, in either case, was then to him unsolved; and his mind sought no analysis of the fact, or solution of the mystery.

It was still long before the slow-moving storm began to give token of its immediate presence by other signs than darkness in the sky, and thunder in the air.

At first, gusts of wind could be seen to sway the tops of the trees to the westward; which, after a momentary release from the clutch of the passing blast, would again bend over, yielding to the power of the giant that again laid hold of them, and with increasing steadiness and might, kept their vast trunks twisted and awry. Onward, and still on, came the forerunning wind. Now in light puffs, it began to whisk past the hamlet. Its cold breath was felt upon the cheek. Anon, it hurried away, and could be seen agitating the brambles and branches on the eastern side of the valley. It tore asunder as it passed, a few flower-buds, and scattered their leaves; and it shook ripe currants from the bushes where they hung in the rude garden attached to the hut. Then again, came a colder and mightier breath of air. Young trees bent before it. All light and movable objects were shaken with rude impetuosity, or lifted from the ground and hurled with violence away. Dust and leaves began to fill the air, and the whole atmosphere, as if moving bodily to the eastward, swept the earth's surface with a harsh rushing sound, growing at each moment more obstreperously audible. Like a cataract, it poured upon the ear in painful intensity. Still no rain had yet fallen. What had passed was the mere antecedent. The blast, loud and violent as it was, was only the precursor of one more mighty.

Those who had watched it up to this time, now took refuge within the cabin. The door was, however, left open; and from it, and from the windows, the scene without continued to be regarded with much interest. The roar of the wind through the woods now rapidly increased. Loud sharp peals of thunder began to break overhead, and seemed to shake the earth to its center. Large drops of rain, like the spent shot of distant musketry, began to patter upon the earth. They were soon followed by a wild discordant sound of the high wind, mingled with thick falling rain, which formed the real commencement of the storm. All before had been skirmishing, this was the grand charge of the elemental army. Suddenly it broke over the strong-timbered dwelling, and while the huge logs of its frame shook, as though a new Samson had laid hold of its pillars, the windows were dashed with cataracts of water, and the outer air became opaque and impenetrable from the rushing mist, and the compactness of the down-falling drops. The stormy discord was complete; the scene most impressive. Peal on peal of thunder broke in the air, like exploding rockets. Sharply and painfully too, did the blue and pale lightning flash across the eye, threatening a general destruction.

During the height of the storm, when confusion and uproar prevailed without, and silence and awe reigned within the cabin, unnoticed by others, and unconsciously to herself, the light form of Lucile drew near to the side of Walcott. Around him she hovered, as a gale-threatened ship will hover near its assured haven. It was, in part, the natural instinct of weakness taking shelter in the shadow of strength. It operated powerfully upon both the girls present; but each had looked in different directions, and Marion had sought out her father, where now, half leaning upon his arm and half inclining her head upon his bosom, she was endeavoring with closed eyes and uplifted hands, to shut out the dazzling blaze of the lightning, which suddenly became more frequent and more startling. The old man, with his long white hair falling upon his shoulders, and his high pale brow lifted to the window, looked the patriarch and the hero that he was. Quietude and repose, were even then the characteristics of his appearance and his bearing; and not even the loudest bursts of the tempest without, seemed to disturb his eye, or to vary the expression of his face.

Brigham, who at first had eyed the coming storm somewhat observantly, had soon manifested his accustomed coolness, and by this time was lying down on a bench in one corner of the hut, fast lapsing into a doze. He only muttered with a yawn that, "he should n't wonder if we got a bit of hail afore the shower was over, as the air smelt mighty coolish."

But Walcott was of an age and of a temperament which inclined him to take more interest in the not unusual, but always impressive scene which was passing. He had taken his station near the door, and watched with attention and even with pleasure the wild war of the elements which raged through the wilderness. He had seen large limbs of trees torn from their hold, and flung at a distance to the earth. He had seen mighty old pines, though so strongly rooted as to be ultimately secure, still rock upon their foundations before the sweeping efflux of the air, and threaten to come at some moment with a vast crash and a wide ruin, to the ground. He had watched the quick scudding clouds overhead, as they moved like flying artillery through the sky, discharging their mighty ordnance, and with loud explosions sending their chained shot through the hearts of oaks, and cleaving in twain other old and lofty trees which had escaped the lightnings of five hundred years. One of these ruinous bolts at length hurtled over an enormous pine which stood within a few rods of the cabin door; and the dark trunk and lofty crown of which had hitherto, through all the wrack, been visible to the inmates of the hut, like a beacon or a tower of strength.

It was just as Lucile came close to Walcott's side that a bright streak of light sped downward upon the venerable tree; and before the gleam of that blinding flash had left her eyes, with a deafening explosion, the old trunk had received its death-stroke. So violent and sudden was the shock, that for the moment, all were stunned. The next instant a more appalling danger threatened them; for almost instantaneously with the flash and report, did Arthur and Lucile become conscious that the enormous mass was toppling over in its fall toward the hut.

There was no time for thought; no space for escape. With a sudden scream the affrighted girl clung to the young man with the instinct of weakness, and an impulse of affection, while a deafening crash bore down upon their place of shelter. Then again followed the sound of pattering rain, rushing wind, and the distant muttering of thunder. The startled occupants of the cabin awoke from their stupor, as if expecting to find themselves in the other world. Thank heaven! It was only an alarm. The tufted branches of the tree only had struck the building, but had not been sufficiently weighty to break it down. The mighty trunk itself had fairly cleared it, and so they were saved. It now lay there like a stricken leviathan.

The peril created by its fall had been so sudden, so inevitable, and so overwhelming that those who were exposed to it had not, so to speak, had time to become fully alarmed before it was passed. There, indeed, might have been seen some pale cheeks and quivering lips. Marion even fainted at the sight and thought of the fearful escape. Brigham had risen and now already stood without the door looking, with curious eye, at the ruin caused by the storm, or the "shower," as he called it, unheeding the rain which deluged his naked head, and the wind which blew his hair wildly about his face.

Gently did Walcott unwind from his neck the arms of the trembling girl who had so suddenly clung to him in the moment of peril. It was even a few seconds before she was fully conscious of what she had done; but then, with a brow blushing scarlet, and almost with tears of shame, she said, in a low tone:

"Forgive me, Mr. Walcott; I have been so frightened that I did not know what I was about."

"There is nothing to forgive," he replied, with warmth. "I could only wish that the danger had been one from which my presence or strength could have shielded you. It gives me unspeakable happiness even to think that you look to me for protection."

Fortunately, Marion was unconscious while these words were exchanged, and until after most of the agitation caused by the alarming incident we have above described had passed away. She might otherwise, perhaps, have noticed the degree of emotion displayed by both Lucile and her affianced lover, and her woman's wit might have enabled her to discern and read signs of growing interest between them, which might have proved as destructive to her hopes and alarming to her heart as the peril of the impending tree; always supposing that her heart partook of that deep interest in the subject, which her actual relations with Walcott would seem to warrant others in believing.

Upon the latter, however, at that time, began to dawn a faint consciousness of the true state of his feelings; and that another was usurping that place in his thoughts which should have been occupied by Marion alone. To Lucile the same twilight of knowledge, causing her at once pain and pleasure, began also to appear. The glory and happiness thus brightening on her soul's horizon, were still clouded by thoughts that her new affection would be an involuntary treachery to her friend; and it was with embarrassment and almost with self-accusation that she withdrew to the side of the still half conscious Marion. The shock of the thunderbolt had lifted a vail from her eyes. All these things had passed in a moment of time—so rapidly, indeed, and with such electrical quickness, that Lucile even assisted at the restoration of the swooning Marion.

By this time the storm began sensibly to diminish in violence. The heaviest and darkest of the clouds had rolled off to the eastward. As Brigham predicted, hail had been mingled with the rain, and the ground was now sown with it as if with crystals. Rivulets of water poured past the door of the cabin. On all sides around could be heard the rush of similar streams, as, in full chorus, like hounds in chase, they speeded on their way. Soon the wind lulled, the sky grew brighter, the thunder departed with the clouds, rumbling heavily in the distance. The little rain that now fell came in pattering drops. The clouds themselves had broken, and spaces of clear sky, like blue water amid the floes and icebergs of an arctic sea, gladdened the sight.

The burly form of Brigham was seen stalking about in the open air; and thither also soon went Walcott to note the ravages made by the storm. A quantity of wreck was strown in every direction—broken branches, and, now and then, fallen trees. Every crevice and low spot of ground poured, like a gutter, with the escaping water. The brook below rushed past like a river. It nearly filled the entire breadth of the valley. The bushes and small trees near it were surrounded by water, and bent before the powerful current; while a little gulf separated the two opposite slopes of the swale. But nightfall was close at hand. It was not until just as the sun was descending behind the Kayaderosseras mountains that the clouds fully lifted; and its last rays were permitted to spread, like a golden mantle, over all the landscape, and, for a moment, to light up the receding storm with its beautiful bow of promise. Anon, all this effulgence was withdrawn. Shadows again crept over the earth, and another summer night, though the day had closed in weeping, came, with gentle approach, softly and soothingly, like an angel of mercy, to hush the tired world to repose.

CHAPTER XVII.

SANDY BRIGHAM.

As the evening was fresh, Brigham caused a fire of pine knots to be lighted, in a large open stone fireplace, within the hut, to dispel the damps, occasioned by the recent storms, while its blaze should shed a ruddy, though flickering and uncertain light through the room. The inmates of the cabin were now all gathered there; and the secure, quiet, and home appearance of the place, was grateful to them, after the agitations and alarms they had just experienced. Through the small eastern windows, the pale moonlight shone, and mingled with the red reflection of the fire. The sound of the swollen and rushing brook could still be plainly heard, as it poured its unaccustomed volume of water away through the darkness.

"How long is it, Brigham," asked Colonel Belden, as all sat pensively within the light, listening to the echoes which resounded from the neighboring forest—"how long is it since you took up your abode in this place?"

"I've been here only since last year," answered Brigham. "Arter the war, things did n't flourish as usual, down there in Stillwater; and so, as Gid. Morgan had got tired of this place, and gave me a good chance, I thought I'd come up and try it. I like it all the better too, because General Schuyler is here, more or less, every summer, and we can now and then talk over old times."

"But," said Colonel Belden, "a man like you ought to have had some position, or some notice by Congress before this time; and it seems to me, if the case had been properly represented, something would have been done."

"Likely enough, colonel," said Brigham; "but there's so many chaps arter the loaves and fishes, that I've never thought enough of my desarts to jine with 'em, and make the trial."

"How so?" asked the colonel; "that one affair near Fort Edward, in visiting Burgoyne's camp, was enough to have got you a thousand acres of land, at the least. I mention land, because Congress is so poor that it can pay in nothing better."

"I have often," said Walcott, interposing, "heard a rumor of that circumstance, and should much like to hear the particulars of it."

"Brigham, I dare say, will have no objection to giving you an account of it," answered Colonel Belden.

"None at all," said Brigham; "and if you'd like to hear how it was done, why, this was the way of it. Arter General Schuyler gave up command; old Gates—excuse me, colonel; that's the way we called him, quite familiar, in those days—old Gates, I say, as a new hand at the bellows, was quite put to it to know what the British General was going to do next. At that time, as you must know, the inemy's army lay in camp, just beyond Fort Edward, where they was trying to recruit and refresh a little, arter crossing the swamp from Skenesborough, and arter the cooling their courage got at Bennington. Well, as I was saying, Gates was regularly nonplushed. He lay down here away toward Stillwater, and did n't dare to stir for fear of goin' wrong, in a case where mistakes would n't answer. But the blood of the country was up, on account of that affair of poor Jinny M'Crea, as you recollect, colonel?"

"You mean the young girl who was murdered by the Indians, when on her way to Burgoyne's camp to meet her lover, I suppose?" answered Colonel Belden.

"Exactly, her I mean," said Brigham. "Well, the people thought that it was all owing to the scalp rewards offered by the British; and so, they was all detarmined on revenge; and, if I might be allowed to express my opinion, it was that, as much as any thing else, that gained the battle of Saratoga. But, not to get ahead of my story, old Gates sends to the committee of safety of Stillwater, and wants a man to go into the British camp, and find out what was in the wind. It so happened just about them days, that I was keeping a place some five miles or so, this side Waterford, on the North River. Don't you remember stoppin' there about that time, on the winter afore, one cold snowy night, colonel?"

"I remember it well," answered Colonel Belden; "for you had to haul me in through a back window, in order to avoid the attention of some English spies who were in the public room."

"Your memory ain't none the worse for wear, any how, colonel," answered Brigham.

"Well, who should I see one fine morning, riding up to my door but a sort of orderly, who gets down and inquires for Mr. Bridgeman.

"'That ain't quite my name, friend,' says I, 'but may be it's me you want, for all.'

"'Do you keep this here tavern?' says he.

"'Yes,' says I, 'but it ain't a tavern. It's a hottel.' I thought I'd come a little of the French on him.

"'Well,' says he, dismounting, in a cool way, 'tavern or hottel, it's all the same to me, if so be you're the man. I've a dispatch from the Comity of Safety at Stillwater for you.'

"So he hands me a letter in which they wanted me to go at once and see Gineral Gates without delay, on public sarvice. To make a long story short, I started for the army the same night, and when I went in to the old Gineral's tent:

"'Is your name Brigham?' says he.

"'Yes,' says I.

"'Can you go to Burgoyne's camp, across the river at Fort Edward, and bring me word what's a goin' on?' says he.

"'Yes,' says I, 'and glad of the job.'

"'When can you start?' says he.

"'Now,' says I.

"'And when can you get back?' says he.

"'That's more than I can say,' says I, thinking to myself, I might be made a tassel at the end of a hemp cord, or a target for a file of men, before I should have the pleasure proposed.

"'Then you know the risk?' continued he.

"'Sartainly,' says I; 'but, in times like these, every man must do his best; and, without braggin', I've a notion I can do this job better than most, if it must be done.'

"'It must be done,' he answered. 'At this time, if any accident happens, the whole country to New York will be open to pillage. Remember the affair of Miss M'Crea.'

"'Gineral,' says I, 'you need n't mention that poor gal, to stir me up. I 'd go, if it was to sarve the country; and talkin' of the cussed Injuns only riles me so I ain't fit for the job.'

"'Well,' says the general, walking about very oneasy, and looking thoughtful, 'I hate to risk a man like you, but somebody *must* go, who is acquainted with the business. I must trust entirely to your discretion. If the English army breaks through my lines, our poor country is lost. Spare no pains, my good sir,' he went on earnest like; 'remember, every thing depends upon committing no blunder. I can not give you any papers, and you must pass both lines as best you can; and there is about as much danger from the one as from the other.'

"Here an orderly comes in, and says the Green Mountain Boys would be down, two thousand strong, in four days.

"'Very well,' says old Gates; and giving me a look, I took it as a hint to leave.

"It was no light job, in them days, to go through the first part of the task I had before me. Lines of sentinels had been posted on all the common ways between the two armies. So I had to make a wide circuit; and I came into the British camp as a fugitive, having managed to get pursued by a lot of chaps, who took me as a scout of the inimy. So my indorsements was good in my new quarters. Some of the officers knew me; and, after no great trouble, I was introduced to the gineral himself.

"'Eh! sir,' says he, 'I am told, my good man, that

you have been driven out of the country on account of your attachment to the king's cause.'

" Something like that, your honor,' says I. 'In fact,' says I, 'the varmints chased me to the very pickets.'

"'I perceive,' said the general, 'that you are a native of this region, and, as such, may be very useful to his majesty.'

"'Yes,' says I, 'no doubt your honor is right. I might be so.'

"Well,' says he, 'are you willing to try?'

"'Whatever I undertake,' says I, 'I try to do my best in, and so your honor will find it in the end.'

"'Does any body know this man?' says Burgoyne, suddenly looking around at the assemblage of officers collected in the marquee.

"'I know him,' says one, 'he keeps a house of entertainment near the Mohawk Fords.'

"'I know him,' says another, 'he hid me one night from a gang of rebels who were in chase.'

"'And I know him,' says a third, 'he gave me a haunch of venison three weeks ago, when we liked to have starved in the mash, this side of Skenesborough.'

"And so betwixt'em all, I got a first rate recommend; and the General being satisfied on that head, goes to cross-examine me as to what I knowed, and could do, useful to him.

"'Bridgeman,' says he, 'for I think that is your name?'

"'No,' says I, 'your honor, that is not my name, but Brigham, if you please,' thinking that if it was worth knowing at all, it was worth knowing correctly.

"'Well then, Brigham,' says he, 'since you will have it so, how many men have these rebels got together?'

"'Five thousand four hundred and fifty one,' says I.

"'How do you know?' says he.

"'I counted 'em,' says I.

"'And where are they,' says he.

"'At Bemis Heights,' says I.

"'Where's that?' he asks.

"'Down the river twelve miles or there away,' says I.

"'On which side?'

"'On the west.'

"'And what are they going to do next?' asked he after a moment's pause.

"'They're a going to wait till they've got together enough to drive you (excuse me) out of the country,' says I; 'and then they'll be a movin' on these here lines.'

"'How many do you suppose that will take?' he asked.

"'About seven thousand,' says I, 'reckoning in the sharp shooters.'

"When I made this answer, I noticed him a smiling at the other officers, and so I knowed he must have had more than that number of men.

"'Well, my good man,' says he, again taking up the talk where we stopt, 'can you tell me how long it will be before these seven thousand men get together?'

"'Sartainly,' said I, reckoning on my fingers and speaking slow. 'As many on 'em has gone to Fort Stanwix, and won't be back for some time, and as the principal help is expected from Vermont, it will take nigh on to a month before they're all in working order.'

"Here I noticed him smiling again to the officers around him; and thinks I to myself, 'Old feller, though your 're mighty close, I 'll get the better on you yet afore we 're through.'

"'How long,' says he, 'would it take for them to reach us?'

"Here he gives another knowing look about him. I thought to myself, it would take no longer for him to reach them, than for them to reach him; so I says,

"'Perhaps, two days, with the irregulars and militia they 've got; though if they try to come up the east bank of the river, it may be two days longer on account of the state of the country.'

"'Then the west bank is the best route?' says he.

"'Sartain,' says I.

"You know, colonel, that if he had kept to the east side of the river he would have had almost a clean sweep through the settlements, to opposite Albany, with no large streams to cross like the outlets of the Mohawk, and no good ground on which a stand could be made against him."

"Arter axin' these questions, the gineral walked about for a while, and then says, suddenly stopping,

"'Do you know the country well?'

"'As well as you know what 's in this tent,' I answered.

"'And who,' says he, after a moment's pause, 'who requested you to get the information which you have given me about the rebel army?'

"'Captain Gracie, says I, 'of his Majesty's 31st regiment of infantry.'

"'Is Captain Gracie present?' asked the general, lookin' round.

"'Yes, sir,' said the captain himself, stepping forward; 'and I can vouch for the truth of much this man says, having passed over the ground he mentions. Of his fidelity I have no doubt, as he once hid me from a pursuing party at his own house.'

"'This speaks well for your loyalty, my good man,' then said the general; 'and for the services you have rendered, and the risk you have run, I hope to reward you. Let some one look to his accommodation.'

"Here I was dismissed, and, though after that I seemed to be moving about quite free in the camp, yet, I noticed, that under the pretense of providing for me, I was more or less watched all the while. The next morning I was again called up for re-examination, and, though many knew me, as I said, yet it was clear I was looked on by the gineral as a rather doubtful character. Still he could n't resist the evidence I got on every side, and, finally, was induced, from my acquaintance with the country, to give me little places and commissions of some consequence and trust.

"I'll say to you, colonel, and to Mr. Walcott, what I would n't like to say abroad, that, on the whole, I'm rather ashamed of the part I acted at that time, and, though you and others, who are knowin' to the facts and to my motives, may make great account of it, yet I never could bring my mind to ask of government any reward for having been a *spy*. So, colonel, there you have the true reason of my silence on the subject."

"Why, sir, you are a noble fellow, and I am proud to know you," exclaimed young Walcott.

"I am much obleeged to you, captain," answered Brigham, much gratified at this evidence of esteem; "but still I can't feel proud when I am a tellin' what I then did. The fact is, I went through the British camp under favor of the confidence they had in me, and found out all its strength and weakness; and from several interviews with the officers and the commander-in-chief, I got a pretty correct notion of what was agoin' to be done. Hows'ever, time pressed, and, as I already knowed the intention was to pass down the right bank of the river, through Stillwater, and that pretty soon, I began to think on the means of getting away agin. This was troublesome, at any time. At night it was even more difficult than by day; and, though I was still treated well, and seemed to be on a good footin', I knowed well that I was watched; and any blunder in the dark, or even stirrin' about after nightfall, was risky business.

"The army was to start on the 16th of September, and this was the night of the 14th. There was just time for me, and I made up my mind, by hook or by crook, to get away the next morning. So I sauntered through the camp, till meeting my old acquaintance, Captain Gracie, I said to him, knowin' he would be busy as a beaver:

"'Captain, would n't you like to take a small shoot to-morrow morning? There 's some capital partridges in the fly, a few miles back.'

"'I'd like it well enough,' said he, 'but we're in such a devil of a hubbub, now that I suspect we are about moving forward, and so I've no time.'

"'Well now,' says I, 'that 's a 'tarnal pity, for I saw some of the finest birds ye ever laid eyes on—so fat and plump. Dare say the general would be delighted to see a half dozen on 'em on his own table.'

"'Do n't talk that way, Brigham,' he says, 'or you'll make me run away, and violate orders, for the sake of a blaze or so, at them.'

"'Well,' says I, 'if you *can't* go, you *can't*, that's all. But that's no reason why I should n't. And so I'd be obleeged to you to get me leave to go out arly to-morrow; and I'll make sure of as fine a game dinner as ever you sat down to.'

"'It's easy enough, I dare say,' said he, 'to get what you ask; but I'm damned if I stir a peg in your cause, unless I am to get a brace, at least, of the birds, as my share of the plunder.'

"'Two on 'em, captain,' says I, 'if you like; and I'll give you my word that if you don't get none, the general himself won't.'

"So upon that, he goes over to the big marquee, and soon comes back with a slip of paper, with the order written on it, as I supposed.

"You may be sure I was up early enough next morning. The daybreak gun had n't yet rolled off its smoke, afore I was ready. To turn aside suspicion, I detarmined, as I hinted, to take the back track, and leave the camp on the north side toward Skenesborough. I found no difficulty in getting away, though I noticed the sentinel I gave the paper to, arter hesitating a little, and eyeing me pretty sharp, called another chap to him, and sent him off. Then he falls to studying the paper again, and arter a few minutes, looking up to where he had sent the chap, he signified that I could go.

"Slinging the gun over my shoulder, I took the north road boldly, and moved off. When about a quarter of a mile away, on looking around, which I did pretty often, I can tell you, I noticed two men on horseback leaving the camp, by the same road which I was followin'. They did not come very fast; but I should have liked it better if they had not come at all. They kept me in sight, and even gained upon me a little. It looked onpleasant. I took it cool, hows'ever, till I come to a little piece of woods, beyond which the road made a sudden turn. Here I quickened my step; but whew! no sooner did I do so, than I sees them fellows put to, whip and spur, as if for life. I had nothing now to do, but to cut a way for myself. I rather consated something had gone wrong lately to give me a bad name in the camp. Perhaps, countin' the men, or takin' too much notice of the cannon, had been disagreeable to 'em. Any how, away I run, but saw they was gaining on me fast. Something must be done, thinks I. In a few seconds I got to the turn in the road. Just there, a small creek crossed it, and was bridged over with rough logs. The banks of it was lined with a few alder bushes. I formed my plans at once.

"It was sartain I could n't keep the road much longer; and the woods was far too open to be a good hidin' place. So that no sooner was I fairly round the bend, where for a minute or so, I would be out of the sight of my pursuers, than I jumped into the thicket, got to the creek, followed it up behind the alders, and crawled under the low log-bridge, just as their horses' hoofs came thunderin' down on it; and I could hear them shout and strike away to get up a little more speed. Their going ahead that way, was a sure sign they had not seen my trick. I could hear the clattering of their horses' feet, for a minute or so, as they swept round the bend in the road; and then, seeming to haul up a little, one on 'em shouts:

"'I say, Tom, where the devil has he gone to?'

"'Eh?' says the other. 'Among the trees on the right, I suppose. Do you ride forward, so as to be sure he ain't hid along the road behind some stump or stone, while I beat this little grove. He could n't have gone the other side, for we saw him plain enough go round the turn here.'

"So saying, one rides forward, and the other turned in among the trees, and soon scoured the little thicket through and through, for it was not much larger than an acre in size. I could see all that went on. At the same time, I was not quite comfortable. They would soon be a doubling on me. When I was n't found ahead, they'd be sure I was behind. So, what they had said gave me a sudden idea. Could n't I creep entirely through the hole formed by the log-way, and come out t'other side, and so get into the woods in that direction, where they would n't think of looking for me. No sooner thought on, than tried. After a little squeezin', and a great deal of mud and water, I got through; and crawling up the little brook for a rod or so, I soon got off far enough to venture on rising again, to trust to my heels. Lucky enough, I did so; for afore I was fairly out of sight, I saw them, like bloodhounds, making for the bridge itself. The dodge was discovered; but I did n't stop to obsarve 'em any longer, making off as fast as two tolerable legs could carry me.

"Well, the long and the short on it was, that arter being chased pretty sharp for half the day, I finally managed to throw them out. Then I had to get across the river, which I did just below Glen's, and traveled through a thick woods for near twenty miles, before reaching the American outposts. There again, I had some trouble in getting admitted and decently treated. But when, at last, I got into the old gineral's quarters, and had a chance to talk with him alone, you ought to have seen how tickled the old chap was. Glad to see me safe, he was, that was something; but then the news I brought seemed to settle all his doubts, and he capered about like a boy.

"I don't know how it was; but, although before that, I had felt like a sneak in the job I was at; yet when I saw how the gineral took it, and how much account he made of it, I began to think I might have desarved something for my pains, arter all. And so, colonel, there's the whole story. There's no use in speakin' of the fight which took place a few days arter. Every body knows about that, and none better than yourself."

Here Brigham paused in his narrative, during which, some time had elapsed. The hour had waxed late, and the small fire in the cabin had smoldered down to embers. The two girls had long before retired to the inner room, and were now locked in the deep and dreamless slumber with which fatigue ever blesses youthful frames.

CHAPTER XVIII.

JOE'S SECOND ATTEMPT AT VENGEANCE.

The night flowed quietly on. The storm had passed away, and left but few marks of its violence behind. The fallen tree, the scattered branches, the shaken fruit and flower-bushes were still visible tokens of its passage. The swollen brook had subsided, and a low ripple had taken the place of the loud gurgle of its late full flood. The moon still shone, wet and watery; though its beams now came in long silvery pencils from the western sky.

All within the cabin, at length, were at rest. But not so without. There, the wilderness was full of creatures broad awake, for plunder or for prey. There too, strangely enough, were human passions, more unappeasable than animal appetites; and unregulated human mind, more cunning, more incalculable, and more to be feared, than the fiercest beast of prey.

Indian Joe had not forgotten the injurious language of Walcott, and conceiving himself to have rendered service, he felt a violent resentment at the ungrateful return it met with. The act which had called forth his rebuke, he could only look upon as a meritorious one. So, when he had left Walcott's presence, he had brooded over his imaginary injuries. The thirst for revenge was strong within him, and could be quenched only by blood. Before the morrow's sun should arise, he was eager to impress upon his contemplated victim some signal marks of his vengeance. For this cause he had arisen in the darkness from the couch where he lay in his own cabin, and made preparations to go forth on his fatal errand.

Slowly and moodily, through the bushes, and the trees still dripping with the waters of the late storm, did he find his way back to the log house of Brigham.

He prowled around the hut, until long after all the lights were extinguished. The silence that prevailed, seemed only to arouse and augment his ferocity. He thought of the peaceful, self-satisfied sleep which now rested upon the spirit of Walcott, and then he thought of the severity and contempt with which he himself had been treated. And why should a pale face, he thought, thus abuse a native of the woods? What right had a being who ate and slept, who walked and ran, who lived and thought, like himself, to be abusive and insolent when awake, and yet to be tranquil as infancy and innocence when asleep, while he himself was restless with passion, and thirsting for revenge?

None but those who have had some opportunity of witnessing it, can fully believe in the much enduring patience with which an American savage will wait for an occasion to retaliate an injury. For hours, then, did poor Joe lie sullenly concealed in the bushes near at hand, so situated as to be able to command a view of almost every thing which took place within the cabin. He saw when the two girls, overcome by weariness had withdrawn from the outer room; and watched where they disposed themselves in the further apartment. He already pondered upon the means of reaching them, should they become necessary to the attainment of his paramount object.

In uncultivated natures, one strong passion almost always has such a preponderance, that when aroused it overbalances and bears down all others; and in such cases no motives can be administered to guide the conduct or attain an end, unless addressed to this one absorbing feeling. In Indian Joe, such was now the case. All respect for Colonel Belden, every impulse of forbearance which his intimacy with, and friendship for Brigham and M'Carty might have awakened, and every feeling of generosity and compassion which the sex, the tender age and great beauty of the two girls might have inspired, and which are usually felt to some degree by all men, however stolid from barbarity, or hardened by vice, were utterly forgotten, or if not forgotten, utterly unheeded.

It was long before he saw the last of the lingerers fling himself down upon a pile of skins, and compose himself as if for sleep. The embers of the fire yet gave forth sufficient light to enable him to discern through the window the relative situations of the inmates of the cabin. The door had been closed and fastened by a rude wooden bar drawn across it on the inside; but the precaution taken in thus closing it and the security it afforded were enough to deter the unskilled savage from any plan which might require him to gain access to the interior through it. The windows, also, were too high and too narrow, to afford any means of getting through, even if the operation could be performed without noise. There seemed to be difficulty in every plan. At one moment he thought of setting fire to the hut itself, and thus sacrificing all. But more stealthy, and more individual revenge accorded better with his savage nature. In a conflagration, moreover, some might escape, and why not Walcott, the youngest and most active? There was still another method which had first occurred to him; and which, next to the pleasure of imbruing his hands in blood, and giving to his very muscles their share of the luxury of murder, he preferred over all others; but which, nevertheless, he hesitated to adopt, on account of the noise by which it would be accompanied; and also, on account of the great likelihood of detection and punishment. His method was none other than shooting his victim where he lay, by firing through the window. The thing was quite practicable. A deliberate aim could be taken, and death would be almost a certain result. Still, for a long while, the murderer hesitated. Like a panther in view of its prey, he still moved many times around the cabin. In the consciousness of possessing the power of complete revenge, and in the contemplation of the object of it, there is a species of fascination, as intense and painful as the fascination of fear. The thoughts of the savage, meanwhile, were all intent upon his purpose. At length he made up his mind to risk all, and adopt the only method of complete retribution which had seemed to him feasible. He placed himself again by the window which commanded a view of the position where Walcott lay. The carefully loaded gun was slowly and gently brought to its position.

Inside of the building, all was silent save the loud breathing of the sleepers. Could they even have dreamed of the danger which lurked so near them, and threatened so soon to burst upon them, how suddenly would sleep have left their eyelids, and clamor and alarm have taken the place of quietude and repose!

The Indian had brought his weapon full to its range, and was feasting his cruel eyes, for a moment, with the sight of his enemy, so completely in his power, when he felt his arm lightly touched, and turning his head quickly, he saw Jacob standing close behind him. The gun dropped from his hold. A superstitious fear went through him, sharp and painful, like an electrical shock; and though his limbs were almost powerless from terror, instinct induced him to make a sudden leap on one side, to escape from the gripe which Jacob seemed inclined to fasten on him.

The effort was vain, for barely had he stirred ere he felt himself wrapped around by the brawny arms of the maniac. He was as helpless as a deer when caught in the slimy folds of a boa constrictor; and he heard the low chuckle of his captor as he felt himself borne rapidly away.

Jacob, as well as the savage, had felt an interest in one of the occupants of the hut. He had not forgotten the beautiful young prisoner who had been rescued from him in the cavern. With a confused, but pertinacious notion that she had, in some way, become his property, or was to be his wife and the companion of his solitary haunts, he had not, for a single instant, abandoned his purpose in respect to her, even when driven from it. At a distance he had followed the departing intruders and had marked all their subsequent movements. He had even closely observed where Lucile was bestowed for the night, with some notion of attempting a re-capture. It was while engaged in his reconnoissances that he had been fired at and slightly wounded by Joe, as the reader is already advised. It was also during this prowling at night that, more wary than the Indian, he had discovered that more than himself were seeking some purpose there. In his mental confusion he conceived that whoever it was he must be in pursuit of the same object as himself. In thwarting him, therefore, he would be defeating a rival; and in destroying him he would only be gratifying one of the instincts of his peculiar type of mental aberration.

From the moment when these ideas occurred to him his attention became fixed upon the conduct and actions of his supposed competitor. He followed him like a shadow, as silent and as inseperable. Up to the very instant when Joe was about to fire, he had refrained from touching him, and he might not have done so even then, but for the vague idea that the shot was designed against, or might injure Lucile. Even after he had made the other sensible of his presence, and had caught him in his arms, he had still, with almost unaccountable forbearance and prudence, refrained from making any noise which might disturb the inmates of the cabin. As for the Indian, he was in such agony of superstitious apprehension, that he could not think of any devices to escape; and it was not in his nature to cry out, or call for help. So the seizure took place almost in silence.

Those within the building slept on, as if nothing but the summer night wind moved around them; and as if the moonbeams lighted up nothing but the vast, green, slumbering and deserted wilderness. No thought of danger disturbed their rest, and they reaped the grateful reward of exertion and fatigue. All the operations of nature seem to be accompanied or followed by their appropriate reactions or compensations. So, a great danger to one of those sleepers had come and gone, without his knowledge. How often in life, must the same thing happen to us all! Who can know the invisible perils which hover in the air, and threaten to fall upon us at every step we take through the world! How many thousands are the causes which may either utterly destroy us, or do us injuries perhaps more unendurable than death! A careful and protecting hand must always shield us during sleep; and an ever overlooking providence must constantly guide us through the blind and dangerous ways of life, until the day of final earthly destiny be come. How few reflect upon this, and how much smaller the number of those who feel grateful for what are called the *ordinary*, but what are in reality, the *inestimable* blessings of life! In the vast machinery of organization and law by which we are surrounded in the world, the least derangement of one of its complicated parts, may crush ourselves or our hopes; may, by removing our friends, leave us alone and without sympathy on earth, or hasten us prematurely from it. Sickness may possess our bodies, poverty and disaster reign in our affairs, disgrace and misconstruction attach to our names, and dwell upon our memories; yet, when none of these things happen, we take the exemption as a part of our due, we give no thought to our unworthiness, and we render up no grateful tribute for the unearned happiness we enjoy. On the contrary, all, even the most favored, are disposed to murmur at their lot. Some unsatisfied ambition, some unfulfilled hope, some ungratified desire, is still the cause or the pretext, of complaints against fortune or against providence.

CHAPTER XIX.

THE MORNING.

When Brigham went out of the hut early the next morning, he was not a little surprised to find, lying upon the ground beneath one of the windows, the gun which Joe had dropped when seized by the maniac. The weapon, of course, was still loaded, and the lock was drawn back, as if ready to be snapped on the instant. The powder in the pan had fallen out; and the menacing flint, like the tooth of a dead wolf, now threatened in vain.

There were, also, on the ground where the weapon was picked up, marks of footsteps; and Brigham even thought that he could discover in some of them, resemblances to the track of Jacob, which he had lately had occasion to follow up so closely, and to study so much. The gun itself he knew belonged to Joe; but why it should be found where it was, seemed mysterious. He soon called M'Carty to consult him upon the case, and to hold a council of advisement and inquiry. When the latter came up, Brigham said to him—

"M'Carty, here's a tarnal strange affair. I found Joe's gun lying under this window all loaded and cocked. Just look at this 'ere trail, and see what you can make of it."

M'Carty did as requested, and after having terminated

that task, he also examined the window itself, looking through it, into the cabin.

"Do you remember," said he, "whereabouts Walcott lay last night?"

"Sartain," said Brigham, "he was over there just opposite us. But why ax such an onmeaning question as that, Jim?"

Jim here put his hands in his pockets, as he sometimes did when in thought, while he walked to and fro for a moment, whistling "Yankee Doodle," in a solemn sort of manner, but winding up at last with a flourish.

"'T ain't onmeaning at all," said he; "but I've got something of a guess as to how the thing got here. But *why* it was left is a puzzler."

"Well, how did it get here then, if you know?" asked Brigham.

"P'raps you did n't hear of the little row the captain had with Joe, yesterday afternoon, about that shootin' business?" suggested M'Carty.

"Yes, I heard something about it, but did n't suppose it was any thing serious."

"Well, may be it was n't," said M'Carty; "but when Joe left, he had on a look I did n't like. I've knowed the critter a long time; and I told the captain to look out for himself."

"Then you think Joe came here to get a crack at Mr. Walcott through the window, do you?" said Brigham; "the murdering thief! If I thought it was true, I'd hang him to the next saplin' to learn him not to come sneakin' about my house. But then how do you account for his gun being left in this odd way? The lock is open, and the primin' is all gone."

"May be you'd find that last upon the ground, by looking," said Jim.

The ground was accordingly examined where the gun had fallen; and, sure enough, faint traces of the powder were to be seen, though some of it had become moist, and mingled with the earth; and the lighter portions of it had been blown away.

"Don't it look mightily as if the critter had dropped the wepon just as he was goin' to shoot?" asked Jim.

"Yes; and I think I know what scared the vicious devil away. Look at this, and this, and this," said Brigham, pointing to where he had discovered the successive impressions made by the lunatic's feet, as he had started away with his burden, the footmarks being more distinct than usual from the weight which he had carried.

M'Carty looked at these traces, as they were pointed out, and he at once acquired the same conception of the case as that which had already struck Brigham.

At this moment, Walcott approached the two men, and without delay they stated to him the discovery they had made, and the construction they put upon it.

"I telled ye, captain, how it would be, when you druv the poor devil off yesterday," said M'Carty.

"Well, it seems no great harm has been done yet," was the reply; "for, according to your own story, he is more likely to be in danger himself from Jacob, than I am from him."

"That's true," said M'Carty; "and as we've a mind to hunt up the crazy fellow at any rate, it will come in our way to look arter poor Joe, though, may be, he's swung to a saplin', or pitched down some hole afore this."

From the cabin now came forth, side by side, the two girls, who, though they had spent the night together, had passed through very different kinds of repose. Exhaustion had done its work upon the frame of Marion; but sleep had also worked its full restoration. She had risen with the freshness of the meadow lily; and she came forth with joy in her heart, and health beaming from her eye. Her companion looked jaded and weary. Her cheek could hardly be said to be pale, for in its center was a crimson flush; but her eyes wore a look of sleeplessness; and it was easy to discover that night had not to her brought its usual balm. Nevertheless, her countenance did not fail to light up with pleasure at the sight of the charming scene which hailed her as she issued from the cabin.

The sun had just surmounted the crest of the thick forest; and its rays poured down, like a golden cascade, upon the spot where Walcott and the other men were standing. Youth and morning must ever possess strong sympathies; and their full force was felt by Lucile, as she stepped forth by the side of her friend, and approached the place where the young man stood, to exchange with him, the morning salutations. The color that mantled in her cheek was deeper than any summer morning, however glorious, is apt to call forth. Feelings of various kinds were busy within, and sent the warm blood, like crimson signals, to her glowing face. She was oppressed by various and almost contradictory feelings. She remembered with something like shame, how she had clung to Walcott the day before; and yet how could she assume a cold and distant demeanor toward one who had so strong claim to gratitude. She was indeed but half conscious of the warmer feeling that was springing up in her heart toward the betrothed of her friend; yet there was a vague accusation from the inward monitor that she would be guilty of treachery toward that friend who leaned so trustingly on her arm, if she gave scope to the emotions of gratitude which she felt to be his due. And yet how could she greet, as a mere acquaintance, one who had done her so great a service? Would he not have a right to despise her as cold and ungrateful? Might she not even wound the feelings of one to whom she owed more than life?

But description moves slow, while time and events are flying forward. Thus, while we have been dwelling upon the scene before us as if it was a still picture, that scene itself, like a moving panorama, has been steadily changing.

"So Mr. Arthur!" exclaimed Marion, after a little pause, "have n't you a word to say to us this morning?"

Arthur had, in fact, like ourselves, been heedless of the lapse of time. He was now startled from his reverie.

"I was only thinking," said he, "how well you two look after your sleep."

"Now you were thinking of no such thing," she said, "for if you had taken the trouble to look you would have seen that Lucile here does *not* look well at all. Poor little thing!" she continued, gently kissing her, "she looks as if she had had no rest at all. It 's that frightful Jacob, I suppose, still disturbing her imagination."

What we see is not always that which meets the bodily eye. The mind makes pictures upon the mind as well as the mind upon the eye.

Arthur, for the first time, now saw that what Marion said was true. Approaching then, he extended his hand to Lucile, and began to make inquiry as to the cause of her obvious sleeplessness or illness.

"P'raps she heard the critter about the hut during the night," said Brigham, coming up, having heard the inquiries of Walcott.

"You do not surely mean to say," asked Lucile, quickly, "that he really was here during the night?"

"Fact, miss," answered Brigham; "but never fear, for he could do no mischief with such chaps as Arthur there, and the rest on us at hand. But it seems, he was not the only one neither, for Joe must have been hanging about as well as he."

"How so?" asked Colonel Belden, who had now joined the group.

"Well, it 's mighty curious, colonel: but we found Joe's gun just under the window there, and he and Jacob must have had something of a scuffle together, judging from appearances. Hows'ever, no harm 's done, so far as we know, except that Joe 's gone, and that may not be much harm neither, the vicious varmint. A whole redskin is bad enough unless you get on the right side of him, and then he'll go through fire and water for you. But you never know where to take these half-breeds."

"Why, what is the matter with Joe, all at once?" asked the colonel. "He was of your party yesterday, and behaved himself very well, and yet you now seem irritated against him?"

"I do n't exactly know," replied Brigham, "what the particular pint is, but he and Mr. Walcott had a bit of a quarrel yesterday, and I conclude that he meant to be ugly. If I should catch the critter sneaking around my primeses again with a gun arter dark, I'd larn him! He ought to be choked!—if Jake ain't done that much for him afore this time. I'll flog the Indian out of him, if ever I get hold on him again!"

Luckily for the young ladies they understood but imperfectly the nature of the new danger which, during the night, had threatened them, or, at all events had hung over one in whom they both felt a deep interest. For the present nothing more was said upon the subject.

There was, however, among the men, some conversation as to what could have brought back the lunatic; but they had not much difficulty in attributing his visit to its true cause. They, therefore, concluded, reasonably enough, that the same inducement might bring him there again.

Meanwhile, what was to be done in reference to Joe? Their theory as to his late presence, and as to what had become of him, was, after all, a mere hypothesis; and he might still be in his own wigwam or, possibly, quietly cultivating his little patch of Indian corn—an occupation for which his mixed blood was supposed to have given him a little taste. It was determined first of all, that some one should be sent thither to ascertain if such was the fact.

While the morning meal was in the course of preparation, therefore, M'Carty went up to the neighboring hamlet of Indian huts; and having informed Catfoot of the state of affairs, engaged his services in ascertaining the presence or absence of Joe.

"Cap'n speak big to Joe, eh?" asked the chief, when M'Carty had finished his story.

"Why, I must say," answered M'Carty, apologetically,

"that he was a little over hasty with him; but he meant no harm; and to my notion, it did n't justify Joe in going to shoot him arterward.

"Joe shoot him," said Catfoot, coolly.

"But he had n't ought to shoot him, just for a little talking to. That ain 't law nor gospel. Why the colonel talks worse than that to me sometimes."

"Joe shoot him—good," replied the Indian.

"I don 't say but he may be right to feel riled, Catfoot," said M'Carty, "but murder is quite another thing. It 's takin' the life of a fellow creature, you see. But the captain is now agreeable to make it all right, and any how, wants to get Joe out of the grip of that cussed catamount, wild Jake, who, he consates, has got hold on him. So if you 've a mind to help a friend, and see the captain do the handsome thing, you can jine us again in the sarch."

"Good," said Catfoot.

Here M'Carty shook him warmly by the hand to seal the compact, and departed on his return. As he was moving away, the Indian watched him for a while, his eye lighted up with an expression which was almost humor, while a half smile for a moment lingered on his usually staid and saturnine face.

"He good—big fool," he muttered to himself; "Joe right—may be cap 'n right too—go see."

Upon this he rose up and started toward Joe's clearing, which, as we have already observed, was nearly a mile distant, and long before the inmates of Brigham's cabin had finished their breakfast, he had performed his errand and returned.

As they got through with their preparations for starting and sallied forth, they found him seated near the Rock Spring, as grave and silent as if he had not been upon a mission, or brought back news.

Walcott himself went first down to meet him.

"Catfoot," said he, as he approached, "I am sorry Joe should have got offended at what I said yesterday; and am more sorry still, if any thing has happened to him. Did you find him at home?"

The Indian shook his head, seeming to consider it unnecessary to waste words upon a mere negative.

"Then we must make search for him," said the young man. "This crazy man must be found and secured; and in looking for one, we can look for both. Are you willing to join us again?"

An affirmative nod was the reply.

"And I hope, my friend," continued Walcott, "that a hasty word will never make enemies of us. Judge me more by what I do, than what I say."

"Good," said the savage, appearing to appreciate the apology which the other was indirectly making for his haste. "Joe not know dat—tell him," continued the Indian, after a pause.

The two now went up the bank, where they found M'Carty and Brigham.

"I guess, captain," said M'Carty, "that one on us had better stay about here in case of accident. It would not do to leave the colonel here alone with the young women."

"True, M'Carty," said Walcott, "and I think Brigham would be the best, and make it the safest. Brigham, I suppose that you would prefer being active with us, but you know that exactly here is the spot where most danger is to be apprehended."

"Very well," replied Brigham, "I'm agreeable; and I'm sure I like the colonel's society well enough to keep him company, always providing it's the best plan. Catfoot and Jim there, will most likely answer your purpose, unless Joe and the crazy man should patch up a treaty, and make war on jint account."

Here Brigham chuckled at his own conceit.

"There's not much risk of that, I fancy," answered Walcott; "but, above all things, you, for one, are the man to stay, and M'Carty may do the same if he likes. Catfoot and myself will be sufficient for the search."

"I'm blessed if I do, though," replied M'Carty, "unless downright ordered. I've had bad luck enough, standing sentry in this here business; and I've no notion trying it a third time."

"You can go, of course, if you like," said Walcott, "and it will be one more chance of success; though Catfoot here has a scent as keen as that of a hound, and with his help I have little doubt of soon getting on the trail."

"Now you are speaking of a hound, Mr. Arthur," said M'Carty, "I wonder what has become of the critter we brought with us. Have you seen him anywhere about, Miss Lucile? for I don't remember seein' him since the first morning, when he led the hunt arter the colonel."

"Sure enough, what has become of him?" was now the general inquiry.

No one had seen him.

Lucile felt some concern at the discovery, for the dog was a particular favorite of hers. The events of the last few days had been so remarkable, that they had driven from her mind all thoughts of her poor four-footed follower; but now came an unpleasant doubt, whether or not the faithful beast was killed or lost.

But while so much was pending, there was no time to indulge in surmises as to the fate of a dog.

The exciting scenes which they had passed through, and the continuous dangers which had beset them, had taken away all inclination on the part of Colonel Belden and the young ladies to remain in their present situation any longer than might be necessary. It was therefore agreed, that, if possible, Walcott should return the same night, and that preparations should be made for starting for Ballston on the morning of the next day.

Meanwhile, the three men, Walcott, Catfoot and M'Carty, now refreshed with a night's rest, and prepared with cold meats and other necessaries, had made their dispositions for starting.

"Arthur, my boy," said Colonel Belden, as they were about going off, "I beg you to run no unnecessary risk; and remember, we are all most anxious to have this unpleasant, but necessary, and most humane business at an end."

"Never fear for me, colonel," said Walcott, "my only anxiety will be on account of yourself and those we leave here behind us. It was my intention to have them safely conducted to Ballston to-day; but this affair of poor Joe seems to require that we should act at once, in his behalf, and endeavor to save him from a fate from which he helped to save our little Lucile. We must all be grateful for that, and I am afraid my own precipitancy has done all the mischief in the present case."

"But, Arthur," said Marion, "may not Joe try to

do you some evil himself, if he is free and meets you alone?"

"It is not very likely," said he; "but I hope to be able to convince him that I meant no harm by a hasty word."

During this colloquy, Lucile had been, for the most part, silent. It was not, however, for lack of interest in the subject, but for lack of a suitable way in which she could express her interest. At last, seeing no other method, and feeling that she was called upon to evince in some manner that she was not indifferent or ungrateful, she walked up to Arthur, gave him her hand, and said:

"You know, Mr. Walcott, already, how grateful I am for your kindness to me; and you must know now, that if any thing happens to you, I shall feel that I am indirectly the cause of it. So I beseech you to be careful what you do, and come back to us—to Marion—as soon as you can. Remember," she added, while her hand trembled in his, "remember, your life and your happiness belong to more than yourself."

Walcott pressed with warmth the hand which she gave him; and after having repeated his assurance to all, of his prudence, and his speedy return, he, with the others, took his departure.

It was not long after their start, before the searching party was again out of sight. Those who remained behind them disposed of themselves in various ways. Brigham undertook the apparently Herculean labor of removing the trunk and limbs of the tree which, during the storm of the preceding night, had, in its fall, come so near crushing his cabin. He first attacked the obstacle with that mighty leveler and civilizer, the ax. It was not long before, yielding to his resounding blows, the great trunk itself was divided into manageable lengths, and cloven into hundreds of small pieces, suitable for fuel. The whole mass, consisting of the long and ponderous shaft, and the wide and bushy top, seemed to melt away, like an icicle before a spring sun. Ere midday, all its unseemly incumbrance had disappeared; and it was now removed, and stowed away in neat piles near at hand, to be used during the succeeding winter.

Meanwhile, Marion had induced Lucile, who seemed to be depressed in spirits, to take short strolls through the neighborhood, endeavoring to enliven her by sprightly conversation, and by pointing out such objects of beauty and interest as were to be found in their situation. They had visited the Indian hamlet, where they had been sufficiently gazed at by the great round eyes of the dusky and dirty young papooses, and simpered at by the broad ugly features and white teeth of the ugly and uncouth squaws. Outside of the huts, lay, in stolid indolence, the lords of these unseemly households, in utter want of occupation, and in utter indifference to surrounding objects. A few, it is true, were absent on hunting excursions, and a few more might also have been engaged in fishing.

The great business of all American tribes, that is to say, war, was at that time dull. Of the white people they were afraid; and there was among them, at this moment, no serious quarrel with any neighboring tribe. Depredations, with desultory, but ferocious slaughter, were the only engagements which could arouse all the elements of their savage natures. So, like a civilized nation destitute of commerce, they were in a state of apathy and decline.

Our young heroines traversed the miserable village with no great interest. Small dogs, now and then, snarled at them by the doorways; and little urchins, six years old, launched at them, as they passed, their little, harmless, blunted arrows. In all they did, and wherever they went, Marion observed that her companion still seemed dull and dispirited. She even began to complain of pain in her head, and of weariness in her limbs. So they again went back to Brigham's cabin. They found the huge tree nearly cut away; and nothing but green twigs bestrewed their path as they returned.

CHAPTER XX.

OLD ACQUAINTANCES.

By this time, it was nearly noon. The atmosphere, as on the day before, was warm and genial, though now free from oppressive sultriness. A gentle breeze could be felt, as it rustled the leaves of the neighboring trees, and poured its cooling breath through the open door and windows of the cotttage.

It was then that the sound of a distant horn was heard which induced all the occupants of the cabin to come forth. It was not a single blast, or even a succession of blasts, as if uttered for the purpose of calling attention, or of giving a notice or a warning. It was rather the leisurely, regulated and metrical note of a bugle. As yet, however, it could only be heard on its louder keys. In a short time the sound seemed to come nearer, or, at all events, could be more distinctly heard. It then became obvious that it was a tune and not a blast which was being blown upon the instrument; and the fact would seem to indicate the approach of a troop, or some procession or party of gayety or pleasure. It came from an easterly direction; and, as nearly as could be determined upon, those who caused it, must be coming up the left bank of the Creek, which here led circuitously toward the Lake.

"That sounds like a trooper's bugle, Brigham," said Colonel Belden; "have you any idea who it can be?"

"I reckon it must be some party from Schuyler's—may be the gineral himself—or, mayhap, the young patroon from Albany. They often come this way and use the tent below. It 's a favorite notion of the old gineral himself."

It was not long after this, before, through the trees, in the distance, could be seen a few banners, then a small equestrian troop, headed by a trumpeter. The horses were, however, mounted by ladies and gentlemen promiscuously, and moved, without order, along the footway or road observable in that direction.

Judging from appearances it was a gay and joyous cavalcade; and, as it came nearer, it became obvious that it was not of a military character, except so far as the trumpet and the pistols of the gentlemen, with now and then a slung rifle, might make it so.

"It is as I supposed," said Brigham; "some folks up to see the gineral from Albany, I reckon, have taken a notion to see that curiosity down there" (pointing to the Rock Spring). "We often have 'em here."

Gayly did the procession come on. When within a few rods of the house, however, it turned obliquely down the bank, and headed for the large military tent or marquee which has already been mentioned, and which had been pitched closely adjoining the spring. Here the cavalcade paused, and soon all were dismounted, and preparations apparently made for immediate occupation of the tent.

It was not long after this before the young people of the newly-arrived party dispersed themselves about the spring, which, as an object of curiosity, while its waters were supposed to be imbued with great sanitary power, was the principal attraction which had induced them to undertake the expedition. Around the broad, brown, conical rock over which its waters bubbled, were collected a group which, in gayety of appearance, in youth and sprightliness might, perhaps, rival many, of the same general character—which visit that same spot in modern times; or, at all events, if it did not rival them, might, at least, serve to suggest, and in some sort of prophetic way, to foreshadow them.

It may be remarked that, excepting the fact that the adjacent grounds are more clear of trees and brush, they have remained for three quarters of a century and up to the present time, almost entirely unaltered and unimproved. A recent visitor can, therefore, easily imagine what must have been the appearance of a troop, such as we have mentioned, at the time of which we are writing.

Colonel Belden and his party had, meanwhile, retired within the shelter of Brigham's cabin. They could, every now and then, hear from where they sat, merry peals of laughter and voices ringing with all the joyous energy of youth. Presently a gay plume, and then a bright, fresh, and blooming face arose from the brink of the slope and was presented to the eye, on the plateau where the hut stood. Then young men came. And thus, in diverging parties, like the crystal streamlets which poured in all directions from the apex of Rock Spring, did the visitors scatter themselves around.

Gladness and merriment reigned everywhere. Some went up to the Indian village, some followed the still course of the brook as it stole on its shadowy way beneath the dark entangled branches of the willows; and some, with freer step, betook themselves to the high open woods, where, with a refreshing sense of vastness, of freedom, and of solitude, each young heart could more readily find its kindred one; and thought and emotion could flow on in conjoined streams.

Among the new comers, Brigham soon found out acquaintances enough. Much to his disappointment however, General Schuyler himself was not there; but instead of him, were one or two men, still young, whom he had known during the recent war as mere boys in service, but who, from gallantry, or family or political influence, had now attained to rank and position. By these, he was at once recognized, and much inquiry and congratulation, nowise pertinent to our story, took place between them.

One of them had attained his military majority; and though still young, and since the peace, withdrawn from active service, he still felt proud of the circumstances which led to his promotion, and kept his memory stored with the stirring events he had witnessed. This young man, whom we will, for lack of a better designation, call Floyd, was a native of the county of Westchester, once the famous "neutral ground." From the convenience of his place of residence to the city of New York, he had some years before, been well, if not intimately acquainted with Colonel Belden and his family. Time, different habits, and different occupations, had, however, for a considerable period separated them. He had known the daughter as a mere child, and he remembered her as possessing a charming figure that gave promise of womanly beauty; and, as gifted with long, soft, flowing ringlets, and gentle blue eyes. In her girlish frolics she had often chosen him for her playfellow, and even sat and prattled upon his knee with the affectionate confidence and engaging vivacity of early years. He was then already a man, and she a child.

But a few years, in one sense, had annihilated the space between them, while in another, it had placed them still further apart. He was still a young man, and she, though the actual difference in their ages remained the same, and would continue the same, to separate them by its interval, like a wall of iron forever, had grown to a full woman's estate; and might now vie for his equal affection, and stand the peer and eligible companion of all of his age and sex.

But these relations were not, at the time thought of by either of the persons concerned. How should they be?

Marion had, as we have said, withdrawn into the cabin on the approach of the strangers, and was now caring, with affecticnate solicitude, for Lucile, who hourly grew more dejected in spirits, and ill in body. Of the presence of Floyd there was, of course, no suspicion and no thought; and, of his former acquaintance, whenever it occurred to her memory at all, she only preserved a faint, though an agreeable trace.

On the other hand, he, although a soldier, had got so far through the world, not only with sound limbs but with a whole heart—the one, perhaps, for gentlemen of his profession, as great a miracle as the other. So that the years of his manhood, being as yet few and happy, had passed lightly over him—had left no wrinkle upon his forehead, and no sadness in his heart. His humor was buoyant and gay; and upon expeditions of pleasure like that in which he was now engaged, he was generally a ruling spirit.

He was among those who had first ascended the bank westward of the spring; and there, having recognized Brigham as an old companion in arms, he had made many inquiries as to his position and present circumstances; and, among other things, learned from him of the presence of Colonel Belden. Leaving his companions for the moment, therefore, he hastened to pay his respects to the old gentleman. He met him at the door, and was immediately recognized and warmly greeted.

"My dear colonel," said Floyd; "the sight of you has much increased the happiness I have in to-day's visit; but I am a little surprised to find that you appear to be so nearly unaccompanied?"

"Not quite alone, my boy," replied Colonel Belden, with a smile. "Not quite alone, for there is an old playfellow of yours here with me."

"Whom do you mean, colonel? Am I to have another surprise?"

"You shall judge for yourself," was the answer, as the old gentleman approached the entrance of the inner apartment, from which he presently returned, leading his daughter by the hand.

"Why, father," said she, "it is Richard Floyd! How delightful to see him here!"

As she said this, she hastened forward, almost forgetting that she was no longer a child; and taking his hand, she had almost kissed him as of old, before she fully recollected that while time had been adding to her years and her stature, it had also been raising up a barrier of formality and propriety between herself and him, which she could not now with impunity throw down. The impulse was nevertheless, strong upon the warm-hearted girl; and she blushed as she caught herself, nearly, *in flagrante delicto.* But no proprieties could prevent her from manifesting the deep and surprised pleasure which she really felt.

As for the young man himself, he was completely taken aback. If he had expected to see the daughter, it was only as a child—one whom he could take up in his arms and kiss. It was as such that she existed in his memory. Instead of that, however, he now beheld a well-grown, though delicately formed, and as he thought, a very charming young lady, rushing toward him, and reclaiming with eagerness, the long interrupted acquaintance. Had her action been completely that of the child he had thought her, and had her arms, as in former days, been thrown affectionately round his neck, he would not at that moment, perhaps, have been able suitably to acknowledge the favor, or even to receive it with the proper degree of grace, such complete possession had surprise taken of him. But young men are not apt, in like situations, to remain long in a state of stupefaction. So that it was but a moment, before Floyd had so far rallied as to say, with some confusion:

"You have taken me in ambush with a vengeance, colonel. I was looking out to see some old companion in arms, but instead of that, I find little Marion—I beg her pardon—I find a young lady, who has so grown as to put the eye at fault in recognizing her."

"She was, at all events, an old companion of yours, if not a companion in arms," replied the colonel.

"And, Mr. Richard," said Marion, "you need not look so sorrowful because you do not find me 'little' any more. I have not grown out of remembrance of you."

"Sorrowful, did you say?" answered Floyd. "You must not mistake astonishment for regret. Think a moment, when last I saw you, I had to stoop to hold your hand or to pat you on the head; and now as we stand, your head is as high as my shoulder, and your heart is almost up to mine."

"Up to yours, indeed," said she, with a laugh; "my heart already appears to be a great way ahead of yours, judging by the length of time it takes you to recollect old friends."

"It is not the heart, but the head that is slow, my little lady," said he.

"The heart should then have quickened the head," said she; "I am sure mine would. And, besides, I am not a 'little lady' any longer, and you must not call me so; for I have a friend here who is smaller than I, and if you give me such a name, you will have none to call her by. Would you like to be shown to her—you who seem to think yourself such a giant?"

"Not now, Marion," said he, "one surprise of this sort will do for the present; and I am well enough satisfied with you, not to be off at once in search of pleasanter company. And so, laying aside this new scheme, and returning to the old one, can you give me some account of yourself during this long lapse of time, so that the history of your progress and adventures may, in some sort, accustom me to the full-grown woman, as you stand before me?"

"For that matter," replied she, "an account of my affairs is easily enough given. But before I begin I must positively introduce you to the little friend I spoke of. There now! don't object, for I insist upon it. She is small enough, and handsome enough, and dear enough, to make all your pleasant little diminutives proper when addressed to her."

Marion now went into the inner apartment, where she endeavored to persuade Lucile to come forth and meet her new, or rather her old acquaintance. She even rallied her on her shyness; setting forth in lively colors the handsome appearance and gracious manners of the young man, and jocosely hinting that it might be a fine occasion to lose her heart, if she had not managed to dispossess herself of that inconvenient commodity already. All these persuasions and rallyings, however, were fruitless. Lucile felt disinclined to the task of meeting strangers; and to the laborious care with which the barriers to acquaintanceship are usually taken down. She therefore persisted in her refusal to go out, so that Marion was at length compelled to leave her and to return alone.

"Where is this famous friend of yours, whose praise you trumpet forth so loudly?" said Floyd. "After all this flourish, is she to form no part in your little pageant?"

"She is afraid of you," answered Marion. "I suppose she heard what a severe critic you are upon people, and trembles lest she should n't pass muster. But, seriously speaking, I am afraid she is a little indisposed. She has been terribly frightened since we came here, and has not yet recovered from the shock."

"And pray what has occurred to alarm her?" asked the young man.

Marion here entered into a detail of the events already known to the reader. Her recital occupied some time. Floyd listened with much attention, and a growing interest. The circumstances were also sufficiently unusual, and, if related by strangers, sufficiently improbable to call forth some expressions of astonishment. When she had finished, he was silent for several minutes, endeavoring to find some solution of a tale so marvelous, and of characters by him hitherto unheard of. The effort was of course a fruitless one, and he soon gave it over in despair. Assuming a gayer humor, he asked,

"And pray Miss Belden, who is this Arthur, who has made himself such a hero, and whose name you mention with so much familiarity?"

"What, Arthur?" she answered, "and don't you really know who he is? Why he is—he is a very old friend of my father's—very indeed—though he is not so very old either."

While making this reply, Marion had hesitated and blushed, when she came to the place where she was about to state in what relation Arthur stood to herself. Though the fact was well known, she, for some cause or other just then, felt a repugnance to its reaching the ears of Floyd, and most especially from her own lips. Besides this, she was not entirely free from the shyness which almost all young persons feel on so delicate a subject. So that in her answer, as we have seen, she evaded the difficulty, and even gave a different coloring to the facts, transmuting the young man from an affianced lover of herself, simply to an ancient friend of her father. It is true that she had never before felt the same reluctance, to the truth being divulged on proper occasions. She had never disavowed it, and what was more, had never before avoided giving a frank and direct answer when interrogated on the subject. In the present instance, however, she urged to herself, that the fact could in no way concern Floyd;

and therefore she felt justified, not in concealing, but in omitting to disclose it. The simple truth was, that it was none of his business. This seemed plain enough, and ought to have been conclusive. But to her it was not. Her soul was candor itself, and the slightest shade of disingenuousness marred its clearness and its beauty like a cloud across the spotless sky. But to any other course she felt, at the moment, an invincible repugnance, not that Arthur in her judgment, was a person to be ashamed of. On the contrary, she thought him worthy to be mated with any one.

All these thoughts and feelings, meanwhile, occupied scarcely a moment of time. They were grouped in her mind, rather as a present consciousness than as a train of reflections.

"But," said Floyd, noticing Marion's slight hesitation, "telling me his name, and his Christian name at that, is not telling me who he is. I begin to suspect there is some mystery in it all, and that the lucky youth is also an old friend of yourself."

Marion was again a little confused, but managed to answer steadily:

"He is, in fact, what you suppose. And, I am sure, when you come to know him, you will like him as well as the rest of us. Lucile almost honored him with her love at sight."

"That must have been delightful," answered Floyd; "but, after all, I suppose the young man did have another name?"

"Well then," she answered, "as you are so impatient to know it, his name is Arthur Walcott."

"Arthur Walcott!" he exclaimed, while his countenance changed and he began to look a little grave. "And how, in the name of all that is unpleasant, has he become so intimate a friend of your family?"

"You seem to know him, then?" she answered, "but I do not like the tone in which you speak of him."

"Yes," he replied; "I have known him for a long time; or, to speak more correctly, I knew him a long time ago. To be frank, I do not wish to say any thing about him because—because, the fact is, we once had a little quarrel, and it ended in—

"Smoke," broke in Colonel Belden, who had heard that part of the conversation which referred to Walcott.

"Yes," answered the young man; "in smoke, as you say; but, to be plain, in the smoke of gunpowder, though neither of us was hurt."

"Oh, Richard!" exclaimed Marion, her old familiarity coming back with the emotion, "what could have induced you two to quarrel? He is all kindness and generosity, and would not so much as harm a cat, if he could help it."

"Maybe not," answered Floyd, "but I thought he had harmed me, notwithstanding. But from subsequent development I have since suspected it just possible that there may have been some misconception between us."

"Such was the fact, you may rest assured," said Colonel Belden. "But I suppose that you are aware that he has resigned?"

"Yes," said the other, "and gone into that rascally profession, the law."

"Look out how you speak in that way before him," said Marion, "or your words may end in smoke again."

"Well, since you wish it," the young man replied, "I will restrain my tongue a little, though I must say that for an active, able, brave young fellow as Walcott undoubtedly is, *or was*, to waste his life among cobwebs and pigeon-holes, strikes me as a sinful perversion of his qualities. And ever since I heard of his doing so, I have disliked to meet him, for I could not help thinking he had, in some sort, disgraced the army by his choice."

"Pooh! pooh! Dick," said Colonel Belden, familiarly; "you are altogether unreasonable about Walcott. He has never disgraced any body except his enemies, and, take my word for it, he has never injured you; and so you will confess before you get away, or I am much mistaken."

Here the conversation turned upon other topics, and an hour or so passed away agreeably to all parties.

CHAPTER XXI.

MR. VALCOUR.

If the reader will take the trouble to recollect, or, if he can not recollect, will be at the pains of turning back and referring to some of the incidents related near the commencement of this story, he will find that the first mischief attempted by wild Jacob was announced by a grayhound that had accompanied the party. Since the fright which the poor dog subsequently got from the crazy man, we have entirely overlooked his movements, or, rather, he has disappeared from our little drama.

At the time of these occurrences, Mr. Valcour, the father of Lucile, was, as has been already intimated, remaining at Ballston, then a place of much more frequent resort than Saratoga.

He had been too feeble to accompany his daughter on the little excursion with Colonel Belden's family, but had urged her to undertake it, thinking that it would be a source of much pleasure and healthful excitement. The day on which they started, had, with him, passed quietly over. He did not expect the immediate return of the party, and was, therefore, in no way disturbed when evening set in without their reappearance. Then some hours were passed by him, in conversation among his acquaintances, after which, and still early in the evening, he had retired to his chamber. The night was a quiet and peaceful one. Those who have, for the first time, found themselves in a retired country hamlet, surrounded by forest, will recollect the overwhelming sense of retirement and isolation from mankind which they experienced. There is something in the prevailing silence, and something more in the slight noises which pervade the air and enforce the notice of the senses, which awakes in the heart new and vivid emotions, refreshing to the jaded mind, and long retained in the memory. The little undulations which agitate the atmosphere, like pebbles or drops of rain falling into a still pond, only seem to create a more profound repose. At least, they give the suggestion of it.

To all these impressions the old man was susceptible. He enjoyed the sylvan scene from his open window. The moonlight, falling on dark green trees, ever a grateful and beautiful spectacle, was to him, at that moment, peculiarly pleasant. From his casement, which opened from a room next above the ground-floor, he could look out, and divide his glances between the shadowy earth below, and the effulgent sky above, studded as it was with pale stars. He paced his room, now and then, slowly pausing at intervals to enjoy that scene of singular repose and loveliness. Standing there, he could hear the low hum of insects, and catch the soft and delicate odor of wild flowers, arising from the blossoming world below, as the dew descended upon it.

As he was passing, and paused by the window, he fancied that he heard a new sound, distant, faint, and low—a sound still different from all the others which arose from the dwellings and the wilderness around him. He listened attentively; but it was not then repeated. He resumed his slow and meditative pace. When again he came along by the open casement, again did that far-off intonation break upon his ear. In a few moments it became more marked; and now it might be taken for the howl of some distant wolf, or for some other of the wild and melancholy sounds which at night sometimes disturb the solitudes of great forests.

Again it sounded forth; but whether from the old man's fancy or not, it seemed to have become more regular, and, if the expression may be pardoned, more humane and familiar than the coarse cry of a wolf, or the sharp wail of a panther.

Though still judging it to be of little or no account, Mr. Valcour, in his sentry-like pacing to and fro, and pausing, could not avoid attending to the ever-swelling and more sonorous outcry.

The little village, or rather hamlet, seemed to be wrapped in repose. No people were astir. In those primitive days, early hours both in retiring to rest and in rising from it, were practiced.

Becoming more and more interested in what he heard, he stationed himself at the window to get some solution of what perplexed him. After being there a short time, he could distinguish, and that plainly, as he thought, that the sound which had so echoed in the distance, and was now poured forth in melancholy sharpness upon the night air closer at hand, was neither more nor less than the prolonged bay or yelp of a hound. Besides, it seemed rapidly approaching; so that soon after, much to his astonishment, and somewhat to his alarm, he imagined that the sound itself was familiar to his ears, and that it was sent forth by his own dog, returning to him in this unwonted and ominous manner. This conjecture turned out to be correct; for in a few minutes after, he got sight of the animal approaching the house. Leaning out of the window, and calling to the dog by name, he saw the latter exhibit signs of recognition.

For the old man to descend and let his faithful follower into the dwelling, was but the work of a moment. When he returned to his room, he endeavored to ascertain by such marks as might be upon the quadruped, whether any, and what circumstance of an unusual character had taken place. In this, he was disappointed. The dog was panting, covered with dirt and moisture, and exhibited other signs of a long run and great fatigue; but there were no marks of violence, no spots of blood, torn skin, or wounded limbs, to indicate that any struggle had taken place. For all this he appeared to be but ill at ease; and though he answered to the caress of his master, and fawned upon him in his gladness; yet he would still walk restlessly about the room, whining piteously, and now and then scratching at the door. Then coming to the old man's side, he would again fawn upon him, and look wistfully into his face. From this he would sometimes turn quickly and walk to the door, looking back, as if he sought to lead the way, and wanted to be followed.

To all these signs the old man was most attentive. He puzzled his brain with useless conjectures, and with more useless apprehensions. A dog is accounted the most faithful of followers—the most reliable and incorruptible of friends; and for what cause this one had thus apparently abandoned his mistress, seemed indeed a mystery. It was not in the nature of the animal to tire of the woods; and it was hardly a possibility that it could have got lost. Could it have wearied of the unenterprising society of ladies, with whom there was but little activity, and no hunting? But then, what was the meaning of those prolonged and mournful howls, which thus, in the depths of night, had heralded its return? What forebodings of instinct, what subtle and instinctive sense of misfortune, had awakened the apprehensions of the poor brute, that he should come thus in the darkness, to announce the mystery to those who might feel interest in its solution?

Mr. Valcour had seen too many vicissitudes in the course of a long life, had been accustomed to too many false alarms and empty premonitions of evil, easily to give way to a sense of unknown calamity. In the present case, however, it was more than himself that he felt to be concerned. His daughter, more precious to his heart than his own life—than all his earthly or future hopes—might be threatened with, or surrounded by dangers, from which the humble energies of a poor dog would be powerless to relieve her, but might not be entirely useless in summoning aid. Long and painfully, and with nervous uneasiness, did the old man ponder on the circumstance.

As yet, he called upon no friend. He thought that his fears might be looked upon as idle, and treated with ridicule, by others not so deeply interested as himself. Still he resolved, on the next morning, if no information arrived, to seek out an explanation by some personal effort. He determined, in that event, to set forth himself; and, even if he had no attendance, to find out his daughter, and assure himself of her safety.

With these resolutions, though with many misgivings, he, at last, sought repose. Sleep, however, to the aged, comes slowly, and lingers reluctantly. Hours on hours passed away without his closing his eyes. The lethargy of age, is not such as to soothe the brain or hush the nerves to quiet. Dull wakefulness haunted the old man on his uneasy couch, like a black-winged phantom, ever brushing his eyelids as they drooped in forgetfulness; and adding coherence to his thoughts, as they sought to mingle in unconnected confusion. Thus uneasily did he lie and toss on his fevered bed of anxiety.

Rosy morning, with its bright and virgin blush, was already crimsoning the east, before full forgetfulness rested upon the troubled spirit of the old man. Then indeed, the wand of sleep would seem to have been waved over him, and to have dropped its dew of repose upon his eyelids. Slumber, that sister of Death, as called and sung by the classic poets, then sat beside his couch, and like a watchful nurse, smoothed his pillow and quieted his uneasy spirit.

Morning came with its wide-spread, pale light. Birds and bees awoke to labor and to song. Sun rays stole under thickly-boughed trees and through closely-drawn curtains. Men and other animated creatures walked abroad. And in the full career of the new-born cycle of light and life, did the old man again awake, unrefreshed by sleep and unsoothed by temporary forgetfulness.

CHAPTER XXII.

JOE IN PERIL.

When Walcott and his two associates, Catfoot and M'Carty, started, for the second time, in pursuit of Jacob, they at first supposed that he might have got back into the cave. Knowing his violence, and the little restraint which even beauty, youth and innocence could exercise upon him, they had but small expectation of finding poor Joe alive. Still the conceits of a crazy man are so erratic—so out of the ordinary course of thought—his conduct is governed by motives so peculiar and incalculable, that all speculation as to what had been done, in the present case, was entirely idle.

As it was now daylight, they had, at first, but little difficulty in following the trail. It did not point or lead to the cave, but kept away to the eastward and southward. From this circumstance they supposed it not unlikely that the fugitive had betaken himself to his old haunt on the brink of the Kayaderosseras valley. In this hypothesis it soon appeared that they were correct. In the course of about an hour they came into the vicinity of that place. Before proceeding further they paused to listen, judging that Jacob, following his usual habit, would, if engaged in mischief, be noisy and uproarious enough to be heard. Having waited, however, for some time without hearing the expected sounds, it was determined to proceed. When they arrived near to the copse, in the midst of which was Jacob's place of abode, Catfoot, by a light touch on the arm, arrested the steps of Walcott, and, pointing forward over the tree-tops, showed a column of smoke rising slowly above the place. It was not a usual thing for Jacob to have a fire there, and especially at that hour in the day. Something remarkable, therefore, was, in all probability, taking place. Could it be possible that he was roasting his unfortunate prisoner alive? In that case some outcry of pain would be heard. And, supposing the prisoner already dead, what cannibal thoughts might be entertained by the maniac? It was shocking to imagine, as well as useless.

So far all was still, and that tall, white, silent, spectral column of smoke seemed to add to the profound hush of the scene. Catfoot was now detailed to move forward and reconnoiter. He dropped softly upon the ground, and, by a rapid and stealthy movement, disappeared beneath the bushes in the direction of the spot over which the smoke arose. Walcott and M'Carty, in the meanwhile, remained perfectly quiet where they stood. It was desirable, not only to prevent any evil which Jacob might contemplate doing to poor Joe, in case it was not already done, but also to secure the person of so dangerous a character to prevent the recurrence of events like those which had recently taken place. For this reason Walcott was proceeding with unusual caution. He knew well that unless he could come suddenly upon him, and in such a way as to render escape difficult, if not impossible, Jacob would burst away from them on being discovered. To pursue, with any hope of overtaking him in a direct chase, was out of the question.

For some time after Catfoot had disappeared beneath the underbrush his two expectant companions heard nothing from him. The smoke still rose above the trees, showing its high column sometimes white and thin, and sometimes heavy and dark, as if wet or fresh fuel was added to the fire from which it sprung. The air, meanwhile, was so motionless that the tall vapor shaft generally seemed nearly perpendicular, and only waved or oscillated in various directions, as a suspended rope will swing with the lightest breath of wind in a still atmosphere.

This extreme quiet rendered it more likely that if Jacob was astir and anywhere near at hand he would soon be heard from. After waiting with patience for a long time Walcott began to think that he was taking unnecessary pains, and that it might all be for nothing. He was on the point of moving forward upon the suspected spot to ascertain directly how affairs stood, when suddenly the Indian re-appeared, and, by a sign, gave them to understand that they should follow him. He went to the right of the course at first taken, as if he intended to turn the position supposed to be occupied by Jacob, and the others followed him with as much silence and caution as possible. After creeping along for some distance they came to the brow of the hill, and passing over it, Catfoot changed his course to the left, and then moved directly toward the place whence the smoke arose.

Where they then were, the hill was exceedingly steep, rough and rocky, and it was with no little difficulty that they made their way forward. The crest of the hill was sharp, like the angle of a wall, and they were careful to keep so far below it, that any person on the upper level, and a short distance back could not see them. Proceeding in this manner, it was not long before they came, as they imagined, within a short distance of the fire, the smoke of which had attracted their attention. They could, in fact, hear its crackling, as dried sticks and twigs seemed to be heaped upon it. The odor of smoke, and the peculiar bitter vegetable smell of burning leaves, now also became perceptible. It was evidently necessary that they should exercise greater care than ever. Keeping close together, what little communication took place between them, was more by looks and signs than by words.

At length they reached a spot where above them, and fringing the edge of the declivity, was a thick line of overhanging bushes. Catfoot thrust these cautiously aside, and disclosed to the others the view beyond.

In the centre of the open space there, was a circle of dried sticks and brush. At one point this was already in flames. In the midst of this circle and securely lashed to a stake driven in the ground, was poor Joe, for whom they were so anxiously looking. Singularly enough, he seemed more indifferent to passing events than they, for he neither moved or spoke; and on a closer inspection, it was discovered that he either was, or feigned to be fast asleep. With the characteristic stoicism of his race, he had witnessed the preparations for his destruction, with the coolness and apparent disregard, which are generated by constitutional phlegm, or a sense of fatality. The meaning of all that had been done around him, he well understood. He felt himself to be a legitimate object of Jacob's vengeance; and now having fallen into his power, he expected nothing less than death, and was in no way surprised at the manner in which it was likely to take place. Like a sentenced convict, therefore, he could, and did sleep soundly, the hour before his execution.

The fire had not yet sufficiently advanced to disturb him by its heat. To a looker on, however, the sight was an appalling one. The young man was eager to rush forward and release the victim at once; but the Indian, more prudent, still restrained him. Up to this time they had seen nothing of Jacob. This doubtless, was the cause of Catfoot's hesitation. But they had not to wait long for him. In a few moments, he was discovered stealthily entering the bushy inclosure from the opposite side, bearing in his arms a quantity of dried bush and sticks, with which to feed the growing fire. Fortunately the fuel, hitherto, had burned but slowly, or the arrival of Walcott and his companions might have been too late. Jacob seemed fully aware of the condition of his victim; and went about preparing the fiery surprise with which he should be awakened, with the same air as that with which school-children play a trick upon a sleeping companion. Moving about on tip-toe, while his eyes sparkled with ferocious joy, he would take the burning brands from one place, to dispose them in another, in such a manner that the fire would communicate more rapidly, and burn more brightly. The fresh armful which he brought was added to the circular pile.

The affair was growing critical, and Walcott was growing more impatient than ever to rush forward at any hazard, in order to save the prisoner from the painful death which so nearly awaited him. He was still, however, restrained by the phlegmatic Indian at his side. Meanwhile, poor Joe, lashed securely to the stake, still slept on, apparently as securely and as sweetly, as a young infant upon the protecting bosom of its mother.

Before interfering, Catfoot seemed waiting for some decisive event. When Jacob had got all the wood arranged to his mind, he stepped toward the thick brush behind which his pursuers lay concealed, and took from beneath a log, a long sharp stake which seemed to have been prepared for the occasion, and which to all appearance was about to be used as an instrument of torture or as a skewer, upon the body of the poor victim. By this time the fire had considerably increased, and the thick smoke which arose from it, mingling with Joe's breath, and the growing heat beginning to affect his naked limbs, he at last awoke.

In his first glance around, there was perceptible the startled look of fear. In an instant after, however, his countenance, which had thus been momentarily disturbed, like a surface of water ruffled by a flaw of wind, settled back, and became quiet and stolid as before. All this Jacob had closely watched, and now that his prisoner was awake and seemingly prepared for whatever might happen, he burst forth loudly in his peculiar and dissonant laughter.

"So ho!" he shouted, "so ho! my fine red bullock! You begin to warm up at last do you? You're not quite ready for the first turn, or I'd give ye a touch of my fork," (here he gave a flourish to the huge stake he bore in his hands). "But wait till you are a little soft on one side like a roast potato, and then I'll jist prick you a little to let out the steam. So! ho! You are nearly ready now are you?"

As he finished this he did in fact move toward the fire, balancing and pointing his formidable toasting fork, as if he was then ready to put his threat into execution. The poor wretch within the fiery circle, gave one rapid glance around, to see if there was yet left him the least chance of relief or escape. None appeared.

Catfoot now silently thrusting aside the bushes in front of him, indicated by a sign to Walcott that he should pass through. This was instantly done. The young man then stepped quickly forward, and just as Jacob had drawn back his powerful arm to pierce the body of his victim with the weapon he carried, Walcott's hand was laid upon his shoulder. The crazy man turned fiercely upon his interrupter, but his eye quailed before the bold determined glance which was bent upon him; his arm dropped, and his whole manner at once became pacific and submissive.

"Mr. Whittaker," said Walcott, "you have carried on this jest long enough. You must not frighten people any more in this way, or by-and-by, they may think you are in earnest. Catfoot," he continued, turning to his companions, "you and M'Carty had better take Joe out of the fire while I have some private conversation with my friend Whittaker here."

This last direction was quite unnecessary, for the two men were already engaged upon the task indicated. Meanwhile, the condition of poor Joe had become critical indeed. While the smoke had grown almost suffocating, the fire itself was beginning to scorch and blister his naked skin. Though he uttered no cry or complaint, and though pride, or obstinacy, or aboriginal superstition, thus sealed his lips, all manifestation of fear and agony could not be suppressed. The scorched flesh quivered, and the fixedness of despair shone in his eye. The arrival of Walcott upon the scene did not entirely reassure him; for Walcott he now regarded as his mortal enemy;

and he looked for no forbearance or kindness at his hands. It was not until the other two men had kicked aside the firebrands around him, and cut the thongs which bound him, that he began to recover hope, and to believe in the reality of his rescue.

Fortunately no great evil had yet been done. With the exception of a little blistering, he found himself so far unscathed. But his limbs were stiff from long confinement; while he was so astounded by his sudden and unexpected release, that for a moment he stood like a man who had fallen asleep, and awoke in another world.

Meanwhile, Walcott did not for a single instant, leave the side of his prisoner; and scarcely did he even turn away his look from him. It was a sort of moral chain by which he kept him fettered. This time he was determined to make sure work, and to allow no escape. The transaction which he had just interrupted, was a sufficient warning against any future negligence, and showed the impropriety and the danger of allowing such a creature any longer to remain at large.

As yet, poor Joe continued to be almost helpless. The reaction of his sudden escape united to the stiffness of his limbs, through which the arrested blood had hardly yet resumed its circulation, rendered him weak and faint to such a degree that he sat down upon a stone hard by, to recover both his thoughts and his strength.

"M'Carty," said Walcott, "be good enough to bring me some of those cords, and some fresh bark. I perceive, sir," he continued, turning to Jacob, "that you have been slightly hurt. We will just put a fresh dressing on the wound, and it will then, doubtless, soon get better."

Jacob's leg was, in fact, just below the knee, already

rudely bandaged up with bark and thongs. The injury had been caused by the bullet fired at him by Joe. The two men soon came up, bearing the required articles. Jacob looked foolish enough, as he regarded his wounded leg, and saw the toils in which he was taken; but as, in furtive glances he every now and then kept watch for an opportunity to escape, there would momentarily shine, in his restless eyes, a baleful and malignant light. But with the hand of Walcott resting firmly upon his shoulder, and his gaze rivetted steadily upon his face, as if to read his intentions, and to be ready to thwart them, the crazy man gave way to the moral force which enveloped him, as a caged lion will refrain from struggling with the unyielding bars of his iron prison.

"Mr. Whittaker," said the young man, at length, "now that you are getting reasonable, let me call your attention to these friends of mine. I believe you have met them before. They will assist me in dressing your wound; and after that, will accompany us to some place where you can be better cared for. Be good enough to sit down on this log for a few moments, while we see what is the matter."

To this request Jacob yielded a reluctant compliance. While the others stood behind, Walcott, stooping down in front, quickly removed the rough binding in which the injured leg was swàthed.

The wound turned out to be more serious than was supposed. The ball had gone quite through the calf of the leg; not indeed so as to touch the bone, or to cut any of the large blood-vessels or tendons, but still so as to make a rough hole through the flesh, which, by this time, had become much irritated and swollen. To judge from appearances, it must have been very painful, especially when Jacob was moving about.

"The wound will have to be probed, I am afraid," said Walcott, looking up, "to ascertain whether or not the ball is lodged inside. The operation will be a very painful one; and it will be necessary for the moment, to tie your arms, Whittaker, so that you can not move while I am engaged. Otherwise, you may interfere with me, you know. You understand, M'Carty?" and Walcott gave the latter a significant look.

"Oh! as for that," broke in Jacob, "I don't mind a scratch. You may cut the leg off if you like. It would be rather pleasant, just by way of variety, you know. Ha! ha! Don't you think so?"

"I do not think so," replied Walcott, "nor do you; and I beg you not to make any more such childish remarks."

In the mean time, the two other men had secured Jacob's hands behind him, and bound them strongly with the cord they had brought. So far so good. The next thing would be, still under pretext of the wounded leg, so to encumber both legs as to prevent him from giving them the slip by running away. Walcott again set himself to examine the injury, and soon discovered, what he had all along supposed, namely, that the ball had passed entirely through. There was thus no occasion for probing. He then caused some fresh plantain-leaves to be pulled; then bruising or mixing them with the soft inner rind of elm bark, he made a kind of mucilaginous poultice, which he applied to the injury. This was bound fast; and over all and around the leg, were lashed a number of splints, intended both to keep the dressing in its place, and to prevent Jacob from running. The latter submitted to all these operations in silence. He was not so wild as to be the dupe of so many pretended cares for his welfare; but he was still overawed, and by some potent moral force, fascinated when being, as he was now, in the immediate presence, and beneath the eye of Walcott.

CHAPTER XXIII.

THE SWORD *vs.* THE GOWN.

"WHY, Dick," said Colonel Belden to his young friend, for he and Floyd were now walking together, at some distance from the hut, "I am sorry to hear you express any ill feeling toward Walcott, and especially against the profession he has chosen."

"Perhaps I am wrong," replied Floyd, "in even hinting any thing against him personally; for, except that we have been in some sort rivals, I don't know but I like him well enough after all. But then, to be a lawyer! Why, colonel, you yourself must think *that* quite inexcusable!"

"On the contrary, sir," said the old man, "on the contrary, I think it the best profession he could have chosen, under the circumstances. Military men are apt, I know, to entertain a poor opinion of legal gentlemen; but take my word for it, there is no good reason for the prejudice. It may be caused by the fact that their duties and occupations are widely different, and each estimates the importance of the other by reference to proficiency in his own calling. While they judge by this rule, it is not surprising that a very considerable degree of mutual contempt should exist between them."

"You don't mean," said Floyd, "to set up for one of their apologists, do you?"

"Certainly not for one of their apologists," answered the other, "nor do I think they need any. So far as talk goes, they are quite able to take care of themselves—a thing which can not always be said of your trade, Dick. And I am also free to observe that, so far as my experience goes, that profession which you seem to hold in so much dislike, comprises in reality a greater proportion of high-minded men, than almost any other. If one of them happens to be a defaulter or a rogue, we never hear the last of it. And this very fact goes to prove the truth of what I say; for dishonesty here would not be accompanied by so much outcry, and followed by such universal execration, were it not that it comes from an unexpected quarter. Half the fortunes in the country are daily entrusted to the care and integrity of these very men of whom you think so poorly, or at least, of whom you speak so lightly."

"Still, sir," answered Floyd, "you confess that they do, now and then, turn out a scamp or so?"

"Just as the army turns out a coward, or the church a hypocrite, and no more. What I claim for the lawyers, is, not that they are naturally more honest than others, for no such distinction can be taken in favor of any class, but that the very nature of their profession is one of trust and confidence—one in which integrity is a necessary ingredient. A lawyer without it, would as soon lose his practice, as an officer without courage would lose his rank."

"But still, sir," persisted Floyd, "what is the reason that such a prejudice exists against them? Can there be all this smoke without any fire?"

"There is no such prejudice except among the ignorant;

or, you will excuse me for saying so, among those, who, like yourself, have had no proper experience, and have not sufficiently reflected upon the subject. It certainly is as honorable to plead for a cause as to fight for it. But, you say, a lawyer advocates the claims of his clients, right or wrong. Suppose it is so. Does the soldier, when he goes into battle, stop to inquire whether his country be in the right or the wrong? If a comparison must be instituted between the two, I should say that it was infinitely more honorable and ennobling, for a reasonable being to advocate a cause—grant it for argument's sake to be a wrong one—by an appeal to the judgment of mankind, than to endeavor to advance it by violence and brute force. Do not mistake me; I have no disposition to depreciate my own profession, but I wish to exhibit, in the most palpable light, the injustice of the prejudices which you seem to have imbibed upon the subject."

"I must confess, sir," said Floyd, after a moment's reflection, "that you have presented the question in an aspect which to me, is entirely new."

"Depend upon it, my young friend," replied the colonel, "the more you think upon the subject, the more will your views accord with mine. The soldier is well in his place. In times of war and danger, he is the bulwark and safeguard of his country. But even in our late war, we can but confess that such men as Henry, Jefferson, Lee and Jay, did as much by their eloquence and wisdom, as any four of our best generals did by their military skill. Yet these men were all lawyers; as were also Hamilton and a host of others, who were the very pillars of the Revolution. Let me say, Dick, that you never should be guilty of ridiculing or denouncing a profession which has rendered such men illustrious, or in which so much genius has been displayed."

"But, sir," still persisted Floyd, "I am not speaking of such men, but of the common run of lawyers, who have always appeared to me to be a mean-spirited, knavish, pettifogging set."

"I don't know where you got your experience, then, for the simple fact is otherwise. Knaves there certainly are among them, and fools too, for that matter. You can not expect every man in the ranks to be fit for a general; nor can you look for a Mansfield in every poor lawyer whom lack of practice has driven into a garret, or whom poverty has forced to seek for clients among the wretched and insolvent. If he sometimes pleads the cause of a rogue, it only shows that the rogue has succeeded in getting a person better and more respectable than himself to speak on his behalf before a hostile community, or to keep him in countenance before his accusers, so that the reins of justice, in the excitement of the moment, may not be drawn too tightly. But I do not intend to go at length into all the questions which may arise in this connection. You ought to have learned by this time that men, in masses, are always alike, and that no necessary and proper calling in life is to be despised."

"Well," replied Floyd, "I may not, perhaps, *despise*, but still I may *dislike* them."

"You *may* do either of these things if you see fit, but you can do neither with justice. A little impartial reflection will convince you that in a community which professes to be governed by law, those who understand it, are the ones to administer it, and, to that extent, are among the props of society; for law, without its proper enforcement is but a useless array of rules. Who are the men that you look to to fill public stations, to be conservators of the peace, members of legislative bodies, the incumbents of administrative and executive offices? Are they not generally lawyers? And without them, how could it be possible, for legislators especially, to get along? You may depend upon it, sir, I am not putting this thing in too strong a light. I am only presenting to you the plain truth, which, it would seem to me, ought to be quite obvious to every man who undertakes to think upon the subject. And yet, my dear fellow, you talk of disliking or looking down upon this profession! It seems to me that such sentiments are very unjust and ill-considered. But we are quite forgetting ourselves in this discussion. I only hope you will think better of Arthur and his calling hereafter. Meanwhile, let us return toward the house to see how they are all getting on there."

"To say truth," answered Floyd, as they moved in the direction indicated, "I begin to feel a little ashamed of my boyish expressions on the subject we have been talking about, and I trust, if you have found my opinions open to some comment, you will not, at least, find me indisposed to correct them. I shall certainly avoid giving offense to Walcott by any reflections upon his present course of life."

"You will confer a favor upon me by not doing so," replied Colonel Belden; "and when you come to look at the subject as I have presented it, and to understand Walcott's position, you will find him to be still a man with feelings as high and honor as bright as if he could yet strut through a camp, or swagger and swear at the head of a squadron of dragoons."

CHAPTER XXIV.

REVELATIONS

In a few moments the group which had attracted Brigham's attention emerged into more open ground, and proved to be, as had been supposed, Walcott, returning with his companions and his prize. They had been compelled to move slowly, as had also been conjectured, in consequence of the bandaged condition of Jacob's injured leg—a condition more attributable, however, to their fears of his escape, than to their anxiety for his welfare.

The sun was already behind the western woods, and the men came on slowly in the gathering shadows. All were silent, either from fatigue, or from being busy with personal reflections.

"And so you've got the critter this time, have ye?" said Brigham, who had gone out to meet them at some distance from the cabin; "had much of a time on't, Jim?"

"None in partic'lar," answered M'Carty, the person addressed; "in fact, rayther a dull affair for all, 'cept Joe here, who came nigh on having a warm spell on't."

Brigham now, for the first time, observed Joe, who was following on in silence, and who, as usual, showed no signs of the feelings with which recent events had inspired him, either upon his countenance or in his manner.

The old soldier and pioneer knew, or thought he knew, the nature of an Indian, and did not, therefore, argue because Joe was quiet, and had assumed his customary manner, that he had forgotten his late feelings of resentment against Walcott. He saw that he kept constantly near to him, and to Jacob. It looked suspicious to his experienced eye; and he resolved not only to watch the savage, but to put the young man again upon his guard. In the course of the walk to the house, he learned the circumstances which had taken place during the early part of the day, in connection with the recapture of the lunatic. In spite of his knowledge of Indian life, he could not, with his own white-man's feelings, help thinking, that if Joe still meditated upon revenge, after what had happened, he must be a devil incarnate. Still no trust was to be put in appearances. And again, why did he hang so closely upon Walcott's footsteps?

On their arrival Colonel Belden greeted the young man with unusual warmth. A serious portion of their difficulties had at length been surmounted. The maniac was secured, and no doubt, with Walcott's co-operation and activity, all things could be put in such train, that they could extricate themselves from their present dilemma, and return to some place where the comforts and care of civilized society could be obtained for the now suffering Lucile. He made the young man speedily acquainted with her illness, and was not a little astonished at the evidence of deep concern which he exhibited.

Meanwhile Brigham accompanied the Indian, Catfoot, for a short distance on his way from the cabin to the village of huts up in the forest.

"Catfoot," said he, "what do you think of Joe?"

The other paused for some time and then said:

"Joe been sick—got well now."

"But," said Brigham, "do you think he'll try any more of his tricks against the captain? Because, you see, I'll have nothing more of the sort done about my primises!"

"Joe no kill—no shoot cap'n now," was the reply of the Indian.

"I hope you're right, old fellow," said Brigham. "But what makes the varmint stick so clus to his heels all the while?"

"Jake there," said Catfoot.

"May be you're right, arter all," said Brigham slowly and thoughtfully; "may be the critter has got human feelin's and wants to help the cap'n keep that wild devil fast."

Pausing for a time, Brigham at length continued: "Catfoot you and I are old friends. I won't thank you for what's been done, but you know that whenever you're in want of anything, and I've got it, or whenever you'd like me to help shoot deer, or any other varmint, I'm your man; and so, good-night."

"Good," said the Indian gravely; and the two separated.

Brigham walked thoughtfully back to his cabin. There he found M'Carty and Joe. The latter unaccountably seemed bent on staying, instead of resorting to his own hut, which was at no great distance.

"So Joe," said Brigham, as he approached, "I hear you had a pretty tight time on't? You must be tol-'able hungry by this time. Suppose we have a bite together."

Brigham then caused to be produced a platter of cold meats, upon which the three men fell to work with their sheath-knives, and did good execution.

The evening by this time was closing in. For a while the men ate in silence. When their hunger was a little appeased, M'Carty said:

"What has happened down here while we was gone? For I see lots of folks down thar at the spring, a makin' a time."

"Nothin'," said Brigham, "but a party over from Schuyler's on a lark. One on 'em, though, is an old acquaintance of mine, Dick Floyd. I knowed him as long ago as '77. He and the old colonel too, was mighty thick. But talkin' of the colonel, he's been oneasy on account of the little French gal, all day; and a wishin' for the cap'n, as you call him, to come back."

"And what's the matter with the gal?" asked M'Carty.

"That's mor'n I can tell," replied Brigham. "She's been in the dumps all the morning in consekens, I suppose, of the troubles yesterday; but this afternoon they've been a talkin' of fever, and what not. Hows'ever, I ain't seen her, and so can't speak for sartain."

Having finished the meal, which Brigham had shared with them more from hospitality than appetite, they rose up. Joe, now for the first time breaking silence, asked:

"Where cap'n?"

"What do you want to see him for now?" asked Brigham.

"No matter," was the reply; "want him, bad."

"Well," said Brigham, "it's seldom a natyve speaks; but to give the devil his due, I'll say this for him, that when he does speak, he generally makes short work on it and has a meanin' to it. So I'll jest say a word to Walcott for ye, to see what'll come on't."

Brigham accordingly went into the cabin to call forth Walcott. When the latter appeared, Joe said:

"Pretty squaw sick, eh? Know what matter? Joe make well."

"You make her well, Joe?" said Walcott. "I wish you could, my good fellow; but I'm afraid you can do nothing."

"Make Joe see squaw, eh?" persisted the savage.

Walcott looked around inquiringly at Brigham, who nodded his head, saying: "It'll do no harm, and I've knowed him to do a deal of good, afore now, though it was in the case of a rheumatis."

In accordance with this opinion, Walcott took the Indian into the cabin; more, however, be it confessed, to comply with the prevailing humor, than from any expectation of good to result from it.

A few moments afterward, Marion came out of the inner room to request Walcott himself to enter. They found the poor sufferer in a pitiable plight. The apartment itself was rude and uncomfortable for one as delicately bred as she was. The pallet where she lay, was in one corner. The yellow light of a tallow candle, which was stuck up in a block of wood, fell upon the flushed and agitated features of the invalid, as she lay there, moaning and restless. At the moment, she was in a state of partial stupor, and did not open her eyes. The Indian had placed himself to examine her appearance, with all imaginable gravity. For a few seconds he held her little white, delicate hand within his own, swarthy from race, and hardened by exposure. It was as if a lily should lay within a cup of bronze. He held it however, but for a moment, and the act seemed to answer the same purpose as the feeling of the pulse—a modern professional accomplishment utterly unknown to this doctor of nature. While that pale, diminutive, untrembling hand had thus for a moment remained in his own, the rude savage, as he bent his harsh brown features over it, seemed to become half-conscious of the vast gulf which separated that refined and delicate organization from his own. No emotion, however, disturbed his features; and but for a single second, was there a puzzled, amazed, admiring look in his dark eyes. He then dropped the hand gently, as one would lay down a piece of delicate workmanship; and turning around, he said to Walcott:

"Joe go now cure him right off, by-and-by."

With this very definite assurance as to the time when his miraculous performance was to be finished, he left the apartment, followed by Walcott, who endeavored to extract from him what he really proposed to do. But his efforts in that direction signally failed, for Joe was as silent as the door-post, and probably would have been quite as unable to explain the mystery of his practice, if he had tried. Leave the building, however, he did, immediately, as if to carry out his purpose, whatever it might be. Walcott, in despair, thought that it would only end in some unmeaning mummery or Indian exorcism; and began almost to regret that he had given consent to the interference of the savage at all. The astute Brigham himself was not a little puzzled. Never hitherto had he known an Indian to become reconciled to his enemy; and, therefore, was he inclined to look with suspicion upon all proceedings by Joe which might affect Walcott or his friends.

After the sick room had been vacated by the men, Marion again returned thither. She sat down by the side of the low couch where the unconscious patient lay. The latter was moaning in her half sleep; but as Marion took her hand, though it was ever so gently, she awoke with a start.

"Was he not here just now?" she said.

"Was not who here just now?" asked Marion as she smoothed the pillow, and sought to compose and caress the prostrate girl.

"He—Arthur," answered Lucile; "I thought he came in to tell me that that horrid man should not come near me any more. Oh! if he would only stay by me, I should not be afraid—and I should be so happy! Oh! so happy!"

And as she spoke thus, clasping her hands, Marion observed that, though her eyes shone with the unnatural light of fever and delirium, they nevertheless filled with tears; showing that after moments of agony and alarm, gentle influences, like ministering angels, surrounded her heart.

"Shall I tell him to come here again, dearest, and stay by you?" she asked.

"Hush! not for the world!" she replied; "do you know I have no right to have him by me? He is so good, so brave, and has done so much for me; but he belongs to Marion, and he can never be mine. Never! never! But—it is a great secret, and you must not tell—I love him! Do you hear? I love him! What do you think of that? I could not tell him for the world. He loves dear Marion so! Oh! gracious heaven!" she exclaimed, as a wild shriek or howl was now suddenly heard near the cabin, "there is that fearful man again! Oh! call him! call Arthur or I shall die of fear!"

As she uttered this, she rose and sat upon the couch. Her eye was unnaturally lustrous with fear and fever combined. Marion herself became alarmed. She went to the door, and finding Walcott in the outer apartment, beckoned him to enter. As he was approaching, Marion said to the invalid:

"Here is Mr. Walcott, dear; he will keep Jacob away, you know. You need not be afraid now, but you can lie down and sleep quietly again."

As the poor girl gazed at the young man, a half consciousness seemed to return to her; and while her face flushed to a deeper crimson than fever had painted upon it, she lay quietly back upon her couch, still keeping her eyes turned upon him, as if to make sure that she was not deluded, and as if fearful that if she should lose him from her sight, he would flit away.

The case had become serious. Here was a delicate girl, away from her immediate relatives, a prey to an unknown but violent febrile attack, and no medical assistance was to be had. Moreover, they were in a rude hut, in the midst of an inhospitable wilderness, and could not command any of the comforts to which she had been accustomed, or even the commonest appliances of a sick room. She might die for lack of timely remedies. Upon whom then would the responsibility fall?

But aside from these considerations, it may well be imagined that the young man was not in a very enviable frame of mind. He felt himself affected by deeper emotions than might have been called up by the reflections we have mentioned. Aside from this, his position was in every way embarrassing. He had, by degrees, become fully conscious of the true nature of his new-born feelings toward the poor sufferer, who was thus calling for his presence, and claiming his protection. The appeal touched a chord in the deepest recesses of his manly nature. Gallantry, generosity, chivalry, admiration, pity and affection, all chained him to the task of consolation and relief. But on the other hand, he was a man of honor; and not for the world, by any consultation of his own feelings merely, would he hazard an act or voluntarily indulge a thought, which could be regarded as a violation of his plighted faith.

As for Marion Belden, she had been so astounded by the unexpected disclosure of Lucile—it had come upon her in the midst of so many other things which required her attention—that she had hardly yet made up her mind whether what had been divulged was one of the wandering vagaries of fever, or whether it lay deeper than the sudden attack, and was one of its causes.

It was not long before Lucile, being quieted by the presence of Walcott, and apparently assured of his watchfulness, fell again into an uneasy sleep. Beside the couch also stood Marion; and those two young people who had so long considered themselves as affianced man and wife, were thus called upon to watch over one whose principal source of suffering, might be the knowledge of that very engagement. Arthur himself felt abashed and embarrassed. The nature of his thoughts could not, of course, be divined by Marion; but he was still afraid, lest by some unguarded act, the deep interest which he felt in the invalid might become apparent.

Marion had, in the mean while, gradually grown thoughtful. She knew—at least she felt sure—that nothing could have been done by Walcott to foster the love of her friend. If she had been disposed to doubt it, the very language of Lucile would have proved it. It was also plain that Lucile would not voluntarily have done any thing to encourage such a sentiment in her own heart.

Still, there were to be remembered the great and numerous perils to which she had been exposed, and from which Arthur had rescued her; and it was easy to divine how gratitude, when so great and absorbing, might unconsciously be changed into a warmer feeling.

Marion was, therefore, inclined to believe that the few wild words of the sick girl were something more than the wanderings of a disturbed brain, and that they had, in reality, given the true picture of a loving, but remorseful heart. Strange to say, she did not feel herself indignant at the thought. She imagined that it was her compassion which absorbed all other emotions, and prevented jealousy from rising in rebellion against the competitor for the love of her betrothed. And then when she thought of the deep affliction into which the blameless Lucile was now plunged, and of the long years of misery which might follow her unhappy passion, she felt that she herself could sacrifice something to prevent it; that she could give up the love and the plighted faith of Arthur to secure so much good.

And yet, was this the feeling of a genuine love? Still did she ponder profoundly, and in deep abstraction, till by degrees, like the dawn of a summer day, the light of a new truth arose upon her mind; and that truth was, that she herself *did not love Arthur!*

There was joy in the discovery; but was there not also

misery? What of Arthur? Could his affection be thus easily slighted, and cast off? The chain which had bound the two was a double one. What though that which she supposed to bind her own heart was discovered to be ruptured, was not the other one still unbroken, and linked forever to the heart of her lover? It was distressful to think of; and she could not for an instant indulge in the thought of sundering the bonds which allied her to him. The idea of his affection was almost a tradition; and for years it had been handed down to her, as a truth as well established as holy writ. She did not doubt it; and she could never seek to shun the effect of it; and yet, from time to time, did she detect herself in the half formed wish, that her last construction of Lucile's words might be the true one, and that Arthur might be won to reciprocate the affection which they implied.

Strange human heart! Whence could arise such a wish, or rather, whence could come the remote suggestion of such a thought? Was no other image mingled with the pictures which her fancy was passing before her mind? Yet she strove to think how generous it would be in herself, were it possible, to be instrumental in bringing consolation to the desponding heart of her friend—how noble to contribute to her happiness by a sacrifice.

But on the other hand, it might be all delusion. She must wait and watch. She must be sure; but when once sure, how would she prepare for the dear Lucile such a delightful surprise—such a glorious self-sacrifice! Yes; she must watch and be sure. And Arthur—he must not be deceived. She must learn whether he could consent to such a new disposition. Ah! generous and noble Arthur! He must be thought of as well.

So did the kind and really unselfish girl think and reason. If any personal consideration mingled with her thoughts, she knew it not.

Meanwhile, she sat down beside the bed, preparing to note each unguarded word which the sleeper might whisper in her dreams. She did not regard herself as establishing an improper espionage into the secret thoughts of her friend; but she rather felt herself to be a kind physician who sets himself to study the type and character of the disease he seeks to cure.

Beckoning Walcott to come near, she, in a whisper, requested him to go out, and quiet Jacob, who, maddened by confinement, had become loud and frantic in his outcry, and whose shouts threatened, at each moment, to reawaken the sleeper.

Walcott, accordingly, left the apartment on the proposed errand.

CHAPTER XXV.

THE PRISONER.

We have omitted to state that when the lunatic was brought in, no suitable place had at first been found in which to confine him. After having been supplied with some cold food which he ravenously devoured, he was taken to one of the log out-buildings, which was small and strong, having originally been used to protect fowls and the smaller domestic animals, from the foxes and wolves, that, in the autumn, and at night, had formerly much abounded in this vicinity. Jacob's hands were again secured behind him; and he was ushered and fastened into this temporary place of confinement.

It was intended to send him away the next morning to some suitable asylum in the more thickly-settled portions of the country. Confinement, whatever its consequences might be to the poor man himself, was now deemed to be absolutely indispensable to public safety. Meanwhile, he had proved to be far from passive and tractable except when Walcott was at hand to overawe him. Even his influence seemed to be limited to the period of his immediate presence. It was only when he felt himself beneath the very eyes of this master that he was disposed to yield. Away from him, and out of his sight, or even behind his back, he affected to scoff at his authority. Thus it was that Walcott's presence was necessary in the making of the various dispositions we have mentioned.

The building in which Jacob was confined was only about ten feet square, and was roughly constructed of logs. The door, after having been closed, was now strongly barricaded. Several circular openings five or six inches in diameter, and as many feet from the ground, answered the purpose of windows.

No sooner was the inmate left to himself than he began to grow frantic, and to rave in a manner unusually violent. Loud soliloquies, shouts, laughter, and even screams followed close upon each other, and formed a wild chorus of harsh and incoherent sounds, poured tumultuously forth upon the still night.

When Walcott went out for the purpose of endeavoring to quiet the uproar, he carried a torch. The moment he stood at the door and so long as his voice was heard outside of the little building, all within was still. After remaining there for some time he returned toward the main house; but no sooner was he out of hearing than the dissonant outcry was renewed. He tried the effect of his presence and absence several times; and finding, at length, that he could do nothing effectual to prevent the annoyance, he gave up the attempt, regretting that some other disposition had not been made, and half inclined to try a change, as it was. But, meanwhile, he concluded to wait, partly in the hope that the tired girl would become accustomed to the noise, and so disregard it; and partly, that as the night grew on, the maniac would himself weary of excitement, and gradually fall asleep.

Very different was the scene where the young man stood, from that which, at the same moment, might have been observed at the tent near the Rock Spring. A bright light illuminated the interior, and shone out through the openings, upon the dark green leaves of the surrounding forest, while the sound of a violin, and voices mingling in merry conversation and in laughter, indicated the kind and degree of amusement which was there taking place.

In obtaining a view of those who were participants in this primitive festivity, we should witness a simplicity of manner, and a style and material of dress, quite different, it may be safely asserted, from any thing seen on the same spot in our days. It is not, however, our purpose to enter upon a description of the personal appearance of those who composed the assemblage, for it would be quite irrelevant to our present purpose. We merely wish to state that the enjoyment was hearty—that the young ladies had cheeks as bright, forms as lithe and pleasing, and eyes as soft and bewitching, as can be found at any modern fashionable soirée, notwithstanding some of them may have been our grandmothers, and their customs and costumes are now, alas! almost a century out of date! But then they were neither old or unfashionable, and gayety and happiness filled their young hearts as fully and exclusively as possible. For the moment, they seemed to entertain no thought of sadness or of misfortune; but to give themselves up to the innocent amusements and pleasures of the hour.

Still, amid the excitement of the dancing, and the sound of the music which regulated it, amid the low hum of conversation, and the occasional burst of merry laughter, could be heard, now and then, the strange shouts with which the maniac continued to beguile his confinement.

"What is it? What can it be?" were questions which, after a while, began to be asked. One would suggest, in reply, that it might be a bear in the neighboring brush, or some panther, disturbed in his prowling by the sight of such an unusual light as now shone in the tent. Another hinted it might be some drunken reveler at the cabin on the upper bank, or some Indian in the village, beside himself from the use of "fire water."

Still there was no satisfactory solution. When, occasionally, some one would pause to listen, the noise was discovered to be prolonged, continuous, persistent. Something unnatural or supernatural seemed to be in it; so that to the timid, even amid that collection of young hearts and thoughtless heads, it was a source of uneasiness.

Floyd himself had been among the first to notice it, but, from constitutional indifference, as well as from a knowledge that they were not far from a considerable collection of Indian habitations, he gave the subject but little thought. In the course of the evening, however, as it still was heard without abatement, and as one continued uselessly to question another, so that a general observation was drawn to the unexplained circumstance, he determined to go up the slope and ascertain for himself the cause of so much outcry. He was, in addition, it must be confessed, a little interested to know how the invalid was faring, and especially was he pleased at any pretext which might afford him an opportunity of seeing Marion again. He was not yet aware that Walcott had returned.

He found the old colonel pacing the floor of the outward apartment alone.

"Good evening, Dick," said the latter as Floyd came in: "it is kind of you to come up to us in our trouble, with all the amusement you have down at the tent. Walcott has got back, and he and Marion are doing what they can to keep the poor girl quiet. She raves much, I am told."

"Pray, colonel," said Floyd, "what is the noise I hear outside? It has been going on this hour, and we have been a little puzzled to make it out."

"That is the poor crazy creature they caught during the day; and, as there was no other secure place in which to confine him, they placed him in an out-building hard by; but he seems to be very uneasy at the restraint put upon him."

Walcott, meanwhile, had returned to the house, and had again been called into the inner room, where his mere presence seemed to exercise a soothing influence upon the invalid.

CHAPTER XXVI.

OLD TIES AND NEW FEELINGS.

It is, perhaps, needless to say, that what Marion had heard from the lips of the sleeper during the absence of Walcott, and during a momentary access of mental aberration to the sick girl, had only gone to confirm the suspicion she had conceived. It now occurred to her that it might be desirable that he should also learn something of what was passing in the mind of the sleeper. Especially, did she wish to observe the effect which any communication of that nature would produce upon him. For this purpose she was not compelled to wait long; for hardly had the young man seated himself by the side of the couch, before Lucile began again to utter some incoherent words. In a short time, what she said became intelligible; and thoughts and sentiments escaped from her fevered lips, which in a moment of full consciousness, she would sooner have died than have uttered.

While Walcott, therefore, in being a listener, expected to hear the mere disconnected moanings of pain and fever, what was his confusion and surprise, to hear instead, the plain avowal of the love for him which the poor girl cherished in her heart. It came upon him so unexpectedly, and seemed to pour upon his mind such a flood of dazzling light, that he felt like a prisoner suddenly transported from a dungeon to the open day. The effulgence was painful even. He felt staggered, confused. The intelligence smote him like a sword thrust, so bright and so lightning-like had it seemed in penetrating his soul. For the moment, he seemed unable to endure the intensity of it. He even turned pale, and felt weak and faint, as the tell-tale blood forsook his cheek and fled to his heart.

"Arthur! Arthur!" exclaimed Marion, starting up in alarm! "what has happened, what is the matter with you?"

"Nothing," said he, "at least—not much. I believe I must be a little unwell myself. Fatigue, perhaps."

We have said that the effect of the disclosure upon Walcott was painful. It was so in the extreme. His own attachment, and the suffering it might cause him were as nothing, when counted against his plighted faith to Marion. But now that the feelings, and possibly the permanent happiness of another were concerned, the case had become different. How could he, by adhering to his vow, crush the hopes, and sear the heart of such a being as Lucile? It was a sense of the suffering which, as he imagined, must result from whatever course he might pursue, that most oppressed and weighed upon him for the moment. Yet with this pang, sharp as it was, came also a balm. The poison of the new hope, if poison it was, was still most sweet and tempting. Had he, at this period of his life, thought as to whose love, of all others in the wide world, he would most have coveted, his choice would have fallen upon the one whose actual love was thus, in the unconscious voice of sleep, tendered to him.

At that time, however, he would listen to no more.

The utterance of sentiments in which he was so deeply concerned began to affect him with a sympathy too painful to be borne. Moreover by thus remaining, he seemed to be obtaining by indirection and espial, a knowledge which could not well come to him openly. Such an act would therefore be apparent treachery to the sleeper. He rose to go.

"It is better," he said, "that I should not remain any longer here, I think. She is ignorant of what she is saying, and probably in her delirium, she has from gratitude, mingled my name with others which she cherishes more nearly."

Marion had watched all in silence. She now felt persuaded that Walcott, at the least, had become deeply interested in the fate of Lucile; and judging of the attractions which might operate upon him in that direction, she did not find it very difficult to believe that his admiration must be as strong as her own. The conviction fast gained upon her, that, without knowing it, the feelings of each had got to be greatly concerned in the affair. And what then? The plain truth—if such it was—might to her be a little harsh, perhaps a little painful. Had she herself been so incapable of inspiring this young man with any other feelings than those of fraternal esteem?

Meanwhile we have left unanswered the half embarrassed and awkward remark of Walcott, as he arose to depart—not that Marion did not reply to it; but that we have been compelled to pause and record some of the thoughts which passed through her mind.

"Whether she raves or not, Arthur," she had calmly replied; "you know that she has desired that you should not be absent—at least not very far. Besides, do not go, for I shall want—I think I shall want, some frank conversation with you myself before long. I have heard and seen enough to make me painfully anxious."

The young man paused—did not leave the room, but turning to her he said,

"My dear and gentle Marion, whatever you have to say, you will find me as sincere and loyal as when our hands were first plighted; as sincere and truthful to you, as when our earthly hopes were first by compact joined together."

"I knew you would be so, Arthur," she said, her eyes filling with tears, as, taking a chair she sat down near him. "I knew it would be so, and therefore come to you above all others, first. I need hardly tell you now that the dear girl who suffers there loves you—loves you deeply. I found it out as you did—and—and if I must say it, I have almost wished that her love might be returned."

All this was said with much hesitation, and with many pauses, and much embarrassment; but still the frank and generous girl was determined to say all.

"Marion," he replied, "you know that my faith is pledged to you; and I do assure you that I have never willingly or consciously swerved from the duty which such an obligation imposes."

"Duty, Arthur, is a cold word to use as between us; and surely it should not have been felt as an obligation, nor should you have looked upon it as imposing any thing which your own feelings did not spontaneously dictate."

"And what then?" he asked, in doubt what construction to put upon her words, while he recollected with some confusion that his own language was calculated to unvail his sentiments too plainly.

"What then?" said she. "Why, you could never have been attached to me in good, downright earnest; and you have been properly punished. You do not now deserve to be loved by such a one as Lucile. Perhaps you will also think that her regard will impose upon you some weighty and irksome obligation?"

Insensibly, thus had the conversation taken such a turn as to seem as if they were discussing not the relations between themselves, but a well understood attachment between the young man and Lucile. It was not without difficulty that he could contemplate himself transferred to this new position. He could scarcely believe his senses. He looked in the countenance of Marion, to discover whether her words covered an ill-timed jest, or a reproaching sarcasm. He did not find indications of either the one or the other.

It was true that the expression of her features was half playful, yet it was also half tearful. Whatever else she might feel, she certainly felt earnestness. She rejoiced in the generous action which she supposed herself to be doing; and yet, womanlike, half regretted the sacrifice she made. Was another to gain and possess the confidence of the man to whom she had been so long bound by so many ties? All the affections are jealous, the weakest as well as the strongest.

"But Marion," replied he, after a long pause, "I will not permit you to make this change on my account. I am sure there may be some misconception in the whole business."

"You shall promise me one thing," said she, interrupting him: "if she" (pointing to Lucile) "does not love you, you shall marry me after all. What do you say to that?" she continued, half laughing through her tears.

"I promise you any thing you ask, dear Marion," replied the young man, appreciating with a heart full of emotion, all the high-minded generosity there was in her act.

Does the reader think the whole circumstance unnatural and incredible? We affirm that the human heart is a profound mystery, made up in its outward developments, of seeming paradoxes and contradictions.

And yet, in this particular case, who can tell? May there not have been some new-born emotion in Marion's heart, and rising like a summer morning upon the horizon of her intelligence, to send its joyous light through all the recesses of her being? What music of a great joy yet unseen, may have been resounding, in advance, in the inmost chambers of her soul? Influences she knew not of, may have guided her thoughts and determined her wishes, as guardian angels were once thought to guide the unconscious footsteps of men.

But now the hour was waxing late. It was time that some final dispositions for the night be made. The invalid, for the moment, was sleeping quietly, all unconscious of the momentous issues affecting her fate which had thus been disposed of. Before leaving the room, Walcott, with much feeling, raised to his lips the hand which Marion had extended to him, in token of continued regard. As he went forth, therefore, his countenance was flushed, and his mind was disturbed with many conflicting emotions.

It will be recollected that for a great portion of the time taken up during the above interview, Floyd and Colonel

Belden had been engaged in conversation in the outer room.

In the confusion which had ensued after the return of Walcott with the maniac in custody, he and Floyd had not met. He was, therefore, taken completely by surprise to find the latter there, insomuch that he stopped short, exclaiming almost unconsciously:

"Major Floyd!"

"Arthur Walcott!" replied the other, almost equally surprised on the instant, although he knew him to be in the house.

After a few moments' delay, however, Floyd came frankly forward, extending his hand, and saying:

"I have to beg pardon for some old passages between us. I feel satisfied that I was entirely in the wrong, and trust that you will receive my regrets in all sincerity and good faith as they are expressed."

"With all my heart, sir," quickly replied Walcott. "And hereafter I hope we shall know each other better than to conceive mutual mistakes so easily."

During this brief colloquy Marion had stood in the door-way, at first anxious as to the issue, but afterward gratified beyond expression at the generous initiative taken by Floyd; and when she saw the two young men shaking hands cordially together, her blush of trepidation became one of happiness.

As soon as the first civilities were passed, Walcott begged to be excused for a few moments as he wished to look a little to the situation of his prisoner. For this purpose he went out; but he had hardly moved from the door before he saw standing unexpectedly before him the dusky form of Joe, who, it seems, was just returning.

"Eh, Joe, is that you?" said Walcott as he distinguished him in the darkness.

"Got him, cap'n," laconically answered the savage.

"Got what?" asked Walcott.

"Medicine—cure pretty squaw, now—right off—by'm by," answered the other.

"Let us see what it is," said Walcott, turning quickly back to the house.

The savage now exhibited to the inmates of the place a collection of plants for which, it would seem, he had been in search.

"What good will these do, and how are we to use them?" asked Colonel Belden, after a moment's pause.

"Do good, eh? Cure squaw, that all," said Joe, answering one of the questions.

"But how shall we use them, I ask?" repeated the colonel.

"Bile 'em—make, what you call him, tea?" said the Indian; "take big drink—be well in mornin'."

The directions, then, were plain enough; but who was to guaranty that the promised results would ensue? How were they to know that the consequences, instead of being favorable, might not be dangerous or fatal? This was the important question. And then the prescription was recommended by a more than half savage—by one who had but recently manifested a most hostile disposition toward one of the persons most deeply concerned in the result. The case was certainly critical. There was a well-grounded apprehension that the remedy might be worse than the disease; but, on the other hand, as if to spur them on to some measures of relief, however desperate, the poor girl was hourly yielding to an unknown fever, more and more violent in its symptoms.

Brigham, who was called in to be advised with, and who was suppcsed to be best acquainted, not only with the temper and intentions of Joe, but with the character of Indian remedies, was decidedly opposed to running the hazard of trying the supposed cure, notwithstanding the kind of voucher which Catfoot had given him for Joe's uprightness of purpose.

Walcott himsèlf, being free from suspicion, and half doubting the story about the Indian's late designs upon himself, was, on the other hand, inclined to try the effect of the decoction. His knowledge of the medicinal virtues of plants was not extensive; but, in the present case, it was sufficient to enable him to feel very confident that none of those recommended were poisonous; and he thought that, at the worst, thcy would be harmless. He had, likewise, much faith in the skill, with which the simple inhabitants of the woods applied the means of cure within their reach. He had often, in his own experience, had occasion to witness their beneficial effects. Moreover, he did not suppose it possible that any one could harbor an evil purpose against a person as innocent as Lucile. He reasoned of others, from what he felt himself.

In regard to the precise character and names of the plants produced, no one present was sufficiently an herbalist, or botanist, to say much. Some of them were unfamiliar even to the eyes of Brigham.

After a brief discussion as to the course to be pursued, Colonel Belden asked:

"What if this medicine should kill the young lady, Joe? What should we do to you then?"

"Joe here, kill him, that all," was the reply.

There was something so confident in his manner that it had the effect of inspiring the others with a little hope, if not with a decided faith; so that it was finally determined that the decoction should be prepared and administered.

The task was, therefore, immediately set about, and it was not long before, for good or for ill, the potion was in readiness and swallowed by the invalid.

Much to the gratification of all, shortly afterward she became quiet and sank into a deep sleep.

Floyd now took his leave, promising to return the next morning after having seen his own party set out, as they intended to do, at an early hour, on their return to Schuyler's.

CHAPTER XXVII.

THE LUNATIC'S ESCAPE.

In a short time after Floyd's departure, all within and without Brigham's cabin became comparatively quiet. The music from the distant tent could no longer be heard. Even the maniac had lapsed into silence; and it was supposed that nature and fatigue had at last surmounted the "seven devils" by which he seemed to be possessed.

The small building where he was confined, was, as we have said, detached from the main house, and stood quite alone. Its general character has been already mentioned. It may, however, be added that its roof was composed of thick timbers, stretched across the top sufficiently near each other to allow a thatch of straw to be laid over all. It was supposed that these stringers were too close together to enable a man to pass up between them. The whole erection, however, was low; and a person could nearly reach the roof when standing beneath the lowest part.

In the arrangements made for the night, M'Carty and Joe (at his own desire) were to act as sentinels upon the place of confinement. It was not known what attempt at violence or escape might be made in the darkness; and it was therefore thought not unadvisable to have a sufficient force at hand.

Walcott himself, though now suffering much from fatigue, and his continued exertions and watchings, could not immediately compose his mind so as to get that sleep and rest which he so much needed. Perhaps the very excess of his fatigue served to keep alive his excitement, and make him wakeful. To quiet his nerves, he even went forth into the open air, and strolled for a while among the trees, inhaling the fresh atmosphere, and enjoying the wide-spread stillness which prevailed. The fragrant air, and the repose of all nature around him, served at once to cool his blood, and to soothe his excited feelings.

After a time, he went back into the house, where he found every body asleep before him. He soon fell into a doze himself, and by degrees, became entirely lost in forgetfulness.

As the night wore on, the two watchmen outside occupied themselves sometimes in such scanty discourse as could be maintained with a person of Joe's taciturn habits. In fact, whatever conversation took place between them was almost entirely kept up by M'Carty, who was as talkative as the other was silent. Nevertheless, the lack of responses, like the lack of applause to an orator, rendered his discourse unsatisfactory to himself, and long periods of silence frequently occurred.

Sometimes, like true sentinels, they paced to and fro, before the entrance to the temporary jail they were set to guard. Their task, to all appearance, was likely to be an easy one, for the prisoner had, at length, become quiet, and had fallen asleep, as they thought, without making any serious effort to escape. They began to congratulate themselves that they should not hear of him again till daylight should call forth his hoarse and ill-omened croak, as it would the musical voices of the birds.

Sometime after midnight, however, when every thing was hushed in the most profound stillness, the quick ear of the savage detected a low and peculiar sound, coming from the place where the prisoner was confined. It was not like the noise of one moving about, or attempting to remove any obstacles, or testing the strength of the fastenings. It was rather a regular sound, like that of a saw, but more smooth and muffled, and without its harshness.

Joe immediately called the attention of his companion to the circumstance. Neither of them could tell from what the noise originated, or what it might import. Their observance of it did not seem to have any effect upon it. If Jacob was busy at any thing, he did not appear to care a rush whether they heard him or not. Meanwhile, the sound gradually increased in rapidity and loudness. The two men moved hastily about the small building, as if securely to invest it on all sides, and to be in a better situation to discover the cause of the disturbance. They went everywhere, and listened at all points, but to no purpose. They well knew that Jacob could, when left to himself, without much difficulty, relieve his hands and arms from the ligatures which bound them; and it was not doubted that in the morning all his limbs would be as free as ever. His immense strength and insensibility to pain made any movement by him in the darkness, all the more noticeable and dangerous.

At length, the Indian found a place where there was a considerable opening between the timbers, and where he could hear what was going on within, more distinctly than at any other point. Here he established himself with aboriginal patience and determination, as it promised to be the most probable place at which to solve the mystery of the unaccountable noise. Not only did he listen, but every moment or so, he applied his eye to the aperture in order to make any discovery which might be possible to the sense of sight.

After a few moments this vigilance was rewarded by his noticing occasional sparks of fire emitted from a certain point within the building. The truth now flashed at once upon his mind; and he conjectured rightly that Jacob was endeavoring to strike a light by a well known method in use among the savages, that is to say, by friction.

Curious, however, to learn what could be the object of it, the two men outside continued to listen and watch in silence. It was not more than a minute afterward, when, instead of occasional sparks, they saw a dull, blue flame rising from among some dry leaves upon the ground. The light emitted from this, though at first but faint, soon increased sufficiently to enable them to observe all the movements of their prisoner. Their curiosity was meanwhile, in no respect diminished. What was to be the purpose of the midnight illumination they could not conjecture. Besides, the material for maintaining it was extremely limited in quantity. The blaze barely sufficed to make visible the sides of the small quadrangle, and as the sticks and rubbish on which it fed would soon be exhausted, the purpose for which it had been kindled must be accomplished soon, if at all.

It was a curious spectacle which they witnessed. The light from that faint fire of leaves striking upon the maniac's grim and uncouth features, from below, like the foot-lights of a theater upon the countenance of a player, showed his wild eyes glittering with cunning and ferocity; while a smile, half of fatuity and half of diabolical mischief, was visible upon the lower portion of his face. He seemed like an untamed beast prowling in his lair, and watching an opportunity for making his escape or doing some act of violence.

Meanwhile the two men, who so closely overlooked his proceedings, had not long to wait before they learned the meaning of all these preparations; for no sooner had he procured fire enough to ignite the end of a small dry stick, than he raised it above his head like a torch, and in a twinkling, set fire to the straw thatch of the roof. The Indian uttered an emphatic "ugh!" of astonishment, and rushed with all his speed toward the main cabin in order to waken Walcott, to get his directions and assistance in the coming crisis. For this, instructions had been already given them. The latter was, accordingly, roused from a deep sleep into which he had fallen, by a rough shake of the shoulder; when, looking up, he saw the swarthy features of Joe bending over him. He sprang up at once.

"Come," said Joe, "come quick. Jake burn house."

At that moment they heard the wild, hoarse laugh of the lunatic from without, pealing through the still night air, as loud as a trumpet, and as discordant and startling as a fire alarm. The two men rushed forth as speedily as possible. They found the roof of the little building already in a full blaze. Inside of it, Jacob was apparently capering and shouting with might and main, in a state of the highest glee at what he had done.

Not a moment was to be lost. It was evident that the

poor wretch would soon be roasted alive where he was. They found M'Carty already hammering away at the fastenings of the door, humanely determined to let the prisoner loose at all hazards. He was now joined in his efforts by the others. Overhead the fire crackled and blazed away with momentarily increasing heat and violence. The merriment of the inmate continued unabated. As always happens under such circumstances, the very haste of the men to get the door open, retarded their movements. They tore away the cross-bars one after another, almost in despair of being able to succeed in time. They could see flakes of burning straw already falling from the roof within the building; and sometimes around or upon the dancing fiend, like a shower of shooting stars around a fallen Lucifer.

Just at the instant when they had got the door partially cleared away, and so suddenly that the act was entirely unanticipated, the maniac made one furious bound at the opening, burst it through with as much apparent ease as that with which a cannon ball breaks a window-sash; and overturning all who stood in his way, he rushed forth, and with wild screams of laughter, disappeared in the darkness.

All this was done in much less time than it could be told in. The three men, who had been utterly confounded or overset by this sudden sortie, which came upon them more like an explosion than the act of a human being, now looked at each other in astonishment. Walcott alone made a start as if in pursuit, but immediately recollected the uselessness of such an attempt at that time, and stopped.

All this noise and uproar had awakened the other occupants of the larger cabin. Brigham now came forth followed by the old colonel, and Marion herself stood alarmed in the doorway. The blaze of the burning thatch cast a bright red light for a long distance around, upon the rusty trunks of the forest trees, or upon the green leaves of their tops.

The scene was one for an artist. The rough and various forms and accouterments of the men, the different expressions of astonishment, curiosity, or alarm, which might have been observed upon their countenances; the pale and delicate face of Marion, as she stood in the portal of the rude log building, and all in the wilderness, at night, and made visible by the lurid reflection of a burning roof, formed a group of objects not often to be met with by the lover of the picturesque.

The view, however, was to be brief; for as the thatch was exceedingly dry, it burned with great rapidity, and was soon consumed, without even setting fire to the timbers upon which it rested. As the flames died away, the whole scene faded into darkness. It seemed to have come and gone like a single flash from a magic lantern. The woods around, again became vocal with the chirrup of toads and the cries of insects. All else was deep hush and solitude, except when occasionally the voice of the retreating lunatic could be heard in its unearthly merriment, ringing from afar.

When the nature of the disturbance, and the result of it had become fully known to all, and as soon as all danger of the fire communicating to the main building had passed away, most of those who had been aroused by it, made arrangements for the second time that night, to retire. M'Carty was secretly cursing fate, or his own inefficiency and want of foresight; and feeling an intense degree of chagrin that an escape for the second time, had now taken place while he was on the watch. The Indian began to feel some return of his old superstitious awe of a being who played such terrible pranks. Walcott was simply annoyed. The labor of the last few days had been rendered unavailing, and must be done over again. He was the last one to retire. He saw that the slightly charred timbers of the burned roof did not blaze up again, and that the fire had in fact, effectually died out. He heard the voice of the wild man gradually lose itself in the distance; and the whole scene became peaceful and undisturbed.

Fortunately Lucile had slept on through all the uproar, and that as quietly as if nothing had occurred. The draft which she had swallowed must have been a potent one, or exhausted nature was avenging itself for too many hours of weariness and watching previously spent without sleep.

Whatever was the cause, her senses remained locked in profound unconsciousness through all the anxieties and disturbances of that night.

CHAPTER XXVIII.

ELECTIVE AFFINITIES.

THE next morning was fair, bright and still. At an early hour, even before sunrise, the party of pleasure which had occupied the tent during the previous night, decamped; and soon after, might have been seen in gay procession, and in high spirits moving to the north-eastward along the rude road-way in which we first introduced it to the notice of the reader. There was the same blowing of trumpets, the same prancing of horses, the same tossing of bright plumes in the air, and the same voices of merriment, now, as then. While the horizon in the east was rosy with the uprising light of day, a thin white line of vapor, some miles distant, stretched its fleece-like, rolling coil of gauze above the bed of Saratoga Lake—marking thus to curious eyes, where that beautiful sheet of water lay, hushed in the moist and dewy repose of unbroken morning. Such banks of fog in these latitudes, are sometimes to be seen in summer, and always in the autumn, at dawn, hanging over lakes and rivers; and in the latter case, giving in the atmosphere a rude reverse of its sinuous outline. These vapory transcripts of the watery features of the country, only fade away when the rays of the ascending sun begin to fall upon them: though often stirred by some auroral breeze they are huddled off in vast squadrons, and disappear among the woods and hills around.

But we have no time fully to trace, or dwell upon all the varying and picturesque objects which might attract the notice of an appreciating eye in the vicinity where our scenes are laid. Many such mornings, and many such views, must be fresh in the recollection of most of our readers.

The sun had been up for a long time, and most of the occupants of Brigham's cabin had gone forth, before Lucile had awoke from the deep sleep into which she had fallen the night before. So profoundly indeed had she slumbered that not the least, most flitting, or remote idea of the events of the last eighteen hours, remained in her mind. Her senses during that period seemed to have been, like drowsy sentinels as they were, all off duty or unmindful of it. The space of time was therefore an utter blank in her existence—a void spanned by no bridge of overarching memories.

But though this period was thus, so to speak, stricken from her existence, it did not carry into oblivion any of the events anterior to it. With them, there was still complete connection. All that had transpired since this eventful expedition was commenced, was fresh in her mind—each individual circumstance was clearly engraved upon her memory in sharp and inerasable outlines. Upon them therefore did her first waking thoughts turn. Each event was passed in review, but all rapidly and successively like a running file of troops. Her mind seemed to take them all in, without pause or interval—or rather seemed to sweep over them, as a skillful hand sweeps the keys of a piano, so that each circumstance, like a note, gave out its peculiar tone, and produced its particular effect, though all so rapidly that a single second sufficed to begin and end the task.

But after these events, what had happened? What was the mystery of her forgetfulness; and how and why came she in the precise position in which she found herself on waking? She was not unwell, at least she did not now feel herself to be so. She rose up and looked out. The day was far advanced, the birds sang by the window, the peaceful trees hung their deep green branches between her and the blue sky above. The whole world seemed to be in repose.

But we must not, or rather we can not, leave her longer alone. As she stood thus in thoughtful silence by the window, she heard a light step behind her; and on turning, saw Marion, who was coming to salute her with a smile as bright and cheerful as the morning itself. Their affectionate greeting was uttered in that universal language, a kiss; which with the young expresses more, and goes more directly to the heart, than any words which have ever been devised by the scholar, or any phrases which have ever been invented by the poet.

"And so, dear, you feel quite well this morning, do you not?" said Marion.

"Well?" answered Lucile, interrogatively; "have I then been ill?"

"Only a little," replied Marion. "Do n't you remember yesterday, when we came back from the Indian village, that you felt low-spirited, and had a slight headache

"I do n't remember any thing about it. I only remember—but I remember it well—coming back from that dreadful cavern with Arthur—with Mr. Walcott; but for all that may have occurred since, I feel as if I had then fallen into a sleep from which I have but this moment awoke."

"Do you mean to say," asked Marion, with surprise, "that you do not remember how Mr. Walcott, as you will call him, went away in search of the crazy man afterward?"

"Oh! yes," exclaimed Lucile, "now that you mention it, I think I do remember something about that. But, Marion, what has been the matter with me? I hope I was not delirious also," she continued, laughing.

"Yes, but you were, though," answered Marion.

"What, I delirious?" asked Lucile, with quick surprise and a little alarm.

"Wild!" answered Marion.

Lucile stood stupefied, and looked the picture of embarrassment, incredulity and affright.

"But," continued her companion, "I will tell you all about it by and by. In the mean time you must let me be your dressing-maid for a little while. I do n't believe you would like to see papa or Arthur in your present plight—and they are anxious to see you, I can tell you that."

But we leave the two thus talking, asking and answering questions, requesting and giving explanations with girlish intimacy and frankness, while we, for a time, look after the course and position of some others concerned in our story.

At an early hour in the morning Walcott had gone out in order to pay his respects to his old friend, though his recent enemy, Floyd, who, as had been arranged, was to stay behind after the party which he accompanied thither had taken its departure.

The two young men, being both of a frank and liberal disposition, soon became as communicative and almost as cordial as they had been of old. The events which had transpired, and the casualties and adventures which had befallen each since their former intimacy, furnished abundant matter of conversation; and, in the interest of it, an hour or so was passed pleasantly enough. After this they returned to Brigham's house where they met Colonel Belden.

We have said that while the two young men were alone together they had conversed freely and without constraint. We should have said that such was the fact upon all subjects excepting one. This topic, which each secretly and instinctively avoided, was, as may readily be surmised, the relations in which they respectively stood to Miss Belden.

Walcott felt anxious, as soon as it was possible, that the old colonel should be made acquainted with the new feelings which had risen up between himself and Marion, like a barrier, to prevent their union; but he also felt that the task of communicating the intelligence was one of great delicacy and of dubious issue.

Until this little cloud on his immediate prospects should be dissipated, he did not feel at liberty to make his own position in reference to the young lady the subject of any conversation with third parties.

For manifold reasons, on the other hand, Floyd was most anxious to know how Walcott stood in the family, but, at the same time, he was conscious that it would be impossible to clear up the subject by a direct inquiry. To both of them, therefore, there was food for much reflection, and room for anxious doubt. The secret truth might be favorable to the wishes of either or each; but, even if so, was it likely that Colonel Belden would look with an approving eye upon the new arrangements which fate was silently shaping forth for them? Was it not rather probable that the plan of marriage between Walcott and his daughter, now in the way of being broken off, was one fixed upon and considered settled, and for their best interests, years before, so that to change it would be to uproot, in the old man's mind, a prejudice of long growth, and difficult of eradication? Was it not likely that in its early determination no thought was given to the feelings with which the parties immediately concerned might regard it?

Upon that subject it is well known that the old and the young have never yet been able to look with the same eye. The old are forever providing for marriages of interest, and the young as constantly think only of marriages of affection. The former forget to allow for the impulses of youth, and seem to think that obvious advantages of a pecuniary and social character, must weigh as strongly at the age of eighteen as they do at eighty; while the latter, in truth, very rarely think of any point but the simple feelings of nature which induce the preference, and which, like a golden halo, outdazzle all other objects.

An experience of six thousand years has not yet corrected the misconceptions of age, or the imprudences of youth on this subject; and were the world ten thousand years old at this moment, it is not at all likely that its octogenarians would be any the wiser herein from their own experience, or that its marriageable young men would be any the more disposed to regulate their connubial arrangements by the experience of others.

It was not to be doubted that Colonel Belden had long contemplated the union of his daughter with Walcott—that it had become incorporated with all his plans for the future. Any change, therefore, would be a great thing for him to consider—a disarrangement of his designs, and, possibly, a disappointment of his hopes. No matter what substitution might be proposed, no matter if the change promised to be better for his daughter in all those particulars in which he considered the true eligibility of a marriage to consist, still the change would be vast, and the contemplation of it, at least in the outset, would be repugnant to his feelings.

There is a period in almost every summer day, shortly after noon, when, as every body's experience will corroborate, the air is peculiarly still, and when all nature seems to invite to repose. It is during this hour that people of torrid latitudes take the well-known *siesta*. It is also then that the hardy, and hard laboring peasant of severer climates lays himself down for a short after dinner sleep—a relaxation from toil, which he enjoys with as keen a zest, and with as high a sense of its luxury, as the brightest-eyed, most tenderly nurtured, and most princely maiden of the Antilles, or the Austral islands. The influences of nature work alike upon the roughest, and upon the most delicate of animated beings—and lay the ox and the gazelle, the peasant and the lady, alike under contribution.

It was at this hushed hour of the midday, when every

thing around was full of repose, and invited to somnolence, that Lucile Valcour and Arthur Walcott were silently walking, side by side, along a solitary, sunlit pathway of the forest. The direction which they had taken was toward the southward from the cabin. Their ramble had originated in a careless, or seemingly careless, chat, and in an unguided and purposeless stroll. They had been lured on by the coolness of the shadows, and now and then by the temptation to cull some fresh wild-flower, as it grew by the side of their path, and filled the grove with its fragrance. It was not by design that, as their conversation went on, they involuntarily sought more and more to be alone. It was because the sentiments which began by degrees to sparkle in their eyes, to flush their cheeks, and to be spoken more and more directly by their lips, were not sentiments which either of them would have desired any other human being to hear or to discover. It was an involuntary, instinctive impulse of secrecy which had guided their footsteps.

And now they were already at some distance from the point whence they had started. It is not for us to lift the vail from feelings which they so sedulously sought to conceal. It is enough for us to know that, despite of all restraints of formality, they now walked not only side by side, but hand in hand. The somnific influences of the hour were unfelt by them. The distant song of birds, which at intervals, and in drowsy notes, was still heard from leafy thickets, seemed as joyous and spirit-stirring to them as the first clarion notes which the same birds had sent forth at daybreak.

Upon the cheek of the girl was a flush which was not

that of fever. In her eye was a light which was not that of delirium.

And yet, for all the potent pleasure which bound them thus in solitary companionship, and for all the words of magnetic significance which betrayed so well to each the passionate happiness of the other, as yet, no words of actual love—at least of their own love—passed between them. Such words would have seemed an utter superfluity. There had been a mingling of sentiment; their sympathies were alike; their thoughts dwelt on kindred topics; and their hopes and feelings flowed in unison. The voices of their hearts had spoken, and, like according notes, sounded harmoniously. In whatever they saw, in whatever they heard, in whatever they thought and uttered, they seemed to discover a common point of interest; and a conviction—a most pleasing, overpowering conviction—had gradually stolen upon the mind of each as to the cause of this wonderful unity of thought and emotion. From what fountain but one, could such mighty happiness flow? Alas! to the heart of youth, there is but one such fountain in the wide, waste, melancholy world; while age has proved, or believes that it has proved, even this to be a delusion—an unsubstantial mirage of the desert. But still, to the young, love, that source of so much hope, is ever sought for, "as the hart panteth after the water-brook." The poisonous drafts which are sometimes partaken from it, are as yet unsuspected. Sweet are those streams to the taste. They are the fabled nectar of the heathen gods—as grateful to the palate as the waters of everlasting life—till the sad lessons of experience have shown how often they become the waters of oblivion, or like the contents of a poisoned chalice, to partake of which leads to early sorrow, or to premature death.

And yet, though the happiness may be unenduring, what heart, though seared by time and worldly care, can fail to sympathise with those emotions of early life? In after years there are none such. They are the high noon of earthly joy. After them, life goes on decayingly and solemnly to its shadowy sunset. Oh! joy of early love! How foolish in the remembrance of the selfish and the worldly-minded; but how embalmed and sacred in the memory of such as appreciate life, and its struggles, its ambitions, and its sorrows, at their true value.

Through the still woods, then, still wandered on that happy young pair. The secret to them had been divulged —not by bashful and timid lips, but by the undeceiving eye, by the electrical touch, by the wide open mirror of harmonious and sympathetic thoughts. As yet each felt it to be a truth—a most pleasing, life-involving truth; but as for the lips—those observers of forms, those servants of interest, those chroniclers of lies—they had not even whispered it.

And yet hand in hand our lovers wandered on. When their hands were at first carelessly joined, it was as if a chain had suddenly linked their several existences together —a seemingly indissoluble and most potent chain. To withdraw their hands, then, might indeed, divide their persons, but the moral links, intangible to the eye, inappreciable to the judgment, would still bind their hearts by their golden weight and magic power. Ah! then why withdraw those agitated and trembling fingers, so lovingly intertwined? Indeed, on behalf of Lucile, the unexplained sensation was as if that small white hand, so given in token of fealty, had found its natural home of protection. Where else could it go, or to what beside so confidingly cling? And thus it was that the entranced girl, in her happiness, still left her hand where her heart would have placed it; and felt as if her very soul, like an overcharged vase, was flowing thence and pouring of its fullness into the very heart of her lover.

Intense indeed was her happiness—intense the happiness of each. No thought of time or place occurred to them. A broken conversation was still imperfectly kept up between them—on indifferent topics—on all topics, but one; but still, in whatever was said, there was the same unvarying, invariable meaning. Who should break the charm, and why should it be broken?

In that joyous hour, earth seemed like what the garden of Eden must have been before it was visited by the evil one. And although its happiness seemed almost unmingled, at intervals, faint glimmerings of remembrance or apprehension would shoot up athwart their minds, as if to recall to their recollection, or give warning to their inexperience, that every thing earthly was evanescent or delusive. But for this, why should tears—tears of happiness, sometimes appear in the young eyes of the tender-hearted girl? Tears unbidden, and apparently uncaused? Alas! there is a solemn whispering of warning arising from the depths of each human soul, even in the moment of its greatest security and highest bliss. Hence, as they are called, "*tears of happiness.*" Is it supposed that angels, in the unclouded sky of everlasting life, ever weep for the intensity of their joy?

During this while, without material pause, did the two young people continue to yield to the impulse, which had thus far urged them on. We do not attempt to chronicle their words. We can not even give a faithful picture of their conduct. Was a fair flower visible near their path? It was soon in the hand, in the hair, or on the bosom of the blushing girl. Was there to be seen a glorious reach of azure sky shining through the tree-tops far away, like a distant aërial lake? It was he that besought her instant attention to it, and found some neighboring hillock, or moss-covered stone to bring it more clearly into view. Was a rough portion of the pathway to be surmounted, or a stony rivulet to be passed? It was his arm that supported her over the difficulties of the one, and guided her footsteps through the intricacies of the other. And how much was to be said between them! Each was to unfold to the other a map of his or her past life, with its lights and shadows, like a landscape; its eminences of hope, and its valleys of sorrow. Thus in their memories lay wide fields of discourse, which years of communion would scarcely suffice to travel over. In nature too, that beautiful and variegated nature, whose myriad objects of wonder surrounded them, what stores of mystery, and what multitudinous topics of thought! And yet, on all these things, their conversation lingered but briefly. As if on the wing, it passed lightly over a wide expanse, and ever, in circular gyrations, came back to dwell upon a theme more grateful to their hearts—a theme, which like the sun in a landscape, illumined all other objects, and gave them life and beauty.

But upon this picture, so pleasing and so genial, we are unable any longer to dwell. The panoramic canvas moves on, and the scene must change.

CHAPTER XXIX.

UNEXPECTED ENCOUNTER.

NEAR Walcott and his companion, for some time past, had been moving an object very different in character and appearance from themselves. It was one well calculated to chase from their minds the halo of their present happiness, and all "castles in the air" for the future. Absorbed, however, as they were in the contemplation of each other and in their own feelings, it so far escaped their attention. This object was neither more or less than our old acquaintance, Jacob, who, for some time, with all the stealth of a cat, and the perseverance of a sleuth-hound, had been spying their movements and hanging upon their footsteps. Not the rustling of a leaf, the fall of an acorn, the crackling of a stick, or the flight of a bird taking suddenly to wing, betrayed his presence or his passage. Long practice had enabled him to move as noiselessly through the forest, as his own shadow.

And during this while he was well worth a little attention; for, as he darted behind the great brown trees, and peered out from leafy bushes, his eyes shone, if possible, more fiercely and maliciously than ever. To add to the formidableness of his aspect, he now carried in his hands a huge bludgeon. It was still rough with unshorn knots and bark. But, notwithstanding its obvious weight and size, its possessor handled it with as much ease as if it had been an ordinary walking-stick. In his grasp it was, most assuredly, a murderous-looking weapon. It might readily fell an ox, and when swung by the brawny arms which now held it, upon whatsoever human head it might descend, it must come with a crushing power, sufficient to produce instant death.

Close upon the footsteps of our two young people did this wild Hercules thus continue to follow, unheard and unseen. A double motive seemed to be actuating him. That he still looked upon Lucile as in some way belonging to himself, was most probable; and that he now began to regard Walcott, not only as a man to be feared, but as one to be avenged upon, might be argued from the formidable preparations he had made to meet him. Besides, until now he had always, from whatever cause it might arise, sought rather to avoid, than to be near the young man. His present conduct, therefore, indicated some change in his disposition.

Meanwhile, he to whom this change was principally important was quite ignorant of it. Had it been otherwise, it would, probably, not have caused him any uneasiness on his own account. He was far too sanguine and self-reliant for that. But it might have occasioned him some apprehension on account of his fair companion, who was too unused to such dangers, and had been too recently in the power of the maniac not to be nervously and, perhaps, hysterically alive to the horrors of his presence.

They had been walking for a long time, and had commenced their return toward the hut. At a little distance a-head of them was a thick copse of scrub pine, through the midst of which the path wound its way. Toward this, as they slowly moved along, Jacob, by a little circuit, hurried forward so as to anticipate them in reaching it. It was a convenient and almost impenetrable ambush. He succeeded in arriving there before them, and still unseen. Here he ensconced himself with all secrecy and care, taking up such a position as would enable him to fall upon his victims with almost certain effect. He waited in silence while they slowly approached.

For them the occasion was not one of haste. With lingering footsteps, and voices modulated to the harmony of the forest echoes, they seemed to have given themselves up to the intoxicating influences of the hour and the occasion. The trees, shrubs, and flowers which they passed, and which tempted them, at every moment, to pause in contemplation of a new beauty, or to dwell upon the varied sentiments suggested by them, were only so far observed as they were the occasion of a ceaseless play and change of fancy in their minds, and as they seemed to cast moving lights and shadows upon their thoughts, as they did upon the leaf-strown earth at their feet.

But, linger as they would, the two young people still advanced, and, at length arrived in front of Jacob's ambush. Yet, even there, the absorbing theme, which had so withdrawn their thoughts from outward objects, continued to occupy them. This theme, however, had not yet been distinctly discussed. Each thought of nothing else, and yet, each shunned to mention it, as if the happiness it involved was too great to believe in, or the disappointment it might occasion would be too bitter to survive. But to them its dazzling luster was still attractive, and around it they continued to flutter, like moths around a candle.

They were now within two circles of danger, the one mental, the other physical. To one, they had been for some time exposed, and they were just treading across the outer verge of the other. Slowly they passed by the fatal place of concealment. It was the moment of peril. Behind them, glided, like a phantom, the ill-omened form of the wild man. Already is his arm upheaved, bearing its ponderous club, when—hark! there rises upon the still air, in sharp, startling echoes, the long, shrill, sonorous cry of a hound! As quickly as if struck by a ball, did Walcott turn in the path. It was just in time! Before him stood the Titanic Jacob, with threatening mien and attitude. But upon him there fell a glance, before which his eye had ever quailed. Like an Arctic winter, it froze him where he stood. His courage and his limbs were stricken with instantaneous inaction, as with a paralysis.

Sternly and steadily did Walcott then approach him. He covered him with his eye, as a hunter does his game. He enveloped him with a magic influence. It was too much for brute force. Mind, the master of the world, was still master here.

With a wild shout of fear, rage, and disappointment, the maniac, by a convulsive effort, broke away from the spell which was being put upon him, and rushed violently through the woods. Loud and discordant cries filled the air, as he disappeared; and some minutes elapsed before the unnatural sounds were silenced by distance. It was not until then that Walcott looked about him to see what had become of his companion. He found her lying upon the ground, pale and motionless. The sudden sight of Jacob, in his menacing attitude, had been too much for her nerves, painfully excitable as they were, after her recent exposure and illness.

The young man was instantly by her side. He knew that she had fainted, and that the danger was not imminent; but the case was sufficiently serious for all that. With quick alarm, he bethought him of what to do. It was but the work of a moment for him to run to a neighboring rivulet, and in the hollow of his hand, to bring a little cool water which he dashed in her face. Kneeling beside her then, he half lifted her in his arms; and while holding her head, with watchful tenderness, he waited for the signs of returning consciousness with painful anxiety. At that moment, he easily forgot his reserve, and words of endearment broke from his lips involuntarily, as he besought her to revive, giving assurance that the danger was past.

In a few minutes she began to breathe again, while her pulse, like a disturbed pendulum, slowly resumed the regularity of its oscillation. Then opening her eyes, with a start, it was some seconds before she appeared to comprehend the situation in which she found herself. She rose up quickly; and in an impulse of gratitude, while the returning blood crimsoned her cheek and forehead, she took his hand in a half caress, while she could not help saying:

"Ah! thank heaven, you are safe after all! It seems to me like a frightful dream. Let us return at once, and no longer be exposed to that dreadful man."

"Yes, safe," he replied; "and you need never be alarmed, for him, when I am with you. You see how he fled."

At this moment a voice, well known to Lucile, was heard behind them, suddenly exclaiming:

"Good God! my daughter, what is all this I see? And what has happened to you, I pray?"

"My father! It is my father!" cried Lucile, as she darted from Walcott, and flung herself, with tears, into the arms of the old man, for it was indeed her father who had come.

Our old acquaintance the dog, too, whose opportune outcry had given warning of Jacob's fell intent, now testified his joy at the meeting by leaping and gamboling around the party, in all ways in which canine gratulation is usually expressed.

"Why, Prince," said Lucile, patting the dog, after the transports of her meeting with her father were over, "where have you been this long time? I am afraid you are but a truant cur of a dog, after all, and I have a great mind not to speak to you."

"You need not think hardly of him, Lucile," said Mr. Valcour; "for if he left you, it was only to come to me to give warning that my presence was necessary (here he glanced slightly at the young man); or perhaps that something had happened to you; for I see that you are pale and ill, my poor child! So come! tell me all about it. But first allow me to greet my friend here."

Walcott, who, after the meeting of the father and daughter, and up to this moment, out of respect for their feelings, had remained somewhat apart, now came forward to salute Mr. Valcour in his turn.

During this proceeding the cheek of the young girl was illumined by a flush a little more marked than usual; but the self-possession of the true lady, and the confidence she felt in the truthfulness and dignity of her feelings, still made her manner composed, and in the eye of a lover at least, more charming than ever.

"He is, sir," she said, as she took Walcott by the hand, and led him to her father; "he is thrice my preserver; and you have to thank him many times, my dear father, for the life of your child."

"Believe not her extravagance, my good sir," said Walcott. "I have done no more than what any man, not to say any gentleman, would have felt himself bound to do under the same circumstances; and I am only too happy to have been the one whose lot it was to be of use in this case."

"But, dear father," she broke in, "you do not know! The story is such a frightful one! Such a dreadful creature has been haunting us! I thought I saw him but now, and it was that—his standing with such a great club, and threatening to strike Mr. Walcott—it was that which made me foolish—made me faint, I believe."

"Such is the fact, sir," said Walcott; "there is a poor maniac wandering in the woods here, who is sometimes a little violent; and but for our timely exertions, he might have done some evil. As your daughter says, he was here but a moment ago, and apparently with some bad purpose. I turned around at the noise made by the dog, and saw him stealing toward us. You yourself must have observed him, or, at least, have heard him, before he got away?"

"It was, I suppose, the strange-looking creature that I took for an Indian as I came up," replied the old man; "he ran off with a horrible outcry. Still, whatever the story may be, it seems too long to be told now. I have, in the mean while, to thank you, sir, for the services which my daughter says you have rendered to her. Believe me, I am more touched by kindness to her, than if it had been extended to myself. You can hardly appreciate how highly I prize a service done to one I cherish so dearly."

As he spoke thus, he laid one of his hands, trembling with emotion, upon the head of his child; while he extended the other cordially to Walcott.

It soon appeared from what Mr. Valcour said, that in traveling through the woods on horseback, the attention of himself and his companion, had been, a short time before, attracted by the uneasy and remarkable conduct of the dog that had accompanied them. He began whining and running about ahead of them, and at last breaking off from the track they were pursuing, ran some distance to the westward, yelping, and with his nose upon the ground as if upon a trail. He did not however go out of sight, but as soon as he discovered that he was not followed paused, turned about, and set up a low howl, as if to beckon pursuit.

Mr. Valcour, who had already been much disturbed by apprehensions for his daughter's safety, though without being able to assign any good reasons for it, still determined to ascertain what these singular movements of the beast might signify. He, therefore, dismounting, followed him for a short distance into the brake. It was at this time that the warning cry of the alarmed brute had so startled Walcott; and, by inducing him instantly to turn about, had most probably saved his life.

All three now directed their course to the spot at which Mr. Valcour had left his horse in charge of his traveling companion. As however, the distance thence to the house of Brigham was not great, they took the beaten track thither on foot, the horses being meanwhile sent forward. This walk afforded them an opportunity to make such explanations as were desired, and Mr. Valcour now heard a full recital of the events which had lately transpired. His astonishment and alarm, even though the danger was past, were extreme.

In particular, was his wonder excited by the rare instinct of the dog, which seemed to have been something superior to intellect itself, in thus apprehending dangers which no human wisdom, could, under the circumstances, have dreamed of. Great also was the old man's thankfulness. With a swelling heart, again and again were his acknowledgments uttered. With what pride, with what pleasure, did Lucile see and hear expressed by her father, some part of the deep gratitude which filled her own heart, but to which, as she thought, she would never be able to give adequate expression.

Walcott himself was greatly pleased at the thought, that, whether deserving or not, his conduct had thus won approval, in a quarter where he now valued approval most.

After a short walk they all reached the open ground. Here they were encountered by Indian Joe.

"Seen big Jake in woods, eh?" he asked of Walcott.

"Yes," said the other; "but why do you ask? But I see you have a gun there. I hope you do n't mean to use it if you meet him?"

"Do n't know," said Joe, coolly.

"Pray do n't be so cross with poor Joe," here interposed Lucile in a whisper, addressing Walcott; for she saw that he was not pleased, and that another quarrel with Joe might take place. The young man was strongly inclined to interfere with the half-expressed purpose of the savage, and that by some positive prohibition; but the voice which now spoke to him came like music over the uprising discord of his heart, and soothed his harsher purpose. Her appealing tones at that moment, proved omnipotent. Within his own heart, sat a sceptered magician, that swayed him with a despotic, though a genial power. Under this strong curb, he refrained from saying any thing more to the half-breed, at that moment; but observed him so far as to note that he went off into the thicket without holding any further discourse with any one, or vouchsafing any further explanation of his designs.

After they had proceeded a little further they were also met by Brigham, who came forward saying to the young people:

"Where the deuce have you been so long? The colonel is in a great way about you. But I can't tell all that's happened sin' ye strayed off. You'll find it out soon enough yourselves, I reckon."

"But," said Walcott, smiling, "you can give us some idea of these new wonders can you not? Nobody else carried off, I hope?"

"No," answered Brigham, "yet stop; now I come to think on 't, there was. Major Floyd was carried off—by his own hoss!"

"You do n't mean to say that he has taken his leave in this abrupt manner?"

"Yes but I do, though," replied Brigham: "can't guess the reason on't. May be an order from head-quarters. But I suppose the old colonel can explain it all.

So come along, you and your friends, for I see you've got another one or so."

"Yes, Brigham," answered Walcott, "this gentleman is Mr. Valcour, the father of the young lady."

"Well," said Brigham, "he'd be welcome even if he was an entire stranger; and so he's sure to be welcome as the father of the young woman. She's a nice and desarving gal, though it's I that say it; and I dare say she has a fond father, since she turns the heads of strapping young fellers like you and me, eh, captain?"

Nice feelings and a delicate address were never the distinguishing characteristics of men of Brigham's stamp. It was not without a blush that Walcott listened to his rude attempts at civility and politeness—a blush partly of pleasure and partly of shame—of pleasure at the intended praise of Lucile, and of shame not only at the rough work he made of it, but at the suspicion that Brigham had already some sort of vague perception of his feelings towards the young lady.

On this point he felt sensitive enough. The idea of his secret sentiments being known—sentiments which he had as yet scarcely dared to avow to himself, gave him the keenest annoyance. Besides he had had no explanation with Colonel Belden, who might, like others, have his eyes open to what was going on about him; and who might not by any means relish either the new state of things, or the nice little arrangement between Walcott and his daughter, by which it had been furthered, if not brought about. It is true the young man desired him to be informed of all these things, and that as speedily as possible; but yet he desired to have it done in a particular way, so that the intelligence would produce neither a shock or a fit of indignation.

It would be infinitely better, he thought, that full explanations should first be given by Marion. He asked himself why it was that the old gentleman was, as Brigham had intimated, anxious for his return? Why also had Major Floyd so suddenly departed? Had the two events any connection? But it was useless to speculate. It was useless also to endeavor to hide from himself that he felt some foreboding. Though he fully justified his own conduct to himself, he was of course, entirely in the dark as to what view the old colonel might take of it. In approaching him therefore, he did so with some of the feelings with which a culprit comes before a judge.

CHAPTER XXX.

AN ENTIRELY NEW PROGRAMME.

As the party drew nigh to the cabin they were met by Colonel Belden, who greeted the father of Lucile with much heartiness and good-will. Some time was, in fact, spent in little courtesies and attentions between them. His manner to Walcott, on the contrary, though not absolutely discourteous, was cool—sufficiently so at all events, to indicate that something was the matter. Besides, Marion had not come forth to meet them. She had remained in the inner apartment. Hither Lucile also soon went, but did not immediately return. No explanation of what had occurred seemed likely, therefore, to be soon attainable: and as the two old gentlemen seemed to have much to say to each other, or at least, talked as continuously and eagerly as if their conversation was important; and as Walcott felt himself kept a little at a distance, he after a few moments, withdrew into the open air. Here he hunted up Brigham again, and endeavored to extract from him something to throw light upon the cool reception he had met with.

"Well," said that worthy individual, rolling a quid of tobacco from one of his cheeks to the other; "as I tell'd ye before, there's no making out exactly what's in the wind, but a man can guess, you know."

"But," said Walcott, "what was it that you saw and know; for perhaps when I hear that, I can form some notion for myself."

"Why, then, Mr. Walcott," said the other, "to tell the business, free and candid; arter you went off, and nobody could tell exactly how, except that the young gal—the black-eyed one, I mean—was gone too— why what should Major Floyd do but contrive to get up another select party for himself; that is to say, himself and the colonel's darter. The old gentleman and me all this while was talking of old times, and paying little or no attention to other matters. Hows'ever, at last he axes for Mary Ann."

"Marion, you mean," interrupted Walcott.

"Well, Marion, then; he axes for her, but she wasn't to be seen. So up he gets, and says he, 'Brigham, did you notice which way Mary Ann (or Marion, as you call her) went?' 'Yes,' says I, 'she and Floyd has gone down toward the rock.' 'And where,' says he, arter that, 'are all the rest on 'em?' 'Why,' says I, 'the captain (that's what most on 'em calls you, you know) the captain and the little gal was out a walkin' some time sin', and ain't got back yet so far as I know.' This makin up two pairs on ye didn't seem to please the old colonel, for he begun to look serious and says, we had better walk out and see that nothin' happened to his darter. From being full of talk and spirits, he begins to get glum and silent as we went; and when we reached the top of the bank, you know, jist where the path winds down between the bushes, he pulls me by the sleeve, and says, 'Wait a minute.' Through the bushes the Rock Spring was plain in sight. Hows'ever no one was near it; but beyond there, where the path follers along the willow bushes clus under the bank, who should we see under a big wide-limbed oak-tree that hung out from the hill, but the very Major and Mary Ann herself, no doubt thinking themselves cosy enough. And what do you think they was a doin' ?"

"I can not imagine, I am sure," said Walcott; "though they are old acquaintances and school-fellows, I believe."

"School-fellows be hanged!" exclaimed Brigham; "if they wasn't a makin of love I'm much mistaken. They went through all the motions mighty nateral, I can tell you. He was at that very minute a kissin her hand. I obsarved the old colonel tremble, and turn a little pale. So says I, feelin it wasn't exactly right for me to be a looking at sich an affair, says I, 'Colonel, perhaps I had better go and look arter the rest, as we've found two on 'em.' 'Do so,' says he; and I went back at once. I see no more on 'em, till a good while arter when the old man came up to the house, and his darter along with him, a cryin' and talkin' as if her heart was going to break. He was mighty glum and stern for all that. Not long arter, up comes Floyd too, but not to go into the house.

"'Brigham,' says he, 'can you get my horse out here in no time?'

"'Yes,' says I, 'but what on arth is in the wind?'

"'Oh! nothing particular,' says he, though I could see he was terribly flurried, and kept walking about in a kind of a rage. So I axed no more questions, but had the hoss brought, which he mounted and rode off as if the devil was behind him. And there you have the whole on 't, except that after that the colonel kept axing for you and walking about as impatient as Floyd had been, and muttering to himself, like. Something has gone wrong all round, but where the loose screw is, p'raps you can tell better than I."

When Brigham had finished his recital, Walcott, also, was considerably disturbed, and paced about uneasily for a few moments.

"I'm blessed!" said Brigham, "if I don't think you've all got walkin'-fits this morning. If it's catching I may as well be off, for fear I shall find myself walking a sentry-beat too, before long. What's got into ye all? Is there any thing a plain man can do to set things to rights?"

"I'm afraid not, my good friend," said Walcott; "I think I know what the matter is, and those concerned will have to settle it among themselves. I am much obliged to you, however, for your friendly intention. I will just take a short turn by myself, and if the colonel asks for me you will find me down by the rock. I wish to think a little before seeing him."

"Sartainly, sir," said Brigham, "any thing you wish. And I hope the trouble, whatever it is, will soon be made up."

In a few minutes afterward Walcott had disappeared, going down the pathway which led to the mineral spring.

When Lucile went into the apartment to which, as we have said, Marion had previously retired, she found the latter sitting with swollen eyes and flushed cheeks, in sadness and despondency, by the window.

"Oh, Lucile!" she exclaimed, "how glad I am to see you! I have been waiting for you so long, and have so much to say to you. Dear papa" (here the tender-hearted girl sobbed bitterly) "has been offended, and I don't know what to say or do!"

"What has he said to you, then?" asked Lucile.

"Oh! it is a long story. He has scolded me for walking out with Major Floyd, and has said very harsh things to Richard himself, poor fellow! Oh! how miserable I am!"

"But," answered Lucile, "what reason had he to scold you? I'm sure Major Floyd seems a very gentlemanly person, and he would do nothing to merit reproach any sooner than Arthur."

"No, indeed, he would not! Why, Lucile, he is the most delicate, the most noble, the most kind-hearted of men!"

"But," said Lucile, suddenly recollecting the supposed relation between her friend and Walcott, and blushing, half with pain at the thought, and half with pleasure at the hope that that relation was soon about to be changed; "but, you do not, of course, like him as you do Arthur?"

"As I do Arthur?" said the other. "Why, Lucile, how can you say such a thing? Why Lucile" (here she rose and caught her blushing companion fast in her arms, then again sat down, holding her on her lap and hugging her to her bosom); "Lucile, you dear, delightful angel! you love Arthur yourself! There now, don't blush and cry so, my poor little darling! He is nothing to me, and he has told me that he loves you so!—so dearly! But, as for me, I am so unhappy!"

It was now the turn of Lucile to become the consoler. At what had just been said her heart had become light, though a tear still trembled in her eye. Her blood now bounded along her veins in joyous pulsations, like dancers to the beat of enlivening music. The melody of happiness was flowing through her whole being, and even the sorrow and dejection of her companion was only a light shadow over the sunshine of bliss which had so suddenly fallen upon her. Oh! joy of joys! she now might love where she knew herself to be loved in return, but without treachery to her friend, and without shame before others! Oh! joy of joys! He, around whom all her bright and loving thoughts had of late so much clustered, was, in turn, enamored of her own poor, undeserving self! What happiness to think of it! How it might be dwelt upon by day, and dreamed of by night!

Nevertheless, toward Marion she felt all the genuine sympathy of a true friend.

"My dear Marion," she exclaimed, "you must—indeed you must—tell me all that gives you sorrow, and you will see how your poor Lucile can love and watch over you!"

"Ah! good and tender heart!" said the other, "I knew I could tell my inmost thought to you. I love (she whispered), I love—do you hear? dearly love Richard! and papa has been so unkind to him, and so severe to me! He said it was dishonorable for him to act as he did, knowing that I was betrothed to Arthur! I told my father that I and Arthur did not love each other; that we had parted; that he belonged to you! But he would not listen to me, made me take his arm, and come away! It was too, too hard! And Richard, dear Richard, I fear has gone away in sorrow, and perhaps in anger! Oh! how I wish I had told papa this morning how it was! But he is so stern—has so set his heart upon my marriage with Arthur, that I dreaded to see how he would think of a change. Oh! I am so, so wretched!"

"Calm yourself, dear Marion; perhaps when he sees Arthur, it will all be explained."

"That is what frightens me too. Arthur is so proud; and papa is so quick, I am afraid something dreadful will be done!"

"No," said Lucile; "be sure nothing dreadful shall be done! I will speak to my father about it; or—or I will speak myself to your father, who has never yet denied me any thing."

We will not, however, for the present, follow the train of mutual condolences and explanations which took place between the two young people. Suffice it to say, that after a long period of weeping, of sympathy, of caressing, and efforts at consolation, the mind of Marion was brought at last to be a little more composed; and she laid herself down to obtain, if possible, a short period of sleep. Lucile watched solicitously by her side. When at length, however, slumber came to close the eyes of the excited sufferer, she softly stole from the room, with the purpose of doing as she had half promised she would. She would see Colonel Belden herself, and at whatever sacrifice of maidenly reserve it might cost, to explain to him the new and true relations, and wishes of all concerned. With this object, she accordingly went forth. In the outer room, she found her father, reclining upon a rude couch of pelts, and tired with his recent journey and exertions, sound asleep. She went gently to his side, kissed his trembling lips, parted the thin white locks on his forehead, and, breathing a prayer of blessing over him, went out.

The day was already over. All objects were dim in the growing shadows of evening. To her listening ear, a universal silence appeared to prevail. During her short sojourn there, she had become accustomed to those sounds which, in the evening, and in the woods, are usually heard; so that they now only seemed a part of the dewy hush of nightfall itself, and in no wise to drown or interfere with whatever other echo might vibrate through the air.

Stepping forth then, with the bright stars just emerging from the pearly luster of the sky, the sound of distant voices did not fail at once to attract her attention. Not doubting that they must be from those whom she sought, she hastened forward.

But before we follow her steps further, we must revert, for a short space, to other events which had lately transpired.

After a long conversation with Mr. Valcour, Colonel Belden had left him and gone forth with the purpose of meeting Arthur Walcott. By inquiry of Brigham, he learned that the young man was somewhere about the Rock Spring, as it was usually called. Thither he at once bent his steps. As he approached, Walcott, who was, in truth, walking there, came forward to meet him.

"You may have observed, sir," the old gentleman began, "that my manner toward you since morning, has slightly changed. I come now for the purpose of having a full explanation; and I will take it upon me to say, that unless some satisfactory solution of affairs be given, my present deportment toward you must, for the future, remain unchanged."

"I am sorry," answered Walcott, "if any thing I have done has caused an unfavorable change in your sentiments toward me. I even think I know to what you would refer. But, to prevent all misapprehension, I beg of you first to state frankly and fully what it is in my conduct that you disapprove."

"I will first ask of you, sir, if it be true that you already divine the cause of my dissatisfaction, whether you think it quite manly or generous, to require me to speak plainly of so delicate a subject as my daughter's affections and her future welfare?"

As we have before had occasions to observe, Walcott's temper was none of the gentlest; and the blood now mounted into his forhead at the words and manner which the old gentleman seemed now inclined to use toward him.

With some effort, however, he managed to restrain his feelings, and he still replied with forbearance.

"I believe then, sir, that you think I have not treated your daughter honorably, or yourself with becoming respect? If this is so, I will give you what explanation I can; and I trust that you will not, in the end, utterly disagree with me."

"That is to say," interrupted the testy colonel, "that you acknowledge my suspicions to be just, and you are willing to ask my permission to sneak out of obligations which you voluntarily assumed."

"Colonel Belden," said the young man, thus severely pushed, and now, in his turn, becoming somewhat excited at the unjust imputations of the other, "Colonel Belden, I am not accustomed to hear language such as you see fit to use, and I beg of you to remember the difference between our ages. If you can not address me except in terms dishonorable for me to listen to, I shall beg the privilege of terminating this painful interview at once, and here."

"Painful to you, no doubt, it is," replied the other; "as painful as any culprit's exposure; but if you suppose that because I am old you can treat my daughter with baseness, or me with contempt you are much mistaken."

"I beg of you, sir, for the sake of your daughter, if not for me," replied Walcott, "to refrain from such language. Justice to her I am determined to render, even though you load me with injurious epithets. When that shall be done, I shall feel more at liberty to meet your personal charges, or to leave you to make them to other ears than mine."

"This is all very fine," replied the irritable old man, not unaffected, however, by the tone and bearing of Walcott; "but where the devil are your excuses? I can hardly believe you have grown to be a craven that will neither explain nor back up his conduct with his courage?"

"I shall certainly not do the last, whether it be necessary or not," said Walcott; "and if you will but hear me for a moment you can better judge of the proper course to be followed in any case."

"Curse me," exclaimed the other, "but this is almost enough to drive one mad! Here you have already had half an hour, and I am no wiser or better satisfied than when I first began."

"Unless you will listen," said Walcott, now determined to bring the interview to a point, "you will never be satisfied. Your daughter and myself were contracted to each other when very young, and when neither of us knew our own minds. We have never been attached to each other as those should be who are to be man and wife.

We are not so now. Our mutual esteem, I trust, is great; but there, all feeling stops. I am now (excuse my directness) deeply attached to another. But even this should not have interfered with my honorable fulfillment of all obligations to you and yours, but that Marion herself, unsolicited by me, and almost against my entreaties, formally released me from all ties, and almost gave me a dismissal. There, sir, you have the whole story, which I could have wished to come from other lips, but which you have thus rudely forced from mine. I am not reprehensible for feelings over which I have no control; but my conduct I could control, and did regulate according to my conventional duty until discharged from it. These are all the circumstances with which I have any concern, and you may now make the most of them."

Having said this the young man turned to move away, for he felt pained and humiliated beyond measure at the views which Colonel Belden seemed determined to take of the matter, and the language he seemed inclined to use in reference to it.

"Stay, young man," Colonel Belden exclaimed, as the other was going off; "am I then plainly to understand that all this silly and romantic arrangement has been made by you and my foolish or generous daughter, and that without consulting me? It is easy enough to delude a girl—to work upon her sympathy, or to awaken her pride; but, sir, you will find that I am not so easily disposed of."

"I don't know," said Walcott, "what you mean by working upon the sympathies of your daughter. God knows I have never done so! But as you do not seem disposed to view the affair reasonably, I shall again beg leave to withdraw."

"How the devil do you expect to withdraw so long as I am here, and insist on your staying till the business is settled? You must take me for an old fool, indeed!"

"I take you, sir," answered Walcott, "for a gentleman who is forgetting the respect due to himself, and a little of what is due to me; but, above all, I take you for the father of Marion."

"Ah! you do all that, do you? Well, then, let me see what it is you propose to do?"

"I propose to leave you, at all events, till you are more yourself."

Walcott here again turned to walk away.

The old man, in bad humor from the beginning, and more so as he felt such to have been the case—as he saw that the plans he had so long dwelt upon, and considered settled, were melting away, like frost-work in the sun—that a new scheme of life for his daughter had been thus unexpectedly opened—irritated, almost beyond control, by all these circumstances, stepped hastily before the young man and, with his cane, was about to strike him—an act which might have been regretted for the life-time of both—when there stepped between him and the object of his animosity another form which induced him to pause.

Before him, in fact, he now saw, in the uncertain light of evening, the person of Lucile Valcour—one of the causes of his suspicions, and, as he imagined, one of the frustraters of his hopes. But he could not strike her—a frail and gentle girl. He could not even find it in his heart to speak harshly to her. In her look and bearing there was so much of confidence, so much goodness, so much that was pure and beautiful, that the anger of the old man was at once dissipated. She did not pause to inquire what had happened. She would not know that any thing unpleasant had taken place. She approached him at once, and, taking one of his hands in hers, she exclaimed:

"You must come with me a little while now, dear sir. We have all missed you so much! It's a pity if I am to be treated any longer in this cavalier way, and not get any attention from you. You used to like me better!"

"Why, Lucile, my poor child, how strangely you talk. You do not know, perhaps, that I was engaged—deeply engaged with Arthur—with Mr. Walcott, and that we have important affairs to settle?"

"Yes, sir, I know all about it," she replied; "but you shall not look sternly at me! You shall not frighten me as you did Marion! There now, be good for a little while! I am determined to stay by you till I see you smile as you used to at me."

"Lucile," said he, "I repeat that you do not know what you are saying, or what you interfere with."

"I know, sir," she replied, with spirit, "that you have unjustly wounded the feelings of the best and tenderest of daughters; that you have almost driven to desperation one of the best and most honorable of men, and are, perhaps, on the brink of doing the same with another; that you are willing to make enemies of all who love and esteem you best, merely for the sake of carrying out an old plan for your daughter's welfare, which could now only make her unhappy for life."

During this short colloquy, Walcott had availed himself of the interruption which it had caused, to take his departure, as he had intended to do before. Meanwhile, the old colonel had been slowly approaching the house, before which they now stood.

"But Marion, the poor deluded, rejected Marion, my daughter, what is to become of her? What will the world say?" he asked, as if for the first time, his mind began to contemplate the possibility of a change, and to consider its consequences.

"Have you been so blind, sir," she asked, "as not to see that she has for a long time, probably unknown to herself, cherished the memory of another much more than she regarded the actual presence of Walcott?"

"Whom do you mean?" the old gentleman asked. "You can not mean Dick, whom I just now drove off, with too much—precipitation, perhaps?"

"Why, whom else could I mean? Did n't you see that he was attached to Marion; and was it kind or just to punish him for his admiration?"

"But, my lively young lady," he replied, "that is not a precise statement of the case; then, I supposed he was treacherously endeavoring to thwart me, and to supplant Arthur; and when I came just now to learn from the latter that it was as good as if it had been an understood thing between them, I confess it was a little too much for my patience."

"But it will not, I hope, be too much for your forgiveness, will it? Promise me that."

"Why, true," he replied, "when I come to think of it, Dick, after all, is a very clever fellow, well-bred, gentlemanly, possessed of fortune enough; and, and—by the Lord! on the whole I think I would rather prefer him! And that infernal Arthur—no, that won't do either. He 's not as bad as that would come to. Perhaps, miss, you'll expect me to apologize to him too?"

"Certainly, sir," she replied confidently, "of course you'll apologize."

"No, I shall do no such thing, then!" he answered.

"But, sir," she said, "recollect that you almost struck him! Think of that! You would not listen to him; you would not accept of his explanation; you drove him to madness by your harshness; and then, you almost—*almost* forgot that you were a gentleman, by attempting to use your cane. Oh! my good sir! Remember, if you had done that—remember, you would never have forgiven either yourself or him, unless he had shot you for it!"

"I believe," he now said, somewhat thoughtfully, "I believe you are right, my little monitor, after all. Arthur was always a little high-spirited, and I should not have pushed him quite so closely. But see if he is now in the house, I must make it all right at once."

Lucile hastened away with a glad heart, but in a moment afterward, returned to say that he was not there. They then made inquiry of Brigham if he had seen him, but found that he had not. All looked about in the vicinity, but he was nowhere visible. At this circumstance, Lucile began to look a little blank. However, she comforted herself with the hope that he must soon return from wherever he might be. So they went into the cabin, and into the room where the impatient Marion was waiting in anxiety to know what had been the result of Lucile's mission. The latter appeared as a messenger of joy and forgiveness. Behind her came Colonel Belden already almost reconciled to the new state of things. With the characteristic selfishness or egotism of age, he had imagined that nobody's views or wishes were to be consulted as much as his own. But now when he found his plans utterly uprooted he yielded before invincible necessity, and began to face the new prospect which arose in the future. It had soon begun to appear to him in colors almost as glowing as those of the last. It was not long before he was in the full tide of pleasing anticipations in regard to it. So many of the unselfish feelings of a father, however, were awakened by the sight of the swollen eyes, the trembling lips, and the sorrowful attitude of his daughter, as he came in, together with her appealing glance of apprehension, that his heart began to relent, and he felt ready to accuse himself of having acted like a brute in his harsh deportment toward her.

As he approached her, one look gave her an assurance of this, and she sprang to his arms exclaiming:

"Oh! my dear, good father! now you forgive and love your foolish and wicked child again! Oh! how good and kind you are! You must never be so severe with me again, dear father! or it will break my heart! But I knew you could not be so long!"

"Hush! my poor child!" said the old man, much affected; "hush! I now know all. You shall not have any more cause for apprehension from me. I see these arrangements are still made in spite of the cares of foolish parents. But there! Don't blush and tremble again; I am not going to chide you a second time."

Thus was the domestic storm which had overshadowed the last few hours, cleared away. All the prospect before the young people seemed now to be fair and promising. No cloud obscured it. No cloud? Stay a moment—

where was Richard?—and where was Arthur? Where was he, who, for the last few days, had been all self-denial and self-sacrifice for others? Was he thus turned away in contumely and contempt, when danger and trouble were over?

He must soon return. So they thought. No one said it; but all thought it. Yet he did not return. Hours passed by. It was late at night. All had sat up, without saying so, for him. At last came the hour of retirement. It was with much uneasiness that Colonel Belden and his daughter betook themselves to rest.

As for Lucile, it is hardly necessary to say that her pillow was bedewed with many tears. She apprehended, she knew not what; and it was long after midnight before sleep, in mercy, wrapt her senses in forgetfulness.

CHAPTER XXXI.

JOE'S WIGWAM.

WALCOTT left the presence of Colonel Belden with a heart swelling with a sense of injustice, and with the proud determination to place distance between himself, and a chance of renewed insult. He had not been fully aware of the long-cherished purpose which had been frustrated by the intrusion of another person upon the scene. He knew however that his own ill-considered designs had been changed. He could not, for all that, make up his mind even to be a distant witness of what he supposed was about to take place. What should he do next? To stay longer at Brigham's was out of the question. Besides, was there really no ground for the colonel's reproaches? Should he not himself, before accepting the dismissal so frankly tendered to him by the daughter, have referred the subject to the father for his ratification and approval? Would it not, at least, have been the more manly course? These questions Walcott could hardly answer satisfactorily to himself. He suspected that his new-born love had increased the facility with which old ties were loosened; and caused the eagerness with which he had availed himself of the door of escape, which Marion had so generously opened for him. These suspicions had much to do in augmenting his present discontent. As yet he did not know of the strong motives under which, unconsciously to herself, Marion had acted Had those motives been known, no chains could have held him to the fulfillment of the early betrothal. Without any other choice himself, the choice of Marion alone would have decided the question irrevocably.

Without regard to the particular course he was pursuing, in a fit of thoughtfulness and abstraction, he still walked away. Before being fully aware of it, he found himself in the dark woods, following a faint and scarcely defined path. His feet could without much difficulty trace it by the soft, smooth surface upon which they trod. As soon as he wandered in the least degree, on either side of it, he encountered brush and brambles; and so was immediately warned to change his course. This he for some time continued to do, without giving much heed to it. His familiarity with forest life made him indifferent to mere darkness, and the mazes of the wilderness. At length, however, the profound stillness began to have an effect even upon him. As his other and more painful emotions subsided, the vast obscurity and silence which enveloped him began to assume a place in his imagination, and to occupy a little of his attention. Then, for the first time, he thought whither his steps could be tending? It was a problem a little difficult to solve. By what compass could his course be determined, in the ocean of darkness he so incautiously attempted to navigate? In which way had he started? He could not tell. What landmarks had he last observed? He recollected none except the spot where he had left Colonel Belden. No moon was shining; but here and there was visible a faint and pale star. Here were the compass and the chart!

The stars! How many, and which, were to be seen? Then did he begin to study that vast volume, over which magicians and astrologers have pored so many ages, and to so little purpose. But his investigations had a more direct and practical object. It was not to pry into the secrets of the future, but to settle an urgent question of the present, that his observations were made. For the purpose of such a solution, they did not prove to be deceptive. After a few moments' consideration he was enabled to decide what course he was following, and by consequence the direction in which he had strayed. He found himself to the south and west of his starting-point. The distance he had gone could not have been great.

But when this question had been settled, a still more important one arose; and that was, where should he now go? While he was pausing and musing upon the subject, he thought he heard a slight sound in the path just behind him. This immediately aroused him to a more lively sense of his present situation. Who or what could it be? He knew the dangers which lurked in the midnight forest too well to be indifferent to their signs. He paused and held his breath to listen. His eyes were now useless sentinels. Upon his sense of hearing alone, must he for the moment depend. The sound which had attracted his attention, faint and low, was heard again once or twice, and then entirely ceased. He continued to listen. It was not repeated.

Here was a dilemma. What should he do? Walk on? By so doing, he would be turning his back to the danger. Should he remain where he was? This would be but a craven way of passing any very long period of time. Should he walk back toward the spot whence the sound proceeded? He knew that if it was some beast of prey, there was less likelihood of attack, when he faced it boldly than in any other position. This course was then determined upon. Quietly but firmly he retraced his steps for a short distance along the path. Suddenly something touched his shoulder. He started but made no outcry. He felt it to be a hand. A voice said:

"Where go, cap'n?"

"Ha! Is that you, Joe?" quietly asked Walcott, though in his sudden relief, he felt his pulse going down, like a sea after a whirlwind.

"Yes, cap'n; but, I say, where go so late?" answered Joe.

"That's what I hardly know myself," answered the young man; "something has happened which prevents me from staying at Brigham's any longer; and I have not yet made up my mind what to do."

Joe listened in silence, and continued to do so for some moments. He then said:

"Why not go to Joe's wigwam? Good to sleep. No got far to go."

"Well, Joe, that's frankly offered. I was just thinking of finding my way up to Catfoot's, but did not know exactly how far it might be. So, as your place, as you say, is close by, I will accept your offer."

Joe now led the way forward. After a short walk, they came into a small open space of ground. Here they found it much lighter. They could discern a cleared area, comprising in all, about an acre. In the center of it, stood a conically shaped hut, so long, and so invariably, the form of the native dwelling of the American savage. The ground adjoining appeared to be under rude cultivation; and in approaching the entrance, they passed through a small patch of growing maize.

After they entered the cabin, a light was soon struck, by the aid of flints. An evening repast of cold meats was produced. Every thing passed nearly in silence. Walcott felt moody and melancholy; and the Indian was taciturn from nature. He was, however, hospitable; and no necessary attention was omitted. Of the cold venison and other rude condiments, such as parched and pounded corn, each partook in silence and moderation.

Was there no danger for Walcott, then, thus to share the hospitality, and to put himself in the power of one who had so lately been guilty of an act of deadly hostility? He felt none. On the contrary, he looked upon the hospitality as a sort of pledge of good faith; for the young man was of an open, brave, and trusting nature, where merely his own safety was concerned. He was self-reliant. Besides, his thoughts were then dwelling on other themes.

What should his plans be for the morrow? for the next week or month? for the long future? Did not the lack of Colonel Belden's consent to its dissolution leave the tie between him and Marion, in some sort, in point of honor at least, in force? He dreaded to think so. And yet, after what had just passed between him and the old man, a resumption of former relations seemed nearly impossible. Had it not, in fact, raised an insurmountable barrier against it? He felt such to be the fact. Until some concessions were made; until some more conciliatory tone should be assumed toward himself, he would certainly never move a step backward toward amity and ancient friendship. Besides, how selfish was it for him, thus to be dwelling upon the effect which his quarrel had produced, and was to produce upon, himself! Was not another now concerned? Ah! the gentle Lucile! How soothingly and graciously did her image then come back to the young man's memory. In that poor hut; on that low pile of skins; in the dull glimmer of the decaying fire, with rudeness, and savageness, and desertion around, the picture which his soul so cherished, made his reveries as bright as noonday, and shone in effulgently upon his heart, like the flash of a distant signal-rocket to a storm-driven ship. Yes, now the question became different. Now the feelings of another must be consulted. Could he then, for a vain quibble upon a mere punctilio, hesitate to take such a course as would insure not only his own happiness, but that of one so dear and deserving as Lucile? He was not the coxcomb to suppose that she felt as deeply interested in the result as himself. He knew that she was essential to his happiness; and he imagined, or rather cherished the hope that his alliance with Marion would be to Lucile a cause of regret, and a source of pain. Thus much the instinct of love taught him. He reasoned with reference to it; and he acted upon it.

But, after all, the question came back, what was to be done? His host manifested no curiosity to pry into his affairs, but had fallen asleep like one whose business for the day was over, and who, until morning, had no other vocation than that of sleeping.

Left then to his reverie, sleep at length fell upon Arthur. The fire grew low, and its dull light shone upon the slumbering forms of the two inmates of the cabin, whose deep, regular breathing showed how profound was the slumber in which they were wrapped. At last the blanket which served as a door to the cabin was slowly and cautiously pulled aside, and the faint light of the smoldering coals shone upon the wild and haggard face of the lunatic, which peered eagerly in. A gleam of ferocious delight shot over his grim countenance as he was assured that his two enemies were now wholly in his power. Cautiously he entered the cabin, his huge form casting a colossal shadow on the poles and bark behind him. His step was light and noiseless as that of a phantom. He bent by turns over each of the sleepers, and gazed into their faces. He wreathed his arms and clenched his hands as if eager to strangle them where they lay. Some invisible influence, nevertheless, withheld him. Perhaps it was the thought of a more complete vengeance.

He now moved toward the decaying fire, and, sitting down by it, cast a few dried leaves among the embers. A momentary blaze threw a brighter light around. The sleepers slept on—the Indian was as motionless, save for the regular heavings of his chest, as if he slept the sleep of death. Walcott, on the other hand, showed signs of uneasiness. He uttered half articulate names. At such times the maniac would lend an attentive ear, and smile as now and then he caught a word.

At length a sudden thought seemed to strike him. He rose up, and taking a half-burned stick that lay in the ashes, went rapidly toward the entrance. In a moment more he had disappeared. At that very instant of time, and almost simultaneous with his disappearance, there arose through the stillness the low, wailing cry of a wild-cat. The Indian started to his feet. Walcott awoke also; and rubbing his eyes, as he sat up, asked what was the matter.

Joe stood in a listening attitude, and only replied by uttering the word "Hark!"

Immediately afterward the same cry was renewed, now louder and more prolonged than before.

"So," said Walcott, "it seems to be nothing but a wild-cat, after all. What makes you stand there that way, Joe, as if you never heard one before?"

The Indian, meanwhile, seemed to be in a state of unusual perplexity. He continued listening and walking about alternately, as if trying to make out something he did not quite understand. For several times was the same cry repeated. It was some minutes before it seemed to die away in the distance. The two men then again lay down and were soon as soundly asleep as before. The incident made but little impression upon Walcott; and as for the savage, though he had seemed to be troubled at the time, it did not keep him awake.

Soon afterward a dull, red light appeared at one corner of the hut, and over it slowly rose a thin column of smoke. Then a whiter and larger flame suddenly shot forth, and began rapidly to spread among the dry and combustible materials of which the tenement was composed. The lunatic, from without, again pulled aside the blanket which hung at the entrance, to gaze in. His hideous features exhibited a broad grin of satisfaction as he watched the rapid increase of the fire, and the continued unconsciousness of the sleepers. The flames soon began to crackle and roar as they caught light puffs of air. Heavy volumes of smoke spread out and filled the apartment.

At this moment, for a second time that night, was the silence broken by the cry of the wild-cat. It seemed to issue from some point close under the side of the cabin, and near to where the two men lay. It struck their ears louder and more startling than ever.

The cloth at the door dropped. The face of Jacob had disappeared. The two inmates were already on their feet. The savage, with an instinct which served him for presence of mind, sprang for his gun and the few articles of value he possessed, which he succeeded in seizing; while Walcott, half blinded and half suffocated by the smoke, groped his way with difficulty to the passage, and managed to get out. Both escaped the danger which had so nearly threatened them.

By this time the fire almost entirely enveloped the hut. In a few seconds more, if not aroused, they must inevitably have perished. But what was the cause of this unexpected conflagration? How could it have originated? Here was the mystery. What was it, also, that so providentially awoke them? They could scarcely imagine.

"That wild-cat has saved our lives, after all, Joe," said Walcott, after a moment.

"Wild-cat?" answered the savage interrogatively. "Don't know—catamount not like fire, don't come so close."

"It is certainly all very strange," said Walcott; "but the most remarkable thing about it is, that we were startled once before by the same cry."

"Can't make him out—too dark for Joe," said the other.

At this time, the woods for some distance around, were illuminated by the light of the fire. The black, tall, and columnar trunks of the older trees, stood out like the pillars of temples. Now and then, afar off could be seen the scudding forms and flashing eyes of the wolves; as startled by the fire, and still attracted to it, they skirted along the outer verge of the light. But another object soon diverted attention from them; for, near to where the two men stood, something suddenly arose from the ground which caused them both to start. It was the form of a man, clothed in the Indian garb, and carrying in his hand a gun. At his back hung an unstrung bow, and a well garnished quiver; and in his belt were stuck his knife and ax. His head was decorated with an eagle's feather; and his countenance was covered with paint curiously put on, one-half of it being tinged with a bright crimson color, and the other half being left untouched. Over his eyes, and across his forehead, were streaks of red and black.

As this remarkable personage slowly approached, in full relief, from the bright light of the fire, Walcott could not help regarding him with unmingled astonishment. Joe, on the contrary, manifested no surprise, uttering quietly, by way of clearing up the matter, the name of the new comer. It was Catfoot. Some time elapsed before the young man could recognize in what stood before him, the form and features of his Indian friend. In his extreme surprise, he was hardly sufficiently self-possessed to give him a greeting. Joe himself said nothing, but began to wear a suspicious and scowling look.

A thought at once occurred to Walcott; could it have been Catfoot that set fire to the hut? And even if he had not done so, he had, at least, been near at hand, and why had he not given timely warning? These suspicions had evidently occurred to Joe also; and he already began to handle his gun with signs of hostility. Observing these manifestations, Catfoot dropped his rifle to the ground, and stood regarding the two men with composure, though without vouchsafing any explanation.

"Catfoot," at length said Walcott, "why are you here and in this strange disguise?"

"Come in war-paint—you see him," was the reply.

"Not to make war on Joe, I hope?" continued Walcott.

"No; Joe put on paint too," replied the other.

"But," said the young man, "I hope you did 'nt set fire to the hut to make Joe put on war-paint?"

To this, the other made no reply, either in contempt of the suspicion indulged against him, or being determined not to answer the indirect inquiry.

"I would not have believed such a thing of you, Catfoot," said Walcott, after a pause, half in sorrow and half in rage.

"Did 'nt do him, tell you. Catfoot no burn wigwam," the Indian now replied, with some energy.

"But you saw it burning, and did not give us any warning?" continued Walcott.

"No hear wild-cat, eh?" said the chief, now turning sharply to Joe, "no hear him, you big fool Injin?"

The latter here fairly dropped his gun in the extremity of his surprise. Light was breaking in upon his mind. The mystery was also clearing up for Walcott. The cry had been uttered by the chief by way of warning. Its very naturalness had deceived the white man, and mystified the Indian, though it had not quite satisfied him. Hence his perplexity. But why had not Catfoot come boldly forward to announce the danger? Why had he gone away? And above all, how did the fire originate? To all the above questions, they received but the one laconic reply, "Wild Jake."

The madman, it would seem, was still held in awe by Catfoot. It was fear of him that had prevented him from continuing his first warning after the lunatic went out; and as the fire had been applied on another side of the hut, he was only actually apprised of it in time to save his friends by a second warning.

But the question now arose, where could Jacob in the mean time have flown to? It was most likely that he was still somewhere near at hand watching the effect of his plans. The three men began now to look sharply about them. The two savages, with the instinct of hounds, at once spread out, examining every thing which might give a clew, and casting quick glances in all directions among the shadowy trees.

A few minutes after they commenced their search, a long dark object arose out of the little field of corn near the burning cabin; and as their eyes fell upon it, they saw it glide rapidly away, while shortly afterward, the usual shrieks and jeers of the lunatic apprised them that it was he himself whom they had started from his lair.

With a speed and power they had no hope of equaling, he soon disappeared among the shadows of the woods. Joe, however, again sent after him a quicker messenger than himself, in the shape of a leaden slug from his rifle; but it was apparently without any result; for as the reverberations of the report died away, the sounds of distant peals of laughter were heard until in their turn they mingled with the hum of insects and the cries of animals, and became indistinguishable.

CHAPTER XXXII.

THE WAR PATH.

THE present village of Saratoga Springs stands, for the most part, upon the lower, and almost level, termination of a long mountain spur. The soil, though soft, is not deep; but is sprinkled thinly over a rough bed of limestone. A little to the northward the rise in the ground becomes very perceptible; and at the distance of a mile or so in that direction, one attains a height which commands a clear view of a wide extent of country.

At the east, and to the south, the land for leagues and leagues away, is almost one dead level; at least, from this elevation, so it appears to the eye. In the former direction in an autumn morning, one can easily trace the long winding course of the far-off Hudson, by the bank of fog which hangs above it; while beyond it, at a vast distance, rises the dim, rolling outline of the Green Mountains. Nearer at hand, like a white cloud in the hazy landscape, lies Saratoga Lake.

But from the eminence we have mentioned, by far the finest and most extensive view lies directly to the south. Thither the spread of the level country, at a first glance, seems almost illimitable. Field and forest, in irregular succession, stretch away in green and golden alternations, till they become commingled and indistinguishable in the distance. On sultry summer days, when mist and smoke are floating in the air, the line of the horizon can hardly be discerned; but on a clear morning, or when the sky is blue, and the cool fresh wind is breathing from the west, the eye discovers, a long way to the southward, and quite above the line on which the horizon is expected to be found, a dim, round, waving line of blue. This is the crest of the Catskill Mountains, nearly one hundred miles away: the mountains where old Hendrick Hudson and his grim companions, are still supposed, on a cloudy evening, to be playing at their old game of bowls! May the echo of their gigantic sport, long resound through those distant wooded valleys, and roll along those ancient enchanted eminences! To the westward, lies a country still beautiful, but more broken, and terminated at a short distance by a high spur of hills, abruptly shutting off the view. Behind them, the sun frequently goes down in a magnificent halo of crimson and gold.

Between the time of which we are writing and the present day, a great change, has, of course taken place, not only in the character of the adjacent country, but in the appearance of this space of elevated ground itself. Then the whole surrounding view was one of wilderness, and the eminence itself was covered with a luxuriant growth of hickories and oaks, whose trunks were covered with moss, and whose vast roots, clinging to the huge rocks at their feet, had resisted the power of rushing winds and heaving frosts, through summer and winter, for hundreds of years. The ground was encumbered with large, broken stones, or rough boulders of granite; from beneath and around which, sprang thick and thorny brambles, and from whose hollows and cavities, green and spotted toads and reptiles, crawled forth to bask in the morning's sun.

Now, the same spot is a rich and cultivated lawn. The trees have disappeared. The rocks have been rolled away to form the foundations of edifices, fences and landmarks. Instead of reptiles, are to be seen groups of peaceful kine grazing in the quiet inclosures. A noble mansion crowns the high ground, and looks off upon the magnificent prospect we have feebly endeavored to describe.

A gentleman, lately deceased, who, during his long and useful career, was no less eminent for his cultivated tastes, than for his courteous manners and his private worth, has made of that once rude and unpromising elevation, one of the most charming places of resort, and one of the most beautiful country-seats which can be imagined.

But our purpose was not to draw a landscape, or even to bring a contrast before the mind of the reader. It was merely to call attention to a scene which was represented at this place a long while ago—a scene which may in some sort serve to give a better idea of the ancient inhabitants of this rude land, of the manners which distinguished them, and of the maxims by which they were guided.

But we have a few more words to say by way of description.

The upland, or elevated ridge of which we have spoken, extends for many miles to the northward, rising higher and higher as it recedes, until it terminates in the rocky and precipitous mountains which surround Lake George. The name by which it was in former days most familiarly known, was, we believe, the Palmertown Mountain. For nearly its whole extent it presents a steep, rough and abrupt front to the eastward.

On that side, and between it and the Hudson river, lies a broad, sandy plain, which was formerly covered with a heavy growth of pine. This plateau is entirely overlooked by the upland spoken of. To a person traveling over it from the eastward, the latter presents a dark, wall-like front in the distance, reminding one of the palissades on the western bank of the Hudson, near New York. Along the top and eastern margin of this mural elevation, formerly extended a well-known and much used Indian pathway or *trail.* It was indeed one of their great highways, being the route traversed by the warlike parties that went to, and came from the great lakes and hunting-grounds of the north. For such a use, it possessed many advantages; it commanded a wide lookout, and was but little exposed to ambuscades; and the woods along the height were a favorite resort of game. Security and a supply of provisions were therefore its great recommendations.

Near to this trail, and about a mile from the present limits of the village of Saratoga, was a rocky boulder, remarkable for its size and height. It may answer the purpose of a natural watch-tower. Let us take up our position upon it, and observe what is passing, at the period in our story at which we have arrived.

We find ourselves on the western side of the pathway, and considerably elevated above it. We can look far away to the eastward, where the morning sun is just making its appearance, with half its disc already above the horizon. The sky is red and effulgent. In the bush, near at hand, we hear the occasional twitter of a bird. Through the open boughs below us, we can trace the indistinct outline of a beaten path. The ground is not visible anywhere; but the pine leaves and twigs are trodden hard and smooth.

The branches of the underbrush do not obstruct the view; but as the path winds among the timber and the rocks, it nowhere presents an extended vista to the eye.

All at once we perceive a long line of moving objects approaching. The distance and the imperfect light prevent us at first from ascertaining its true character; but as it comes nearer, we perceive that it is a file of Indian warriors, coming on, at a long, steady trot, up the pathway. They present a motley, but at the same time, a picturesque appearance; and there is seriousness and significance of purpose in their aspect.

The foremost man is our old acquaintance, Catfoot. The garb and paint with which he is now bedecked, set off to great advantage his muscular frame and fine athletic limbs. On his head, and plaited in with his hair, is a tuft of feathers. A rude sort of cloak or mantle, composed of differently colored panther skins, is thrown over his shoulders, and secured round his waist by a strong cord of twisted sinews. A similar cord secures it loosely to his throat. His broad chest itself is exposed, covered with hieroglyphical objects, rudely painted upon it, no doubt, having reference to the immediate expedition in which he is engaged. From his waist depends a short skirt or frock, terminating at the knees; and his feet are protected as usual by moccasins, fastened around his ankles by a thong, and ornamented with colored beads.

Behind him, follow the others in single file. Each is fantastically set off, though none wears a plume of feathers except the leader. The others generally have their hair gathered and tied in a single tuft on the top of the head. All are provided with weapons, and some with fire-arms. Where these last are not to be seen, are still the bow and arrow, the formidable tomahawk, and the inevitable scalping knife. In short, the whole body of savages is fully equipped for war. As they pass by, no look apparently is turned to the right or to the left. Gravity and singleness of purpose are depicted on their countenances, and are even indicated in their gait and movements.

And now, like a long mottled snake, the winding, articulated file of men goes up the acclivity further on, twisting itself around rocks and other obstructions, and preserving its uniform velocity, whatever the nature of the ground may be. In a moment more the dusky armament has gone by, and disappeared. Woe to the unprotected settlement upon which that merciless train of savages shall descend, with a purpose as fell as that of the reptile its motions imitate!

But the days, fortunately, when such enemies were let loose on civilized communities were already passed away. The war now on foot was only one of the incessant feuds which took place among the native tribes—feuds which no treaty or example could suppress or mitigate, and in which cunning and stratagem, cruelty and ferocity, went forth to meet their like in the enemy they encountered.

On the evening before, a runner from some distant station had arrived with news which set all the warriors of the hamlet on foot and away thus early in the morning. Among them our friend Catfoot, of whose good faith, prowess, and forest skill, we have had a little taste, is disappearing, to engage in struggles and enterprises peculiar to his race. The row of silent warriors has passed with as little noise as the rustling of a lady's dress through the aisles of a church; and now, in the distance, as the last brown and tufted scalp goes out of sight behind yonder rocks, repose again takes possession of the scene. The whole was but a passing and almost a silent pageant. In a few moments it has come and gone, and it has hardly disappeared before the dilatory morning sun, like a ship unmoored, swings clear of the horizon and sails slowly away on its diurnal voyage through the sky.

The small Indian village, of which mention has from time to time been made, was now comparatively deserted. All the males capable of action had joined the expedition whose departure has just been noted. The old men, women, children and dogs, were the occupants who were left behind; and, although the population was thus materially diminished, those who remained seemed capable of making quite as much clatter and noise as all who had been there before.

Upon a fallen tree near one of the huts Walcott and Indian Joe were sitting, engaged in earnest conversation. After the burning of the hut on the night before, both had come up to the village, where they at present found themselves. In doing so, Walcott had been enabled to thank Catfoot for his disinterested assistance, and to press upon him such tokens of his good feeling as would not offend the pride of the chief. They had, accordingly, parted in high good will toward each other, and with mutual esteem. Indian Joe could not be persuaded to join the war-party. Some motive more powerful than love of war restrained him. What it was will appear in due time.

"Joe," said Walcott, as they sat side by side, "what do you say to a hunt after this crazy man again, one of these days? He has done a great deal of mischief already, and, unless he is caught, he is likely to do much more."

"When you want go?" asked the other.

"I can not now say," replied Walcott; "it would be well to have Brigham along, and I do not like to try it until the people at his house have gone away, when there will be nothing to be feared on their account."

"Cap'n," said the Indian, "Jake burn Joe's wigwam."

"Well, what if he did?" asked Walcott.

"I shoot Jake, that 's all," replied the other, doggedly.

"I hope you will not do it, Joe; remember he is crazy, and do n't know what he is about."

"Do n't know—tink he de debbill, so shoot him if can."

Walcott endeavored, but in vain, to dissuade the savage from the resolution upon which he seemed to be fixed; but did not again attempt to assume a peremptory tone, after what had lately passed between them, and after the ill effects of his former effort in that way.

While they were yet talking, the voice of Brigham was heard, speaking in loud and familiar tones to the old crones and impish urchins he met, as he came along.

"Hooray!" he exclaimed, "old mother white-top. How 's yer roomatiz this mornin'? And so loping Hank has gone off with the rest, the varmint! I hope he left you plenty of deer-meat and fish before startin'. But, I say, hain't none on ye seen Joe anywhere about? For I'm telled he did n't jine the scalpin'-party. And there's the captain, that some on ye must have fell in with, for he 's missin' ever sin' last night when he went out for a walk, like. Heh! what? and so he 's here, is he? With Joe, too, I suppose?"

Talking in this way, Brigham soon came in sight of those for whom he was seeking.

"You make as much noise as a company of marching recruits, Brigham," said Walcott, rising up and going forward to meet him. "You herald your approach by trumpet, if not by drum."

"I wish then, Mr. Walcott," he answered, "that you had heralded your whereabouts in the same plain way, for I've been on the sarch for ye these two hours."

"And you have found me out at last, my friend, and so what is it you want?"

"Oh! you're wanted by others than me, and have been inquired arter more than a little. The case is here. You know—or if you do n't know, I can now tell ye—that your friend, Major Floyd, took horse yesterday afternoon and started for Schuyler's. He went off sudden, like a lighted fusee, and nobody knew much on 't till they saw the dust of his horse's heels risin' behind him, like smoke. Well, so far so good; but this morning what do we see but his horse quietly grazin' near the house as if nothing had happened. But, you see, the misfortin' on it was that he had the saddle on him still, though now turned under him, and with the bridle draggin' about his neck, and broke in two. It looked mighty queer. I hope it ain't no more of that cussed Jake's doin's, for if I thought it was, I'd shoot him myself! I'm told he's burned you out, Joe, clean and clear? But, to come to the business in hand, somebody must start at once after the poor Major, and see what has happened. I hoped to find Catfoot, but the 'tarnal fool has got some scent of Canada Injuns in his nostrils, and you might as well try to keep a wolf from fresh meat as to stop him. So, you see, what are we to do?"

"Is there any horse left at the sheds fit to be mounted?" asked Walcott.

"Yes, there 's one good, strong roadster, but we want a pair, and there ain't any other fit to keep up with this one."

"Then," said Walcott, "I'll take this one and go alone. It will be all that is required. You can remain—one of us *must* remain behind. I 'll be back in a very short time; but in the meanwhile, let us hurry down to the house."

They accordingly started in that direction. As they proceeded, Walcott recollected what, for the moment, had been driven from his mind by the news in regard to Floyd—namely, the ill-footing upon which he stood with Colonel Belden, and that it might be very unpleasant to meet him.

"Brigham," said he, "I don't exactly like to meet the colonel now; he and I had some high words yesterday, and I hardly know how to manage it. I suppose he is naturally anxious a little about the fate of Floyd?"

"Oh! you be hanged about meetin' the colonel!" said Brigham. "He 'll be glad enough to see you, depend on't; and whether he will or not, his darter has been a cryin' and going on all the morning to find you. She seems to take the news mighty bad; and I half thought she 'd be off in the pursuit herself alone, one spell."

"Yes, I suppose she is much alarmed about it. They are old play-fellows, I believe, she and Floyd," said Walcott.

"Much alarmed?" replied Brigham; "I should think she was, if takin' on dreadful, is any sign on 't. Why she's been a cryin' as if her heart was ready to break. But from the dry way you talk about it, one would think you 'd walked among these people with your eyes shut."

"What is it you are driving at, Brigham? What was to be seen that has escaped me?"

"Come now, you 're makin' fun of me!" said Brigham. "Do you mean to say that you think her anxiety is only as to the fate of her school-fellow? Why she did n't make so much ado when the other gal was in the cave with Jake."

These questions began at last to start a new train of thought in Walcott's mind. He had never before endeavored to consider the subject in the new light which now broke upon him. The state of things implied by Brigham was certainly not improbable; nay, when he came to think of the matter, was highly probable—was almost a certainty.

Shall we say that a twinge—a very slight twinge—of regret, or jealousy, or annoyance, or something of that nature, was felt by the young man, as the thought took possession of his mind that, after all, Marion had made no sacrifice in giving him up; but had been all the while following out the secret bent of her own heart? Alas! such is human nature. What he could most have wished, when he found it to have actually occurred, still occasioned him pain. But generosity and justice soon got the better of less worthy feelings. His vanity had been wounded; but the wound was a cure for the many apprehensions he had entertained. His own qualifications had not proved so dazzling as to outshine those of all others; yet, he now found the door thrown wide open for his own egress from an "entangling alliance;" and his course for the future was as free as that of an uncaged bird. He was free even to place his heart again in thraldom—a thraldom in which he would delight to be involved. To his awakened imagination, gentle eyes shone on him as he thought of it, and cheeks that he loved to look upon flushed with pleasure, as he should relate the joyful news of his own freedom to choose.

But all these thoughts passed silently in his breast as he went along. With respect to every human being, there are always two worlds; the one, without, which he can look at with his eyes, and hear with his ears, and appreciate with all his senses; the other, within himself, which he can only contemplate with the organs of his mind. These worlds are often widely dissimilar. The outer one may be a desert; the inner one, a gorgeous palace, glittering with gold and effulgent with light; the outer one may be the wide, open, solitary sea; the inner one, green fields, a sunlit cottage, a vine clambering up a wall, loaded with grapes, or redolent of the perfume of flowers. So it was with Walcott. He was traversing a rude forest pathway; bushes and half-decayed stumps lined the track, towering, mossy trees hung solemn and shadowy above him; there was rudeness, savageness, primevalness around him. Within him—what was *there?* Glorious, most joyous, and most hopeful pictures. How his eye lit up! It was not the cold wild scene around him, that thus kindled his glances; it was the moving panorama of thought and fancy—the luster of the spirit-world, that thus shone out through the windows of his soul!

At the cabin of Brigham, they found all, as they had anticipated, in much alarm, at the uncertain fate of Floyd. And yet, all did not feel the force of the possible castastrophe in the same degree. Marion and Lucile were certainly, on this point, not alike. Lucile, constitution-

16*

ally the more excitable, the more mercurial, the more passionate, was now the calmer of the two. The old colonel himself, partly from real interest, and partly out of sympathy with others, seemed quite agitated and impatient. The office of consoler and soother fell upon Lucile. Her companion, ordinarily the stately and dignified Marion, in deep tribulation and tears, was now walking to and fro, asking ceaseless and useless questions, and uttering constant and unavailing exclamations of alarm and conjecture.

No sooner did Walcott appear, than she hastened to him, and taking his hand, said:

"Dearest Arthur, you will go after him at once, will you not? You and he were once dear friends; and he thinks so much of you yet; that is—unless—but while we are here talking, he may have been murdered, or he may have been thrown from his horse, and be suffering or dying for want of help! But," she added, her eyes swimming with tears, as she spoke, "we will try and hope for better things, and must trust to you to see where he is, and, if possible, to save him. Will you hasten, dearest Arthur, for my sake, for the sake of your old friend, Marion?"

"My poor girl!" he replied, "did you think it necessary to use all these entreaties to induce me to look after the fate of my friend? Be of good heart, Marion. If he is alive, I will soon find him; and there is much reason to believe that nothing serious has happened. And so, not to waste any more time, I must bid you a hasty adieu, and go on my mission. Colonel Belden, I hope I do not meet or leave you entertaining hard opinions of me?"

"Who? I?" exclaimed the old man; "not at all, my

dear boy. But now I come to think of it; I must have been overhasty and unreasonable yesterday; and I ask your pardon for it. So, my dear fellow, let us now see what we can do for poor Floyd."

"With all my heart, sir," said Walcott, much pleased at the turn his own affairs had taken; "and for that purpose," he continued, "I must at once mount, and be off, as I perceive that Brigham has got me a horse in readiness. He will act as sentinel and guard here, while I am away. So a short good-by to you all!"

In those days, the course which was followed, in traveling between Saratoga and Schuyler's, was not the same as that along which the public highway at present extends. The latter, pursuing a more direct line, crosses a portion of the tract of low and marshy ground, commonly known as "Bear Swamp." The former, on the contrary, made a considerable circuit to the northward, so as to follow the margin of the dry and rolling upland. Going eastward, the low meadows, and the creek which led into, and through them, were kept at some distance to the right. This northerly detour commenced about two miles from the springs.

This was the route followed by Floyd when he had ridden away on the evening before. At that time he was laboring under no small degree of excitement, as may be well supposed. His feelings had been cut to the quick; and he felt intensely chagrined at the turn affairs had taken. Among other information, rudely communicated to him at that time by Colonel Belden, was the fact, of which he had been previously ignorant, that Marion was, and had been for some time actually affianced to Walcott! The news itself had been to him a great shock; and all the subsequent ill-nature and rough language of the old man had passed for nothing as compared with that. It drowned all minor ideas. Marion engaged! This fact was more than all else. He thus needed no hint to hurry him away. The impulse was already powerful enough. Floyd was an honorable man. If Marion was thus plighted to another, he would do no act to break the tie, to cause it to be regretted, or to render the duties it imposed either irksome or less pleasing. So he had nothing to do but to take his departure, and that as speedily as possible.

But as he rode away, heedless of all outward objects, the thought would obtrude itself upon his mind, whether, after all, Marion could really have her heart interested in the engagement which had been formed? If so, how could he satisfactorily account for her conduct toward himself? How could he explain the blush which mantled her cheek, the joy which shone in her eye at his own approach? the trembling of her hand as he took it in his? and those thousand other nameless signs of an interest deeper than that of fraternal regard? All these had impressed themselves deeply upon his own feelings at the moment; and he had had no doubting conviction of their import. They are among the signs which those deeply concerned rarely misapprehend; they are like telegraphic signals which send their meaning across the deep and narrow gulf which separates all human souls, and prove that an indissoluble union has overspanned the chasm, and that there is thereafter for the two hearts thus united, but one earthly fate!

No! Marion could not love Walcott! So thought and reasoned Floyd. He was not suspicious. His mind was free from the little mists which obscure the vision of the envious and the jealous. He imagined that he saw with as much lucidness as if glass was the outer wall of Marion's soul, what was passing within it. At that moment he felt that each warm pulse of her heart beat for him—for himself alone! The betrothal was then a mystery—a mistake. She was not one to deceive. She would never give her hand to one, and her faith and affections to another. There must be some doubt to clear up, some mischance to correct. But whatever it was, he could not help thinking that there was still some hope for himself. By degrees, as he thus dwelt on the more pleasing aspect of his circumstances, the ill-humor which had at first hurried him away with so much violence, subsided; and the rapidity of his progress became proportionately lessened. The horse, from proceeding at a wild gallop, gradually diminished his pace, till he had dropped into a steady walk.

At the place where Floyd was now riding, the road or bridle-path was just on the edge of the solid ground—on the dividing-line, so to speak, between that and the marsh. It was shadowed by thick trees, over the roots of which the horse would sometimes stumble as he passed along. To the right, lay the close and tangled alder swamps, impassable for horse, and almost so for man. In the other direction the forest was open, though from the closeness of the overhanging boughs, and the fullness of the foliage, it lay in sober and silent shadow. Its aspect was peaceful in the extreme.

While he was thus wrapt in profound revery upon a subject, which to one of his age always possesses an interest most personal and absorbing, he did not observe that as he moved slowly along, allowing the bridle to lay loosely on the horse's neck, a dusky form would now and then be partly visible from behind some tree or bush, to the left; or that the tuft of a scalp-lock would occasionally rise from behind a rock or fallen log, while quick, fierce and threatening eyes, marked his progress, and followed his course. Occasionally also, like gray phantoms, fleet forms would glide forward from one cover to another, coming nearer to him at each step and tending toward a point in the road, where it wound around a small knoll. Every thing, however, passed as quietly and unnoticed by the rider, as if those objects, generally so suspicious in the forest, had merely formed a part of the landscape, or as if they were no more to be feared than timid hares changing their hiding-places in the dusk.

When he reached the knoll, and just as he lightly pulled the rein to change his direction there, the form of a tall and fierce-looking savage sprang up in his path. The frightened horse snorted, and reared into the air. The Indian armed apparently with nothing more than his tomahawk and knife, rushed at once toward the animal's head, with the evident purpose of catching the bridle, and thus bringing himself to close quarters with the rider. At the same time he uttered the formidable Indian war-whoop, which was immediately answered by others around, until the air was filled with the frightful din. In his purpose, he was at first, however, disappointed; for the horse had almost instantly been reduced to subjection and control by Floyd, who caused him to make a lateral spring so as to swing himself beyond the reach of the savage. In an instant also he drew from his holsters a horseman's pistol, which he leveled at his assailant and snapped; but which, owing to the dampness of the priming, did not go off. Finding himself disappointed in this, and seeing his enemies increasing in numbers around him, he at once rose in his stirrups, and with his whole force, hurled the useless weapon full at the head of his immediate enemy. It took effect, and the latter was felled to the ground by the force of the blow.

Floyd had but an instant to consider. Ahead of him were several others, now barring his way, and rapidly approaching. His remaining pistol was probably as useless as the one he had thrown away. He had still his heavy dragoon's cutlass, this he immediately drew, and turning his horse's head suddenly about, spurred forward in an attempt to effect an escape in that direction. He had however gone but a few rods before he found that the ambush had been complete; for before him, and directly in the path, were several of his enemies bent on stopping his progress at all hazards. Nevertheless, he drove at them at full speed, now well aware that none but a desperate remedy could save him. The bridle was again flung down, while with his left hand he drew forth from the holster the unused pistol. Like its mate it was found useless as a fire-arm. The powder flashed in the pan. Still he clubbed the refractory weapon, determined if possible to make it serve as good a purpose as the other. As he came fearlessly up toward the group of savages drawn up across the path, they seemed a little daunted by the impetuosity of his approach; and the two who immediately confronted him, stepped aside. One of them was stunned and overthrown by a blow from the pistol; and the other while striking with his ax at the horse's neck, received a sword-cut in the arm, which caused him at once to drop the weapon and run howling away.

Floyd began to entertain hopes of escape. He cheered forward his horse, now as excited as himself, for the woods behind and around him still rang with the wild cries of the pursuers. No shot had yet been fired. He had in fact, seen no guns among them. Here was also a ground for hope. In a few seconds afterward, however, at a spot where the road became a little rough, he suddenly felt a hot, painful shock in the flesh of his right arm. His strength seemed paralyzed. The sword fell from his hand. A sharp arrow-head had pierced the muscle, and the shaft still hung in the wound. His blood was flowing over its flinty point, and dying its feathery shaft. He also heard other messengers of death of a like nature, rushing past him. His position was most critical; and at each moment he expected to be struck to the heart. In case another savage should be found in his path, he would be powerless to assail him and could only hope to ride him down.

While in this very crisis between hope and fear, when a few seconds would place him beyond the danger or make him its victim, at a point where the ground was a little soft, another athletic Indian sprang from the bushes, and endeavored to seize the horse by the rein. The animal again shied, and in doing so, stumbled over some projecting roots, and in his speed, came near falling broad on his side. As it was, the shock was so sudden that, the saddle turned under him, and Floyd was thrown with great violence in the midst of the path. Unfortunately, or perhaps fortunately, his head struck one of the rough roots, and deprived him of immediate consciousness. The frightened horse meanwhile again scrambled up, and snorting wildly, made off as fast as his legs would carry him.

As the young man lay senseless and helpless on the ground now stained with his blood, his immediate assailant approached with the apparent purpose of making sure work, and finishing him. His knife and hatchet were already brandished for this object, when his hand was stayed by another, who from his demeanor and his dress, appeared to exercise authority among them. Thus the young man's life was for the moment, saved; but if one were to judge from the looks of those who now gathered around him, it was not with any benevolent purpose.

The chief, for such he was, bore marks of having taken part in the fray; for there was a large contusion on his face, now swollen and bloody, which added much to the natural ferocity of his expression. This was probably the work of one of the discarded pistols. Uttering a few words in his native tongue to his followers, he pointed to the prostrate but still living form of their prisoner. They now, as if in obedience to the command which they received, lifted him up and bore him away, following the chief. Their course, after leading up the creek for a short distance, crossed it as well as the low swale of alders, and came out upon a spot already somewhat known to the reader.

As to the injured man, the arrow had been left in the wound it had made, and the pain which it caused aroused him, at last, from the stunning effects of his fall. It was with a deep sigh of anguish that he at length opened his eyes. The scene around him, to his bewildered faculties, was new and strange. It was some time before he could recollect how he had been brought to his present condition. The truth, however, at length began to dawn upon him, and he became aware that he was the captive of his late assailants.

Though suffering terribly from the unextracted arrow, he still composed himself sufficiently to observe what was going on around him. Where the party had halted there was a small space of open ground; and here he was set down. As he recovered the use of his senses more fully, his suffering became more acute, and he could not help requesting those around him to withdraw the arrow, the pain of which was almost intolerable as it swung in the loose opening it had made, and caused the blood to flow copiously from it. The savages, however, only laughed at his expressions of pain, and were indifferent to his entreaties.

Meanwhile, they conversed but little among themselves, and that in their own dialect. Floyd endeavored himself to extract the arrow from the wound, but found the task difficult. It could not be drawn backward on account of the roughness of the flinty head, and to draw it forward was to pull the harsh and tantalising quills which lined the shaft through the raw and quivering flesh. Either course was fraught with almost unendurable pain. He tried them in vain, while at every effort and grimace which he made, his tormenters but laughed the more. They even gathered around him, as if to enjoy the scene. Old, grim, and solemn-featured warriors allowed their rough faces to betray a smile at the sufferings of their captured foe. Floyd now and then could distinguish the word "Squaw" uttered by them in a tone of contempt. Already nearly maddened with pain, he became furious at the sight of their inhuman cruelty, and at the thought that his irrepressible anguish made him the object of their derision. In a sudden paroxysm he seized the tormenting arrow in his left hand and attempted to break it. It bent double in his powerful and desperate grasp, but the tough hickory would not break. In a fury he then bent the stubborn withe to his mouth and actually succeeded in gnawing it off with his teeth. In a moment more it was withdrawn from his arm. The flint head he flung, in impotent fury, at his tormentors.

While he had been thus engaged they had become silent. His strength in doubling up the stout walnut, and his resolution in biting it away, at last, had excited in the bosoms of those who surrounded him, a feeling very different from contempt.

"There!" exclaimed the young man, "you damned gang of grinning wolves, take that for your amusement! I'll pay you off with hickory applied to your yelling throats if I ever get free from you again!"

They did not seem to understand him, nor, probably, would they have cared if they had. They made no movement except what was necessary to keep him securely within their reach. Meanwhile, as well from his loss of blood as from extreme suffering, Floyd began to feel a little reaction after his sudden excitement, and grew somewhat faint. He was compelled to sit down, feeling sick and dizzy. His hand trembled as he leaned his head upon it, and he almost imagined that his last hour had come.

After a while, however, the faintness having to some degree passed over, he rose up and contrived to walk down to the brook, where, in the cool clear water, he bathed his aching and now swelling arm, and slaked the thirst caused by the fever of his wound. In these operations he was not impeded but was merely watched. Escape, at present, was out of the question; and he felt that any attempt at it would be worse than useless. He, therefore, after a while, returned to the place where the others were gathered, and being in less pain and more composed, had a better opportunity to make some observations as to the numbers and character of his captors.

That they did not belong to the neighborhood he was already convinced; and, on a more careful inspection, he became satisfied that they were, what were then generally known as Canada or Huron Indians, a race almost always hostile to those of the district which they were now traversing. This supposition accounted for their attack on himself. A white man was always an enemy, and most especially in an enemy's country.

At a short distance from the place where he was sitting, he observed a group of the older men of the party, apparently engaged in deliberation. Beyond them, and a rod or so higher up the bank, was an enormous pine-tree which attracted his attention, not only from its size, but from the circumstance of its leaning over at a great inclination, so much so as to create an unpleasant impression of its being about to fall. At its base was a thicket so close as to be impenetrable to the eye.

As the council continued, various members of it, from time to time, pointed toward their prisoner; and he rightly enough conjectured that he himself was the subject of their deliberations. His suffering, which was lately so intense, and which had not yet entirely abated, had this good effect, that it withdrew his mind from the contemplation of the dangers which, probably, awaited him, or, at least, rendered him partially indifferent to them.

But it was not long before the little conclave closed its ominous session. The pipe, which seems to be the source from which all savage as well as much civilized wisdom is derived, had only twice performed the circuit of the council before its members had, apparently, come to a conclusion, and broke up.

Soon afterward, a few of the younger men, approaching Floyd, gave him to understand that he must rise and follow them. Knowing the folly of resistance, he complied, although he was entirely at a loss as to what it meant. They led him to a small isolated tree a few paces distant. The sapling was not larger than his own arm. They speedily hacked it off, at about five feet from the ground, with their tomahawks. While some were engaged in this, others, from the thick marsh close by, had cut long. pliant twigs of willow, which they bruised and twisted till they acquired almost the flexibility of ropes. Floyd began to have some unpleasant anticipations as to what was coming. The truncated tree formed a stake to which it was obvious enough they intended to lash him. What further designs they might have, he could not, of course, surmise, but, evidently, cruelty would be their prevailing characteristics. The spot was near the bottom of the slope, and around the sapling, to which preparations were being made to fasten him, was a small space of level ground, covered with a smooth green sod. As they began to pass the withes and some strings of sinew around the chest of the poor young man he looked wistfully but vainly about him to see if any aid was at hand, or if the least chance for escape was left him. Though weak and faint, he would not have hesitated, urged as he was by extreme desperation, to adopt any means of relief, however doubtful or dangerous. Not the slightest chance, however, seemed to occur; and in a few seconds he was securely bound, and became as helpless as an ox in the shambles. His back was toward the stream, so that, as he stood, he nearly faced the hill. Almost in front of him, therefore, the high, overleaning pine-tree before mentioned, lifted its ponderous bulk.

In moments of extreme peril, or of strong excitement, objects of unusual appearance are apt to impress themselves upon the fancy, and to make a permanent lodgment upon the memory. For this reason the attention of Floyd was almost unconsciously turned to the inclining pine, though his thoughts were flying far and wide on a thousand other subjects. For this reason, also, for years afterward, did the recollection of that striking object in the wilderness remain vivid and clear in his mind, forming one of the most prominent points in his mental picture of the dangers which that day beset him.

No sooner was the fastening fully completed than a circle of yelling young savages, with wild outcries and brandished weapons, began to dance about him. The little conclave of senators was again formed, but nearer to the place of sacrifice; and while some were engaged in smoking, others had begun a low, guttural chant, which the poor victim might well take for his death-song. He was brave, and, although he felt the invincible repugnance to death which all, and especially the young and strong, experience, he resolved to meet his fate, whatever it might be, with the courage of a man; and if he could not die like a stoic, he would, at least, endeavor to die like a soldier.

But as yet, no further violence had been done him. Once or twice some one had seized him by the hair; and with discordant yells, had swung a knife or ax with murderous import before his face. To produce fear and mortal apprehension, was among the luxuries of their savage executions. Momentarily he expected to feel the fatal blow descending upon his unprotected head. He almost wished it might be soon, so that the horror should be ended. It was not, however, with any reckless feeling, that such a wish came into his mind. On the contrary, in that extreme hour, his heart felt oppressed with prayerful longings and unuttered entreaties to heaven. If death must come, he only hoped its agonies might be short. Around him the band of exulting murderers now circled in their fantastic dance, more rapidly and wildly than ever. Some even, with playful malice, to augment his fears, hurled their hatchets at the tree to which he was tied; they would often graze near him, and often strike into the quivering sapling. Others, again, with mocking menaces, would stand before him, and with fixed aim, and a steady sweep of the arm, threaten to send their axes into his body, as they had sent them into the tree. The torture for the poor young man was extreme. In spite of himself, cold drops of perspiration would gather upon his forehead.

But this could not long continue. In the midst of the scene, at length there came a lull, as one of his most powerful tormentors approached him, seeming to be detailed for some special duty. Amid profound silence he took his position a few paces in front of the prisoner, holding a heavy tomahawk in his hand. This done, the chant of death was again resumed; to which the selected executioner began a sort of solemn, solitary dance, but without materially changing his position. The object seemed to be to fix the attention and to attract the gaze of the victim before the fatal blow should be struck; and in spite of all he could do, Floyd soon felt his looks drawn by a kind of fascination in the required direction.

As he gazed, another object suddenly met his sight. It was the gigantic form of Wild Jacob, emerging silently and stealthily from the bushes at the base of the overhanging tree. With caution, but with great celerity, and unseen by the savages, whose attention was absorbed by the interest of the expected execution, he stole forward, bearing in his hand an enormous bludgeon. Floyd had never before seen him, and at first almost fancied him to be a creature of his own imagination, or some monster of the woods, thus strangely risen from their recesses. His eyes remained fixed upon the fantastic figure, partly in expectant curiosity, and partly in the distraction caused by the apprehension of immediate death.

What it might portend, was of course a mystery; and before the young man even acquired a definite impression of the circumstance, a change came over all around him; for with the scream of an infuriated demon, the wild-man suddenly burst through the chanting circle of the old men, scattering them to the right and left, while with one sweep of his heavy club he struck to the ground the savage who so immediately threatened the life of Floyd. In less time than it takes to describe it, the others with shouts of terror, were scattered like chaff before their insane pursuer; and although many were knocked over in the first few seconds, the whole gang soon managed to scramble up and disappear, with the exception of the one who had been first struck, and who had fallen to rise no more.

The whole seemed to be but the work of a moment. The scene almost magically changed; and Floyd, before he was quite able to comprehend how, found his fetters cut loose, and himself at liberty; but so great was the reaction, that in his exhausted condition, he could not move from the spot. He endeavored to look around in order to thank his strange deliverer, but his tongue seemed as if glued to his jaws and refused utterance; he endeavored to walk, but his limbs were powerless and could not perform their office; and meanwhile a dizzy sense of weakness came over him, and he fell fainting to the ground.

The ignorant are always superstitious, and the American savages were no exception to the rule. By all their customs, teachings and traditions, as we have several times before had occasion to observe, they were led to consider a person either of a weak, or of a disordered intellect, as one to be looked upon with awe, if not with fear. He was supposed to hold communion with beings of the land of spirits; and in some instances it was imagined that they invested him with supernatural powers, or came to his aid in moments of difficulty—fighting his battles, like unseen legions of angels.

Every thing, therefore, in the appearance of Jacob, as he suddenly came down upon the assemblage of Hurons, had been calculated to inspire them with fear. His terrific outcries, his enormous strength, and miraculous activity, combined with their superstitions, were too much for the coolest heads and stoutest hearts among them. Thus it was that they gave way so suddenly before him, and vanished like a mist before a strong wind.

As the last of the dusky fugitives disappeared from the scene, the momentary silence of the forest was broken by a strange and uncouth noise. The madman had flung himself down at full length upon the summit of a gray rock that commanded a view of the scene of his late exploit, and rolled from side to side as if convulsed with merriment at the mischief which he thought he had occasioned. He seemed to consider this his crowning exploit, and his laughter was louder and harsher than ever.

Floyd still lay pale and motionless upon the grass where he had fallen. Not far from him rested the body of the savage who had been brained in the madman's first onset. He, too, was pale; but mingled with the dusky tint of his features, was the livid hue of death. Clotted blood covered his scalp, and in congealed, purple drops, stood on his forehead and his cheeks. In his hand was still clutched the threatening ax. An expression of cruelty still sat upon his countenance. It was the latest emotion which had passed over it, and its traces were thus left behind, fixed there until the dissolving hand of decay should turn all to dust and obliterate alike the mold of the absent soul, and the moral depicted upon it.

After a short time Jacob left the rock where he had gone to give vent to his merriment, and to watch the retreat of his discomfitted enemies, and returned to the spot where the two bodies still lay. He examined each of them. But there was a language in the appalling image of dissolution which became intelligible even to his unsettled mind. It spoke, not directly and plainly to his understanding, but indirectly and confusedly to his whole being, and affected him, as it will affect the unthinking animal, through his instincts, and by a sort of electrical agency through all his senses, and through every nerve and fiber of his frame. Death is a disturbance and a shock to all animated nature. The fiery horse that would trample unhesitatingly upon a living man, will start and turn aside with instinctive fear from his lifeless remains. So it was with Jacob. No sooner had he bent over the prostrate Indian than, with signs of alarm, he recoiled from the corpse, though his head was still turned, and his eyes were bent upon it. Fear took possession of him—whitened his lips, enlarged his wild, wide-open eyes, and shook his iron muscles, as the wind will shake a slender reed.

With Floyd, however, it was different. Though he was still in a swoon, and, to a careless observer, as lifeless as the other, the more acute instincts of Jacob at once discerned that he was not dead. Notwithstanding the destructive tendencies of this mindless creature he acted according to no rule, and his course could never be conjectured in advance. Accordingly, through some inexplicable freak, he now lifted up the body, and with many tokens of tenderness and care, bore it up the bank. Parting the bushes he deposited it in the secret hut of boughs already described and known to the reader. This done, he turned and left the place in silence, though the vagrant thoughts which flitted over the desert of his mind seemed to find expression in a continual whispering, which moved his lips indeed, but which, to one not close to him, was quite inaudible. After getting in the open space he again bent his looks, with many signs of fear, toward the spot where the dead Indian lay, and cautiously avoiding it, and turning stealthily up the bank, he soon leaped away with his usual precipitation, and disappeared amid the gathering shadows of evening.

When Floyd returned to his senses he found himself alone and in darkness. By a determined effort he was, at length, able to recall to his recollection the events that had happened up to the time when Jacob had so suddenly made his appearance. But beyond that all was darkness in his memory, as complete as that which now met his outward vision.

After a brief interval he rose up to grope about; and, by dint of searching, he finally succeeded in detecting a place of egress from his leafy prison, and in emerging into the open air. As he did so, the night wind felt chilly to his fevered frame, and he shuddered as its first breath blew moist and cold upon him.

Stepping a few paces down the slope, Floyd, by the aid of star-light, was soon enabled to discover the stake to which he had lately been bound. The train of recollections which the sight of this evoked, well-nigh made his memory of the recent events complete. He knew himself to be still near the scene of his late perils, and found that he was now apparently safe, though alone and faint from suffering and loss of blood. Some friendly arm it must have been that had thus interfered to effect his deliverance, and to deposit him in the place of seclusion and repose in which he had awakened. Turning back, he again stood at the base of the leaning tree, and while there a low sound caught his attentive ear. It proceeded from some place near that which he had lately left, where he had come so near being offered up as a sacrifice. It seemed to be something like the noise made by a man or animal walking cautiously over the leaves. He did not dare to move, or to make any sound, lest it might be some of his late enemies returned to reconnoiter. Meanwhile, the character of the sound changed; though still muffled and low, it appeared more like the tramp of several persons than of one. Soon after it seemed gradually to recede and to become less and less distinguishable. Then again it ceased altogether; and in the place of it a low, wailing chant, as of many voices, disturbed the solemnity of the night. To Floyd all this was quite inexplicable. He knew not that his late persecutors had thus, in stealth, and under cover of the night, returned to bear off the body of their slain comrade.

After this all soon became silent again, save the usual noises of the forest—as much to be expected as the roar of the surf upon the sea-coast—and, after many painful reflections upon his own situation, the young man thought he could do no better than avail himself of the shelter he had at hand, and wait the return of morning.

CHAPTER XXXIII.

FATE OF THE LUNATIC.

We must now again call attention to the proceedings of other parties connected with our story. We will, for a brief space, follow the course of Walcott. His old experience and especially his late practice, had made him familiar with the signs of the woods; and, when there, had imparted to him something of the sharpness and sagacity of the aborigines in following a trail. As he went down the road, therefore, which led eastward toward Schuyler's, his eyes were constantly bent upon the ground, where he easily traced signs of Floyd's passage. This continued to be the case until he came as far as the knoll, where the attack had, in reality, commenced. There the sudden cessation of the horse's foot-prints, and the signs of violent and rapid leaping and turning, were plainly visible. It was there, then, that Walcott began to examine every thing with the greatest care; and in order to prevent any mistake, he dismounted and went forward on the road to see if, by any chance, the footsteps could be found anywhere beyond. On this point he was soon satisfied, and with a little diligence, after returning, he soon discovered evidence of the horse's actually turning back, and that, apparently, at a rapid pace. He also marked the spot where the last mêlée had taken place, and observed that some heavy object must there have fallen to the ground, which was, in various places, stained with bloody discoloration.

So far all was plain, but being unaccustomed to follow the slight marks which the Indians in their stealth and caution, generally left behind them, he was thrown out and was at fault, at the spot where the party had diverged from the path, and turned to carry their prisoner to the south bank of the creek. While he was here busily engaged in looking for the lost trail, and scanning the ground and even the borders and bed of the little stream, he heard a familiar voice calling:

"Halloo there! Walcott! what are you looking for? Lost any money?"

Walcott started with surprise and pleasure; and as he looked up, he saw, a few rods from him, and coming down the slope, the figure of Floyd himself.

"No, Dick," answered Walcott, "but somebody else thought she had lost what was more precious to her than money, and she sent me to look for it."

"Well," said Dick, laughing, "but you did n't expect to find it in the creek did you?"

"I expect to see it there in a moment," answered Walcott, "and that as soon as you attempt to cross over. But my dear fellow, what does all this mean? Your arm tied up, clothes bloody and torn! You have n't been so foolish as to tumble off your horse, have you?"

"Something like that, I believe," said Floyd, "but I can't say certainly whether I fell off or was knocked off."

"Knocked off?" asked Walcott; "pray who would knock you off? But tell me all about it at once."

"But," said Floyd, "the story will keep for a little while. Besides, it's a long one; and to own the truth, I am at this moment far from comfortable. This confounded arm of mine gives me a good deal of trouble, and I would like as soon as possible, to get where it can be dressed."

"In that case," said Walcott, "it's lucky I brought along a nag strong enough to carry us both back; for you don't look as if you could manage to get along very rapidly alone. So let us mount and be off, and you can tell me your story as we return."

So saying, the two young men after a little ado, contrived to place themselves on the back of the horse, and then started for the house of Brigham. During their journey Floyd gave a brief detail of the events which had befallen him since leaving the spring on the night before. Walcott was greatly surprised that any violence should have been committed by the savages, as all who were supposed to be in the neighborhood made professions of friendship and good-will to the whites.

"As for that," said Floyd, when reminded of the circumstance, "I do not think that this gang belonged to this vicinity at all. A good many things induced me to suppose it was a marauding party of Hurons."

"Hurons!" exclaimed Walcott; "then that accounts for Catfoot's leaving the village at the head of a war-party this morning; and I venture to say, if your Canadian redskins do not look to it, they will find some unpleasant embarrassment on their way back home."

"Then you think," said Floyd, slightly changing the course of the conversation, "that it was the man you call Wild Jacob who gave them such a fright?"

"Unquestionably it was he," replied Walcott, "for your description proves it beyond a doubt. Besides there is no other person in this part of the country who could perform such a feat."

"What I marvel at most," said Floyd, "judging of the man by the reputation he bears, is, that he has been found doing a good action, in spite of all the horrors that are related of him."

"As for that," said Walcott, "it is just as the humor strikes him. Had he met you alone he might have endeavored to perform the office which the Hurons sought to accomplish on you. It seems to satisfy him if he can find any object on which to spend his superabundant fury and strength. But did he not kill any of them, think you?"

"One, I thought, must surely be dead; but this morning I could find nothing of him. The wolves could not, certainly, so soon have eaten him entirely up."

"Not likely;" said Walcott, "but the simple explanation of it is that his companions have probably returned and borne away the body during the darkness."

Thus conversing and entertaining, among other things, no little apprehension at the idea that a band of hostile savages had been, and were still so near to those in whom each of them now felt so deep an interest, they made what haste they could to get back to the cabin. Meanwhile, Floyd's arm had become extremely painful; and although he made no complaint, the motion of the horse was a perpetual torture to him, and sent the cold drops of perspiration to his forehead.

But we will forbear any endeavors to depict the joy which was felt and expressed at his safety, when at last he dismounted at the door of the house. Marion, though alarmed and anxious on account of his wound, was still radiant, through her tears, with pleasure and gratitude that nothing fatal had happened.

Although Colonel Belden had designed to remove from the Spring, and return to Ballston without further material delay, the accident which had befallen Floyd, and the new relations in which he was likely to stand to him, necessarily produced a change in the arrangements. The wound was not dangerous, but the arm, nevertheless, became much swollen, and was exceedingly painful. Apprehensions were entertained that it might terminate in fever; but the great loss of blood which the young man had sustained, probably saved him from it. Indian Joe, also, was again the physician; and his remedies, whether beneficial or not, were used, and the arm by degrees got better.

In the mean time, several days elapsed, during which the movements of our principal personages were somewhat restricted, owing, not only to fear of their old enemy, Jacob, but of their new and more dangerous neighbors, the Hurons. Walcott, however, was but little restrained by the one consideration or by the other. Of Jacob he, of course, entertained no apprehensions whatever, considering the influence which he had been hitherto able to exercise over him; and as to the hostile Indians, he felt strong confidence that the movements of Catfoot would soon send them skulking back to their distant retreats in the great northern forests. So he hunted, and fished, and rambled about as usual. In his shorter strolls, however, he was now sometimes accompanied by another. It will, perhaps, require no great stretch of the imagination for the reader to divine who this companion was.

During this interval, on a fine morning, at an hour

when the summer dew had just risen from the grass and the leaves—at the balmiest, and most beautiful, and most exhilarating period of the day, the two young people had strayed away a longer distance than usual from the cabin. The place at which they found themselves was near the spot where Walcott was first introduced to the notice of the reader. That spot, it will be recollected, was on the sandy level, or plateau, eastward of the little marsh, near the westerly margin of which Congress Spring was subsequently discovered. The bank which here descended from the upper level toward the swamp, was covered with fern and wild-flowers, so fresh and blooming that their perfume could be perceived for some distance around. On this slope, and a few feet below its upper margin, Walcott might, at this time, have been seen, as with careless leisure he culled, from time to time, the small, fresh blossoms that grew in wild profusion around him. Still further down the steep bank his companion, in a freak of adventure, and in the exuberance of her happpiness had clambered, in order to find buds of rarer hue and finer perfume than those which grew above. At that time each had no thought except for the other, and a hopeful calm, as peaceful as that of all nature around them, reigned in their hearts.

But, here again, we are compelled, with regret, to introduce an unpleasant change in this pleasing picture.

It so happened that Jacob, the lunatic, in the pertinacious constancy of his caprices, had still lingered in the neighborhood. No fixed designs restrained him; but habit, which rules with animals as well as with men, had operated upon his neutral nature. On the morning in question it was by chance that he found himself near the bank where Walcott and Lucile were standing. No sooner did his eye light upon them than a sudden train of recollection seemed to be fired within him. Almost immediately he set himself to watch their movements, and to steal closer upon them; and as his look fell on the young man, his usual malicious smile disappeared, but in the place of it was a scowl of timid but murderous malignancy. With the stillness of a snow-flake he crept nearer and nearer. His usual weapon, the terrific club, was still in his hands. By dint of patient watching he soon succeeded in reaching, unseen, the edge of the declivity just above where Walcott stood. It was just then that the young man was facing his fair companion, to whom some playful words were being addressed. His back was consequently turned toward the danger which threatened him. Lucile, on the contrary, laughing as she replied, looked up, with blushes and smiles, like shower and sunshine, on her beautiful face; but as she did so, Walcott observed, suddenly, that her eye became fixed and staring, that her cheek turned pale as ashes, and that a faint cry broke from her parted lips. Meanwhile, he heard a slight rustling behind him. He turned, but before he could fully discern what was there, a heavy, uncouth object fell to the ground just above him, while the woods around simultaneously resounded to the sharp, ringing report of a rifle! The lunatic lay dead and motionless at Walcott's feet! The murderous club was still clenched in his hands.

In a moment after, Indian Joe, carrying a discharged gun, coolly and unconcernedly approached the spot. His shot had taken effect just as the club had been raised, with murderous purpose, over the young man's head. That was the last of the wild, hopeless wanderer, "Crazy Jacob."

CHAPTER XXXIV.

CONCLUSION.

On the eastern bank of the Hudson river, a few miles above Spuyten Duyvel creek, surrounded by a belt of old trees, may now be found a small field or inclosure, in the midst of which is a hillock commanding an extensive view in either direction up and down the river. Upon that knoll, the curious may find a few blackened stones around the margin of an ancient cellar, besides the remnants of a chimney-stack and fire-place. Within it are tall weeds; and vegetation has crept over every spot where mold has gathered, thus softening or hiding the ruin.

Standing near that spot, at this time, one can count, of a fair summer day, when a fresh wind is blowing, perhaps two hundred vessels, dotting the wide expanse of the stream, as the pale wings and breasts of flocks of wild, white pigeons sometimes speck the deep, still azure of a vernal sky. Vast steamers, like floating palaces, every few moments, send their black columns of smoke, in long curves, into the glassy atmosphere. Underneath the shore, also, every hour or so, the rush of ponderous railway trains is heard, rumbling like earthquakes, as they burst through the wind, and their echoes die sullenly away in the distance.

Looking inland from the same spot, through the branches

of the open trees, and rising in round hemispherical elevations above the tree-tops, one sees a rolling country receding and growing higher as it recedes, clothed in verdure, wrapped in ripe harvests, crowned with sumptuous villas, and glittering and glowing in all the beauty, refinement, and rural pomp, of careful culture and civilized wealth.

The scene was not always the same. In 1787, a few weeks after the events related in the last chapter, the broad river with its magnificent palissades, the high hills, and the blue distant mountains, were indeed the same as now; but on the bosom of the water, perhaps not more than one or two lazy sail could be seen in the course of an entire day. The stillness was never disturbed by the echoes of the loud-breathing steamboat, floating by, like a panting leviathan. The surrounding country, almost everywhere, was deeply wrapt in a mantle of green, for the forest was not yet shorn from the face of the earth. A few widely scattered country-seats, lay embowered along the shore, and only indicated their positions by thin lines of smoke, sent up like beacons from the clearings where they lay. No swift-winged railway train startled the fisherman, as he hung lazily on the gray rocks which projected into the water. Summer-houses, also, were built out from the shore, like sentry-boxes, and within their cool recesses, the drowsy sojourner could hear beneath him the gurgle of the restless tide, and from the window, watch the shining backs of the rolling porpoises, as in countless platoons, they filed, in solemn order, along their watery path.

But where the old ruin, the blackened stones, the half-filled cellar, the decayed chimney-stack and fallen hearth are now faintly traceable, there stood a capacious, and, for the period, a stately mansion. Its high portico facing the river, was sustained by six square columns. In front lay a small terrace of earth, supported by masonry, its area filled with rose-bushes and other flowering shrubs, and its corners ornamented with tall vases of white marble. From this portal, a wide pathway led down to the river-bank. It was flagged with broad flat stones, and lined with rows of box, and small pines and mountain ash. Past the doorway itself, also swept a wide carriage-track, bordered like the walk with shrubbery, and over-spread with a layer of finely-broken slate. The lawn was covered with a carpet of bright green grass; and a few deer could now and then be seen browsing upon the tender buds of the young trees or bounding lightly across the open spaces.

But our attention is now particularly drawn to what was passing within the mansion itself. On both sides of the wide hall, were high, broad folding-doors of solid mahogany, which were all now swung back, disclosing, on either hand, lofty and capacious parlors. These were decorated according to the fashion of the times. On the southern side of the house, the sunlight of a warm fore-noon was stealing through the green venetian blinds; while through the open lattice-work without, the soft south wind percolated, laden as it was, with the sweet odor of the honeysuckle, which climbed the outer case-ment. The place was altogether charming. It was for-tunately not unoccupied.

Several groups were standing or sitting in various parts of the saloon. In one corner, was our old acquaintance Colonel Belden, somewhat more carefully dressed than when we last saw him in the wilderness; while his long flowing white hair hung over his shoulders. A smile of pleasure and of courtesy, illuminated his fine face. Before him stood another figure, not so venerable in respect to years, but more so in respect to costume. He was dressed in the imposing robes of a minister of the English church, which, with the surplice and bands, plainly betrayed his vocation.

The two stood courteously conversing, while each held in his hand a still untasted glass of golden wine.

But whom have we here, on the other side of the apartment? She is so richly dressed—is so surrounded with the civilized ornaments and appliances of the lady, that we can hardly recognize in her our little heroine of the forest, the spring, and the cave. And yet it is herself. By her side stands Walcott. In her hand, and in her hair, are small clusters of flowers, even more beautiful than those she once gathered on the steep borders of the alder-swamp, now the "vale of statues" at Saratoga.

But there is still another group, who are passing out to the portico. The reader can well imagine of whom it is composed. He—for the two were now man and wife—finds himself bound, not to the sacrificial stake to be hooted and tortured by grinning savages, but with voluntary ligaments equally strong, to a gentle and beautiful being, who will but love and honor him, "so long as they both shall live."

THE END.

THE

OLD VICARAGE.

A NOVEL.

BY MRS. HUBBACK,
AUTHORESS OF
"THE WIFE'S SISTER," "MAY AND DECEMBER,"
ETC. ETC.

NEW YORK:
W. P. FETRIDGE & CO., PUBLISHERS,
FRANKLIN SQUARE.

MY FIRST SEASON.

BY

BEATRICE REYNOLDS.

EDITED BY THE AUTHOR OF

"COUNTERPARTS," AND "CHARLES AUCHESTER."

NEW YORK:
W. P. FETRIDGE & CO., FRANKLIN SQUARE.

HAGAR THE MARTYR;

OR,

PASSION AND REALITY.

A TALE OF THE NORTH AND SOUTH.

BY

MRS. H. MARION STEPHENS.

WILL IS DESTINY.

Alas! O, alas! for the trusting heart,
When its fairy dream is o'er;
When it learns that to trust is to be deceived—
Finds the things most false which it most believed!
Alas! for it dreams no more!

NEW YORK:
PUBLISHED BY W. P. FETRIDGE & CO.,
FRANKLIN SQUARE.

HOME SCENES AND HOME SOUNDS;

OR,

THE WORLD FROM MY WINDOW.

BY

H. MARION STEPHENS.

NEW YORK:
PUBLISHED BY W. P. FETRIDGE & CO.,
FRANKLIN SQUARE.

EVENTIDE

A SERIES OF

TALES AND POEMS.

BY

EFFIE AFTON.

"I never gaze
Upon the evening, but a tide of awe,
And love, and wonder, from the Infinite,
Swells up within me, as the running brine
From the smooth-glistening, wide-heaving sea,
Grows in the creeks and channels of a stream,
Until it threats its banks. It is not joy,—
'T is sadness more divine."

ALEXANDER SMITH.

NEW YORK:
PUBLISHED BY W. P. FETRIDGE & CO.,
FRANKLIN SQUARE.

Little Folks' Own:

STORIES, SKETCHES, POEMS, AND PARAGRAPHS,

DESIGNED TO

AMUSE AND BENEFIT THE YOUNG

BY

MRS. L. S. GOODWIN.

NEW YORK:
PUBLISHED BY W. P. FETRIDGE & CO.,
FRANKLIN SQUARE.

www.ingramcontent.com/pod-product-compliance
Lightning Source LLC
LaVergne TN
LVHW020109110826
845151LV00001B/113

* 9 7 8 1 4 2 5 5 4 3 9 2 1 *